# THE
# GUILT
# WITHIN

Published in Australia by
Freevoice Publishing
PO Box 1448, Noosaville, QLD 4566
mm27@bigpond.net.au

First published in Australia 2023
Copyright © Mandy Morris 2022



National Library of Australia Cataloguing in Publication entry

 A catalogue record for this
book is available from the
National Library of Australia

ISBN: 978-0-6456575-0-0 (paperback)
ISBN: 978-0-6456575-3-1 (hardback)
ISBN: 978-0-6456575-1-7 (epub)

Cover photography and design by Stephanie Leo
Interior typesetting by Sophie White

Printed by Ingram Spark

# THE
# GUILT
# WITHIN

MANDY MORRIS

# CHAPTER 1

'What the hell?' *I can't... I can't hold my toothbrush... Oh... Oh god, I'm so drowsy. So... so drowsy...*

~ ~ ~

*This is all my fault... all my fault! Tout est ma faute... c'est ma faute! We should never have come back. How could she... how could my mother betray me! What a fool I was to trust her! My own flesh and blood has sabotaged my love and happiness for her own greedy gains.*

I curse myself over and over as we run for our lives from the charging horses and soldiers. I am terrified, and my legs are trembling so much that I can barely run. Luca grips my hand tightly and pulls me along, but I can't keep up. As we get to the bottom of the steep sand dune, he pulls me onto his back and carries me. The wind is blowing a gale, and the ocean is roaring. When we finally reach the top, fear consumes me when I see the wild, grey ocean below.

He puts me down, grabs my hand, and we run down to the

beach. My legs are still trembling, and my heart is pounding. I try to appear brave, but I'm panicking that I'll never make it. I've never been so scared, but I've got to be strong. The only way to get to our cove past the impenetrable headland is by sea; to do that, we desperately need an outgoing tide.

Luca grimaces as he examines the ocean. 'The tide has not even begun to recede, and the waves are massive; it may be a while before we can leave, but we must be ready. I think we have managed to lose the soldiers for now, at least.'

We undress, hide our clothes under a rock, and Luca huddles me into his body. He nestles his head into my neck, inhales deeply and whispers into my ear, 'I love to breathe you, mon amour!'

'Oh, mon amour, how I long to be up at our cove, cocooned within your arms. Cocooné dans tes bras.'

As the waves break on the shore, freezing gusts of wind dump sea spray all over us, and I shiver uncontrollably. Luca hugs me tightly, and we wait as the tide slowly ebbs from the rocky cliffs at the headland. He whispers into my ear, 'We have to follow the tides, Rianne. Suis les marées, Rianne. The tides and the currents are key to our freedom.'

Luca leads me towards the headland, where the waves are crashing high over the rocks. He tries to hide his concern. 'You have done it before, Rianne. You can do it again. The force of the outgoing tide will carry us beyond the headland to the caverns. The soldiers will never be able to reach us there.'

We climb onto a rock, and he points out past the headland. 'See the dark horizontal line in the distance? That is the strong northerly current. We need to aim for this current, Rianne, so we will be swept along till we reach the caverns on the other side, and once the tide changes again, we can easily swim to our cove.'

I nod apprehensively, and he reassures me again. 'We will soon be free, mon amour!' His eyes light up. 'In our sanctuary!'

Luca's eyes sparkle as he creates a picture of how perfect our life will be when we get to our cove. I can't hear a word he is saying, but I understand his passion and blind belief, and I desperately want to believe it too, but I am utterly terrified as I glare out at these ferocious waves. The last time, the waves were calm and the tide was right, and we didn't have soldiers chasing us.

Luca pulls a thin piece of leather from his wrist, then gently twists my long, tangled hair into a tight knot and ties it on my head. I turn and face him, and he lifts me above his head. I feel rapturous and close my eyes, savouring the moment as he slowly lowers me, kissing my stomach, my breasts, and my lips. Our desire is intense but is quickly brought to an abrupt halt when the waves smash against the rocks and saturate us.

The tide is receding so slowly, and I know he is fearful now by the way he's biting at his bottom lip. He stares into my eyes intensely. 'The breathing technique we practised, Rianne, it is so important now. We must dive as deep as possible to escape these waves.'

I am shivering profusely, and he pulls me protectively close again as we stand in the shallows, waiting.

Suddenly, the horses' squeals are piercingly loud.

*Oh god! Oh, mon dieu. I'm too scared to look back. They must be so close.*

Luca pulls me onto his back. 'We've got to go now, Rianne. Remember, deep, slow, calm breaths.'

I take a deep breath, hold tightly to Luca, and we dive as one, deep beneath the waves. As we plunge deeper and deeper, I cling as tightly as I can to him, but the tremendous force of the ocean forces us straight back up to the surface.

Huge waves keep dumping on us until finally, we are forced apart. Luca calls to me from beyond the swell, but I can't see him, and the unrelenting waves keep pushing me back to the shore. I shake uncontrollably and try to propel myself back out, kicking wildly. I am almost free when something warm thumps against my body, and I turn in horror to see a soldier being sucked out by a rip.

Haunting, shrill cries from the horses get louder and louder. The soldiers are whipping them, trying to force them into the ocean, but the horses are rearing high into the air, trying to escape. Some horses and riders have been dumped back onto the shore among the rocks and heavy swathes of seaweed.

Utterly terrified and out of breath, the breaking waves rush at me, but Luca's words—'Our sanctuary, Rianne!'—give me the strength to keep going.

From beyond the break, Luca tries to get to me. With a deep breath, I dive beneath the waves. The soldiers are close behind, and I swim frantically until a hand grips my leg, and I am jerked backwards. Pulled half out of the water, I twist and squirm as I glimpse the contorted face of a soldier. I kick wildly at his hand until he finally loses his grip.

Finally, the northerly current grasps me; this current is our only chance for escape. I calm my breathing as I am propelled away, relaxing into the flow, but it loses momentum as a massive wave forms underneath me. Lifted high in the water, the wave grips me tight, spinning me out of control, and finally pummels me to the ocean floor. I surrender my last breath to the sea, but it spits me from its deadly grip, smashing me onto the shore.

Disoriented and confused, I open my eyes to vibrant flowers as Luca cocoons me within his arms. We have made it to our cove. I snuggle back into him and pull his arms around me... when suddenly the roar of the ocean and the sharp sting of the sand being whipped up by the wind and I realise where I am. I gasp for breath and try to remain perfectly still at the sound of approaching footsteps. *Soldiers...*

Tangled up in seaweed, I desperately hope they cannot see

me amongst the camouflage of rocks and debris.

A shadow passes over my eyes as the footsteps stop.

The soldiers are close, and I can't help but open my eyes. My heart pounds as two soldiers tower over me, grinning wickedly. Panicked, I crawl frantically back towards the ocean but their firm hold on my hair jerks me back. The soldiers snigger, and they yell into my face, 'Il est mort! Il est mort! Il est mort!'

*No! Non! Non!* They drag me back again, shouting again, 'He is dead! He is dead! He is dead!'

I do not believe what they say, and I lunge for the ocean to be with my lover. I have nothing left to live for.

The soldiers' shouting fades. My head spins. And then, from beyond the waves, a voice. *'Follow the tides, Rianne! Suis les marées, Rianne!'*

With a final surge of strength, I am fearless in my fight to reach my lover, his voice calling for me from beyond the waves.

~~~

*I... I killed... I killed him...*

Melissa jerks violently and instinctively grasps her neck in sheer terror. *Oh my god, what just happened? It was utterly horrifying. I've been trapped in that nightmarish hell the entire night! Oh god! I can't open my eyes. Oh... Oh... And now I can't move. Where am I? There's something hard and cold under my body; I must be on the floor of my bathroom again! Oh no! Not again! Putain de merde... Nom de dieu... What... What does that mean? What is happening? Why can't I move? What was that fucking nightmare!*

Strange words from her nightmare niggle at her. *Ill... Ill laymor! Yan... Reeyan! Swee... sweelaymaray! Fuck—what do they mean?*

Trying desperately to make sense of the words, she whispers as many as she can remember. 'Ill lay mor... Swee... Sweelaymaray. Sweemarianne.' Her mind becomes muddled
~~~

as she becomes more fully awake until almost all the words vanish. *Sweelaymaray, sweelay... What was it? Come on, think!*

Closing her eyes, Melissa tries desperately to conjure the images that felt so real just a moment ago. Fragments flash in black and white, strobe-like. *It was freezing and there were horses rearing up... aggressive soldiers screaming at me. Illaymore... Ill lay more... Ill lay more? What? What does that mean?*

Melissa's had this dream before, and while she waits for the paralysis to subside, she once again tries to recall the words. She yells at herself in one of the few French sentences she knows. *Tu es une imbécile, Melissa! You are an idiot! An imbécile! Why can't I remember? Sweemarianne. Sweet Marianne? Oh god, now I've lost it. Lamerr...? Or la mer? Isn't that the word for sea in French? Suis les marées? Suis... Mer... Rianne...*

Now she has that song going round and round in her head.

*"So long, Marianne..."*

'Great. Now I can't get that song out of my head!'

*"So long, Marianne..."*

'Fuck, Melissa! Concentrate!' She curses, knowing very soon she will be totally distracted by her busy life.

Finally, when she can move again, Melissa reaches for her phone, scrolls through her messages and sees a text from her son. *Oh god, Zac is already on his way! He can't see me like this! What's happening to me? Why is this happening? Putain... Fuck, I need to get organised!*

~ ~ ~

Zac slams his laptop shut and slides it forcefully to the other side of the kitchen bench. He calls out to his mother as she emerges from the pool. 'Hey Mum, do you want a bottle of water or anything? Ugh, I can't stand physiology! I don't care how fucking body parts function or what they do! I hate this course! It's bullshit!'

Melissa tilts her head to the side to clear the water out of her ear and smiles sympathetically at her son. 'If you don't like it, why don't you study something you do like?'

Zac shrugs indifferently. 'Dad thinks it's important for the business. I... it's not so bad, it's just hard at the moment. I'll get used to it.'

Melissa puts her arm around his shoulders. 'It's your life, Zac. Do something that lights you up. I want *you* to be happy.'

'You know me, Mum, I'll be fine. Just have to get through these exams, and it'll be smooth sailing! I'll be a Doctor of Pharmacy like my old man in no time. I'm just having a whinge.'

'Your happiness is so important to me. It's up to you to do what you want. Can I get you a smoothie? Something to eat?'

Zac smiles and nods. 'A strawberry smoothie would be super sick.'

Melissa pulls a big container of frozen strawberries from the freezer.

Zac grins. 'Yes! A big one would be sweet.' Melissa nods with a smile, and Zac's expression suddenly turns serious. 'I hear the shit hit the fan with Granddad. He's giving Dad a really hard time. What's happened?'

Melissa sighs. 'Oh I don't know. Why don't you ask your father, or, better still, ask his father?'

Zac throws his head back, laughing loudly. 'Not only is it almost impossible to pin Dad down nowadays but he also doesn't seem to want to tell me anything about the business. Come on, Mum! Your lovely big sister recently told me why the Laing Family Trust was set up! Yes, believe it or not, she told me after a lot of persuasion.'

Melissa eyes her son suspiciously. 'Really? What did Lilly tell you?'

'That your father had worked out your mother only married him for his family's money. He'd always vowed he wouldn't accept his inheritance because he hated his parents, so he very cleverly put it all into the Family Trust Fund for you and Lilly. So, Jean had to sign away her rights to it or he wouldn't accept the inheritance from his parents at all.'

'Did Lilly really tell you all that?'

Zac takes over making the smoothies. 'Yes, Mum, she did. And from what I hear, Jean thinks she got screwed pretty bad.'

'Well, no, not exactly,' Melissa says with a frown. 'I don't know how many times Lilly and I had to hear about it after Dad died. We ended up telling her she could have it all, but she preferred playing the martyr and tried very hard to make us always feel guilty about it. Although she doesn't stop telling us that we should get rid of the Trustees but Lilly and I wouldn't have a clue how to handle the finances... Anyhow, Dad left her everything else, so don't worry; Jean has been really well looked after—'

'Then why is Granddad freaking out at Dad?'

Melissa screws up her face. 'Brian's freaking out?'

'Yes, and Dad won't say why.'

Melissa drums her fingers on the bench. 'Maybe it's because Billy's invested a lot of time and money into this latest wonder drug, the antidepressant he's been developing, but it hasn't been approved.' Melissa raises her voice to be heard over the thrum of the mixer. 'The Therapeutic... the TGA or whatever the government body is that controls the pharmaceutical industry said they need to do miles more tests, which will cost a lot more money, before they'll approve it. I don't understand why your grandfather is so furious. The business is just having a few problems. I don't think Brian likes his clever little son to fail.' She looks Zac in the eye. 'And yes, your dad is a very clever man. When he took the company over from his father, Blatt Pharmaceuticals as it used to be called, was going bust, and your dad managed to rescue it.'

'So has Dad lost a lot of money or something?'

Melissa finds two glasses from the cupboard and places them on the bench. 'Well, after the Family Trust funded the last set of trials, the trustees pulled back future funding as there have been all sorts of problems. The financial side of it is really complicated and, as you know, Lilly and I are both completely hopeless as far as finances are concerned. Neither of us would have a clue. But let's not worry about that. There's nothing we can do, and I am sure your dad will work something out. He always does. Please don't worry about it. You have enough going on with all your studies.'

Zac fills the two glasses, and quickly sips the froth that is spilling over the top. 'I hope everything is okay, he seems pretty stressed.' He glances back at his laptop. 'Fuck, I hate this Chemistry shit!'

Melissa gives him a quick hug, and as she heads to her bedroom to change, yells back to him, 'Let me know if you need anything from the supermarket?' She returns shortly after pulling at her jeans and complaining. 'God, I've put on so much weight! I feel enormous.'

She sees Zac quickly raise his eyebrow and as usual he ignores her gripes about her insecurities. Still, she complains again loudly. 'I've got so fat!'

Zac keeps his head down but this time, he responds, 'Mum, you're not fat.'

'Well, I feel so uncomfortable in all of my jeans.'

Zac's long, fair hair covers most of his face and he continues working with his head down. 'Mum, you're not fat.' He looks up, grins at her and teases, 'That's what you're looking for, isn't it?'

She pinches at the flesh hanging over her jeans. 'Ha ha. No, that wasn't what I was looking for. I just don't understand...' She wanders back to her bedroom, stepping over a pile of jeans and tries another pair. She gets them halfway up and starts jumping. 'Why are they all so tight?'

Zac laughs out loudly as he sees his mum falling backwards onto her bed with a coat hanger hooked through the zip of her jeans.

'Aha! Now you agree with me!' She smiles then pleads, 'No, please don't agree with me. I think I must have shrunk them all in the wash.'

Zac grins. 'You might have put on a bit of weight, but you don't look fat. Maybe you were just too skinny before!'

Melissa smirks at her son. 'I love you. Je t'aime beaucoup. Where did you come from?'

Zac grabs an old photo album from the dresser and sits on the end of her bed. He stops when he sees an old photo of Melissa and Billy on their wedding day. 'Whoa, check this out! Dad looks cool, but you were really under Jean's thumb, weren't you? You look grunt... You just don't look right with that hair and make-up.'

'Grunt must mean bad, doesn't it?'

'Grunt can be good or bad, but in this case, you're right. It means bad. Ha ha.'

Melissa cringes at the photo. 'I look shocking. I think the first time I ever stood up to my mother was when you were a toddler. I was terrified, I can tell you, but it was the best thing I ever did. She's laid off me quite a lot since then. I wish I could destroy all the wedding photos, but your dad looks so good. Mum even got our photo into the local paper, and I just wanted to die.'

Zac laughs. 'Do you still have it?'

'No. I threw it out, but of course she still has a copy, haven't you seen it at her place? Anyway, I don't want to think about her.' She sighs loudly, 'Oh, I wish you weren't always so busy with your studies.'

'Me too. It'd be sick if we could all go to the shack next weekend. Heaps of people are coming up. They're forecasting a really big swell.'

'What about your dad?'

'He's always away for work.'

Melissa nods. 'Oh yes. God, I can barely keep up with his schedule.'

'Has… has Dad got a lot of business in Auckland lately?'

'Not that I know of, but he's all over the place.'

Melissa tries one last time to yank her jeans on. 'Oh, let's forget all this and go and have something lovely and fattening to eat. It's a bit late to go to the supermarket, so I'll just change into something a bit more comfortable.'

As Zac leaves the room, Billy's voice comes roaring through the house. 'For Cahrist's sake, Melissa! Are you ever going to change that broken light bulb? It's dark out here, I almost tripped up the step!'

Melissa quickly throws a dress on and races down the hall to the kitchen as Billy stumbles into the house, briefcase in hand and obviously drunk. 'So, catching up with your dad went well, did it?'

'Sure, sure… you know what he's like.'

*Don't I ever!*

'But that's not the point. Can you please fix that bloody light bulb? I almost killed myself!'

'Well, luckily you didn't, and you're here for another day to save the world from death and disease!'

'Gee, thanks for the sympathy.'

Melissa sighs. 'I'm not feeling very sympathetic at the moment. I've put on so much weight, none of my clothes fit.'

A smile creeps onto Billy's face, and he chuckles like a teenager. 'Yes, I knew you would. And you'll probably put on a lot more too.' His chuckles turn louder and he pulls up her dress, grabbing at the flesh around her stomach.

Melissa slaps his hands away, glaring. 'What?'

'Your thyroid was seriously overactive,' he says with a grin.

'The medication Gerry prescribed will slow your metabolism, and bring it down to where it should be, so of course you'll put on weight.'

'What do you mean, *to where it should be?* What? To some arbitrary level decided by Gerry?'

'No, Melissa, it's not an arbitrary level.'

Zac appears and gives Billy a quick hug then turns to Melissa. 'What's happened?'

'I don't know,' she says, trying to be calm. 'About six months ago I felt a little dizzy and your dad thought I'd better see his mate, Gerry, who's an endocrinologist, who said I have a severe case of hyperthyroidism. So, he put me on these tablets and said I'll need to stay on them for at least two years and I'm supposed to do all of this further testing.'

Billy grins. 'Well, I am sure if Gerry thinks...'

Annoyed by her husband's enjoyment of the situation, Melissa rushes from the room, heads straight to her bathroom cabinet, and throws the entire bottle of thyroid tablets down the drain. *Well, that'll fix the problem and I'll be back in my jeans in no time!*

When she returns to the kitchen, Zac and Billy are discussing a bike race Billy is competing in on Sunday. She waits for their conversation to finish. 'Well, isn't that just dandy that I'm going to be putting on even more weight just because I was a little dizzy for one day.'

Billy adds jovially, 'You'll just have to watch what you eat from now on, and how much you drink with your girlfriends. And no more regular pizzas and sweets with your son!'

Zac laughs. 'Well, that's not going to happen, is it, Mumma?'

'No way, Zac. I wouldn't miss our pizza nights.' She turns to Billy. 'I'm just curious as to why you or Gerry didn't tell me this was going to happen?'

'Well, would you have taken the medication if you knew?'

Zac clears his throat. 'Would you take it if *you* knew, Dad?'

Billy moves away, and again Zac tries to lighten the mood. 'So… pizza everyone?'

'Well,' Billy says, wearing a snide expression. 'I think she may need to do a lot more exercise than she currently does, which I think, apart from a tiny bit of swimming here and there, is zero, isn't it, honey? I bought her a bike so we could go riding together, but I don't think she's—' He stops when he sees her frowning and cuddles her. Although Melissa is angry with him, she lets him stay close to keep the peace. 'How about we all head down the coast the weekend after next, Zac? You and I can do all the theme parks, and your sister and Mum can catch up on a film or some retail therapy?'

Melissa sees the relief on Zac's face that another fight has been avoided, and her son replies, 'I think that can be arranged, old man! and I wouldn't mind smashing your arse at the rifle range again too.' He hugs Melissa, trying to encourage her to get excited. 'You like those big, long, speedy waterslides, don't you, Mum?'

Melissa gives her son a smile. 'Well, Chloe and I do like the waterslides but we don't like the queues. Will it be busy that weekend?'

Zac checks the calendar on his phone. 'Ah, I'm not sure I can do it that weekend, I have an exam the following Monday.'

Billy shakes his head. 'If you have exams, we'll definitely not be going. Your studies should be your priority. Actually, shouldn't you be heading back? It's getting late.'

~ ~ ~

Working on a logo for one of her regular clients, Melissa is startled to hear Billy's car pulling into the driveway. *Oh god, what time is it? I haven't got any dinner ready. Putain!* She rushes to the kitchen, opens the fridge and curses. 'What have I done all day? I think I spent half the day, daydreaming out into the forest, listening to the neighbour's German shepherd barking.'

Billy drops his brief case on the bench, kisses her on the cheek and heads up the hall to his little drinks trolley in the sitting room. 'I'm having a whisky, would you like a gin and tonic or a wine?'

He doesn't wait for her to answer so she calls after him. 'No thanks, I've got lots of work to do tonight.' She glances at a recent photo of her kids on the fridge. *God, I miss them not being here all the time. Our home was always so vibrant and alive when Zac and Chloe were still living here.*

Zac had left home just over a year ago to study in Brisbane and although both kids return home regularly, she feels quite lost since her youngest, Chloe, also went to study in Brisbane six months ago.

Billy yells something from the sitting room, but she ignores him as memories of one of Zac's recent stays with her, comes back to her. Billy was away, and she'd had such a lovely week with her son... but... *why did I mess up?* Her face begins to heat up, and she squeezes her eyes shut, trying to escape the memory but it keeps nagging at her. *He looked so strangely at me when he asked if I was okay.*

Melissa had responded quickly. 'Absolutely! I'm great. I just had the most beautiful dream where I was in these underwater caves—'

'Do you remember me coming home last night?'

Melissa was sure she'd been asleep, but the horror of discovering Zac and his friends, Tom and Sean, had found her cowering under the kitchen bench, was extremely mortifying.

Her eyes had been "weird" he'd said, like she'd been in a trance, but all she remembered was the beautiful dream. The shame. *Oh god, the shame.* Then apologising for scaring him, begging him not to tell his father... only to discover Billy had told both Zac and Chloe that she had done this regularly.

Zac's hug had done nothing to quell her anger at Billy for telling the kids.

Interrupted by Billy's entrance into the kitchen, her mind is abruptly brought back to the present. 'Whoa,' he exclaims, 'you look like you've seen a ghost!' Ignoring his remark, she gives a nonchalant shrug as he seizes the remote, flicks on the TV, and settles onto the couch with a generous pour of whisky.

The kitchen and living room walls come alive with a mesmerizing display of shimmering reflections as the pool cleaner springs to life. Her phone rings, displaying an image of her good friend, Elle. Melissa swiftly answers, 'No, I'm sorry, I don't think I'll make it to the beach in the morning; I've got to finish some work for one of my old clients by tomorrow afternoon. But are we still on for dinner at yours tomorrow night? Great! Got any ideas for what I can make for dinner tonight when the fridge and cupboards are almost bare...? Ah, that's brilliant; I forgot I bought them!' She shares a laugh at Elle's witty sarcasm. 'You're hilarious. I have to go now. See you tomorrow night.'

Melissa quietly removes frozen chicken mornay pies from the freezer, hides the containers in the bin and puts the pies in the oven. *Ah, that will make him happy.*

~ ~ ~

Melissa flinches as the sunlight wakes her. She buries herself deeper into her bed, determined to remain in this reality where she is experiencing intense love. Even as it fades, the sensual aroma of the sea lingers, as does the sense of warm, comforting security and passion. *Suis les marées... suis les marées.* Soft words linger as she relaxes, settles her breathing, and drifts off again.

Surrounded by a forest of towering trees, she runs faster and faster until she lifts off the ground. She soars higher and higher until she is above the treetops, in harmony with the wind. Exhilarated at this feeling of total weightlessness, she sails over the edge of the cliffs. Lured by the glistening ocean below, she shifts her momentum and dives. She glides gracefully through the water, following a man through a series of underwater caves. *Who is this man? It's so perfect! C'est tellement parfait. So divine!*

A loud, distant sound disturbs her, and she fights the strong urge to wake from this dream-reality. *Suis les marées... suis les marées...* The voice becomes louder, more aggressive until suddenly she is plucked out of the current to the surface, Billy's voice destroying the magic. *No... No... Non... Putain de merde.*

'Melissa! MELISSA! You've fucking ruined a whole heap of my important work that I left in the sitting room! Again! This is happening way too often. I can't take it!'

# CHAPTER 2

Cigarette in her mouth, bottle of wine in one hand and two glasses in the other, Elle directs Melissa to her living room. 'Ooh la la. You're looking a bit worse for wear. Ca va? Comment ves-tu? Are we communicating in French tonight?'

Melissa laughs. 'I barely understand a word, but I just keep coming out with it... weird. But I think you asked me how I am? Well, I can tell you, I have definitely been better. How are you? What's going on with your family?'

After Elle deftly refuses to speak of her family, the two sip their wine and gaze out the large, plate-glass window to the pinkish-blue sky and the golden sun blazing over the ocean in the distance. They bask in the moment until Elle guides the conversation to Melissa's nightmares.

Melissa takes a moment and then responds dispassionately. 'Staring, paralysed, naked in the foetal position, or staring... almost comatose in a cowering, defensive position. According to Billy, this is how he's found me after I've had one of these destructive nightmares. Sounds great, doesn't it?' She shakes her head. 'When Billy was away, Zac found me cowering under the kitchen bench... Fuck! I hope I wasn't naked! He didn't say.'

Elle looks at her sympathetically. 'I hope not, that would be a bit embarrassing.' She exhales a thick plume of smoke. 'So, what does Billy do when he finds you like that?'

Melissa swirls the wine in her glass, stares into its depths. 'He's usually so gentle and loving that no matter how much I hate him in that moment, I feel so cared for, and... and I'm desperate for any affection, no matter how small it is. Something in me softens. I just feel so incredibly relieved to be out of the nightmare and be taken back to bed. I suppose I sound like the abused wife who keeps going back for the wee bit of love.'

Elle raises her eyebrows quickly and then motions for Melissa to continue.

'But that love is fleeting. I can't stand it anymore. We should never have been together. I know there were good times, especially when the kids were young, but the bad memories crush any of the good. In photos, we look like the happy family... but all I seem to remember is the bad. Maybe I'm always looking for the bad.'

Elle nudges her. 'Or maybe photos don't actually tell the real story. We pose for the camera with our cheesy faces. Anyway, you're always telling me positive stories about your kids and your dad and Lilly. And of course your grandmother—'

'Oh, aye, Gran!' Melissa smiles. 'To be sure, to be sure.'

'Right, food!' Elle announces suddenly, and directs Melissa back to the kitchen, where they both start making dinner. 'Sounds like it's time you called it a day, Liss. Maybe Billy is somehow creating your nightmares? You're not happy; why stay now that the kids are no longer living at home?'

'If only it were that easy. The kids would be devastated. They love him so much, and they'd blame me. He's great to them.'

'Surely they're a bit suspicious about Janet?'

'No, they just think she's his colleague and I've never been able to prove anything. He always has some plausible explanation and they think their father's a saint.'

Elle rolls her eyes, then grabs her wine glass. 'Really? I mean really?'

Melissa cringes, knowing what Elle thinks of Billy. 'Really! I just can't risk it. Zac and Chloe are so important to me. Honestly, Billy would make out that I'm going mad. Like he always does.'

'Hmm.' Elle muses for a moment then her eyes narrow. 'Bullshit!'

Melissa grins at her friend's outburst. 'To tell you the truth, I really just don't care. I made my bed and now I have to sleep in it.'

Elle slings an arm around Melissa's shoulders. 'I'm sure you're wrong. Honestly? Your kids must sense it.'

'I don't know. But... remember when Saskia finally left Sam and started seeing Raymond?'

Elle nods, crushing the garlic as Melissa dices an onion.

'Her kids didn't talk to her for years after, even though Sam had countless affairs. Sam manipulated their kids' emotions. Even when she offered to leave Raymond, they still refused to see her and—'

'Yeah, well, Saskia must have crap kids, but your kids adore you.'

Melissa forces a smile. 'I just cannot take that risk, especially at this time in their lives when they might be meeting the love of their life! To miss that would kill me.'

'I think they may have given up on the happy family idea quite a while ago, Liss!'

'I don't know... but I guess we better finish making the dinner.'

The kitchen is heady with the scent of garlic and onion. Melissa refills their glasses and splashes a good helping of the ruby liquid into the pasta sauce. 'There just seems to be no easy way out,' she says, blinking back tears. 'Whatever I tell the kids, Billy would undermine me, he's done it so many times.'

'I don't think you're giving your kids enough credit,' Elle

protests. 'They're not five anymore.' Elle lights another cigarette. 'Surely, they must see what Billy's like? They certainly know what your mother is like; they're always making jokes about her. I have a feeling they're a lot more aware than you realise. They're young adults now, Liss. They've left home. They'll be okay.'

Taking their seats on stools pulled up to the kitchen bench, they toast each other. Melissa sighs. 'I should never have married him. I should have told my mother to fuck off way back then, but… I wouldn't have my beautiful kids without him.' She takes a gulp of her wine. 'I don't know how my mother has such power over me, and over everyone else for that matter. I still don't stand up to her as much as I should.'

'I'll stand up to her for you; she doesn't scare me. Although, that over-filled face is a little scary,' Elle jokes, then stares directly into Melissa's eyes. 'You have to leave him, Liss.'

Tears well in Melissa's eyes and she nods. 'I know, but I also know I'll never have the courage to do it. I've thought about it often but I get myself into such a state worrying about the kids.'

Elle opens another bottle of red and pours the wine as Melissa continues. 'Sometimes, I think I'll just bundle myself off to the shack and live out the rest of my days there. My best memories are being there with my kids, and when Lilly and I were young there with Dad. I wish my sister lived back here.'

'Liss, why *don't* you bundle yourself off to the shack? You deserve to be happy. Billy's like an overgrown child.'

Melissa heaves another sigh. 'I know. I cringe whenever he's around my friends. Aish used to call him Manchi—short for Man-Child.' She brushes at her tears. 'I couldn't stand having to share Chloe and Zac, especially as they're so busy with their lives and their studies. They love coming back to their family home, to their own bedrooms, and to see the two of us. Maybe… maybe I'm afraid of being on my own.'

Elle laughs. 'With your looks, sweetie, you'd be snapped up in a second!'

'Ha!'

Elle swirls the rest of the wine around her glass, lights another cigarette, and on a waft of smoke says, 'Well, then, little fifties-housewife, enjoy your lot.'

'But I *am* a little, hard-done-by, fifties-housewife!'

Elle smiles and gently adds, 'Maybe one day you'll experience what it's like to have some power in your life.'

'Oh god, power... that's only for the menfolk.'

Elle hugs her. 'I really love you, Liss, and I hate seeing you like this. Are you sure Billy isn't up to something? I mean he—'

'I know... Aisha's been all over me too, but I've been checking his passport, and he's often a million miles away when it happens... and... and why, after we've been together for a million years, there's no reason—'

Elle pulls a funny face. 'I know it would be weird... Okay, let's drop it. We gotta work this out.'

Melissa reaches over and hugs her. 'I know. I love you guys. You're so dear to me... well, let's focus on dinner and a heart-rending film tonight.'

They clink their glasses together. 'Cheers!'

~ ~ ~

Rolling waves, squawking seagulls and the bright sunlight wake Melissa. She pulls a cushion over her eyes. *Okay, I'm at Elle's on the couch. I can remember the start of the movie but... nothing else. Let's hope I haven't messed with anything!*

Melissa rises and quickly checks for any damage she may have caused through the night. Everything looks just as it should in the apartment, and Melissa breathes a sigh of relief.

Elle bounces in through the front door with two takeaway coffees and sits beside Melissa on the couch. 'Okay, drink your coffee, then we're going for a long walk along the beach.'

Melissa checks the time and smiles awkwardly. 'Wish I could but I have grocery shopping to do. Billy's back tonight and, as usual, I have no food. I've really got out of the habit of cooking since the kids left.'

'I can very easily imagine that! Okay, I might get you to drop me at the headland on your way home.'

~ ~ ~

Melissa becomes transfixed by the glistening ocean as she drops Elle off. She always imagined she would live by the ocean and the longing has never left her, but Billy had other plans. He wanted to be near his business. The arguments had gone on for months before they were married. They hadn't talked to each other for weeks until Billy came up with the compromise.

Land in the hinterland that wasn't far from beaches, close to her family's beach shack, with the highway nearby for Billy. Since Melissa's Family Trust was funding the build, she designed their home with the help of an architect. Billy's only specification was an enclosed formal sitting room, unlike the rest of the house, which was open plan. He had inherited an entire old-fashioned bar fit-out with a drinks trolley and a cabinet with a built-in refrigerator. The forest was the backdrop, but the focus was the 20-metre swimming pool. Old, solid timber flooring continued throughout the entire house and around the pool. Reflections from the water throughout the house were critical to the design.

CHAPTER 3

Melissa frowns heavily as she becomes horrifyingly aware she is lying wet, naked and huddled in the foetal position on her bathroom floor. Billy gently pulls up her eyelid and directs his penlight into her eye. She cringes. *Not again! Not again! Why did he have to come back today and find me!*

She'd assured Billy a week ago that she could fix these nightmares with a natural cure, but he'd hit the roof. 'You have a serious medical condition, Melissa! You could hurt yourself or me or the kids. You cannot diagnose yourself from the internet!'

Always critical of Melissa's alternative health remedies, he scoffed, 'What did you diagnose yourself with last week? Parasomnia! And this week it's... pavor nocturnus! You need to be diagnosed by somebody who knows what they are doing!'

Melissa closes her eyes as Billy checks her over, then covers her in her bathrobe and quietly whispers in her ear, 'We're going to get you better, honey. I'll secure you a bed at Chevallum. You know James is a specialist in this field, he'll sort this all out. I know you agree this has gone on long enough. You're happy with this arrangement, aren't you?'

She knows Billy. She knows this isn't a question.

An intense pain surges through her forehead as vivid

scenes flash in her mind. She sees herself fixated, staring at her reflection in the expansive ensuite mirror. Suddenly, she witnesses herself repeatedly bashing her head against it, exclaiming in confusion, 'What the hell! Que diable!'

She struggles for the memory but all that comes are vague images of hideous, angry soldiers abusing her, the squeals of horses, and the pounding surf.

With a shaking hand, she touches a golf-ball-size swelling on her forehead, and the pain in her head confirms the flashback was real. *God, what was that? It's all so mixed up!*

Scenes from the nightmare return – vivid and vengeful. Aggressive soldiers. Threats. She claws for the memories as they fade, and all she can hear is one phrase on repeat: *Suis les marées... Suis les marées... Suis les marées...*

Billy's face fills her vision, and he smiles sympathetically. 'Are you okay for me to carry you to the bed, honey?'

She smiles and nods. *Thank you. Thank you! I'm so exhausted. Je suis tellement épuisée. I just want to be cocooned within your arms and sleep forever.* He places her on the bed and lies behind her. Pulling her close, he wraps his legs and arms around her, gently stroking her face.

Melissa jerks back as the weight of his arm presses on her ribs and as he pulls away, she pleads with him, 'No. Please hold me. My ribs will be okay... I really need you to protect me. Please hold me tight.'

Despite recoiling from his touch, she is overwhelmed with fear and confusion, craving the comfort of love and protection at that moment. She reluctantly snuggles closer to him, gradually succumbing to sleep. However, the strong odour of Billy's whisky nauseates her, eliciting a desire to vomit. *Oh Billy, you stink... tu pues. The smell of your whisky makes me want to vomit. L'odeur de ton whisky me donne envie de vomir... Je suis tellement fatiguée... I'm so tired...*

~ ~ ~

Melissa senses somebody standing over her. Slowly, she opens her eyes to find Billy putting a cup of tea on her bedside table.

Her fear subsides a little as he sits on the bed, his medi-kit ready to tend to her cuts. He kisses her on the forehead. 'Do you remember me coming into the bathroom last night?'

She shakes her head. 'No—'

'I tried to stop you from hurting yourself and you became really violent with me too.'

'Oh god, no. I'm so sorry. I'm so sorry.' She feels genuinely sorry for him and so ashamed that she was violent and could never remember anything.

'It's okay. I know you're unwell,' he says gently. 'We're going to get you better.' He picks her up and carries her through the house to the garage where his SUV waits. 'I've got all your things – moisturiser, toothpaste, toothbrush, phone, laptop and chargers, some nightshirts...' She listens to him announce the extensive list of things he's packed. *What the hell? Que diable? How long do you plan on leaving me in this place?* 'We're going to get you better, honey, don't you worry. I know there's going to be something... something simple to fix you... James Press is a sleep specialist, he'll sort you out. I love you, honey.'

~ ~ ~

Billy drives carefully around the bends along the coastline road to the hospital, mindful of her injuries. The sky is heavy and grey; the sea mesmerising.

The nightmare of the soldiers and the foreign words niggle at her. *Suis les marées! Rianne! Il est mort!* But all the other words are gone now. She's feeling disheartened and extremely vulnerable. She hates that it is Billy picking up the pieces.

When they arrive at Chevallum, Melissa cowers at the

building and what awaits inside. The thought of Billy's old school friend and med-school crony, Dr James Press, looking after her makes her shudder. Melissa doesn't trust the sleazebag. With Billy's jealousy, it makes little sense that he would leave her under the care of "Sleazy Press" even if he is some great Respiratory and Sleep Specialist. What makes even less sense is why Melissa was smashing her head against the mirror. *What the fuck? C'est quoi ce bordel?*

Yet, as Billy carries Melissa into Chevallum, it was the memory of a party at home a few months ago, that comes back to her. James, she was sure, was coming on to her. How on Earth, after all these years, did he think she would ever want him? If only James knew just how much she's always found his immaculate appearance and arrogant demeanour so absolutely abhorrent.

Now, she sits shivering in the crisp, white, open-backed gown the hospital provided, and waits in a small, sparse cubicle. She draws her thin, bruised legs up to her chest, eyeing Billy. As the wait stretches out, Billy becomes agitated, glancing repeatedly out through the curtains. He expected VIP treatment and now he's making a point of giving every staff member that comes even remotely close, an earful of his discontent.

Melissa hugs her legs, and rocks impulsively on the sticky vinyl stretcher. Gazing blankly into space, she searches her memories for clues of last night's harrowing events. It's increasingly hard to focus, and she soon realises Billy is clicking his fingers in front of her eyes and whispering something in her ear.

'Honey, you look like a psycho queen.' He chuckles. 'Snap out of it or I'll have to have you committed.'

*Ah, the caring husband. Did he really just say that?*

With Billy being part of the medical establishment, this possibility is distinctly worrying, but she continues to focus on her own thoughts until Billy blows his stinking breath hard into her eyes.

'For god's sake, Billy, go! I'll be okay. I don't trust Sleazy Press, but if I have to do this, I can look after myself.'

Billy grits his teeth trying to control himself. 'I'm not going anywhere. I need to know they're going to look after you.'

'Just *go*. You're embarrassing.'

Instantly, his lips tighten and his nostrils flare. '*Embarrassing? Me? You're* the embarrassing one here, with your freakish antics and your—'

'Sorry, I didn't mean that,' she says, wearily. 'But you're stressing me out. I just... don't like him.'

Billy's gaze softens. 'You'll be okay, honey. He's the best in his field and honestly, I think you imagine things. You must have imagined James... well, not everyone wants to get you into bed!'

Melissa doesn't want to argue, especially where it would be so easy for Press to overhear. If Billy knew how many times Press had asked her out when she was dating Billy, they wouldn't be such good mates.

Billy shakes his head slightly, narrows his eyes and continues. 'Anyhow, we need him now. He'll work this out, and we'll have you home in no time, sleeping soundly *through* the night. We'll leave the little psychopath here. You just need some medication and you'll be right.'

*Why the fuck am I here? No. I have to get out of here. No more pills.*

Natural remedies was what she wanted, and Aisha—Melissa's oldest friend—was just as passionate about natural healing and had provided many suggestions and therapies on how to fix the problem but so far nothing had worked.

In a quiet voice, she suggests, 'Aisha still thinks we'll find a natural alternative—'

Billy almost growls at the mention of Aisha. 'What would she know? When did she graduate from med school? And what—'

He stops his rant when a nurse walks past, and he raises his voice, 'I'd like to see Dr Press right now. If he knew we were here, I'm sure he wouldn't have us wait like this. We're personal friends. Where the hell is he?'

A sharp squeak of shoe-rubber on the floor punctuates the nurse's spin to face them. She sucks in a breath and replies with all the composure of a bulldog on the end of its chain. 'I don't think your yelling…' She bites down on the rest of the reply, and offers a strained smile. 'We're doing our best, sir. Please wait patiently with your wife.' And with another squeak of her shoes, she walks on.

Left without an avenue for argument, but having seen her name tag, Billy shouts after her, 'I'll be damn well speaking with your superiors, Nurse Dodd.'

Melissa rolls her eyes. Confident Billy won't seriously try to commit her to a psychiatric institution, she rocks back and forth not just for comfort, but to piss him off. She tries to gather her jumbled thoughts as Billy paces. Sweat seeps through the front of his business shirt, creating bat-like patterns on his rounded stomach. He launches a string of complaints at a passing intern that reminds her so much of her mother. Jean is always right. *Always*.

The similarities between Jean and Billy often make Melissa cringe and she finally snaps. 'Billy, just go! I'll be fine.' Though she isn't so sure about this last part, she certainly wants him gone. 'Go! You need to get back to your work. I'll be a good little automaton and take all the pills the clever little doctors give me.'

'Christ, Melissa, don't you know when to stop? How do you think it makes me look when my wife self-medicates with guff she reads about on the internet, or gets from her pseudo hippy guru?'

'Aisha is my best friend, and she is not a pseudo hippy guru. We research natural remedies together, and as I recall, you were happy when we fixed your tinnitus with onion oil!'

Billy sighs and reluctantly acknowledges that it was true. It had worked.

'Okay,' she says. 'Let's allow this good doctor to cast his magic, and you won't have to watch me have another meltdown.'

'Who got you here today? After last night, I thought you would have been a bit more—'

'I'm sorry. All right... I'll do what they want.'

'It'll be okay, honey,' Billy says, sensing he's won. 'The doctors here will keep an eye on you, and their equipment is state-of-the-art. We'll get you some meds, and you'll be sleeping properly and out of this crazy phase in no time.'

Melissa raises her eyebrows, smirks and says sarcastically. 'My little crazy phase, hey Billy... State-of-the-art? Really Billy? Looks more like the twentieth century to me. But I hope you're right about the sleep because I am completely and utterly drained.'

He cuddles her. 'Well, let's hope they can fix you, and can you please try and be nice to James. He and his father may just be one of our biggest investors into Redlicht's—'

'Oh god, Billy, I am really not in any state—'

'Melissa?' Nurse Dodd peers around the curtain. Ignoring Billy's scornful glance, she continues without skipping a beat. 'Dr Press is ready to see you now.'

~ ~ ~

The room has a bed, a wash basin with a mirror above it, small cameras set up to view all angles, and a monitor connected to a load of cords. Feeling like a rabbit caught in a spotlight, she scans the room, taking note of the cameras set high in each corner. She just wants to sleep. They can do whatever they want, just let her sleep.

Nurse Dodd departs, and a few moments later James appears wearing a dazzling white medical coat that accentuates his golden tan and his head of tight blond curls.

He reaches forward and grabs Melissa around the waist. She grimaces. *Don't aim for the lips like you usually do, Dr Sleazebag!*

James kisses her perfectly on the lips. 'Hi, Melissa. Oh, you have made a bit of a mess of yourself!'

She rolls her eyes and covers the bruising on her forehead with her hand as Nurse Dodd re-enters the room. 'Okay, Melissa, I'll get you all organised for the night.'

James turns to her. 'I'll handle this one.'

Nurse Dodd frowns, and with a shrug, leaves, returning moments later to announce James has an emergency in 301.

James sighs. 'Can't Dr Sutcliff handle it?'

'No, sir, he's left for the evening. There're only a couple of interns, and they asked for you.'

James reluctantly leaves much to Melissa's relief. *An emergency in 301. Putain! Fuck! Get me out of here. What kind of emergency?*

Nurse Dodd raises her eyebrows at Melissa. 'Well, you must be good friends. Never, in all my years of nursing have I seen a doctor offer to do any menial tasks.'

Melissa senses her sarcasm and responds in kind. 'Well, Nurse Dodd, I'm pleased he won't be stooping on my account.'

Nurse Dodd smiles at her. 'Call me Suzie; everyone does. Except the doctors, of course. They use our title and expect us to use theirs. Have you been to the bathroom, cleaned your teeth etcetera?'

Melissa nods.

Suzie helps her to the edge of the bed. 'Let's set you up then!'

Lights seem to be flickering behind the mirror above the basin. *Ah, a two-way mirror. In case the cameras miss something. At the very least, the staff on night shift should get a good show.* She shivers as Suzie secures the cold, sticky pads of the electrodes to her head, neck and torso. The cords are already tangling and she feels faint. *Mon dieu... I feel claustrophobic... je me sens claustrophobe...* She breathes deeply, trying to calm herself, as Suzie reveals a large syringe.

'What the hell is that for? I don't know whether I can do this... all these cords and now this. What is it?'

'This is what's been ordered.' She checks the notes and nods. 'Everyone who comes in after some sort of trauma gets a jab. It helps calm you and get things back to normal. Once you've settled down, we can figure out your normal sleep patterns, and hopefully get to the root of what's causing your problem.' Without waiting for Melissa's reply, she administers the injection. 'Okay, Melissa, that's got you ready. Here's your buzzer should you need the toilet or any assistance.'

Although Suzie dims the lights before she leaves, the small, red LEDs on the cameras make Melissa feel more visible than ever.

'Be careful not to tug on the cords too much or they'll pull at your skin, or worse, they'll disconnect, and we'll lose the data. You have a good night's rest, love.'

Melissa tries to smile agreeably as the damage is already done. *Not bloody likely. How am I going to get to sleep with all this crap on? Some of them have detached already.*

After many attempts, Melissa untangles herself and pulls the small blanket up to her shoulders but now her feet are exposed. *Great. Just great.*

She curls up in a ball, shivering. 'Sure you can spare the blanket? How am I meant to get to sleep with—'

Dizziness overwhelms her. *Oh, what was in that injection? I... what... not... this...*

~ ~ ~

Melissa stirs slightly and senses a presence in her room, she fights to open her eyes, but they feel as heavy as the rest of her. She's paralysed, and fear consumes her. The soft pat of rubber-soled shoes nears. Someone is moving slowly, treading particularly carefully.

A shadow passes over her. A waft of warm air brushes her cheek. Suddenly freed from her paralysis, she flails, striking at whatever she can reach. Heavy pressure against her neck has her fight against the chokehold. Gasping for breath, the sound of a shattering cup disorientates her. She can hear distant screams.

*It's me. I'm screaming... and I'm babbling something that I don't understand.*

A glint of light in her peripheral vision draws her gaze. There's a syringe in James's hand. *No! Get away from me!*

Melissa manages to get one leg free, and kicks James.

A stinging pain surges in her neck, and she knows no more.

~ ~ ~

Melissa watches Billy through the open door of the monitoring room the next morning. Her husband sniggers as he watches footage of Melissa fighting off an imaginary assailant and almost strangling herself in the tangle of cords. When she sees the delight on his face as he views the spectacle of her trauma, Melissa marches into the room. 'Glad to see you enjoying that.'

Billy jolts in his seat. 'Sorry, honey, it was just funny. That kick you gave James—'

'It wasn't funny. And I *know* there was—'

'James,' Billy says, ignoring her. 'I told you it'd be a spectacle.'

'Bill,' James says with a serious tone. 'We think your wife was experiencing something we call confabulation; a disorder in which a person distorts or misinterprets their memories. We see it quite often. First, she accused me of attacking her and kicked me. Then she accused one of the young orderlies. She was hysterical, babbling something incomprehensible. If we hadn't sedated her, she could have done herself or one of us some serious harm.'

'You're telling me! You should see our house most mornings.'

Billy stands as another doctor arrives.

'Ah, Bill, you know Dr Owen Sutcliff, don't you? He's collating what he can from the tiny bit of information we've gathered from the tests so far. Mind you, we lost a significant amount when Nurse Dodd pulled the cords from the machine. An expensive machine that's now damaged.'

After handshakes are exchanged, Dr Sutcliff turns his attention to Melissa. 'We did get a bit of data, Melissa. You are definitely experiencing severe hallucinatory distress. It's not that uncommon. Please sit down and have a look.'

Melissa gratefully takes a seat. 'Oh god, I don't feel well.' She knows the footage won't show what was going on behind her. *I'm sure there was someone in there. But everyone will just think I'm imagining it.*

On the screen is an image of herself tangled in the chords. There's no-one else in the room. Confused, she stands. 'This is really weird. I don't know... I was sure there was someone there and I felt paralysed... I don't... I'm... I'm just going to collect my things.'

As she departs, Billy jokes, 'Judging by that kick you gave James, I don't think you were paralysed.'

James laughs. 'I can't get over all of the babbling she—'

'Enough,' Dr Sutcliffe interjects authoritatively. 'You two are behaving like children.' Melissa raises her eyebrows and shoots a glare at Billy before making her exit.

Packing her toiletries bag, Nurse Dodd enters her room rather sheepishly. 'I do hope you'll be all right, love. You did seem very confused last night, accusing the doctor of trying to strangle you. I assure you; we were trying to save you. You really got yourself all caught up and you were in quite a state.'

'I really thought I was being strangled, I'm sorry.'

'Never mind, you just get yourself well, Melissa.' She quickly vanishes when Billy arrives.

'Sorry I laughed about the kick you gave James,' Billy says. He tries to cuddle her, but she pulls away in pain, rubbing at the injection site like an animal licking a wound. 'You certainly put on a performance. At least we have proof you do go pretty psycho.'

'I bet you would too, Billy, if someone was molesting—' She stops short. *Is this the drug? Or is this my mind messing with me? It can't be... surely?*

'Oh god, what now?' Billy complains loudly as James pops his head in the doorway.

Feeling light-headed, Melissa sits on the bed while Billy and James discuss her situation as if she weren't present. She's transfixed by the strings of dark bruises down the sides of her thighs. A sense of déjà vu creeps over her. She gasps, throws her arms up defensively, and slips to the floor. 'Mon bébé est mort... My baby is dead... Je te méprise, Guillaume... I despise you, William,' she murmurs as her head spins. She closes her eyes and turns her face to the floor. *Guillaume? Mon bébé? Where did that come from? What are Billy and James whispering about?*

~ ~ ~

...Seagulls drift lazily on the warm sea breeze, rising and falling almost in unison with the outgoing tide. Late afternoon light glistens in ripples all around as we talk and laugh just beyond the waves. Luca pulls me close. 'I love you more than anyone could ever imagine being loved! Not in their wildest dreams could anyone love someone as much as I love you!'

'Oh mon amour, I feel the same way too.'

He lifts me above the water and kisses my stomach and then slowly lowers me and cradles me in his arms.

The waves lap seductively at our bodies and without uttering a word, we each feel the tug of the outgoing tide. He tells me we must go, and he pulls me onto his back, my long hair flowing in a gentle trail behind us, blending harmoniously with the motion of the sea.

Luca leads me deeper through a maze of underwater caves and into a bright cavern within the rocky outcrop. Turquoise and gold reflections sparkle all over the mossy walls of the cavern, and water droplets fall from delicate stalactites creating an exquisite melody.

As he lifts my naked body onto the smooth rocks, an ecstasy rises within me. Our desire for each other is overwhelming. The motion of the tide sets the perfect tempo…

We lie in each other's arms for hours, and in his arms, I feel his love. I feel protected.

The waves crash on the outer walls of the cavern… and a bright light suddenly stings my eyes…

Melissa's frown deepens as she desperately tries to hold onto her dream. *I want to feel his kiss. I want to stay here with him.* She frowns even harder, forcing her eyes shut as the blinding brightness intensifies and peculiar noises whisk him away from her.

~ ~ ~

Melissa desperately tries to stay in this dream reality, but Billy's loud peeing sound and the bright light from her bathroom are too disturbing. She's in her bed. *God, that felt so real! Dieu, c'était si réel! Si beau… So beautiful and so real.* She buries herself deeper beneath the covers only to be disturbed a moment later by Billy's bellowing.

'Hoy!'

She ignores him until he pulls the quilt down.

He hands her a glass of water. 'While I'm away, don't forget to take all your pills. Zac should be here soon.'

'Aye, aye, sir. I'll take me wee pills and be better in ta morning, aye, Billy me boy. I must admit the pain tablets are workin' a treat. When do I take anoter dose, moit I ask yer?'

'Really? Do I have to listen to your woeful impersonation of your psycho grandmother all the time? It's either that or your woeful French—'

'I adored my gran,' Melissa snaps. 'Always will, and yes, she was Irish and proud of her heritage. Unlike my mother, Gran was such an amazing woman, way ahead of her time.'

'Your sister with her beloved guru, and your grandma are both wonderfully psycho, you mean?'

'Leave Lilly alone. You'll never understand what a precious soul she is.'

Billy rolls his eyes and tries to kiss her on the lips, but as she flinches, he quickly kisses her on the forehead and walks out of the room.

'You could only be so lucky to have had two people in your family like them,' Melissa hisses at his back. 'As for my mother, you can have her! She'd probably marry you at the drop of a hat. And she hates her Irish descent. Totally ashamed, the wee lassie is.'

*And you'd be nowhere without our Trust to fund your little wonder drug! Wrapping our mother around your finger and getting her to put pressure on us all the time. How on Earth I ever got away with the kids having my surname still shocks me! You must have hated it… or was it the shame of Blatt Pharmaceuticals going bust that did it?*

Melissa sighs with relief when she hears Billy's car back out of the drive. She looks out to the garden where large, grey storm clouds billow overhead. A loud crack of thunder resounds through her room. She smiles as she reminisces celebrating the wild lightning storms with her kids over the years. How they'd loved the thunderstorms as they'd sit on the deck under the balcony and watch the storms pass overhead.

'God, I'm tired.' Reaching over the side of the bed, she

rummages around in her bag, 'Oh bugger, where have I left my phone... Why am I so dizzy... Je suis fatigu*ée*... I'm tired...'

She drops the bag back to the floor and within seconds, she is out to it.

~ ~ ~

Unsure how long she has slept or even what day it is, Melissa stumbles to the shower. Still battered and bruised from a recent destructive nightmare episode, she crouches and lets the water run over her. She tries to make her way to the bath but her legs buckle beneath her, and she falls flat onto the tiles. 'Putain! Merde! Fuck! What the...' *Why do I feel so heavy and weak? I just need to get back to the damned bed. What concoction have they got me on?*

Once more she tries to get up but she collapses again. 'Down! Down! Down!'

*Down, down, down,*
*The king has lost his crown,*
*You got what you deserved though your mind still remains the same...*

Melissa sings the words to herself as the song slowly comes back to her. That night would have been the happiest of her life. Her first date with this beautiful boy she had been secretly in love with for such a long time. He and his friends had sung that song at a beach bonfire. *What was his name? I can't remember if he even told me. And why can't I remember him properly?* He had exuded such confidence behind his guitar, yet he'd shown such a vulnerability, which she had loved.

Everything is hazy but Melissa remembers his white, sun-bleached hair, and an endearing nervousness. She had fallen so badly for him and suffered so much when she never heard from him again. Melissa hadn't slept for months afterwards.

She closes her eyes tight. *Why can't I remember his beautiful face? All I can remember is his white, sun-bleached hair and the way his eyes lit up with almost every word he spoke.* Even decades later, she still shivers at how openly he had divulged his feelings for her. Open, honest, gentle. She had fallen instantly in love.

*Why can't I remember his face?* Melissa remembers nagging him to play another song on his guitar and then felt so embarrassed as he played that song with her name in it. She might not remember his face but she giggles as she remembers some of the song's words.

*'Oh, Melissa, you may be close to home...*<br>
*Oh, Melissa, hear what I'm saying...*<br>
*Oh, Melissa, you're stuck inside ...*<br>
*Oh, Melissa, think about what I am saying...'*

It was as if time had stood still that evening. Nothing else had mattered. They'd danced and laughed for hours and then talked so deeply. *I felt instantly connected with him... I even have shivers remembering that wonderful night.*

Then her memories transform into the nightmare of what happened when Billy had arrived in a jealous rage.

Screeching tyres, the stink of burnt rubber, the explosive BANG! She remembers so clearly Billy's bright yellow car wrapped around the trunk of a massive tree, and Billy lying lifeless on the road, covered in blood. The memory still haunts her, especially the agonising sting of everyone's scornful eyes, and worst of all, her mother's glaring face and slanderous words. 'This is all your fault, Melissa! This is *all your fault!'*

*Fuck. No! Please don't go there! I gotta get organised. Zac will be here any minute!*

Melissa forces herself up, gets dressed, and just as she is about to put on her mascara, Zac comes racing into her bedroom demanding that she comes with him.

As soon as they arrive at the lookout, Zac jumps out of the car, buzzing with excitement. 'Check this out! Have you ever seen a thunderstorm like that, Mum? The storm over the ocean looks like a huge stage with characters coming to life from the explosive lightning show.'

Melissa's eyes widen and she shakes her head. 'Wow, Zac, I think that is the most impressive display I've ever seen.'

Zac looks pleased with himself. 'I know! It's wild! It looks like the entire production has been choreographed!' The storm picks up, and the rain starts to pelt down. Zac yells out, 'I think that's our cue. Let's go into town and watch the storm under shelter! My shout for one of the cheapie beachside cafes for dinner!'

~ ~ ~

Zac races back in from the garage searching for his phone. 'I'll be back next weekend, Mum. I'm sure you're on the up and up! No more nightmares, okay! I'll see you next weekend. Cokehead... I mean, your little baby girl will be here a bit later tonight. You be good now, you hear? Ha ha. Love you, Mum.' He nods, smiles, waits a moment, and adds, 'And I love you, Zac.'

He looks at her cheekily and she smiles and hugs him tightly, 'I love you... Je t'aime beaucoup, beaucoup, beaucoup, mon ami! And yes, I will be good. You really didn't need to stay for the entire week but thank you. It was wonderful spending time with you.'

Once Zac leaves, Melissa puts the kettle on and is distracted by the small forest at the rear of their property. Since she was a child, Melissa had a regular dream about flying. She would be walking down a country path, and as she picked up her pace, she would raise her arms and take flight. Melissa smiles and tries to conjure the feeling. She instinctively puts her arms out—

'Fuuuck!' Steam from the kettle scalds her arm.

After running it under cold water, she pours a cup of tea, gathers that morning's pills from her bedside table, and heads back to her study to complete the logo she's working on but her gaze is constantly captured by something out in the garden. *What is so captivating out there? Why can't I concentrate on my work? I've been working on this for hours and I've not made any progress.*

Remembering that Chloe is coming for dinner, Melissa rouses herself to start the evening meal. *I feel totally wasted.* But she's determined to cook up some healthy dishes so Chloe can take them back for Zac as well.

She scrolls through a music list on her phone and puts on a song by Rodriguez. Turning the stereo up loud, she tries to motivate herself by dancing and singing along at the top of her voice.

> *'Sugarman, won't you hurry*
> *Cause I'm tired of these scenes...*
> *Jumpers, coke, suis les marées.'*

'What the hell? Suis les marées... Suis les marées! Where did that come from?' She rewinds the song and listens to it from the beginning but before long she becomes distracted again. She sings along to another song as she pulls out some salad ingredients from the fridge. 'My happiness is... is...' She stares out into the garden as she slices some onions. 'Suis les marées... Suis les marées... Suis les marées... What the hell?'

She sings the song to herself again:

> *'Silver magic ships you carry,*
> *Jumpers, coke, suis les marées.'*

'What the hell are the lyrics.' She checks on her phone. 'Jumpers, coke, sweet Mary Jane.'

As she turns to get more ingredients from the fridge, an overwhelming feeling of exhaustion hits her, and she nearly collapses. *Oh god, here we go!* She pulls herself around the bench and falls onto the couch. Her sigh is the last thing she hears before falling asleep.

What seems like only minutes later, a noise stirs her. Night has fallen, and slowly waking from a dream, words ring in her head. 'Suis les marées... Il est mort...Vous détendre. Détendre?' she whispers. 'What does that mean?' She yells at herself. 'Tu es une imbécile, Melissa.'

*What were those words? Suis les marées... Det... Vous détendre.* She opens her laptop and searches a few combinations of letters, and finally finds détendre, which means loosen. *Well, that makes it so much clearer—NOT!*

She hears Chloe's car pull up in the drive, and rushes to greet her daughter. 'Vous détendre.'

Chloe laughs. 'What's with all the French? Oh, Mum, it's *so* good to see you.'

Melissa hugs Chloe. 'It's so good to see you too. I don't actually know about the French. I keep having these strange dreams and then random words come to me. C'est dans le couer ma belle, petite fille... Whoa! Not quite sure what that means... something about the heart and beautiful, little girl.'

While Chloe takes her bags to her room, Melissa throws a store-bought lasagne into the oven. *So much for all of the healthy meals I wanted to prepare!*

Chloe sits up at the kitchen bench, and smiles. 'So, what do the medical people think you have?'

Melissa shakes her head. 'They've diagnosed me with something called confabulation. They say I distort my memories. But... I think it's more like amnesic episodes, where I black out and can't remember a thing.'

Chloe bites at the side of her thumbnail. 'And what about the paralysis?'

'They think I imagine that. But they've given me some new medication and they think I'll be better in no time.'

'I'm sure you won't be pleased about that!'

'God, no. I have an assortment of drugs to take now. And they're making me so tired and groggy. But don't worry, I'm going to get over all of this, my beautiful girl.'

Chloe wipes some tears from her cheeks. 'I'm really worried about you Mum. You've never had anything wrong with you.'

Melissa makes her way around the benchtop and hugs Chloe. 'Please don't be upset. How about we sit out by the pool while we wait for dinner?'

~ ~ ~

Melissa stirs slightly, finding solace as he cradles her face in his gentle hands and kisses her passionately. *Suis les marées... Suis les marées...* Her happiness intensifies as they are about to become more intimate when a strange, loud sound disturbs the euphoria. *No. No. I can no longer feel his lips.*

A toilet seat being thrown back forcefully against a ceramic cistern followed by noisy peeing. *Oh, fuck you, Billy! Why don't you jump up and down on the bed as well! Or better still, on my head!*

She rolls over and stares blankly at the hazy-green glow on the clock beside her bed, and although the numbers 6.19 shine crisply, all she sees is a verdant phosphorescent light before her eyes, like a rush of fish were swimming by.

That sense of euphoria returns and once again she floats away, seeking the ocean she knows lies just beyond reality. She smiles serenely as she finds her way back through a maze of caves when soft kisses trail up her neck, cocooned here within his arms. She slowly turns her head to kiss him again when suddenly she sees Billy about to kiss her. *No! No! Non! C'est mal... tellement mal... This feels wrong... so wrong.*

She tries to subtly move away but he becomes more amorous. Melissa flinches as he presses on her body, still bruised from a recent destructive nightmare. Oblivious to her remonstrations, he manoeuvres himself on top of her. *You are such an idiot. Tu es un imbécile.* She complains when he leans on her ribs. Her hope that this may turn him off earns nothing but a quick apology, and he proceeds more carefully. His kisses, his scent... it's all so wrong. Repulsed, she longs to be away from him and back in her dream.

Succumbing to the inevitable, she waits impatiently for Billy to finish. Once done, he rolls away and snarls, 'You know what would be nice, Melissa? If *you* initiated sex for once!'

Melissa rolls over. 'I was having the most beautiful dream—'

'Great. And here I was thinking that maybe I'd pleased you for once.' He waits for a reaction but when nothing is forthcoming, he adds, 'Well, it's been nice having a good night's sleep for a change. Those meds must be doing their job.' He puts her meds and a glass of water on her bedside table.

'Take the blue pill, Melissa. The blue pill!'

He ignores her sarcasm and starts dressing. She closes her eyes, conjuring the images of her dream again, and whilst knowing Billy really isn't interested, she continues telling him about it. 'I've never felt as free as I just did in that dream. I was deep in the ocean, and it felt like I could stay under the water forever. And this beautiful man... he was—'

'Stop it,' Billy growls.

'I'm sorry. It just felt so real. Such a beautiful place, unlike anything I could even imagine. These caves were luminescent, glowing in colours I can't even describe. So beautiful... and there was—'

Sensing her husband's anger she stops and eyes her meds. She *had* been sleeping better of late, and the enchanting dreams weren't unwelcome but there was a big downside – the meds made her sluggish, and she couldn't remember one day from the next.

Melissa glares as she gulps down the pills.

Billy raises his eyebrows disdainfully. 'They're not real, you know. You're wasting your time trying to remember them all the time.'

'Oh, I'm sure they're meaningful in some way. Maybe we

exist in a different reality while we're asleep, like a whole other dimension. I believe dreams can enlighten us if we could remember them. Sometimes, it's like I've been there before; they're so real. I'm sure this other reality could be real. *Je suis sûre que cette autre réalité pourrait être réelle.*'

Billy scoffs. 'You sure aren't off in another dimension when you're having one of your psychotic nightmares. The mess you leave behind is most definitely smack-bang in the middle of our reality. Make sure you take your meds as prescribed. You can't deny they're working. Also Melissa, can you cut it with the bullshit language.' Barely taking a breath, he continues. 'I'm glad I don't remember my dreams. Matter of fact, I don't think I even have them. Good that, because I just haven't got the time to sit around all day pondering their meaning.'

He smiles at her. 'Well, I have to get going. I love you, honey.' And with that, he leans in to kiss her, senses it is unwelcome so he kisses her on the forehead, turns and leaves for work.

She screws up her face as he closes the door. *And Melissa, can you cut it with the bullshit language. Non, Billy, I can't... I like it. I love it... I love it and fuck you. Je l'aime... Je l'aime et te baise. I am sorry... Je suis désolée... désolée... désolée!* She flops back into the comfort of her bed with relief and tries to rekindle her dream but her eyes soon become heavy, and her limbs feel as if they are falling through the bed. She is far too tired to chase it, *je suis fatiguée... I'm so, so tired...* and she slips into the oblivion of sleep.

CHAPTER 4

Hang gliders and kite-surfers fill the sky with their bright colours. The beach is alive with swimmers and surfers and children playing in the sand. Melissa sits alone amongst the crowd, watching a kite-surfer brave the heights. His feats remind her of her recurring dream of flying and she envies the man riding the wind, envies his freedom.

She had needed to get out of the house. The sharp words and cruel barbs Billy had thrown at her at yesterday's party still stung. Even with Aisha and Elle at her side, Billy had still been his obnoxious, insulting self. Oh, but not to his colleague, Janet. Melissa scoffed to herself. *Colleague, sure. Is that what they're calling it these days?*

A bank of ominous clouds barrels over the top of the headland, bringing with it frigid gusts of wind. Those on the beach pack up quickly and race away, herded toward the carpark by stinging sand. Melissa should go too, but she's mesmerised by the kite-surfer gliding perilously close to the headland. Her gut clenches as she watches. 'He's not going to make it...'

At what seems the last possible second, he veers away and lands safely at the other end of the beach. Melissa releases a pent-up breath, shakes her head, and pushes to her feet as thunder rumbles overhead. As much as she'd love to dance beneath the promise of pelting rain, it is time to leave. Not that she needs to get home for Billy, he is on another business trip. Likely with Janet. But she's promised Aisha she'll head over for dinner, and right now, a large glass of wine sounds just perfect.

~ ~ ~

Exhilarated after his kitesurf, Matthew struggles with his gear as the voracious winds keep trying to drag him out to sea. One of the few surfers still out in the huge swell yells out to him, 'That was awesome!'

Matthew laughs as he responds. 'Yeah it was a blast, but I was freaking out as I neared the headland. Didn't think I was going to land it in time.'

He gathers his gear and races to his car, granules of sand hitting him like tiny bullets. Matthew packs his equipment, and when he jumps into the car, sees six missed calls from Manuela. *Oh, fuck! I was supposed to call her!*

When Mathew returns her calls, she frantically talks over him. 'Darling, I've been trying to get onto you for hours. I got the call from Derek and Andy Merton; they want to meet with us. This will be huge! Can you come to Gaston's now?'

'On my way.'

He has no time to change, so arrives at Gaston's wearing a t-shirt and wet boardshorts. He grabs a thin piece of plaited leather from his wrist and ties his hair back. Salsa music plays loudly in the garden as he makes his way through the crowd. Manuela's long, dark hair shines brightly under the dappled sunlight, and her flamboyant nature and sexy accent is, as usual, attracting attention. She stands tall in a tight-fitting red dress that showcases her curvaceous figure, and she dwarfs the two men standing either side of her in their business suits.

Matthew greets her with a quick kiss as she whispers, 'Darling, they love you!' He shakes hands with the two gentlemen and Manuela pops the cork on a bottle of champagne. She pours each of them a glass and announces. 'I think this new marina design is cause for a celebration!'

Matthew grins at her. 'Manuela finds many causes for celebration! We seem to drink a lot of champagne.'

Manuela tucks her arm under Matthew's, pulls him close and laughs. 'Well, if I didn't, you would be head down in your office or out on the tools all day long.' She looks to Derek and Andy. 'Anyhow, aclamaciones, saluti, prost! Cheers everyone!'

CHAPTER 5

Melissa watches Zac towel-off after coming in from the pool and senses something's not quite right with him.

'What is it?' she asks.

'I think you need to say something to Chloe about Oscar. He's such a fuckwit... and she's always upset—'

'She's been having more problems with him...' Melissa trails off to the distinct sound of Chloe's car pulling up. 'I forgot to tell you she's coming here now.'

Chloe rushes into the house with tears in her eyes, embraces her mother.

Zac gives his sister a small smile. 'You okay?'

She nods, tears rolling down her cheeks. He gives her a quick hug, grabs his laptop, and lies down on the couch near the kitchen.

Melissa quickly covers the quiche on the bench and grabs a bottle of water. 'I just made a simple dinner in case we feel like it a bit later.'

They head out to the garden and sit with their feet dangling in the pool. Chloe stops for a moment and looks around. 'God, I miss that sound.' They close their eyes and listen for a moment, then Chloe moves around to lay her head in her mother's lap.

'I miss the sounds of the crickets and frogs, even the cane toads. It sounds like a huge coffee percolator... and makes me so homesick.'

Melissa moves Chloe's long, dark hair away from her face and strokes her cheek. Tears well in her daughter's eyes, and Chloe sits up, takes a deep breath, and finally tells her mother about Oscar.

Melissa pulls her daughter close. 'I'm sorry, my beautiful girl. I'm so sorry. Are you ever really happy with him? I don't want to interfere in your relationship, my mother was so interfering—'

'Mum, you are not remotely like your mother. I want your advice.'

'Well... I would trust your instincts, even if you can't prove anything. I don't know Oscar well, but I wish he would treat you better. Are you really happy with him?'

Chloe smiles awkwardly. 'I don't know. Sometimes I think I couldn't be happier, other times...' She shrugs. 'You've always said to follow your heart and I think I am.'

*Yes, follow your heart but not with him. He's so like your father... Oscar's not the one for you. Oscar n'est pas celui qu'il vous faut. Melissa! Stop this French and concentrate!*

They sit for a while longer, talking, feet swishing in the water until Billy's yell from the garage resounds through the house.

'That's great, Melissa!'

Chloe flinches.

'It's okay. Wait here, he'll be upset about—'

'Melissa!'

Chloe shakes her head, jumps up, and runs into the house. She grabs Zac, and the two scamper up the hall to her room.

Billy stalks into the house and spots her by the pool. 'You didn't bother to turn up to your appointment with Gerry today. He's a very important colleague of mine. He thinks you have a really serious problem with your thyroid, and he needs to do more tests. How do you think it makes me look when my wife just doesn't turn up?'

Melissa thought Billy would be upset the Laing Family Trust refused to give him any more funding, not this. She heads inside, hoping to calm him. 'I cancelled the appointment last week. I don't have any of the symptoms anymore and to be honest, I hardly had any symptoms to begin with. I've been doing a yoga exercise Lilly told me about that's specifically aimed at balancing the thyroid. I've been doing it for a few weeks now and it's working. I'm losing weight too. But of course, Gerry didn't want to hear about that, did he—'

'God, you're an idiot! Do you really think he wants to hear all about your little yoga fucking exercise?'

'Wait here.' Melissa races out of the room, ignoring Billy's strangling gesture. She returns and hands Billy test results. 'I knew you'd be angry, so I've had several blood tests.'

Billy snatches the papers and checks through them carefully.

'And,' Melissa retorts angrily, 'As you can see, every one of these tests shows I don't have any sign of a thyroid problem!'

Billy huffs as he carefully checks the results.

'Funny, the doctor did say I have a high level of—'

'And who did you get to check these results for you? Obviously, Gerry didn't.'

'A local doctor at the Junction Medical Centre.'

'We don't *have* a local doctor. You're not going to some dodgy quack, for god's sake. You whinged about that bunch of no-hopers some years back, as I recall.'

'Well, I wasn't going to drive all the way down the coast just to get Gerry to do it!' Billy storms out of the room and she yells after him, 'Aren't any of you... you... you medical people interested to know about something that might be a cure for thyroid problems? Rather than just pushing drugs down our throats.' He doesn't respond. 'You want to know what the cure is for hyperthyroidism? It's called the "inversion pose". Very simple to do, and thank you for your concern.'

Billy stands seething in the hallway. 'Yes, thanks Melissa. We'll have to get you writing a paper for a medical journal about your conclusive results.'

~ ~ ~

Zac and Chloe cringe every time their parents raise their voices. Zac looks at Chloe despondently and whispers, 'Why doesn't he just leave her and be with Janet? He spends more time with her and—'

'Because Mum would be sad. He's great when—'

'Yes, he's great when he's alone with us, but as soon as he's around Mum, he gets frustrated and—'

'I think they love each other; they're just going through a bad time and he's stressed because of the business.'

Zac rolls his eyes and continues to whisper. 'Why doesn't he just give up on this fucking "wonder drug"? Jean's always putting pressure on Mum and Lilly to let him have more funds to put into it, but it just seems to be a money pit!'

'I don't know, Zac. I trust him, he brought his family's company back from almost bankruptcy. I think he's had to prove himself to Granddad and this will be his goldmine. He's worked so hard for it. I love them both and—' She stops short as they both notice their parents have stopped arguing. 'Ah, okay, I think this is our cue. Let's go.'

~ ~ ~

Melissa notes how Billy's face lights up as he sees the kids. 'Ah, I'm glad we've got you both here. I've been thinking we need a family holiday somewhere. Anyone got any ideas? Queenstown? Los Angeles? Paris?'

Chloe jumps into his arms excitedly. 'What about Portugal? That's the latest rage, I hear!'

Zac screws his face up. 'Nah, what about Hawaii or Bali?'

Melissa looks on happily at how excited her kids are but she doesn't know how she would cope with a holiday. *I feel so dazed most of the time.* She tries to join in the excitement. 'Maybe we should check out the surf in Portugal, Zac, and then that may suit us all.'

Zac grins widely. 'Great idea! That could really work! I'm happy to go anywhere in the world so long as there's surf.' He grabs his bag off the couch. 'I've got to head back to Brissie now but once I get my exam timetable, I'll let you know.'

Chloe hugs her mother. 'I have to go now too.'

Melissa and Billy wave as their kids drive away, then Billy turns around and picks Melissa up in his arms. 'Don't forget we're having the party here tomorrow night and I have some important people coming.'

'Yes, I know Billy, I have caterers set to go, and they'll organise the alcohol as well.' She studies him, relieved that he's not upset about the Trust's refusal to sink any more funds into his wonder drug. He must be banking on the people coming here tomorrow night.

He carries her inside, sits her up on to the bench and kisses her. 'This is going to be the big one, babe! I can feel it! I love you!'

She smiles as she edges herself off the bench. 'That's great, Billy. Love you too.'

He pulls her towards himself and stares into her eyes. 'Would it hurt for you to say it occasionally without me saying it first?'

'Sorry. Désolée... Oops. I'm sorry I'm just really tired and I need to rest.'

CHAPTER 6

Dappled sunlight filters through the leaves of the forest onto Melissa's eyelids as she lies completely still, smiling serenely. She nestles back as strong arms wrap around her. Soft words echo: Suis les marées... Suis les marée... Suis les marées... She breathes slowly and deeply into the strangely familiar, sugary scent from the cotton trees.

Her euphoria begins to dissipate as a dark shadow passes over her eyes, and she feels herself dragged farther and farther from this man she loves. She tries to stay here, in his arms, but he fades... fades until finally, she can no longer feel him.

*No... non.... non... let me stay here.* But this is just another elusive dream, and her reality has just jumped back into bed and is forcefully manoeuvring his hands around her hips and pulling her in to his body. She pulls away. 'Please, Billy, not now.'

Like a small child that hasn't got his way, Billy springs out of bed and yells, 'It's time to get up, dreamer! I was sure you were dead before; I thought you'd stopped breathing!'

There are occasions when she does feel Billy's love, especially after she's had a nightmare but the majority of the time her husband is like a spoilt child. She inhales deeply as a calmness engulfs her and she drifts back to her enchanting dream, huddled within *his* arms where she feels loved and protected. Her breathing slows further, immersed in this other world... in her dream world where the scent is sweet... *oh, what is that? qu'est-ce que c'est... la puanteur de ton whisky... the stench of whisky, oh how vile...* she quickly jerks backwards and opens her eyes.

Billy gasps. 'Fuck. I was sure you were dead this time, Melissa. One day you'll hold your breath too long and you'll kill yourself.'

She ignores him.

He smirks at her. 'So, I'm guessing you had one or two more glasses of wine than you should have last night, huh? You know you shouldn't overindulge while you're on the medication.'

*Oh god, I forgot about the party. I have to cut back on the wine! What happened? Why can't I remember much of the entire evening?* She curses herself as bits and pieces come to her... of Billy pouring her glass after glass. She sits up at the side of the bed and pulls the sheet around herself. 'Perhaps you shouldn't have been refilling my glass all night with that expensive wine then! Those pompous, self-important...! My god, I needed the wine just to get through the night. Why do you get so jealous? One minute you're telling me to impress them and the next you're bailing me up and telling me I'm trying to seduce them! To tell you the truth, Billy, I'd rather not see them!'

'I bailed you up?' Billy scoffs. 'I think your memory may be playing tricks on you again.'

She stares at him incredulously. 'Are you *kidding* me? Check with James. He'll confirm it. It was him you were getting so insanely jealous of. He could see you start in on me. We've got to get some cameras installed—'

'Yes, I agree. We need them all over the house, especially in our ensuite and the sitting room. I've got a company upgrading them at Redlicht's so I'll send them here too.'

'Hallelujah. But honestly, Billy, the other week you're telling me how fat I am... I'm like a dugong and now you think all these men are interested in me! I don't get it.' Melissa pulls the sheet tighter around her. 'Believe what you want, I don't care, but for god's sake, no more parties. You never know, Billy, I may just turn psycho while all these important people are in the house!' She takes a calming breath. 'And stop scaring me awake. It's not funny. I like to wake naturally, especially when I've had a late night and—'

'Honey, I just don't want you to miss the best part of the day. And would it hurt you to come and see me compete occasionally?'

Dressed in his fluorescent bike racing gear, Billy sits on the end of the bed, rummaging around in his sports bag and setting aside his cleats and jersey. 'A little encouragement now and then wouldn't hurt, would it? I love you, honey, and I want you to be proud of me. I'm racing really well, and I'd love you to see me. It seems everyone else has partners there to cheer them on.'

'I'm sorry, Billy I just... I'm not terribly well. I'll come again soon, I promise.'

'Well, the kids are coming.'

'I know; they're coming here for lunch afterwards.'

'They're really starting to get into cheering for their old man. We might even make a competitive sportsman of Zac yet.'

Melissa shakes her head. 'He surfs with his friends, Billy. That's what he loves. He doesn't need to compete.' Making her way unsteadily to the bathroom, she opens the vanity cabinet and rummages for some headache tablets. *You are an imbécile, Billy. If you and your father have your way, Zac will be taking over yours and your father's pharmaceutical world as well! And I think you already destroyed any competitive drive he may ever have had when he was ten, telling him in front of everybody that he was playing soccer like a girl!*

She returns to bed, props herself up on the pillows and pulls the cover around herself. 'The best part of my day differs from yours, Billy. I've never been a morning person and I'm not going to start being one now. I don't have time at the moment to stand around all morning on the side of the road while you ride back and forth every half an hour. I've got so much work to finish. Lucien is expecting this big job to be completed soon, so I'm going to need to shake off this blasted headache and get onto it.'

Billy scoffs. 'I don't know why you bloody bother working; you know you don't have to. I can provide for us all, more than adequately.'

Melissa sighs loudly. 'Oh, are we going to start that again? Okay, well, I like working. I find it fulfilling and interesting and, well, I hope you're right about this wonder drug and the other stuff you're working on because a lot of money has gone into it—'

'You have to spend a bit of money and don't you worry, very soon the Trustees will be eating humble pie. James's father is very interested in investing a lot of money, and we know he's no idiot. Well, don't forget to take all your bloody pills! Perhaps if you were more of a morning person, you'd be a bit more like the rest of us and not destroy the house with your night-time antics!' With that, he clacks noisily out of the room in his bike shoes.

Melissa pulls the covers over her head.

CHAPTER 7

The rain is pelting down as Melissa sleeps serenely, completely oblivious to the storm brewing outside. She frowns at the clap of thunder; rolls over and falls back to sleep until Billy's yelling becomes louder. Louder. 'You've got a hell of a lot of cleaning up to do! In your study this time!'

The door to the garage slams. *Shit... merde, merde, merde. What have I done this time?*

She slowly runs her hands over her body, wincing at the bruising on her forehead, her ribs, and her elbows. The destructive nightmares have returned despite the new meds. As Billy's car backs out of the garage, she stumbles out of bed and heads to her study.

Her drawing lamp has been smashed, her chair knocked over, and her drafting table has been relieved of its contents. A mess of papers, pens and pencils are scattered over the floor. *How could this have happened? I've been taking all the pills, even though they make me so fucking drowsy, they're meant to stop this!* She remembers feeling frustrated with her work just before the guests arrived but she would never do this. *Why do we have to have so many of these parties all the time?*

Shouting obscenities at the room, she rights her chair and

sits down. Tears sting her eyes and her confidence wanes. Any strength she might have had to talk herself out of this depressive spiral is now gone. She can do little more than sag dejectedly onto her desk and sob into her arms. She doesn't remember coming in here last night, but she does remember Sharon being snarly when James's father kept talking to her. And Melissa clearly remembers Billy's jealousy.

Cameras. She needs the cameras set up to see what's actually happening, to prove she's not going mad. *Or maybe I am mad. Who knows, but if Billy doesn't get the cameras here soon, I'm definitely going to get onto it.*

Melissa flattens out the crumpled papers, cursing herself. *Lucien wanted these drawings today.* Tossing the ruined drawings into the bin, she's relieved to find her favourite design is still in good condition as it was left on the glass of the printer.

She's still bitterly disappointed in herself, and majorly pissed off at Billy. *Surely he knows I'd do anything to stop this from happening. I am even taking the prescribed meds.* Melissa opens a new pad, grabs a piece of charcoal and begins to draw.

The process calms her; the charcoal becomes a direct extension of her mind, and she draws her thoughts almost before they become conscious. She stares out to the rear of their property, her mind foggy, and quickly drifts off to sleep.

When she wakes, she finds a few spartan lines of a man she somehow feels she knows. Peculiar waves of nostalgia wash over her. The drawing is her own, but she has no recollection of having sketched it or who this man is. There's a hollowness inside her as she tries to evoke a memory, but the sound of Billy returning evokes overwhelming sadness.

CHAPTER 8

Non compos mentis! Non compos mentis!

The unfamiliar words reverberate in Melissa's head. *Compos mentis* means sane or something like that. *Non... compos mentis?* Insane! Her eyelids feel weighted down, and she has no idea where she is. She can't move. No matter how much she tries. She can hear something moving closer. Closer. *I know someone's here.*

Her heart pounds heavily as she musters all her strength to open her eyes. She gasps when she sees rapid patterns from the pool's reflections onto the large glass doors of her bedroom. *Fuck! Putain! Merde! There must be someone in the pool.* Her knees are huddled into her chest, but she cannot move them. She tries to scream but no sound escapes her.

Terror grips her as she sees the shadow of someone deep in the garden, hiding amongst the trees. *Oh god, who is it? Who is it!* It's moving now. Quickly. Hiding deeper amongst the trees. Melissa keeps her eyes focused steadily to where she last saw the shadow move but as the clouds shift in front of the moon, the shadow disappears into the darkness.

A cold sensation envelops her body, and she shivers as she's able to move slightly. *How on Earth did I get out here? What happened tonight?* Her heart falters as a disturbing image flashes shutter-quick in her mind, of strange, filthy-looking men screaming at her. *Who were they?*

She keeps her eyes fixed on the garden, and her terror outweighs all else, even her anger and disgust at her husband. *Please, Billy, get me out of here!* Melissa struggles to free herself from her paralysis and manages to clench her hand. Slowly, so very slowly, she drags herself to her hands and knees, and crawls back inside the house. With monumental effort driven by panic, she locks the large glass bedroom door behind her. She scrambles over to the bed. 'Billy, oh god, Billy, help me! Help me!'

It takes a moment for her to realise Billy is away. *Why aren't you ever here when I need you?*

Wet, naked, and shivering, she breaks down as she pulls herself onto the bed. *Why can't you be here, Billy?* She reaches for her bag and grabs her phone. *Police. I've got to call the police!* But dark spots invade her vision, creeping in at the edges, and the phone drops from her hand and the darkness becomes absolute.

~ ~ ~

Melissa wakes with a fright to the sound of her neighbour's dog barking. She opens one eye and sees the forest beyond the pool deck. Someone was out there last night, she's sure of it. She knows she didn't imagine it.

As weak as Melissa feels, an insatiable hunger takes hold and she struggles out of bed with her eyes half closed. She stumbles through her house to the kitchen, puts some coffee on and grabs a handful of leftover pizza from the fridge. Dizzy and weak, she slides down the front of the fridge to the floor and sits staring out into the forest, trying to piece together fragments of memory. *I'm sure I was paralysed and someone was watching me. I'm sure of it.* She doesn't remember how she got there, but in the light of day, she's now glad Billy is away.

A box of modelling wax she'd bought weeks ago for the new installation she's designed for Gaston's, is sitting unopened on the bench. She needs to get those models made but the wax is rock hard. Her fingers and hands are too weak, so she puts it in a pan on a low heat to soften it.

While waiting, she grabs her coffee, finds a pair of binoculars, leans against the glass doors and focuses all around the pool area. 'Nothing but leaves, leaves and more fucking leaves.' She pans the area and focuses in through the forest to the neighbouring properties. 'Nothing but trees, trees and more fucking trees. Fuck! What happened out there last night?' She heads outside for a closer look but a pungent smell stops her, and she rushes back inside to find flames scorching the kitchen cupboards. 'Fuck! Putain de merde!'

She mops up the wax that's bubbling all over the cooktop, and glimpses the clock on the microwave to see it's already 11.30am. 'Oh bugger, I give up! I'll just call Lucien and tell him I'm fucking hopeless.'

After searching the entire house, she finally finds her phone under her bed and has vague memories of passing out before being able to call the police. *Why can't I remember anything?*

While her phone is charging, she calls Lucien. 'I'm so sorry. I still haven't got the models ready—'

'Oh, mon amour,' Lucien interrupts with his strong French accent. 'You showed me all the drawings and Adam said you discussed it with him, so I have already given Nash's the go ahead. I love them! They will be installed next week. Please don't worry, I trust you emphatically, Melissa. You have to take it easy, my girl.'

After thanking him and ending the call, she sighs with relief, throws a few clean towels over the cupboards to try and hide the scorching, and collapses on the couch near the kitchen bench.

~ ~ ~

Moonlight shines brightly through the curtains as Melissa angles her sketchpad towards the windows and takes another look at the drawing she's been playing with. She's taken to using the quiet, dark hours to conjure a likeness of this man who appears in all her dreams. She can never see him clearly, but she feels some kind of connection. Relaxing and willing something in her cellular memory to spring forth, she sits with charcoal to paper and slowly, the image appears. It's a young man she doesn't know. In the beauty and stillness of the night, a melancholy fills her. Perhaps what she yearns for doesn't exist in this world.

There's a dull ache behind her eyes, and her mind seems filled with fog. The indignation she feels towards her husband creeps back like a vine squeezing around her heart, barbs sinking deep before making its way to her temples. *What else is in these concoctions James has me on?* She feels like a fucking zombie all the time! Can't focus or remember anything anymore. *I've had enough of this!*

Putting her drawing aside, she marches to the bathroom, grabs the bottle of tablets, and tips them down the drain. Inspired, the second lot of tablets follow the first.

'Fuck you, Billy! Va te faire foutre, Billy,' she whispers. 'I'll be fucked if I'm taking another one of these poisons. You say your meds are helping with the nightmares but I'm still having the same amount of "psycho nights", and now I'm a zombie through the day as well.' She shakes her head. 'Not anymore.'

# CHAPTER 9

'Whoa, Mum, I love it!'

Chloe slides into the booth beside her mother, Zac opposite her, and nods towards Gaston's new installation. She whistles with approval at the three large, brightly-lit, old-fashioned gas pumps. 'I really love them, Mum! I didn't realise they were going to be so big. The glossy red is perfect. They look like three big Gaston's flexing their biceps, competing with each other. Lucien is over the moon with them too!'

Zac smiles and flexes his biceps. 'Yep, they look brilliant, Mum. Did you model them on me?'

'Yes, definitely, Zac. You were the inspiration.' Melissa grins at her children. 'I'm so glad you both like them. I've been so nervous, especially as they're so big and bold.'

Chloe cuddles her. 'Well, they're great.' She gestures to a group of people who have stopped in front of the display. 'Well, they're certainly intrigued with them. How on Earth did you do this with everything that's going on for you?'

Melissa shrugs. 'I've been working on the design for quite a while. Adam from Nash's Steelworks is amazing; he helped me nut it all out and they created and installed them so quickly.'

Chloe stares wistfully at the display. 'Wow. I hope I'll get to do installations one day too.'

Melissa kisses the top of her daughter's head. 'I'd love you to work on an installation with me one day. Next time, I'll get you involved. How's your course going?'

'I don't know,' Chloe says with a despondent shrug. 'I'm not really enjoying it. I hardly ever get pen in hand anymore; everything is done on the computer. I loved that little hand-drawn... you know, the spiralling design you did on Bombetta's menus? Can you show me how to do that again? We get hardly any freehand work.'

Melissa grabs a napkin. 'Sure, I'd love to. I've been obsessed doodling this design since I was a child. It's a kind of spiral.... Well, it starts off as a spiral and then into a treble clef and then around into an ampersand. And you have to do it with one stroke. Zac, will you order some tapas while we're waiting for your dad?'

Zac bows his head. 'Oui oui, ma jolie mère. Je meurs de faim. Ha ha.'

'Ooh la la. What does that mean?'

'I quickly translated it on my phone. It means "yes, beautiful mother. I'm starving." We might have to take a trip to France at the rate I'm going.'

'Lilly and I went to the south of France with our dad when we were very young. I'd love to go back one day.'

'Sweet, so long as there's surf, I'm in.'

'My dad was a mad keen surfer, so there was always surf. I think it was Biarritz. I don't remember my mother being there; she was probably off getting more plastic surgery.'

Chloe scoffs and pouts her lips. 'That'd be right.' She hands Melissa an art liner.

Melissa draws the design quickly and then slowly demonstrates it to Chloe. She hands the pen to Chloe, and holds her hand over her daughter's, demonstrating the movement.

'What's that on your wrist?' Melissa asks. 'Did you draw that on?' It looks for all the world like a four-leaf clover.

Chloe pulls her arm away. 'I designed it, it's a tattoo.'

Melissa chuckles. 'No scrubbing it off then?'

Zac flops back into his seat. 'That looks grunt, Cokehead. Why didn't you get something cool?'

Melissa rolls her eyes at him. 'Oh, I know what you were trying to say: why did she get anything at all on her beautiful skin?'

Zac rolls his eyes right back at her. 'No, I *mean*, why didn't she get something really cool like a scorpion or one of those tribal tattoos?'

Chloe throws one of Zac's expressions back at him. 'Can we just have a bit of shut-mouth from you!' She laughs. 'Shut-mouth! But don't worry, big brother, I have plans for more tattoos, and I didn't forget you. I'm going to get a tree with our family's names on it, on my hip.'

Zac laughs. 'What about Oscar? He hasn't made the tree yet?'

She pushes him and adds, 'Not quite yet. I'd be in and out having to get his name erased all the time—'

'So,' Melissa says, stopping her children. She examines her daughter's wrist again then breaks into a tragic Irish accent. 'So, tell me, wee lassie, did ya get tha' four leaf clover because we've got Irish blood?'

Chloe huffs and extends her arm above the table. 'See? It's shaped like two entwined love hearts. And no matter which way you look at it, one is an M and the other is a W. For Melissa and William.'

'Aww, isn't that sweet?' Zac teases.

Chloe glares. 'Oh, fuck off!'

Melissa bumps her shoulder against her daughter's. 'You're very sweet to go through all that pain for your father and me.'

'Yeah, Mum,' Chloe says. 'I can tell you're really happy about it. I love you guys and I want you to always love each other.'

Melissa notices Billy approaching and responds quickly. 'I know you do, and we love you too—'

'Speaking of Dad, here he comes now,' Zac says, raising his eyebrows at his sister, and moving over in the booth to make room for his father.

Billy walks towards them, eyebrows raised and a smirk on his face, tilting his head away slightly as he walks past Melissa's gas-pump installation. Chloe hides her wrist in her lap but while Billy is on the warpath, it's Melissa who's clearly in his sights. 'God, you're a nightmare! Have you kids seen the kitchen? I think your mother is trying to burn the house down now. What on Earth—'

'Yes, they've seen it,' Melissa interrupts. 'I've organised the—' She stops short as he's clearly not interested in what she was going to say.

Zac motions past his dad. 'Looks like some of our food's arrived. I ordered extra pepperoni for you, old man.'

Taking a long, deliberate breath, Billy shakes his head and takes a seat, helping himself to a slice of pizza. Between bites, he feigns resignation, rolling his eyes at Chloe and Zac for effect.

Chloe points to the installation. 'How cool is it, Dad?'

Billy grimaces. 'Yeah?' He pauses for a while, awaiting any kind of agreement. None is forthcoming. 'Yeah, can we fill up? Is it a drive-through?' Before anyone can speak, he adds, 'I'm kidding! I'm kidding!'

Chloe points at the installation. 'I don't think you get it, Dad. Let me explain, as I'm a bona fide design student now,' she says with a laugh. 'The gas pump connection helps people remember the name as they'll get a great visual of these really cool, old-fashioned gas pumps. And the cute little cartoon character—Gaston, from *Beauty and the Beast*—well, no one will ever forget that name! And the place is booming so something is working.

It's just lucky we have Mum or we wouldn't get a table for ages. Lucien says they're fully booked for the next couple of months.'

Billy's eyes dart from table to table, and it's clear to Melissa he's trying to find something to use against her success. 'Well, maybe it's the fact they have bloody great food! Speaking of which, I'd love an oversized steak and chips! I'm over this health kick your mum has me on.' He smiles happily at his kids.

Chloe takes a breath. 'Speaking of health kicks, look what I've had done, Dad.' She exposes her wrist rather nervously.

Billy almost chokes on his pizza slice. 'Health kicks! Good god, have all the women in this family gone nuts?' Seeing her face drop, he mellows. 'Little flower, what have you gone and done to yourself?' He looks at Melissa, accusation spreading across his face. 'Did you know she was going to get this?'

Zac releases a weary sigh. 'Everyone has them these days, Dad. I'm thinking of getting one too. Dragon sleeves, which stretch over the shoulder blades and down both arms, but I'll make sure you can't see it when I'm wearing a business shirt. I can show you a picture of what I want.' He sees the frown on his dad's face and adds. 'I'm kidding.'

Melissa smiles at her boy, who is once again being the family peacemaker.

Billy shudders and forces another large piece of pizza into his mouth, and Chloe quietly explains the meaning of her tattoo. 'It's only tiny, Dad.'

'In better news,' Billy says, realising this is a fight he can't win. 'How about you come skiing with me to Queenstown in July? I've got a big conference on and I thought we could all have a week or so together.'

Zac and Chloe cheer, high-fiving each other across the table.

Billy raises his hands to quiet them. 'It's all dependent on whether your mum can ever get away. She told me a couple of days ago that it won't be an easy task—'

'I'm sorry,' Melissa says quickly. 'I just wasn't feeling great that day and I was worried when a whole lot of work came in… I didn't say no. I'd definitely love to get away with you all.'

~ ~ ~

After an eventful afternoon at the beach, Melissa and Elle clink cocktails at the surf club. Melissa eyes the six cocktails lined up along the bar. 'Whoa! Three each!'

Elle smiles cheekily. 'Happy hour! Half price! Think of all the savings.'

Melissa laughs. 'Let me pay for all these savings. Please!'

Elle pushes Melissa's bag closed. 'This is my shout. You always pay, and now I have this huge new deal coming up. Baby, I'm going to be in the money!'

Melissa raises her glass. 'Yes, here's to you, clever girl.'

Elle drains the rest of her drink.

Melissa sips her heavily decorated cocktail, and looks out at the ocean. 'That was great for me. I still have a bit of a blocked ear, but it really cleared my head and sinuses.' She raises her glass again. 'And thank you for the show.'

'Ah, yes, my breasts will be the talk of the town.'

Melissa chuckles at the memory of Elle being pummelled by the waves and losing her bikini top.

Elle laughs along with Melissa and pulls her stool close. 'You look amazing today!'

Melissa smiles shyly. 'Thank you. I'm feeling great at the moment.'

'Well, you look amazing, we just have to get rid of these fucking nightmares for you. Sorry. But what the fuck is with them?'

Melissa grimaces. 'I wish I knew. I had a brain scan recently and it came back clear. I'm not quite sure about my mental state. What if I do have some sort of psychiatric—'

'Rubbish! You are exactly the same as you've always been, apart from these bloody nightmares. I really think it's terrible that Billy told your kids you have a psychiatric illness. I wouldn't put up with that—'

'Darling, you wouldn't put up with much of anything!'

Elle pokes Melissa playfully. 'Probably why I'm still single! But you sure are right there. Life's too short to put up with this shit! But really, telling your kids?'

Melissa sighs. 'I don't know exactly what he's said to them, but I'm sure it isn't good. I don't want to involve them, especially as I'm still having these destructive and totally amnesic episodes. What would I say? "Kids, trust me, I'm completely normal… so just ignore the destruction of any of your precious things, which I can't even remember destroying—"'

Elle puts her hand over Melissa's mouth and pulls her close. 'Well, to me you are completely normal. Perhaps a bit on the skinny side and a bit battered and bruised… You haven't looked your normal, vibrant self for a while but when I talk to you, you're the same as you've always been. You know, totally loony! No, seriously, you're amazing. And Aish and Aaron think the same. God knows what these nightmares are about, but you are completely sane, my girl!'

Melissa grimaces and takes a sip of her drink.

'Please don't stay on your own anymore. I can't believe Billy leaves you alone all the time when your kids aren't around. You honestly have to stay with me or Aish or someone.' She stares into Melissa's eyes waiting for agreement.

Melissa nods. 'Thank you. I don't feel as though I'm unsafe, and I really do love being on my own, but I'll stay tonight, especially after I finish all of these Alabama Slammers!'

'Billy should be there helping you to deal with the nightmares not galivanting all over the world. He keeps telling you to stay on the meds even though they're obviously not helping.' Elle shakes her head. 'You two are such opposites. He's all about conventional medicine whereas you'd prefer to tip those pills down the sink. For god's sake, you don't have to stick together unhappily ever after!'

Melissa shrugs, downs the rest of her cocktail and picks up the next. *Unhappily ever after indeed.*

# CHAPTER 10

'Are you sure you won't have a drink?' Billy yells back down the hallway as he heads up to the sitting room to his little drinks trolley to replenish his whisky.

'No thanks,' Melissa calls back. 'I have lots of work to get done.'

He returns with a bottle of wine and a grin on his face while he fills a glass and passes it to her. She raises her eyebrows, sees the determination in his eyes and decides it's not worth the fight. Melissa takes the wine while she continues to work on her laptop on the couch.

Billy sits next to her and flicks through the TV channels and stops for a moment on a sexually explicit scene. Sensing this may arouse him, and that this will inevitably involve her, Melissa slams her laptop shut, puts the wine glass down and jumps up from the couch. 'I've just thought of the best idea for this new client.'

Billy immediately scoffs, 'Oh, no, not another one! You couldn't beat the gas station pumps, could you, or what was it? —the dump truck for Delicious Dumplings?'

Ignoring his sarcasm, she hurries to her study and closes the door. She gathers several large designs from her desk and spreads them over the floor to make his entry as difficult as possible. She sits down at her desk and only moments later the door opens slowly and Billy sneaks in behind her.

Melissa keeps her head down, rolls her eyes. 'By the way, I thought the dump trucks were corny too, but the client wanted something gimmicky because they loved the gas pumps. For what it's worth, the dumplings are huge now!'

'I know, honey, it was a joke! I've actually bought some recently and the business is booming—'

'I'll probably be a while,' Melissa says, keeping her head down and pretending to be engrossed in her work.

Not dissuaded in any way, Billy creeps up behind her and rubs himself against the back of her head while she continues to draw. She cringes and sighs loudly enough for him to hear.

Of course, Billy ignores her. He takes his penis out of his pants and rubs it against her neck.

'God, Billy! What the fuck! I've got so much work on!'

'Come on, its Sunday!'

Realising she's not going to get rid of him any other way, she sighs.

Billy smiles at her, picks her up in his arms, and carries her to the bed. He lifts her slip up over her breasts, kneels beside the bed and kisses up her body. *Oh god this is unbearable. Oh mon dieu c'est insupportable.*

As he nears her face, he obviously sees her disinterest. 'Making love to you is like fucking a stunned mullet, Melissa.'

'Fuck off!' Melissa growls. 'And are you kidding? I *told* you I was in the middle of something! You think only your work is important and mine is nothing—'

'I'm sorry, I'm sorry, honey, you do great work,' Billy apologizes then proceeds gently until his breathing becomes more and more intense as he concentrates on his impending ejaculation.

Melissa is sickened. *Why does he have to breathe all over me!* Her hair becomes trapped under the weight of his elbow and as she tries to push his arm away, a horrifying image of an obese, hairy man forcing himself on her, flashes before her eyes. She shudders violently. 'What in hell's name was that? Qu'est-ce que c'était que ça?'

Billy's breathing intensifies and finally he reaches release. 'What? What the fuck? What... was... what? For Cahrist's sake... Melissa?'

'I don't know what it was! But it was... it was disgusting! Frightening!' She closes her eyes, and clutches at her neck protectively, trying to remember. *It was like he was trying to strangle me. I felt so claustrophobic... Je me sentais tellement claustrophique. Oh... I feel sick!*

Billy kisses her on each breast before rolling off her. 'It was probably just your over-active imagination. Forget about it.' The sour odour of his whisky-breath has permeated their room and she's finding it hard to breathe. Melissa gets up, finds the bottle of wine in the living room, and creeps quietly outside to slide into the pool, washing any remnants of Billy and the obese creature from her mind and body. She dives deep. *Oh, how I love this hollow silence.*

Unwilling to return to bed before she's sure Billy is asleep, she floats on her back and lets her ears fill with water as she relaxes into the gentle rhythm of her heartbeat. Being cocooned by the water like this always calms her. As if she could drift into any reality she chooses. She floats like this for what feels like hours, projecting her dreams onto the stars.

~ ~ ~

Melissa flings an arm over her eyes to ward off the sunlight as she hears Billy screaming at her. 'I don't have time to deal with this, Melissa! I have a plane to catch. I thought you said you could drive me, but that isn't going to happen, is it? Look at you!'

The birds are loud in the background, and the deck is cold beneath her body. She realises she's out by the pool.

When she moves her arm from her eyes, Billy grimaces down at her. 'Look at you! Do you remember me trying to bring you back inside last night? You were so aggressive and ranting as usual, so I literally just had to throw a blanket on you and leave you here. Next time, I'll call an ambulance and they'll find someone to deal with you. Probably lock you up.'

Melissa says nothing as she tries to process his words.

With a sigh, Billy gently picks her up and carries her back to bed. He kisses her on the forehead. 'We're going to have to do something about this, it's killing me! This could have been fatal! I've made you a cup of tea, but I have to run. I'll be back in a few days, I'll let you know when. Go stay at your mother's, the kids can't be here and I really think you'll have to cut down on the drink… especially with the medication. You shouldn't be alone. I love you so much, honey, but I can't miss this opportunity.'

Once he's gone, she sighs loudly. She remembers floating in the pool and staring up at the stars, but nothing after that. *Fuck, I'm tired. Je suis fatiguée. So, so fatiguée.* She rolls over and just as she is about to fall asleep her phone rings. She fumbles for it on the bedside table, sees it's Billy, and lets the call go to voicemail.

'Just leave me be, Billy, for god's sake. And I'd rather live on the street than ever stay with my mother again!'

CHAPTER 11

Billy throws his suitcase on the bed, lifts Melissa in his arms and spins her around. 'This is going to be the big one, babe! The Auckland crew are just about on board.' He squeezes her tightly then puts her down. Excitement lights his eyes. 'I had the major shareholders of one of the largest pharmaceutical companies in New Zealand eating out of my hand... *literally* eating out of my hand.'

Melissa rolls her eyes subtly. *I'm sure they were* literally *eating out of your hand, Billy.* She helps unpack his suitcase while he takes his toiletry bag to the bathroom.

'You should have seen them, honey! They were like putty in my hand. They just hung on my every word. You should have seen me up there presenting to this huge audience. I'm sure you would have been so impressed. It was just like the Melbourne presentation... Hello, can you hear me?'

Billy peers out of the bathroom to see Melissa sitting on the end of the bed. 'Are you listening... Why are you looking at me like that?'

She shakes the brand-new box of condoms she found in the bottom of his suitcase. *Look at that guilty face! Regarde ce visage coupable. Coupable!* She couldn't count how many times she's seen that guilty face. But no doubt, he'll have an alibi, an excuse, he always does! And god knows, she isn't up for another argument.

He reaches for the condoms. 'Great to see you're so happy about my good news, Melissa!' She eyes him suspiciously as he grabs the box. 'What? They're Gerry's condoms, for god's sake! If you had Elle's in your suitcase, I wouldn't go psycho. I have so much on my plate at the moment and now I have to put up with this on my first weekend off in I don't know how long.'

'You know, Billy, I would have believed you if you'd said they were Nigel's; at least he'd have a reason to hide them from his wife. But Gerry has been single forever, so he was a bad choice.'

She ignores Billy as he continues ranting childishly at the top of his voice, happy to be taking the heat off himself and happy that his wife doesn't seem to notice how he thinks he's turned the situation around.

'Have you seen my riding jersey? I don't know how many times I've told you not to wash them in hot water; they're shrunk to the shithouse!'

'They stink of sweat, and I don't use hot water...' Realising she may have missed an opportunity to upset him, she adds, 'Or maybe you've put on a bit of pudge?'

'Fuck off, Melissa!'

'Ah, of course. It was okay to mock me when...' She shakes her head.

Billy picks up a tube of toothpaste in their bathroom and yells, 'What the fuck is this Bentonite toothpaste?'

Melissa yells back, 'Try it. It's much healthier for us.'

'You know what bentonite is, don't you? It's dirt! *Dirt!* No thanks. Where's our usual toothpaste?'

'I threw it out. Just try it, I think you'll like it.'

'No, I won't. I've been using the same toothpaste since I was a kid and I don't intend to change now.' Billy struggles to get his jersey on. 'What the fuck...? I can't get this on!'

'Perhaps you need to order a couple of sizes bigger to accommodate your fuller figure.'

'Oh, fuck off, Melissa. I just don't know why we can't have a cleaner to do the washing, and somebody to do the gardening and the pool—'

'I get people in to help when we need them and always before your parties. I don't want people here all the time. I like to be able to swim naked when I want to. I like my own space and I think I keep on top of everything.'

'Yeah, well, maybe I'd like it all to be done more regularly and more thoroughly and—'

'Okay, well maybe I'll set up a little office at the shack and you can have cleaners and whoever you want here all the time and—'

'No! I'm-I'm sorry, honey,' he says quickly. 'You're doing a great job. I need you here supporting me.'

She shrugs and storms out, making her way to the pool. The water is refreshing, but within minutes she can hear him running around the house, accusing her of misplacing this or breaking that. She dives deep to avoid hearing him until it is almost silent apart from the sound of her heartbeat. She sees his silhouette at the edge of the pool as she is about to come up. *Oh bugger!* Totally out of breath, she springs to the surface and he pounces, yelling angrily into her face. 'You're a fucking dugong, Melissa! Actually, you remind me of a dugong in a lot of ways—a big lump just lolling around in the water all day.'

'A big lump? Actually, Billy, I'm back to the weight I was when you married me and I don't have the beach to surf in, do I? So I do like to *loll* around as you so kindly refer to it, in the pool all day.'

He growls as he storms away, and she yells after him. 'And yes, Billy, I'm like a *dugong* because I don't ever want to hear you!'

~ ~ ~

Billy's car screeches into the driveway and he races into the house. Melissa closes the refrigerator door as he approaches with his hands behind his back and a big smile on his face.

'Well,' she says, 'somebody looks mighty pleased with himself.'

'I am pretty pleased with myself. I just won a race against a bunch of guys half my age. I wish you would come and see me.'

'And what have you got behind your back, pray tell?'

He grins, kisses her and then presents her with a small bag. 'A beautiful piece of jewellery for my beautiful wife!' She opens the bag, suspicious. *Ah, this is about the condoms! Chloe must have told you about this necklace I saw recently. Another "guilt gift" to add to my collection.* The last guilt gift was her expensive, horrendously-bright, aqua-coloured car she received after she saw Billy in town with Janet. Of course, he had an alibi even though guilt was written all over both their faces. The aqua car had just confirmed it.

Melissa had gone through an aqua period. She had towels and notepads and clothing in the colour. But never would she have bought an aqua-coloured car—an expensive spectacle. She loved her old car, and she hadn't wanted this showy monstrosity. It was enough that Billy had his little showy sports car.

Unfortunately, Zac and Chloe had been with him when he presented Melissa with the car. And she'd been mortified at having to drive around in it. 'Wow, it's bright...' she'd said, but sensing the kids' disappointment, had quickly gushed, 'Oh, it's so beautiful. So much better than my old, dull car!'

She'd just wanted to cry.

# CHAPTER 12

Melissa gathers the dirty dishes from the table on Elle's balcony. 'Wow, that's such a beautiful view of the moon over the ocean. It looks almost golden and so huge.' She sighs. 'I miss being by the beach.'

Elle stands and stretches. 'Yes, it is pretty spectacular, isn't it?' She gulps down her wine, butts out her cigarette and holds the empty wine bottle up to the light. 'What happened to that? I wouldn't mind another drop, would you?'

'I'm sure another drop won't hurt the seasoned drinker you keep telling us you are!' Melissa takes the dishes in and returns with another bottle of wine.

Elle quickly refills their glasses and holds Melissa's hand. 'I still don't get why you went back! Billy gets really heavy with you because he hasn't got all the funding he needs for his bloody "wonder drug" and you finally pluck up the guts to walk out and now you're back again. What on Earth—'

'I know, I know.' Melissa blows her hair out of her eyes and stares out over the ocean. 'I just felt sorry for him. He was literally crying... He's so frightened of his blasted father—'

'Liss, he's a grown man. I don't get you. It's okay for him to heavy you but now you feel sorry for him because his father heavies him? Oh, Liss, why did you go back?'

'I felt sick worrying about how I was going to tell the kids. I just felt so sorry for him and I still feel so weak… If these bloody erratic nightmares would stop… It all just felt so overwhelming.' Melissa takes a large gulp of her wine. 'I need to do it when I'm over these bloody nightmares and strong again.'

'Next time, you come and move in with me. I'll help you through it.'

Melissa takes another large sip of wine. 'Next time, I'll drive straight here. Oh, I'm feeling a bit wobbly. I think I may have had a bit too much wine. How about we snuggle up on the couch? I'm still keen to look at this film we've attempted to watch three times.'

After changing into matching pyjamas, both of them considerably drunk, they sit arm in arm on the couch and as the film begins, Elle nods off. But Melissa can't stop going over and over why she went back to Billy. *You know why. You know exactly why. Because Billy would have made himself the hero and her the bad guy.* She couldn't jeopardize her relationship with Chloe and Zac.

She tries to tune in to the film and although for all the world it seemed like she was watching it, images of time spent with her father was all she could see, and she lets the memories wash over her…

…Melissa and Lilly wrestling their dad on the floor… Her father treading water just beyond the swell, waiting for them to jump off the rocks so he could help them onto the waves… She'd always loved cuddling up to her dad while he read them bedtime stories. She'd felt so loved and protected, but Jean put an end to that. 'They're old enough to read to themselves.'

How quickly that tenderness recoils when she carries through each of those scenarios in her mind to their actual endings. Melissa could once again feel the sting of her mother's glare as she stood like an ogre in the doorway, narrowing her eyes at her husband and chastising him for spoiling the girls with frivolous things. Her mother scowling at their father as he played with his children for hours whilst she sunbaked on the sand, far more concerned about retaining her "Miss Bikini" figure and tan.

The memory that hurt her the most was the wrestling getting cut short because her mother thought it improper for fathers to handle their daughters that way. She'll never forgive her mother for making her father feel ashamed!

*God, I hate her!*

~ ~ ~

Rising early, Melissa is relieved that Elle's house seems just as they left it the night before—stained wine glasses, a dirty ashtray, and a sink full of dishes. Still, she checks each room to make sure she hasn't had an amnesic episode and wrecked some priceless something-or-other.

Elle ventures out and pours a coffee from the freshly brewed pot. 'Not a creature stirred, not even a mouse,' she says, and offers Melissa a cup of steaming coffee.

Melissa extends her hands with an awkward smile.

Elle smirks. 'Whoa, they're shaking!'

'Yes, it's been a while since I've had that much wine.'

'You did indulge me! But I really think giving up those pills was the best thing you could've done. You are finally unzombiefied! Ha! I'm sure that's a word. Well, if it isn't, it should be! With any luck, the worst thing you're going to have to deal with today is a hangover.'

'Yes, I've got a smashing one of those,' she said, taking the coffee with a nod of thanks. 'I think a brisk ocean dip will fix it.'

'Not for me! I need to sweat it out! Okay, after breakfast, I'll race you to the headland, I'll run and you swim!'

Melissa scoffs. 'And I can't imagine who will win! Unless, of course, I can attach myself to a strong current and then I could easily win to the other side of the headland.'

'Yes, those currents freak me out. I bet you could win if it goes the right way.'

'I knew a surfer once that used to study the ocean so carefully and he'd win all the competitions. Oh that reminds me… Oh… nope. I can't remember what I was going to say.'

~ ~ ~

'Miss Bikini,' Elle says as the two women sip their coffee and gather together the makings of breakfast. 'Tell me more about her.'

'The nightmare of my life—Jeannie Bikini! She sent me a photo the other day of her crowning glory. Like I haven't seen it hundreds of times before.' Melissa finds the photo on her phone and Elle examines it.

'Wow, she was beautiful. I see where you and Lilly get your looks.'

Melissa's uncomfortable with the compliment. 'I don't see any resemblance to either of us.' She examines the image of her mother and shakes her head.

Elle takes another look. 'You look like a more beautiful, fair-haired version of her. Lilly looks like a more beautiful, dark-haired version.'

'Oh, Jean would hate to hear that; she thinks we got our father's looks.'

'Well, I think you're both much better versions of her. What a shame she's destroyed her looks with too many nips and tucks and fillers and whatever else she does. Anyhow, tell me more.'

'I don't know.' Melissa shrugs. 'She sure did have a lot of men interested but Lilly is sure Jean married our father for his family's money. What she didn't know is Dad hated his parents and swore he'd never touch any of their money, and he kept true to his word. He wouldn't accept his inheritance *but* he set up the Trust for Lilly and me, and once we were of age, we could access it. He always supported our family with his own income, and very well too.'

'From what I've seen, your mum sure never went without.'

'You've got that right. Lilly thinks Dad had woken up to the fact Mum married him for his parents' money, so it was kind of retribution, perhaps. Although, I can't imagine my father being like that. I think he was too proud to accept it; he told his parents often enough they could shove their money. So, I guess the Trust was the best compromise, but not for my mother, obviously.'

They sit in silence, staring into their empty coffee cups and playing with the breakfast crumbs on their plates. Elle's phone vibrates, and after she reads the text, she jumps up, eyes alight. 'Oh la la! Whoa! Shit! No, what is it that you say? Merde! Putain! Fuck! Fuck! Fuck! I gotta go! It happened! It fucking happened! My latest jewellery collection has just been accepted into one of the largest retail franchises in the southern hemisphere. Whoa! This is going to be huge. Oh my god!' She pulls Melissa up and they dance and jump together in the small living room.

~ ~ ~

On her way home from Elle's apartment, Melissa is totally burnt out. She has so much work to finish. *Why did I drink so much! I have to remember to rework the Chapman design today! Oh, and I must remember to change the background to red too!* She yells, 'Remember! Remember, Melissa—change to red! Okay, now I just need some crappy food and then I'll be okay again.' She drives straight to the kiosk on the river, orders a large serve of fries and a thick shake, makes a note to herself about the Chapman design on her phone and drives home along the coast road.

As she pulls into her driveway, she's thankful Billy's away for the day for his cycling event—she really has to get some work done. As she walks past her bedroom, she looks longingly at her bed. 'Wouldn't I just love to hop back in there right now.' She opens the door to her study and then backtracks... *Just a short nap, then I'm going to work.*

What feels like only minutes has been almost the entire day, when she hears Billy's car pull into the drive. *Oh god, am I gonna get an earful!* She quickly jumps out of bed, washes her face, straightens the bed so it looks undisturbed, and sneaks to her study.

When he calls out, she's amazed at how upbeat he sounds, so she ventures down to the kitchen.

He picks her up, grinning widely. 'I won the cycling competition against a huge pack of guys, most of them only Zac's age. I thought you might like a night off from cooking, so I picked up some of your favourite Indian takeaway and I've got a bottle of your favourite white, from Yarra Valley too.'

Relieved for the moment, she manages to engage him in fairly friendly conversation, even though she is secretly dreading what she knows will come next. What always comes after a win.

They sit out on the pool deck and drink and eat as Billy describes his big win. 'You should have seen me, I just literally took off from the pack.' He shows her some footage of the event on his phone as he describes the entire race.

Melissa is distracted, trying to remember how he described one of their last sexual encounters. *What was it? Oh, I know; it's like fucking a stuffed mullet! Oh no it wasn't it was a stunned mullet!* She glances at him while he continues to describe the race. *Stunned Mullet. That would be a great name for Lucien's new seafood restaurant. Stunned Mullet! I like it!*

As Billy finishes off another whisky, Melissa goes to the

bathroom and as she is cleaning her teeth, Billy takes her brush out of her hand and carries her to the bed. He undresses her and very quickly, he is jolting up and down on her. His movements become increasingly aggressive as he gets closer to release. As his breathing becomes more unbearable, she turns her head away. *The stench of your whisky makes me want to vomit. La puanteur de ton whisky me donne envie de vomir.* She tries to think about her new design. *Remember to change it to red... au rouge—* The same horrifying obese, hairy man flashes before her eyes. She shakes her head violently trying to escape the image. *Nom de dieu de merde... God damn it!*

Melissa clearly sees varicose veins all over his back from the mirror built into the ceiling of an old-fashioned, four-poster bed. She squeezes her eyes shut and shakes her head as she tries to shake the image of the same man she'd seen the last time she had sex with Billy. 'I've got to get out of here! The... the smell of the whisky is unbearable... insupportable...'

'I'm so glad you enjoyed—'

She ignores him, scrambles out of bed, runs and dives into the pool.

~ ~ ~

Melissa sighs with relief as she pulls into the drive of her beloved beach shack at Third Point. She feels at home now, protected by the thick maze of trees that surround her here. This is her sanctuary; she's happy here. Melissa loves the old Queenslander with its beautiful, wrap-around veranda hidden amongst the curvaceous cotton trees. She gets out of the car on shaky legs but is relieved to be here, away from her home, away from the nightmares. Away from the guilt of waking to the aftermath of the constant destructive nightmares.

She sits on the veranda and breathes in the sea air, listening to the sound of the ocean, and then heads along the well-worn track she's walked since she was a child. At the top of the dune, she looks out at the sea. Exhaling loudly, the tears come. The gusty wind helps to fill her lungs and she finds a flat rock to sit upon, gulping in the air to try and calm herself. Smothered by confusion and all the disappointments of what is happening to her is almost too much to bear. *Why can't everything just go back to normal?*

As if the seascape is playing out her thoughts, the overcast sky closes in around her and a fog of resignation settles in her heart. Drawing her legs up, she wraps her arms around them and sits staring out at the sea, chewing at the side of her thumbnail.

She sits for hours, deep in thought, until finally she's calm and heads slowly back to the shack. As she nears, worry sets in. *What day is it? Fuck! It's Friday.* Suddenly, a text comes in from Billy: *Don't forget we're entertaining tonight. Very important people. Get the best whisky and shiraz you can find.*

The calmness instantly disappears.

Melissa's heart pounds, and she runs down the path, gets into her car and races home again, cursing. 'I'm not well enough to entertain your fucking guests! Oh, why did I say yes? Why do I always say yes?

'Okay, I'll get some of those... those... No! Fuck it! I'll get, Last Minute Caterers. They'll do everything! Okay, calm down, Melissa, it'll be okay. He'll be okay... As long as he has his expensive booze and his cronies, especially the ones who invest, he's okay. Fuck, what's the time? Oh, no!'

~ ~ ~

Melissa wakes late the next morning in a daze. The entire previous night is a complete blur. She lies on her bed for a moment trying to remember the evening but struggles to recall any of it. She drags herself out of bed, glad Billy has already left. Melissa clears away the remaining bottles and plates, wracking her brain to remember any of last night. She vaguely recalls welcoming the first few guests – Nigel and Sue, and James and Sharon. *Sharon was in a yellow floral dress and was even more snarly than usual. It would be a nightmare being with him, but I wish she wouldn't come.* Melissa knows Sharon hates her. And Melissa remembers Nigel had dyed his eyebrows way too dark and brought his usual half-bottle of wine for he and his wife... *Oh yeah, Billy made quite a funny joke about it.*

*And I remember... I'm sure I remember... fuck. I'm sure I remember James coming on to me in my bedroom... What?* No! Billy watches him like a hawk and Melissa is sure Sharon would have been on to him. It's weird that Billy hasn't accused her of trying to seduce James for a long time. Now they're best buddies, he likely doesn't care, especially if James's father invests in the business.

*Why can't I remember clearly? I'll have to cut down on the wine. And I have to remember to get those cameras installed!*

CHAPTER 13

In a trance-like state, Melissa stands firm against the force of the waves. Lured by the distant voices calling to her from beyond the swell, she dives into the water. She knows the currents well, knows how treacherous they can be, but today she's determined. It draws her in, and she succumbs, breathless, to its almighty power, gliding as one within its course. Melissa loves the feeling of weightlessness and freedom as it carries her farther and farther out to sea. She feels at peace until an image of her children calling her back shakes something deep within her and she suddenly bursts out of the water, gasping for breath.

The immense power of the current still pulls her out, and she quickly swims sideways to escape it. A large swell forms, and with strong strokes, she catches the wave and it carries her back to shore. As she nears, a crowd of onlookers watches. Melissa stays in the shallows, trying to hide, but realises they're not going away, and that their numbers are only likely to increase.

Embarrassed, she covers her face and runs naked up the beach, grabbing her clothes as she races away. What was she thinking? She'd felt this intense lure from the ocean, and then... then... *Why the fuck would I do that? Oh god, I hope nobody I know witnessed it or taped it on their phone.*

She has to get well. And quickly.

Melissa curses herself over and over. A deep sadness overwhelms her. *What the fuck was I doing?* As she gets over the dune towards the shack, she's embraced with a calmness. A flood of tears roll down her cheeks. *Why is this happening to me? What day is it?* Just as she's about to head inside, a vague feeling surfaces. It's Thursday, Chloe's regular dinner night. *I need to get my shit together.*

As Melissa drives home in a panic, Billy calls her phone then texts: Don't forget your daughter is coming tonight.

Melissa arrives just as Chloe pulls into the driveway. She waits until her daughter has gone inside then quickly puts on her bathers, creeps around the side of the house and slides quietly into the pool.

It doesn't take long before her daughter joins Melissa outside. They chat quietly, but Melissa can hardly concentrate. *What was I doing at Third Point? Oh god, I hope nobody finds out!*

She tries hard to concentrate on Chloe's words, and manages to engage in conversation until Chloe's eyes well with tears. Melissa pulls herself out of the pool and hugs her daughter. 'What's the matter, beautiful girl?'

'Dad is really worried about you. He told us you may have... have some kind of serious psychiatric problem.' Melissa pulls Chloe close. *Fuck serious psychiatric problems... non compos mentis...* She cannot believe that Billy would want to worry the kids, but she's pretty sure it's payback for not sticking to the prescribed meds he believes will fix her.

Melissa puts on a brave face. 'Oh, you know Dad, forever the medical man. He's making a mountain out of a molehill—oh, I got it right that time!' She smiles at Chloe's small huff of laughter. 'Now listen, beautiful girl, I definitely don't have psychiatric problems, I'm just having some nightmare issues, which I'm getting under control.'

Chloe hugs her tight. 'Are you really sure you're okay? I love you, Mum. I don't want anything to happen to you.'

'I love you too, and I swear I'm okay. I really don't want you to worry about me. Promise me?'

Chloe stares straight into her eyes. 'Are you sure? Because I do worry about you, Mum, and so does Zac. Are you really sure you have it under control?'

'I'm sure. I feel fine most of the time. Occasionally, I have a bad night. But enough about me. How about we go and make some food?'

They throw some leftovers together and sit at the kitchen bench to eat, but Melissa is struggling to concentrate, wondering what else Billy has said to the kids. *Your mother has severe mental issues. It runs in her family. Her father even refused to accept his own inheritance... What a fool! Quel fou! Fou! Fou! Fucking fou!'*

Melissa blocks Billy's voice out, but she can't stop worrying about the incident in the ocean earlier. *Why would I do that? Did anyone film me? Putain de merde.* She hears Chloe pouring her heart out about her problems with Oscar, and Melissa finally listens attentively. She has subtly tried to tell Chloe what she thinks of Oscar, but, unfortunately, her daughter is blinded by his good looks.

CHAPTER 14

Melissa and Aisha set their towels up on the dunes, away from the families and children playing near the tideline.

Melissa stares for a moment out towards the headland. 'Suis les marées... oops... these words just come from nowhere. Lucien told me that means follow the tides in French. Not quite sure why to follow the tides, but it sounds nice.'

Aisha grins. 'I'm afraid French wasn't my strongest subject at school, unfortunately, since *you*, my good friend, keep coming out with it. Bonjour mes belle amie... ha that's about all I've got.'

'It's so good to see you, Aish,' Melissa says, wiggling her bottom into the sand to get comfortable, then giving up and flopping on her back. 'No, French wasn't my strong suit either, but I just unconsciously keep coming out with it.'

'I'm thrilled you could come. I haven't seen you for ages.'

Silence stretches between them.

'Liss... are you okay? You look really drained. I've left so many messages for you—'

'God, I'm sorry, Aish. I've... I've had a lot of these blasted nightmares lately. And I know what you're thinking but nearly every time Billy has been out of the country. I just don't know what to do anymore. I thought the medications were going to work but I ended up a total zombie.' She gives an awkward smile. 'When Billy is there, he says he tries to calm me down, but I become hysterical, and I won't let him anywhere near me. Recently, I had this golf-ball-sized lump from smashing my head into the mirrored wall in our bathroom—'

'Really?' Aisha tilts her head, and frowns heavily. 'That's so horrible, Liss. Do you remember doing it?'

Melissa shakes her head. 'No, but I keep having these flashbacks where I can clearly see myself smashing my head and I can see him being gentle with me and I just look at him with such hatred.'

Aisha hugs her tightly. 'Oh, Liss, I'm sorry. I wish you would let me try and be there for you.'

'You are so sweet, but I never know when it may happen. It might not happen for several weeks, and just as I think I'm over it, it'll happen several times a week.'

'Well, you must stay when Billy is away and the kids are not there. We could have fun like old times and go to the shack.'

Melissa leans over and hugs her. 'Thank you so much for caring. James—'

Aisha laughs and gestures with her little finger at the size of James's penis. 'So what has the genius doctor diagnosed you with?'

Melissa smirks. 'Ha ha, yes, James says I've got something called confabulation, which is a disturbed memory or something. He says that somehow, I'm *creating* memories. But that doesn't account for the loss of memory… or the paralysis, which he thinks I imagine. And the medications he gave me are a total nightmare. Zac came across another disorder he thinks sounds more like what I have… cas… or mas… oh, I don't know if it helps to have the name if they don't have a cure.'

Aisha smiles. 'Zac's a beautiful boy. They're both beautiful kids.'

'Yes, he and Chloe have been so supportive and kind to me.'

'I'm so sorry, Liss. I wish I could help you.'

Flipping over to lie on her stomach, Melissa buries her head in her arms. 'Fuck, Aish, I don't know what to do. I constantly trash the place during these nightmares, and only remember tiny snippets but I have no idea *why* I'm doing it. I don't get it. I feel so fucked up! Billy thinks I have a serious mental problem and... maybe some sort of schizophrenia or something—'

'Oh, don't be ridiculous,' Aisha scoffs. 'You obviously have a problem with these nightmares, but the rest of the time you're completely fine. Well, you know my opinion of Bully making sure you took all those pills when they were really making—'

'Yes, I know. But I stopped taking them quite a while ago, remember?'

'Yeah, but how long does it take for them to get out of your system? God, it was like you were living in a drug lab with all those pills lined up on your kitchen bench!'

Melissa scoops a handful of sand and watches it run through her fingers. 'I actually believed they were helping for a while, but it was short-lived.'

'What about yoga to help you to de-stress? Has Lilly got any ideas?'

'She hasn't come up with anything yet, except that the kids and I should come and live with her and she'll find a cure! Oh, and by the way, I haven't told Billy I'm not taking any of the meds James put me on.'

'No, of course not.'

'You know, it's funny, but when I have a night without a nightmare, Billy puts it down to the meds! But when I *do* have a nightmare he says, oh, well, they take time to work because I hadn't taken them as directed!'

Aisha snorts. 'That's so typical of Bully.'

'Don't I know it! But I've been in such a bad way again recently, I don't know what to do. I really thought the nightmares were over, and then there I am again, picking up the pieces. Last time, it was the beautiful, enamel sculpture Lilly made for me, and the other month it was a whole lot of designs I'd been working on. When it's some of Billy's important papers, he certainly lets me know! I never seem to destroy much of Chloe or Zac's things, or maybe they just don't complain.'

'Maybe it is some sort of allergy to something or a bump on the head. I don't suppose you remember bumping your head?

'Nope.'

'Ah well... we're going to get you better, Liss, promise.'

They relax together in silence, and Melissa turns to sit and stare out at the ocean.

It's Aisha who finally breaks the silence. 'So, what exactly happens when you have one of these nightmares?'

Melissa shrugs, watching the play of sunlight on the ocean. 'I don't remember anything at all. I just wake up and find myself lying naked on the floor, often feeling paralysed, unable to remember anything. I know I see things just before I regain consciousness. It's frustrating, as I think they're important, but my mind just gets so muddled and I can never remember them clearly. All I know is that the memories are in there somewhere...' She takes a shuddering breath. 'I'm scared that Billy will just ignore me now so that if I really hurt myself it's an excuse to take me back to Chevallum. He really believes James can help me but my life is horrible in that zombie state.'

'Well, you know my thoughts, Liss; Bully by name, bully by nature.'

Melissa rolls her eyes, finding it difficult to disagree with her friend's quip.

'He runs hot and cold, doesn't he? He gives you a lot of shit, but... he also idolises you.' Aisha shrugs. 'Surely, he'd never let you get hurt.'

'Well, I certainly don't think he idolizes me, but... yeah,

I don't think he would either; he's actually really gentle and caring after I've had a nightmare. When he helps me back to bed and cuddles me, I feel so protected. I know he's a pain but I... but I get so frightened... I really need him at the moment.' Melissa sighs and stares out to sea. 'I really... I really want to tell... oh I don't know, I'm so tired... trop fatiguée.'

'Liss, what is it? What's the matter?'

Melissa bites at her lip before she speaks. 'There is something. But I don't want you to freak out. It's a bit distressing.'

'Oh god, what is it?'

'And please, I really don't want you to share this with anyone else.'

'You know you can trust me.'

'I know, but I'm worried you'll be concerned, and I want you to trust me because somehow, I feel I'm in control of it. And... to tell you the truth, nothing can help me short of locking me up, and you know how claustrophobic I get. Just the thought sends shivers down my spine.'

'Yes, I sure do know how claustrophobic you get. We had to climb twelve-storeys last year to avoid the lift, but okay, you're really scaring me now about this. But I promise.'

Melissa takes a calming breath. 'Well, for the last six months or so... on several occasions, I've found myself standing waist-deep, naked, at Third Point.' She looks to her friend for reassurance. Aisha cuddles her and smiles softly. Feeling reassured, Melissa continues. 'It's weird. I feel this huge yearning, and then I have no idea what I'm doing.'

'Oh, Liss, that's really distressing. You could get caught in the currents out there and drown. Please don't be alone anymore. I'd love to stay at the shack with you, or we'd love to have you stay at ours.'

Melissa grimaces. 'He's away so often, and I love being on my own—'

'Well, I think while this is going on, make sure you have someone with you when you're at the shack especially. I'm sure Elle would love to join you too. Or wait for your kids before you go there.'

'Okay. I don't want it happening again either.'

'I don't want you being alone at all, even at your own home.'

'Don't worry, the kids are home often.'

'God, maybe you've been hypnotised by someone. One of your many admirers perhaps!'

'Ha! You're the one with all the admirers!'

'But seriously, Liss, this is really worrying.'

'I know but I just don't know what it is. But I do…' Melissa senses her friend's fear, and decides not to go any further. She smiles and stares back at the ocean.

'You *do* what? What were you about to say before I lost you?'

Melissa takes Aisha's hand and gives it a squeeze. 'I don't remember what I was going to say. I'm sorry I'm so vague. But Aish, I can promise you this, I *am* going to get through this. I've been through some awful times, especially with that mother of mine—'

'She's a difficult woman, isn't she? I remember the shit she would give you and Lilly all the time about the Trust. I don't know how many times you offered it to her, but I think she just wanted you both to feel guilty.'

'I agree. She was a nightmare. Still is. The only time Lilly ever hears from her is when she is bad-mouthing the trustees and reminding us that we are hopeless at the financials.'

'Anyhow, come on, tell me more. You're feeling this calling out to the sea, and then…? What then? Come on!'

'I'm sure it won't happen again. It's really weird, I just feel I'm being drawn to the ocean by this powerful force I don't understand, and it feels so exhilarating and just as I am about to totally succumb to the ocean, I get these visions of Chloe and Zac calling me back and I can't get out of the water quick enough!'

'Oh, Liss, this is really frightening.'

'It's okay, I promise. I'm more worried about the crowds of people gathered on the beach to see this freak show. Some have even taken photos. I'm just waiting for the day I make the headlines in the local paper... or the police take me away for indecency. I don't know what I can do. If Billy or James ever found out, I'm sure they'd have me committed.'

'Well, we have to find something for you—fast. How about we go on a lovely, relaxing holiday. We'd be able to keep an eye on you. A nice little beach up north or something.'

'I'd love that so much, but I've just taken on a whole lot of work. I feel so much better when I'm working. There's not so much time to dwell on things. I'd love to go somewhere maybe towards the end of next month when the kids have time off too.'

Aisha grins. 'Okay, let's do it. Maybe see when all our kids are free, and we can work around them. And definitely no husbands!'

Melissa smirks. 'Oh, is Aaron counted as a husband?'

'Yes, I guess so. Ah, he's a good man. I did well there. Not so sure about my kids though.' She chuckles. 'Ethan is still the perfect child as always, but Ruby still goes off the rails regularly. She called me in the middle of the night, totally out of it, wanting me to pick her up, and it took her about an hour to work out where she was. I think I need to get that tracking app for her. At least she isn't getting into trouble at school anymore.'

Melissa smiles. 'She's a beautiful kid. She'll calm down. Chloe has settled down pretty much, as far as she tells me and she does tell me quite a lot, sometimes way too much, and then I worry. She's definitely calmed down since she's been going out with Oscar. Although I'm not mad about him, I must admit; he's always upsetting her.'

Aisha raises her eyebrows and grins.

'What? Why are you looking like that?'

'Well, he's a little Billy, isn't he!'

Melissa cringes. 'I've been thinking the exact same thing! I try to gently steer her away and Zac has been onto her about him, but she doesn't seem to hear us. Ah well, we can't live their lives for them. It must be those impeccable looks because it just can't be his personality.'

Aisha nods in agreement. 'I find him most disagreeable! Ha ha... But really, he does seem to big-note himself all the time from what I've seen. I bet Bully loves him!'

Melissa laughs. 'Yep, loves him!'

After sitting for hours amongst the dunes, an onshore breeze picks up and the sand starts to whip about them, stinging their legs and faces. Deciding they've had enough, they head to a nearby cafe to see out the afternoon.

~ ~ ~

Blinking from the change in the light, they take a moment to adjust to their new surroundings. Heading towards the counter, Aisha turns. 'I know you're probably keen to give this conversation a rest, but when does Bully get home from his latest jaunt? Are Chloe or Zac around?'

The barista behind the counter smiles as they approach. 'What can I get for you ladies this afternoon?'

Aisha grins at Melissa. 'Not too early for a wine, is it? Or do you want a coffee?'

'Ah, yeah, I better have a coffee. I have a lot of work to catch up on. And Billy gets home tonight.'

They place their order, and Aisha steers them toward a table. 'Oh, that's good. I know you love your own space but just while this is going on, promise me you'll stay with us or Elle when your kids and Billy's away. Promise me?'

'I have so much work to do, it would make it really hard. But

I'll let you know.'

'We love you and we're worried about you, Liss. I still really think you should get security cameras installed—'

'Billy is onto it apparently. He thinks it may frighten me into getting back to Chevallum.'

Aisha contorts her face. 'Well, that wasn't what I had in mind. I thought you may be able to work out what's triggering you. Oh yeah, I've been meaning to ask, what happened about that irregularity in your bloods the doctor at the Junction found?'

Melissa sighs. 'Billy got one of his colleagues to check it out and they sent it to another pathologist, but it didn't turn out to be anything.'

'Oh, I'm sorry, I was hoping that was going to solve all your problems.'

Melissa takes Aisha's hand. 'Now, you promise you won't tell anyone about the weird, naked woman in the sea? I'd die if my kids found out.'

'Of course, Liss. You know I wouldn't. Let's hope it doesn't happen again. I wish you'd make sure someone is always with you.'

Aisha glances at the time on her phone and bites down on her lip. 'Oh no, I just remembered; we have the new building designer coming tonight. We got rid of the last lot; they were an absolute nightmare. I haven't met him yet but Aaron is so happy; this new guy has transformed the design and now it's going to cost us about half for the build, and half in power costs just because of the orientation and raising the house a little. And we're also going to get a huge view of the cane fields and sunsets that we didn't even realise we had before. I'd better run. I'll get the new designs to you, too; we'd love any ideas you may have. Oh, blast; I have to pick Ruby up too. I gotta run!'

She hitches up her little white dress, revealing long, tanned legs, and dashes down the road to her car.

~~~

Racing home with Ruby in the passenger seat, Aisha smiles at the heavy Goth-style makeup running down her daughter's face and the loud music she can hear playing through her daughter's headphones. Aisha panics when she looks at the time, and the more she panics, the more red lights she hits. She breathes deeply. *Ah, Aaron will be okay. Nothing much ever phases him!*

She pulls into her driveway and sees Aaron waving as the building designer departs. 'Well, that must have been our great new designer. Bugger, I missed him!'

Aisha tries to get a look at him but the large design sheets and tubes he's carrying cover his face as he struggles to put them into the back of his car. All she can see is that he's a tall, strong-looking man with shoulder-length dark hair. She gets out of her car and instantly her three large, muddy dogs charge towards her. She tries to protect her white dress from their onslaught but relents quite happily to their playfulness. After a moment, Aisha stares curiously as she notices the designer's car is still sitting out the front. Unable to see much through the tinted windows, she smiles just as her dogs force her to the ground. Now covered in mud, she wrestles with them for a while and then picks herself up again. A few moments later, the designer's car pulls away.

~~~

Matthew drives home, feeling a strange sense of déjà vu after seeing Aisha. He turns into his street, spots his sister's car among the trees in front of his house, and curses. 'Can't she *ever* not be here?'

He enters his house with his arms full of tubes and sheets of designs, throws everything onto his desk and smiles at his sister. 'Where's Monty?'

'I think I heard him barking out in the bush as I walked in.'

Matthew opens the back door and is instantly accosted by Monty, his German shepherd. He crouches to play with his dog but feels agitated and stares at the trees in the rear garden.

Jane joins him outside and looks at him curiously. 'Whoa—you look like you've seen a ghost!'

He reflects silently for a moment and replies, 'Yes... I have. Um... I'm sorry but I'm really busy. I have a huge workload at the moment—'

'What sort of a ghost? A good ghost or a bad ghost?'

He shrugs and continues to stare out at the trees curiously, deep in thought. 'I don't know.'

'Oh, come on, big brother—you have to move on! And you promised me you'd come tonight. Please. I worry about you. You're working too hard. I think Manuela is great for you and she's lovely, but she drives you too hard. Please!' She grabs his face between her hands and stares into his eyes until he realises she's not going to go away, finally he nods.

She hugs him. 'Great! Pick me up at about eight-thirty. I'm sure you'll like these people.'

Creativity seems like a distant memory to Melissa as she spends another day feeling sluggish and depressed. She does her best to work on her most recent commission but finds herself staring out the windows to the forest beyond, totally lost in this haze her life has become.

Before she knows it, she hears Billy entering through the front door, surprised that his workday is actually done. Melissa takes stock of the day's work; she's been at her desk the entire day and is disheartened to see her sketch is less than half-finished. *Where did the day go?*

Billy fills the doorway of her study with his presence. He raises his eyebrows, feigns a smile. 'Have you made an appointment with the psychiatrist?'

Melissa's mental exhaustion is too great to bother lying to him anymore. Coming up with any kind of excuse will tax her beyond her capacities, so staring up at him blankly, she just shakes her head.

Billy breathes in deeply and tightens his lips. 'You know, I really don't have time for your psycho antics anymore. I've got some really big things going on at work and I need to be able to focus.' He shakes a box of tablets at her. 'I went by James's practice and picked up that script. You need to make sure you take them as directed this time. I wish you'd go back to Chevallum.'

The last appointment she'd had with James, he'd made her feel so bad about the stress her nightmares were causing Billy and the kids, so she'd succumbed to a new lot of medications, which James had assured her wouldn't have any nasty side effects, assured her the new pills would definitely help this time.

With no energy left to fight either of them anymore, she follows Billy to the kitchen. He slams his briefcase on the bench, pops a couple of large red tablets out of their blister pack, and hands them to her with a glass of water. Satisfied that he's seen her take the meds, he pulls her close. 'I worry about you having all these episodes, particularly as I am away so often. I'm working my butt off... You may have a nice little trust fund, Melissa, and you do make a bit of money with your work, but with how our family goes through money, I need to work very hard now. I can assure you that if it weren't so crucial for the business, I'd always be here to look after you. I love you, honey.' He kisses her cheek. 'I really care about you, you know.'

While his words of earlier still hurt—her "psycho antics"— she catches herself before snapping at him. 'Thanks, Billy.'

He snatches up his briefcase and heads up the hall to the sitting room to pour himself a whisky, calling out as he goes, 'How long will dinner be?'

*It'd be a lot fucking sooner if you helped! I work too, you know! Well, as much as I can manage with the meds and everything else that's going on in my life! I'm sure I'd manage with whatever money I make, and with the Trust, we'd be fine.*

She suddenly remembers she'd forgotten to clean up the mess she made during last night's episode. She covers her ears and cringes, waiting for the barrage of abuse.

He yells as he opens the door. 'For Cahrist's sake, Melissa! I bloody hope these meds work! Fuck, you made a mess this time. You really need to go back to Chevallum, so they can work out what's wrong with you!'

She doesn't respond, hoping he'll leave her alone, but soon she hears the clinking of ice against the glass as he approaches and stands with a whisky in his hand, waiting for an answer. 'Well?'

'I can't go there again.'

'What are you saying, Melissa? Are we just going to let this continue?'

She lowers her head and mutters, 'No.'

'Look, they just need you for a couple of days to get all the information required to work out what's going on with you. I can't keep living like this; it's really wearing me down. Please go, honey. You've had about three nightmares this past week. They can help you. I love you so much, honey, I need to know that you're going to be okay.'

'You know I don't do it intentionally. I was really good there for a couple of weeks—'

'For god's sake, woman! A couple of weeks without a psycho attack is not "doing really good"! You need to see this from my point of view!'

'I know, I know,' she mutters. 'I think it might be better if I move to the shack for a while.'

Billy snarls. 'Always trying to get to the shack, aren't we, Melissa? And who do you want to share your little shack with, hmm? Got anyone in mind? I'd like to know why you always want to go there. I am...' He stops himself abruptly and she looks at him, deeply curious, before he continues. 'There's no-one to help you there. You could end up topping yourself... jumping off the headland—'

'Why do you think I always want to go to there? What is it *exactly* that you think I get up to? I'm so curious, and I have been for a long time. Can you tell me... or is it just the whisky talking?'

'You need to see a professional. I can't cope with you anymore, with all of the sleepless nights and the other week some of my work destroyed. Who knows whether you'll burn the house down next time. This has to stop.'

Melissa closes her eyes and breathes deeply to calm the anger brewing in her belly. 'I'm not going to Chevallum again. I want it to stop but—'

'Can you at least go to see the psychiatrist James referred you to?'

A compromise. She can do a compromise to at least shut him up. 'Okay... I will. I'll make an appointment soon and I'll try these new meds—'

'Soon? When is soon, Melissa?'

A wave of dizziness hits her and she falls onto the arm of the couch. *I do need help!* She holds herself together in front of Billy, but she's imploding inside.

Billy stares at her, and Melissa can't decipher his expression. 'Are you okay, honey? You look really pale? You really need help with this. You need to take the meds as prescribed or you'll end up worse. I just don't see a natural cure working for this. This psychiatrist, Dr Pymble, James says he's great.' Billy heads back up to the sitting room, yelling back to her, 'You're going to give him a go, aren't you?'

Melissa rises slowly off the couch, follows him up the hall to the sitting room and cringes when she sees the damage again. Broken bottles are piled on top of the drinks trolley, the carpet is covered with shards of glass, and the room stinks of alcohol. *I don't even remember coming in here last night. What have I done all day? I remember getting the brush and shovel this morning but somehow... somehow... the whole day is just a blur.*

Billy throws his hands up at the mess and raises his eyebrows. 'What have you done all day! You'll need to replace my alcohol.' He reaches into the back of the cupboard and pulls out a bottle of his expensive whisky. 'You're just lucky I stashed some out of your reach and you missed this one. This one is a beauty and really reasonably priced! Thirty-eight years old!'

~ ~ ~

In the bathroom, quietly preparing for bed, Melissa is taken aback by the sight of the dark circles under her eyes, and the remnants of bruising on her forehead. 'No more nightmares fer yew now; ya hear, lassie?' she says to her reflection in the mirror.

'What?' Billy calls from the bedroom.

She winces. 'Nothing.'

Billy comes back into the bathroom and watches Melissa from the doorway as she dips her toothbrush into a small glass bottle of coconut oil. He raises his eyebrows, and she explains. 'I'm trying to limit any chemicals—'

Billy shakes his head. 'What? I thought that was why you had the dirtpaste... the bentonite toothpaste?'

'I'm trying this as well.'

'Well, I certainly don't want to have coconut breath nor dirt breath for that matter.' He grunts and goes back to bed.

She sticks her middle finger up aggressively after him and finishes brushing her teeth. Melissa stares deeply into the mirror, becomes mesmerised by her own image until it fades and a hazy light seems to wash over her eyes before she suddenly gets the feeling that someone is watching her. *Who's there? What do you want from me?* She blinks and shakes her head.

She takes a quick look into the bedroom, checking to see if Billy has gone to sleep. Facing herself again in the mirror, she warns her reflection in a whisper, 'No nightmares tonight! Got it? None!'

From the bedroom, she hears a gruff voice. 'For god's sake, no performances tonight, okay? I have an extremely important day tomorrow.'

Melissa imitates him, talking in a whisper to her reflection, 'No performances tonight, okay? I'm an extremely impartant parson.'

~ ~ ~

Waves lap seductively at our bodies, as we stand chest-deep together in the ocean. For many hours we wade and talk and laugh in the water, and then without uttering a word, Luca pulls gently on my arm as we're drawn into the strong current. We hold tightly to each other and allow the ocean to take us, enjoying the soaring sensation through the water as we pass the steep, rocky headland. As we approach the overhanging rocks at the outcrop, we catch our breath and he pulls me onto his back, swims us deeper and deeper through schools of colourful fish and wild sea life. My long hair flows in a wave-like motion behind us, echoing the gentle movement of the sea. I hold tightly to his strong, firm body as we surge through the water. My desire for him becomes insatiable as my body presses tightly against his, as he guides me down under a rock ledge and through a narrow opening.

We emerge up into a cavern hidden inside the outcrop, and I'm instantly captivated by the sparkling reflections of the water and the beauty all around me. I pull myself up onto a smooth rock ledge and dangle my legs in the water. A moment later, Luca effortlessly pulls himself up onto the ledge. He holds me tight, inhales deeply and whispers, 'I could breathe you forever, mon amour.'

We lie down on the moist, mossy rock and he kisses my neck, moves slowly over my breasts to my stomach. My yearning for him is fierce as he caresses me and gently pulls me on top of him...

We lie for hours watching the tide change and the danger of

being dragged out of the cavern and smashed onto the rocks has finally passed. Elated, he picks me up, throws me in the air and kisses my stomach over and over again, smiling. Then he slowly lowers me back down. We look across to our serene sanctuary and he whispers, 'Je t'aime, beaucoup.'

He takes my hand in his and leads me out of the cavern. I want to be with him so desperately, but I'm suddenly worried about my mother and I turn to him, 'Oh mon amour, I cannot leave now, I have to see my mother once more so that she knows I will be safe. Then we will return.'

Luca shakes his head, fearful. 'Oh, non, mon amour! C'est trop dangereux! It is too dangerous! Your mother has forbidden us to marry. You know she will make you marry her cousin.'

'No, Luca. My mother would never do that and when Guillaume finds out that I am with child, *your child*, he will not wish to marry me.'

'Non, Rianne! He is obsessed with you! Il est obsèdé par toi!' Luca looks at me sadly and shakes his head, 'Oh non, mon amour. Your mother is devious. Ta mère est sournoise. Sournoise!'

Tears well in his eyes, and he looks at me pleading. 'Non mon amour. Tu vois la vie en rose. La vie en rose! Rianne. You see life through rose-coloured glasses.' He picks me up, kisses my stomach and reluctantly carries me back to the cavern, and we wait for the changing tide.

~ ~ ~

Melissa feels warm and secure cocooned within his arms. Soft, sweet words linger. *La vie... tu vois la vie en rose... you see life through rose-coloured glasses.* She snuggles back into him as a stinging, cold sensation runs down her back. She presses her back hard against the cold, mirrored wall. *Quoi... Où suis-je? What... What does that mean? Where on Earth am I?* She keeps trying to make herself as small as possible under the thick seaweed. She wants to be swallowed by the ocean but it keeps forcing her back to the shore. Back to the... cold, hard surfaces of the bathroom. She tucks her legs up, clamps her hand over her mouth and stifles a scream as a rush of air and the sweaty smell of horses hits her. Melissa pulls seaweed back away from her eyes, and what she glimpses beyond her camouflage is so deeply distressing. Standing not more than three feet directly in front of her is an ugly old woman holding out a cape shouting. 'Ma fille est vivante!' *My daughter is alive. What... who is she... how... how do I understand her... She's my mother?*

A weird sound and an artificial light drags Melissa away from this shore. *What was that! My mother? Where in god's name was I?* She looks up to see Billy frowning down at her, shaking his head, and all that she can think is, *I'm home.* Billy's voice is like background noise, complaining about how aggressive she'd been towards him. He picks her up, muttering something about not following the prescribed dose of medication as he carries her back to bed.

Billy pulls her in tight to his body. *Thank god you're here, Billy. That was terrifying... C'était terrifiant... Putain! I remember I was even strangled and raped, and then... and then filthy men screamed at me. And that woman... that woman. Oh, stop thinking about it.* She sighs and snuggles back firmly into him, finally feeling safe. Her eyes catch on the clock beside her bed: 17.20. She's supposed to go to Elle's for dinner, but she's just too exhausted. *Sorry Elle and Aish, I don't have the energy to do anything.*

Voices in Melissa's head sound angry... like someone is screaming at her. She tries to ignore them as she settles into sleep, but it's unsettling. She's still frightened; she needs to feel protected from these nightmares. Her mind feels so chaotic. *La vie en rose... la vie en rose... what on Earth is that? A life... a life of roses... god, I don't know. Too tired... too tired to remember. Oh, mon dieu, Billy, the stench of the whisky. Oh yuck... I'm way too tired. Je suis trop fatiguée.*

~ ~ ~

Aisha lets herself into Elle's apartment, a plate of food in one hand and a bottle of wine under her arm. She puts the food in the fridge, and as she grabs three of the ritual wine glasses, Elle calls out, 'I couldn't wait! Very stressful day. Just get glasses for the two of you. I've got a bottle here. Come and see this sensational sunset!'

She joins Elle on the floor in front of the couch, and they admire the sunset through the large plate-glass window. They sit mesmerised by the pink-blue sky, chatting while they wait for Melissa to arrive.

Elle grabs her phone and checks the time. 'I'm really worried about these fucking nightmares. She's having them regularly again. One minute she's on top of the world and the next... what the fuck? I really want to get to the bottom of what is going on.'

Aisha nods in agreement. 'I don't think all this medication she's back on is helping.'

Elle extinguishes her cigarette and excitedly shares her suspicion. 'No, I reckon Billy's got something to do with it!'

Aisha frowns and sips her wine. 'Ah, don't worry, I thought so too, totally, but I'm afraid Liss already checked his passport when this first started to happen and he was in London or Toronto or somewhere, but a long way away. I'd have liked it to have been Billy so she'd finally get rid of him.'

'I can't believe she's hung in there so long.'

Aisha reaches over and squeezes Elle's arm. 'I know. Blame it on those beautiful kids of hers.'

'But they've left home. I still think it could be him. He's in the pharmaceutical industry.'

Aisha sips her wine. 'I don't know... Billy's definitely a dick, but why after all these years? I don't think he would do something like this. Surely not? I mean he has his jealous streak but he has no reason to be jealous. She barely leaves her home. He idolises her, always has... even though he has a terrible way of showing it. I think... I think he's always wanted to be her hero but he's definitely not that. I think he's actually insecure with her, and he covers it by putting her down all the time.'

Elle replenishes the food platter and refills their glasses. 'Well, I'm afraid I'm like a dog at a bone. Actually, my sisters used to call me "Dogatabone" because I always have to get to the bottom of everything. And, unfortunately, I do.'

'Why "unfortunately"?'

Elle shrugs, exhaling a plume of smoke. 'My sisters had a real problem with it. They thought I should let well enough alone. That I was being a pain. Maybe I should have been a detective; no, perhaps a barrister instead of a bloody jewellery designer. A jewellery designer that hates jewellery. Brilliant, aren't I?'

Aisha laughs. 'Yes, a brilliant jewellery designer... and a great cook, and good-looking, and the loveliest, kindest—'

'Okay, okay,' Elle says, and Aisha laughs at her friend, who is always uncomfortable with compliments. 'Now, sorry, can you remind me again; why did she marry him?'

Aisha rolls her eyes. 'I can't quite fathom it nowadays, but her mother was ferocious, and I have my suspicions—'

'What? Tell me. Tell me.'

'Oh, I don't know...'

'Come on, just tell me. What's with that face?'

Aisha isn't sure what she should share and decides on a different direction. 'Oh... um... Lilly was overseas in her commune, and Julie and I—Julie was a good friend of ours from school—well, we were terrified of Jean as well. Melissa's mother just had such control over her.'

'That's really weird for a mother to...' Elle hesitates, and her eyes go wide. 'Was she pregnant?'

'Oh dear, dog at a bone! I can't believe you don't know the whole story. But no, she was definitely not pregnant.'

'I know bits and pieces, but I just don't totally get why they're together.'

'Me either. And I can tell you, I did try to make her see sense but Liss changed a lot after the accident.'

Elle stubbed out her cigarette and returned to her wine. 'I did hear he was very attractive and very popular back in the day, and...' Elle winces, 'I must admit I thought he was really quite attractive when I first met him, but then he opened his mouth... you know those men who big-note themselves all... ah who cares... anyway, go on.'

Aisha cast a glance toward the front door, but still no sign of Melissa. She sighs and continues. 'Well, her mother was very impressed with Billy's family. She forced Liss to go to all his sporting competitions even though Liss hated them. The only time I ever remember Jean being nice to Liss was when she started dating Billy, and I remember she was livid when Liss broke up with him.'

'Weird.'

'Very. Liss had told Billy clearly that it was over, but then the accident happened and that changed everything.'

'Just one second.' Elle jumps up and runs to the kitchen to get her pack of cigarettes. 'I can't get my head around it. It was like she was forced into marrying him.'

Aisha closes her eyes and shudders. 'God, Billy's accident was a nightmare. It was the only reason they got married. After it happened, Liss was under a huge amount of pressure from her mother.'

'Why? What happened? Ooh, hang on; I think this calls for another bottle. I thought Liss would be here by now. But that's okay, we can just talk about her instead,' she says with a laugh, and checks her phone as she returns with another bottle. 'Still no message from her.'

Aisha stares at the ceiling, trying to remember how everything had unfolded all those years ago. 'Well, we were only about fifteen or sixteen. Liss had just recently broken up with Billy and she'd been invited to this beach party by this gorgeous boy with white, surfie hair. People were playing music, sitting around a huge bonfire having a great time. Liss looked so happy, you could see that she was mad about this boy. They both looked so into each other, but I was worried.'

'Why?'

Aisha takes a large sip of her red wine, fortifying herself. 'I was worried because on my way to the party, I saw Billy with Jean on the veranda of the shack. I desperately wanted to warn Liss, and then suddenly out of nowhere Billy turned up and all hell broke loose. I'm absolutely sure it was Jean who told Billy that Liss was at the party, she was obsessed with Billy's family.'

'Why was that?'

Aisha's eyes widen. 'His family were big, wealthy socialites with a huge pharmaceutical company. Blatt Pharmaceuticals.'

Elle nudges her. 'Ha ha. Oh that's right, Billy Blatt... it sounds kind of comical.'

'I know, it suits him, doesn't it? Now, where was I... oh yes. So, anyhow, Billy storms into the party, totally freaks out at Liss. He was seething, and the look he gave Liss's date... I've never seen anyone so angry. He was swearing loudly and carrying on. *Everyone* stopped. We were all frightened by what he might do, and then he seemed to stop, and he took a big breath... it was like he was trying to control himself, his anger. Anyhow, Liss was trying to calm him and then he basically just threw her into the bushes in front of everybody and stormed off in a rage.'

Elle shakes her head. 'Liss told me about the jealous tirades where he'd storm off in his car and she'd be freaking out that he might kill someone on the road.' She shakes her head again, takes a big gulp of wine. 'Anyway, continue.'

'She chased after him but she was back in no time, looking really shaken. Everyone told her to forget about him—the general consensus being that Billy was a dick and she should just get on with enjoying the party. And next thing, we heard tyres screeching and a huge bang, like an explosion.'

'Well, that'd be a party stopper, wouldn't it?'

Aisha tries not to laugh at her friend's quip. 'Yes, it sure did. He'd driven straight into a tree.'

'I can just see Billy doing something stupid like that,' Elle says, lighting up a cigarette. 'He was pretty hurt, wasn't he?'

Aisha nods. 'Seriously injured. Thank god Liss hadn't gone with him or she'd be dead. The major impact was on the passenger side.'

'He really is a dick... a real dick! I like that word. It suits him.'

'You're not wrong, but poor Liss felt so guilty. She blamed herself for *his* stupid accident. Jean gave her hell about it, too, and completely dominated her life from then on. Liss hardly got to see any of us at all. Julie and I were her only remaining links to the outside world, and Lilly was overseas living in a commune where they didn't have telephones. So, it was guilt. Bloody guilt. She allowed herself to be guilted into marrying Billy.'

Elle raises her eyebrows, encouraging Aisha to continue.

Aisha grimaces. 'I wish I could have stopped her... but, she's such a softie, or she would have left him years ago. And of course, Jean was highly skilled at getting her own way. She was scary, and I mean *really* scary.'

Aisha gulps down some more wine and laughs. 'Talking about scary, have you seen her latest surgery? I think they pulled the skin on the sides of her forehead too tight and now she has a permanent frown.'

Elle laughs. 'I know. She looks terrible. I try not to look at her as I find myself staring a bit too closely, which she doesn't like. She stares back at me and scowls. I don't think she likes me much.'

'Oh, don't worry; she doesn't like anyone much. She hates me and Aaron, and can you believe she hates her own granddaughter?'

'Ah yes, good girl, Chloe! She won't put up with her grandmother's bullshit. Enough detouring, continue.'

'Well, Bully was in a really bad way after his accident. He was lucky he didn't die. And even without Jean telling Liss repeatedly that it was completely Liss's fault, she felt responsible, she felt sorry for him. He was really messed up. It was the end of any hope of him going on to a professional sporting career. He was in rehab for probably about a year. We hardly saw Liss at all.'

'Really?'

Aisha reflects for a moment and adds, 'I think Billy tried to redeem himself to his father after his stupid accident. He studied really hard so that eventually he could help re-build the crumbling family empire. I'm sure he got a lot of help from friends of his father's, but he is also fiercely competitive, as we all know.'

'Yeah, don't we just. He's such a show-off. I'm sure he thinks I'm attracted to him.'

'Ha ha, me too.' Aisha sighs. 'I don't know, I think Liss has always lived with the fear that he could do something similar again in a jealous rage and possibly not survive the next time. Or kill her or the kids along with him!'

Elle refills their glasses, checks her phone where it's charging in the kitchen.

'Anything from Liss?'

'Not yet, if she's not here in the next half an hour, I think we should call her. Now, answer me this: why did she feel so guilty? She'd already broken up with Billy and she wasn't driving the damn car. They were both so young? It almost sounds like an arranged marriage.'

'Logically, Liss knew it wasn't her fault, but she couldn't shake it and she was kind of weird at the time... and she was so controlled by Jean, who would take Liss to the hospital to see him almost every day. Sometimes, I'd go with her, but I hated it. Jean would heap attention on Billy; she even talked to the nurses about his condition. And before she'd leave, she'd give Liss this horrible cold stare. It was like she was saying, "This is all your fault, so you just sit there and make it right!" And she'd swish around with her nose in the air and stalk out.'

Elle refills their glasses and plays some music. 'I really can't stand her. I find it hard to be around her— Okay, Aish, what's that face for? Come on, get it off your chest.'

Aisha screws up her face. 'Okay, you promise never to repeat this as I've never said anything to anyone including Liss... and I don't have any evidence.'

Elle nods and raises her glass. 'I swear on red wine.'

Aisha snorts at her friend but raises her glass as well. With a sigh, she continues. 'I don't know but I've always been suspicious that Jean began sedating Liss after the accident. I can't be sure, but Liss just wasn't the same afterwards.'

'Could it have been shock from the accident?'

'Maybe but something just felt... off. Overnight, Liss went from this sparkly-eyed, bubbly girl to melancholic and kind of lifeless. I know it was a shock for her, but she was like it for ages. I just wouldn't put it past Jean. She slowly came back to her old self, but it seemed like it took such a long time.'

'I guess we'll probably never know, but I wouldn't put it past Jean either. You don't think she could have anything to do with what is happening to Liss now, do you? No... it's ridiculous, they rarely see each other anymore.'

'What reason would she have? No, I'm sure not. She's too

busy on her overseas cruises.'

'Did you notice how Jean was with Billy at the barbeque? Anyone would think she was in love with him.'

'Yes, I did notice. It's quite sickening.'

'So… Billy's the only guy Liss's ever been with, right?'

'Yep.'

'I cannot, in my wildest dreams, imagine what that would be like.'

'Yeah,' Aisha says with a sigh. 'She'd only just turned twenty when they got married.'

Elle's phone rings and she races to the kitchen to answer it. 'That'll be Melissa,' she says and takes the call. She frowns as she comes back to the living room. 'That was Billy. He said she's in a bad way and can't get out of bed. He sounded really worried.'

Aisha sighs. 'I wondered if she'd make it. I spoke to her yesterday and she didn't sound good.'

~ ~ ~

Aisha frowns as she wakes early the next morning, feeling a little shaky. When she opens her eyes, she finds Elle in her full gym gear about to leave. She calls after her, 'Wait for me. Let's go and have an early morning swim. I need to get rid of this hangover.'

'Okay. We'll head down to the beach. You can swim, and I'll run.'

'Great, and then I think we should call around to Liss's don't you?'

'Yes, definitely. A quick swim and a quick jog and we'll grab some croissants and—'

'Perfect but we'll have to go to Lemaire's. Liss only likes their croissants.'

The two women, feeling considerably better after their morning exercise arrive at Melissa's house as Billy is pulling out of the drive in his little sports car.

He lowers his window and smiles. 'Howdy, girls. She's pretty good today. She's out in the pool. The house is open, go on in. I was supposed to be flying out to Copenhagen this morning for a very important meeting, but I've delayed it till after the weekend when Zac will take over. Hopefully, he can handle her. I think we need someone with her all the time at the moment as she won't go back to Chevallum. I'll tell you girls, it's taking its toll on me.'

They smile awkwardly as he drives away and as soon as he is out of sight, Aisha puts the back of her hand up to her forehead melodramatically. 'Oh, I tell you girls, it's taking its toll on me. But I am such a hero, I'll get through it somehow! I'll soldier on!'

As they walk out towards the pool, Elle laughs and sings, 'Billy you're such a hero, you're such a pain in the arse. Billy you're such a...'

Melissa bobs her head above the pool and smiles.

Aisha laughs. 'That's what I like to see!' She immediately strips off to her bikini and runs and jumps in the pool.

Elle drops the croissants onto the kitchen bench. 'What the hell!' She quickly strips, runs naked toward the pool, and yells as she jumps into the water. 'Ha, I didn't bring a cossie! Ah well, bombs away!' She resurfaces near Melissa. 'Sorry, I thought I'd be sitting beside your bed attending to your every whim.'

Melissa laughs. 'I'm so sorry girls. I was just so knocked out. I'm not doing very well at the moment. I'm frightened to go to sleep—'

'Liss...' Aisha hugs Melissa. 'This is so frustrating. You've never been sick in your life and now this is happening. Although, this only just occurred to me this morning. Remember when we were probably about eleven or twelve, and I'd sleep over at your house and sometimes you did these weird things in the middle of the night? Do you remember?'

Melissa frowns and then nods slowly as the memories return. 'Oh yeah! I remember you telling me that I did weird things, but I could never remember the next day. Ah yes... and Jean treated me like a lunatic telling me that I would sometimes try to get out of the house in the middle of the night, but I could never remember anything.'

Aisha splashes water at Melissa. 'One night you were trying to force something into our old video machine and when I asked you what you were doing you freaked out at me and then you hopped back in bed. When I asked you about it the next day, you had no idea.' She tilts her head, studying Melissa. 'I wonder if this could be connected.'

Melissa smiles awkwardly. 'I don't know. I wish it were as simple as it was back then. I didn't ever smash stuff or smash myself. Did I?'

'No... no, you didn't. But I do vaguely remember you babbling a couple of times.'

'Apparently, I do a lot of babbling nowadays. Maybe it is connected.'

Melissa props her arms on the side of the pool, slowly kicking her feet. 'I don't know what's happening to me. Sometimes, I have these vivid nightmares and I feel as though I'm really a part of them, and I feel like I could wake myself and escape but somehow, I want to stay there. I try to concentrate so I'll remember when I wake but it just gets so muddled. And then I have these recurring dreams where I'm with this beautiful man and we're swimming and I feel so amazing, and he is so... so...' She shrugs. 'They feel so real. I try so hard to understand what's going on but my mind just can't handle it.'

Elle sighs. 'Okay, so you just need to erase the part of the brain giving you the terrifying nightmares and stimulate your brain to focus on the euphoric ones. Now, how to do that I wonder...' Elle frowns then her eyes widen comically. 'Actually,

I think there is a procedure they can do to stimulate parts of your brain! Maybe little Jamesy does it. Oh, but I think it sounds a bit dangerous.'

Aisha agrees. 'Yes, way too dangerous. Maybe as soon as you wake, you should write down exactly what you remember, or even record your thoughts on your phone.'

Melissa shakes her head. 'As much as I'd like to, I don't seem to be able to hold on to the memory at all. I just know that sometimes I'm desperately trying to escape, and other times I feel this intense love and I desperately want to... just be swept away.'

## CHAPTER 16

Melissa can feel an intense heat searing into her cheek. *Why is my face burning? Where am I? Oh, merde, my head hurts. What's happened? Oh god, I have to move.* A broken shard of mirror ricochets a scorching beam of light directly onto her face. Finally, she musters all her energy to move her head slightly to escape the burning light's path. While she waits for the paralysis to wear off, she watches the changing patterns on the mirror behind the vanity. A spattering of blood and drops of moisture slide slowly down the tiles, and she sees shapes that look like human faces coming to life.

The scent of coconut oil wafts through the air, triggering unsettling images within her mind. A tall, naked man emerges, obscured by the thick veil of steam, leaving his face indiscernible. Frowning deeply, she fights hard to ward off another disturbing image of dirty, aggressive men pulling her hair. *What is this?* She closes her eyes, trying to rid herself of the images, but they're kept alive by the scent of coconut oil. She opens her eyes wide and breathes out forcefully until the images finally disappear.

Melissa looks towards her bath. If only she had the strength, she'd love so badly to have a hot bath and soak this nightmare away. *What are those stains all over the bath?*

Birds and other wildlife stir loudly outside as the sun cuts through the bathroom door. She looks longingly at her bed with its puffy, white quilt, and now all she wants is to be buried deep beneath it.

*I gotta get out of here.* She concentrates, forcing feeling back into her limbs until she is finally able to move her arms and legs. Melissa manages to get into a crouch. She feels dizzy and weak and the frightening images of these men pulling her hair disorient her and she falls to the floor again. Determined to get to her bed, she grabs the edge of the basin and just as she is about to stand, Billy's voice startles her, and she flinches.

He grimaces when he finds her cowering beneath the vanity basin. 'I despair of you, Melissa!' He scowls as he takes in the state of the bathroom. 'Having fun, are we?' He picks up a piece of broken mirror and holds it up to her face and yells, 'Have a look at yourself! I saw your meds in the bin! Do you really think your natural bullshit is going to fix you? It smells like a fucking piña colada in here! I hope I'm not about to blow this huge deal in Copenhagen just because my wife is a psycho—'

He stops himself, takes a deep breath. 'When are you going to realise you have a really serious condition? Are you trying to sabotage my work? I told you how important this meeting was for me, but how can I leave you like this?'

Unable to respond, she listens to him go on and on; the more he speaks, the more she's repulsed by him. *How can you say I am trying to sabotage your work? The Trust has been contributing for years, you complete imbécile.* She tries to move but the pain radiating through her body is all too much.

When Billy accuses her again, Melissa finally musters all her energy. 'What the hell? The Trust has been helping fund a lot of your work for years!'

Billy inhales sharply before he suddenly softens. 'Don't you worry, your *precious* Trust will be paid back everything very soon. The Trustees will be sorry they haven't invested.'

'I'm sure they'll manage without—'

'Yeah. Yeah. Yeah. Like I told you, Redlicht's is really close now to having the most advanced anti-depressant in the world—one with fewer side effects than any other product on the market—but you're just so critical of everything. There are people in the world that need this, you know. You could do with it.'

Melissa gives him nothing but stony silence, and that silence has Billy change his approach. 'Honey, this is all getting too much. Confabulation, or whatever it is you have, is serious. You really need help. *Professional* help. Help you can't tip down the drain or throw in the bin. The kids are really worried about you, and about me. I love you, honey, and so do the kids; we all just want to see you get better.'

Slowly, Melissa closes her eyes. *What have you been telling the kids? I knew you'd try to turn them against me somehow. Why don't you just leave me? I would love you to just leave me. Do it right now.*

Billy picks her up. 'I want you to love me, Melissa, and to be proud of me, but you are so anti-everything I ever tell you. Sometimes, I feel like you just married me out of guilt and you've never loved me!' He puts her down on the bed and gently strokes her face, 'Honey, you need help. This is killing us both.'

*You are killing me, Billy. I am so over you... but what am I doing to the kids... I'd rather die than lose Chloe and Zac.* That guilt is what drives a knife right to her heart, and the words just spill from her. 'I can't take it anymore,' she sobs. 'I don't want to be like this! I'm frightened. I don't know what's happening to me, I really don't. I don't want to be like this anymore. I'll take whatever I have to, to make this go away. I want it to go away, I really do. I'm going to take the meds as prescribed. I am... I am.'

Zac has been watching his mother deteriorate for months now, but in the past couple of weeks, she has declined dramatically and looks like some kind of junkie. She seems peaceful, but she is lifeless. Whenever he comes home, she is either in her bed or on the couch in the sitting room, sleeping with the curtains closed. Zac had tried many times to get her into the pool, which he knows she loves, but she never had the energy. He's tried to get her to see Aisha and Elle, but she pretended she had work to do. He knew that she hadn't done any work for weeks. His father kept assuring Zac and Chloe that their mother was improving, but he was only seeing her decline rapidly.

Zac's phone vibrates; it's a message from his ex-girlfriend, Emma, inviting him to a party. He's happy they've reconnected recently, but he flinches as he remembers their short relationship when they were only sixteen and how horribly it had ended. He and Emma had been in his bedroom one day when his father arrived home unexpectedly.

'Why is Zac's door closed? Who is he with?'

His mother had tried to placate his dad. 'Relax, he's with that cute girl he's been dating.'

No one had been prepared for his father's response. 'God,

not that angry little creature with no redeeming features?'

Zac had reached for Emma, seen the tears falling down her face. He could hear his mother trying to lead his father to the other end of the house, saying in a quieter voice, 'Billy! Give them a break. I think she's just shy.'

His father had responded loudly, 'Tell me you don't care if he dates that little tart!'

Zac had tried to apologize to Emma as they'd slipped out around the side of the house to her bike, but she'd ridden off quickly without looking back.

Zac was furious with his father and had crept back into the house to listen. He could hear his mum whispering angrily, 'Billy, they could have heard you! What the hell? Now she's a tart? We've only met her a couple of times and we've hardly even said a word to her. Really, a *tart*? Give them a break!'

'Be honest, Melissa—as if you're happy about her for your beloved Zac!'

'I can honestly tell you that from the bottom of my heart, I'm incredibly happy for him. If he cares for her then that's all that matters, and if he thinks she's great then I trust his judgement.'

'Bullshit! You judge her just as much as I do. She's just so wrong!'

'Ha! Look how wrong you were about *me*, Billy!'

'Actually, I wasn't wrong about you. Believe it or not, Melissa, I think you're wonderful, and I love you.'

'Wow! Well, isn't that lovely. But at least Zac isn't going to be rushing down the aisle like we did. He wants to travel the world.'

Sitting here, now, in silence with his mother, Zac realises with a sick feeling that he loves his father and wants his approval, but that he's also afraid of him.

*God knows why I can't stand up to him. He used to physically tear us away from Mum, telling us she was crazy or incompetent or that she was having an affair or some other messed-up thing.* The image of his mum falling to her knees in front of the house, pleading with his father not to take he and his sister away, still unnerves him. And his fear of his father is still there. How Zac wishes he could tell his dad how much he hates his studies, but from experience, Zac knows that won't end well.

He leans his head back on the couch wanting to block the memories, but his father's voice rings clearly. 'If you don't want to win, Zac, let's go home! If you want to play like a girl, let's just go!'

Zac was only about ten at the time, and his father had taken his childhood soccer game so seriously. He would never forget his dad's glare when Zac had missed the deciding goal for the match. The humiliation in front of his entire team when he couldn't stop the tears. Zac had hated competitive sports from that day on.

He looks up at his mum on the couch, looking so peaceful in a kind of drugged-out euphoria. *God, Mum, what's happening to you? This has been going on for so long now. When are you going to get better?* It doesn't help that his mother looks totally doped up like... like a heroin addict!

His mum opens her eyes, smiles and nudges him gently with her foot. 'Hey there, sunshine of my life.'

'Hi, Mum. How are you feeling?' Trying to cover up his concern, he reaches up and hugs her. He holds her for a while and a gentle sigh seeps from her lips.

'Hmm... okay, I guess.'

'Would you like some water?'

'Mmm... that would be great.'

Hearing the door open, he glances over to see Chloe. She looks worried but forces a smile in their mother's direction and motions for him to join her and their dad in the kitchen.

Zac grins at his mum. 'I think Dad's going to cook up a storm.'

She smirks, closes her eyes. 'I'll be back in a minute with some water for you.'

When Zac enters the kitchen, his father is leaning against the fridge with a whisky in his hand. He motions for Zac to come closer and says in a hushed voice, 'Zac, look, I was just saying to your sister that I know you're both worried, but the medication is doing its job. Your mum hasn't had an outburst for a couple of weeks now. I tell you; I was worried about myself there for a while and what she might do to me in the middle of the—'

'She's practically comatose,' Zac shouts. 'Of course, she hasn't had an outburst; she can barely get off the couch!'

His dad blinks rapidly then softens. 'Sorry, son, but well, you know your mother. Ever Miss Natural. She kept quartering the dose if she bothered to take them at all. Meds just aren't designed to work like that. It's no wonder she was relapsing all over the place. This may be something she'll need to be on for a long time—'

'No...' Chloe's eyes widen. 'You mean she'll be like this for...? Dad, she *can't!* She looks terrible!'

Zac's shoulders slump. He tries to hide the quiver in his voice. 'I don't want... Dad, I mean, you know more about this stuff than us but she looks like a junkie. I'm frightened for her.'

'She's okay! Just keep encouraging her to stay on the medication. Dr Press... I mean, James, says it will take a bit of time to balance out and she'll get used to them. She'll be better soon, you'll see.'

'But she looks so weak,' Zac says. 'Her eyes aren't the same. It doesn't feel right, Dad. Surely there's something other than pharmaceuticals that can fix her. I've heard about some interesting alternative therapies at uni—'

'Dammit, Zac, you're starting to sound like your mother!'

'We're in shock!' Zac snaps. 'Every time we come home it's like more and more of her has gone. Oh shit, I forgot to get her water.' Zac rushes off and takes his mother a glass of water.

He sits with her for a moment, having to help her hold the glass as she drinks when Chloe cries out from the kitchen. 'Dad, she's like a zombie!'

'Better than a psychopath!'

Zac tries to cover up what was just said but his mother has drifted off again.

When Zac comes back into the kitchen, Chloe suggests the three of them make dinner and as she turns away Zac sees her wiping her tears. He goes to comfort her, but his Dad picks her up and hugs her, saying in a reassuring voice, 'Don't you worry, my little girl, I'm going to get her better very soon, you'll see. Oh, and did I mention I happen to have two almost brand-new laptops in my car for you both? And that I also got you that new program you wanted, Chloe?'

'Thanks, Dad,' they both reply, doing their best to appreciate the generous gifts.

'I only want the best for my kids.' He grins. 'Now, how about we go and get a bite at the Indian and we can bring some back for Mum.'

Chloe pulls back. 'Um, no Dad, sorry. I think I'll stay here and eat with Mum.'

Zac agrees. 'Yeah, Dad, maybe you and I should go and bring some home for everyone.'

Melissa's body jerks and her heart pounds as she wakes suddenly to Billy coughing and spluttering in the bathroom. *Why does he have to make those sounds?* She can't remember how she got into bed, but she is happy to be here and happy she hasn't had a nightmare for many weeks. But Chloe's words echo through her head. *'Dad, she's like a zombie!'*

Those words had shaken Melissa, and she was absolutely determined to get herself better. *I have to do something.* Once Billy has gone, she will... she will... Oh god, she's so tired.

*Dad, she's like a zombie! Dad, she's like a zombie!*

Chloe's words continue to torment her, and she tosses and turns until she finally drifts off to sleep again.

It's mid-morning when she wakes, and she heads to her bathroom and splashes cold water on her face. Life like this just isn't worth living. She stares at herself in the mirror, a look of determination on her face. 'I am going to fix this fucking problem! NOW! Je vais régler ce putain de problème. MAINTENANT! Where on *Earth* does this French come from? Does it even make sense... who knows. Putain de merde... I don't know.'

Opening the search engine on her computer, she looks up

the pharmaceuticals she's taking and finds a list of side effects as long as her arm. 'I'm not surprised to see that lethargy is one of them. Fuck, arrhythmia as well!' The more she reads, the more frustrated and disillusioned she becomes.

Stabbing at the keyboard through her tears, she types, "blackout nightmares".

The first page of results is unhelpful. *No, it's not a rock band! I mean nightmares... blacking out... amnesic nightmares.* She hammers even harder on the keys. *How to get rid of fucking, fucked up...* She backspaces, takes a breath, and begins again. *Okay, let's try "destructive nightmare causes".* She yells at her laptop, 'Will you please tell me, oh great and knowledgeable internet, how the hell I can get rid of them?'

A quick look at the list of results and it's apparent that reducing stress and avoiding spicy foods before bed is not what she's looking for. She gives up and opens her emails to find one from Zac.

Hey Mumma,

I spoke to my psych lecturer today and he thought that possibly a hypnotherapist could help you and recommended a guy by the name of Rahid, who just happens to have an office on the coast. Worth a try. Also, here's a couple of other things I've heard that might be worth looking into as well. I've had a quick look, but I have exams so thought I would share these with you quickly.

OBE – out-of-body experiences.

PLR – past life regression. I found out about these past life regression workshops in Delhi, which I thought might be helpful. You and I could take a trip and visit Lilly. Just a thought. Wouldn't mind a trip to India. There's lots of good surf spots too. Ha ha.

I love you.

Zac.

*Oh, you are sweet, Zac.*

Rahid's office is right in the Junction, and it really would be fun to take Zac and Chloe to visit Lilly in India. Melissa next looks at past life regression workshops in Delhi – Aritarana PLR, and it looked like they endorse a PLR centre in Queensland – the Castillo Clinic.

She clicks on the link to the Castillo Clinic and scrolls through the hundreds of client testimonials. All positive. If the testimonials are legitimate, Melissa thinks she's found what she's looking for.

*"I did PLR at the Castillo Clinic ten years ago and can still say that it is the most amazing, life-changing experience anyone could ever have." Peter Johnstone, Rockhampton.*

They even have full names and phone numbers. It all sounds amazing. Melissa writes down Castillo's name and just as she is about to shut down her computer, she reads something about release pods and hallucinogens. 'Oh, now that sounds a bit scary.'

~ ~ ~

As Melissa drives into the Junction, something nags at her. *What did I need to do in the Junction... there was something I wanted to do! Oh blast... oh yeah, I know ... I want to see the doctor that Zac recommended.*

She finds the office and is told by his receptionist that Doctor Rahid isn't seeing new clients at the moment but that he recommends his self-hypnosis recordings. She buys the one the receptionist suggests, and within hours Melissa is lying on a rug near her bed, listening.

She tries to listen to the tape but is distracted and exhausted and cannot concentrate on the words or on what she needs to do to hypnotise herself.

She pulls at the quilt hanging over the edge of her bed and

rolls over so that it flops down on top of her. *So tired. So very, very, tired... très, très, très fatiguée!*

Curling up, she sleeps for hours.

# CHAPTER 19

Manuela races up to Matthew, puts her arm through his, and ushers him to a table in the garden at Gaston's. She introduces him to their new clients – two men both dressed in neat, casual attire. They shake hands and just as they are about to sit, the older of the two men launches into business. 'We are so happy with your new design for the eco-retirement village, but we just have a couple of questions before we sign off on it. We love the concept of the shared garden, but we're curious as to how you think it will work.'

Matthew is about to answer but is distracted by the sound of two women laughing hysterically as they enter the garden. *Oh shit. It's definitely them! Fuck. Concentrate! Concentrate!*

The men are waiting for his answer. Matthew has been developing this concept for a couple of years and now as he is about to sign off on it, he can't think straight. *Okay, get this done. This is what you've been working towards. Concentrate!* But he can't keep his eyes off the two women who are greeted excitedly by Lucien.

After what seems an eternity but is likely just seconds, he finally turns back to his clients. 'Yes... we would definitely expect some clients won't be able, or interested in attending to their plot and we have that covered…' His mind blanks again as the two women are now chatting right next to his table. Matthew apologizes, and Manuela quickly takes over as he races to the bathroom.

~ ~ ~

Lucien ushers Melissa and Aisha to a table before he wanders off to get them some drinks. Melissa laughs again, continuing their conversation. 'I don't think I've ever been that embarrassed in my life! I never went back to that dentist again—'

'I don't blame you,' Aisha says. 'That happy gas was really weird for you.'

'I'm sure the dentist was glad to never see me again, either!'

'Well, you seem a lot brighter than the last time I saw you,' Aisha says, giving Melissa a hug.

Lucien returns quickly with their drinks and kisses them both. 'I have the most amazing entrees I know you'll both love. I have already ordered them for you. Everything is on the house, so order what you want. I must get back, but Melissa, I want you to know, "Stunned Mullet" is great. I will await your new designs.'

Aisha tilts her head to the side and frowns questioningly. 'Stunned Mullet?'

'He's opening a new seafood restaurant at the Point, and he's going to call it that—'

'That's great, Liss. Stunned Mullet, I love it.'

'Oh really? I wasn't so sure. I guess it's a bit of fun…Oh yeah, I'm sorry I haven't had a look at your new house designs yet. How is it all going?'

'Aaron and I are both over the moon about it, but we'd still love your input.'

'Well, I love all your ideas so far, and I'd love to have a look at the plans. When can I get them from you?'

'I think we're getting them at the end of the week, so you'll have to come over and have a look. I'd love your opinion. And have I told you how amazing...' Aisha pauses and points to Melissa's gas pump installation. 'This is? Wow! You're so clever! Even with all the shit going on in your life you manage to do this as well. Look, people are even taking their photos in front of them.'

'Thanks, Aish. As you well know, I'm not very good with compliments.

'Oh, don't I know it... you are hopeless at—'

'Anyhow, Nashy was great at pulling it all together. I do quite like them.'

'Well, I'm glad you're finally out and about. And you are going to do the yoga class? I think it could really help. I know you don't think you're really stressed but maybe you just don't realise.'

Melissa smiles. 'Yes, I'm looking forward to it. I'm going in the morning. I'm determined to get myself better again. I actually haven't had a nightmare for weeks now.'

~ ~ ~

The timer triggers the automatic pool cleaner and it quickly gathers momentum, creating wild, shimmering patterns throughout the kitchen and living room. Zac's phone vibrates, and before answering, he raises his eyebrows, holds the screen up to Chloe and whispers, 'You see, Auckland!' He walks away as he answers the phone, 'Hey, Dad...'

Zac hears his mother's car pull into the driveway, quickly finishes talking to his father and follows Chloe out.

Melissa smiles as her kids take all of the shopping bags from her. Empty-handed, she stands behind the couch and clumsily tries to balance on one leg with the palms of her hands joined together above her head. 'Guess where I've been today?'

Zac and Chloe respond together. 'We can't imagine!'

Chloe copies her mother, trying to balance with the sole of her foot tucked up onto the thigh of her standing leg. They try several times but keep over-balancing until they burst out laughing. 'We are *hopeless*,' Melissa says. 'Why is this so hard?'

Chloe shakes her head. 'It's a lot harder than it looks.'

Melissa stops and leans against the kitchen bench. 'I couldn't do anything right, but wow did I humiliate myself! I must be the most immature adult. We were all bending over and somebody let out the longest, noisiest fart I have ever heard and literally nobody batted an eyelid! Except, of course, for your immature mother. I absolutely could not help myself.'

Chloe's face lights up. 'Oh, Mum, you're such a child! Losing it over a *fart?* We'll never be able to let you out on your own again!'

'I've had this problem all my life. The more serious the situation, the more likely I am to crack up. Lilly and I used to get into so much trouble when we were young. Jean would be angry with us over the most stupid things and we wouldn't be able to contain ourselves; we'd just crack up. And Dad only encouraged us, which of course infuriated Jean even more.'

Chloe gasps melodramatically. 'Jean didn't see the humour in it and join in?'

Melissa throws her arms around her kids and draws them to her. The three of them stand close together for a few moments, hugging.

A moment later, Chloe gasps again, only this time it's tinged with worry as her daughter runs fingers over Melissa's ribs. 'God, Mum. We seriously need to fatten you up. Or maybe you could just order in some of our yummy cheesy pizzas every night?'

'Ha! Yes – home-delivered pizzas! I'm starving. Where's my phone?'

'Will you order for your dad as well. He was supposed to be

back hours ago.'

Zac nods as he scrolls through his phone for the number. 'No problem. Pepperoni with extra anchovies.'

'You're so much better than the last time we saw you, Mum,' Chloe says.

Melissa pats her daughter's arm reassuringly. 'Please don't worry about me. That makes me sad. I know your father is away a lot, but I see you both so often. I enjoy being on my own sometimes, and I've been really good. I'm going to come down and have a city weekend with both of you when you don't have too much on.'

'That would be so nice. My housemates are pigs, though, so we might want to stay somewhere else. I'm thinking about moving out when the lease is up.'

'Oh, that's a shame. It feels like you just moved in.'

'I know, but Chiara and I really want to get a place together. And by the way, why is Dad away so much? I thought he'd given up on his wonder drug. I thought—'

'God, no. He's received a lot of interest in it again just recently, and there are two really successful drug manufacturers overseas that may want to invest. But you know your father – anything he does, he has to excel at it, so he will make it work, I'm sure... je suis sûre.'

'Oh la la and yeah, that's all great, but it also means he'll probably be away more often. I don't know, Mum, you're so up and down. One minute you're full of life and it's like nothing is wrong, and the next you're having a psychotic episode or you're like a zombie. Zac and I really worry about you when you're alone.'

'Oh, ma belle fille, my beautiful girl, you're so sweet. But honestly, I'm hardly ever on my own; I see you two, and I often stay over at Aisha's or at Elle's. I'm feeling a lot better at the moment. I still do jobs here and there for my old clients, and that keeps me busy. And of course, I see your grandmother… well, from time to time. Thankfully she loves those cruises.'

Chloe acknowledges her grandmother with a condescending sneer. 'I bet she's very understanding about what's going on for you.'

Melissa nods. 'Oh, very!' She imitates her mother's voice. '"Just snap out of it, Melissa. What is all this carry-on about?"' Melissa rolls her eyes. 'It's either that or she starts telling me there's something seriously wrong with me. She's got it both ways.'

Chloe's phone rings. 'Oh, I just have to take this.'

Melissa is so proud Chloe stands up to Jean – nobody else ever seemed able. Chloe would be polite enough, but Jean just couldn't manage to manipulate her granddaughter like she could everyone else. *If only we all had Chloe's strength! Now she just needs the strength to get rid of Oscar.*

Chloe finishes her call and picks up some of Melissa's designs from the kitchen bench. 'These designs for Bombetta's look fantastic.'

'Really? I wasn't very happy with them. But that's so lovely to hear, you may be the only one that likes it. How is your folio coming along?'

'Not very well at this point, but I think I'll get everything done in time. I'll yell out if I need your help with anything.'

'I'd love to help you.'

~ ~ ~

Hours later, the sound of Billy's inebriated voice bellows from beyond the garage door, alerting Chloe and Zac. They look at each other and almost in unison whisper, 'This doesn't sound good,' and race to their rooms.

Billy storms into the house. 'More fucking lights not working, Melissa! Can you ever get around to replacing a globe?'

Melissa clutches at her neck and sighs.

Billy frowns, contorts his face, and imitates her clutching his neck. 'Why do you always clasp your hands under your neck so melodramatically? Anyone would think I try to strangle you.'

'I don't know, Billy, I didn't know I did it.'

'Well, you do it a lot, and it makes me feel bad and—'

'Anyway, I only changed the globe about a month ago! They're not made to last nowadays.' Sad to see Chloe and Zac scampering off when their father arrives, Melissa retaliates. 'Welcome back, Billy; so nice to see you after your trip. How was Melbourne? Or where was it you've just been?'

He lifts the leg of his trousers, expecting to reveal an injury, and swiftly lowers it back down when he finds nothing. 'Oh, I'm sorry,' he explains, 'I just banged my shin. Hello, honey, nice to see you too.' He leans over and kisses her on the lips.

She pulls away and points to the pizza box. 'Well, there's your dinner. We couldn't wait any longer. Zac ordered your usual.' Anger wells up inside her when he complains that the pizza is soggy. She finally snaps. 'How about I give you some peace, then, Billy? I'll go to the shack for a week or so and you won't have to put up with my incompetence!'

Just as she anticipated, rage dawns on Billy's face as soon as she mentions the shack.

'That fucking shack! I've had it with that fucking shack! Let's sell it and buy something new along the coastline with views and—'

'For one,' Melissa continues calmly, 'we can't sell the shack even if I wanted to, as it's Lilly's as well, and it's also tied up with the Trust, as you know. And two, the kids and I love it. The shack *is* falling apart a bit, and I was wanting to spend time there and deal with the repairs.'

Billy tries to sidle up to her and stumbles.

She moves away from him. 'I hope you didn't drive—'

He sighs. 'No, I didn't drive.'

'Well, how did you get here?'

He ignores her question. 'Please don't go to the shack. I need you *here* at the moment. I'm trying to get some of my old Uni buddies on board and I'd like to have some dinner parties over the next few months. See if we can sieve out any more potential investors...'

He heads up the corridor to the sitting room and returns to the kitchen with a large whisky on ice, his voice booming around the house. 'This is going to be the big one, babe! I really want to tell you about the deal we are about to make with one of the biggest—'

'I was just on my way to bed,' she says, trying to quieten him; she is so sick and tired of hearing about it. 'Can you tell us all about it in the morning?'

Melissa makes her way to the bedroom. *This is gonna be the big one, babe! When in god's name is "the big one" ever going to happen? Tu es un imbécile Billy! Un imbécile!*

# CHAPTER 20

A cool breeze slowly wakes Melissa and she frowns as she is taken away from her serene dream. *Suis les marées... Suis les marées...* Before opening her eyes, she tries to work out where she is. Once she realises, she pats the bed behind her. *That's right, Billy is still in Copenhagen. Ah, it's so nice with him away.* Her phone rings, and she fumbles on her bedside table to find it. She shudders, rolls her eyes and screws up her face when she sees it's Billy and lets it go to voicemail. She pulls the sheet over her head and tries to go back to sleep, back to her serene dream, but the ding from text messages keep disturbing her and she reaches for her phone, turns the volume off and tries to go back to sleep again. Now it's the vibrating that disturbs her. 'How do you turn the vibration off!' She yells and throws her phone to the other side of the room, but she's seen the time and is determined to get some work done. She rolls out of bed, has a quick shower, grabs a coffee and heads to her study.

She works happily undisturbed for hours, producing work of which she's immensely proud. 'God, that was the best day's work I've had for a long time. Now it's time to eat.'

She turns off her lamp, stands and stretches, and just as she's about to go to the kitchen, the ringtone on her computer trills.

Melissa sits down again and smiles when she sees Lilly on the screen singing, 'Happy birthday, dear sis! Happy birthday, dear sis! Happy... that will do, won't it?' Lilly says with a laugh.

'Yes, that will do.' She smiles at her sister. 'I got so carried away with work I actually forgot it was my birthday.'

They laugh and chat for hours, and finally Lilly says, 'I love you, sis. I'd better let you go. I'm sure your family and friends are probably all trying to call you. Give the kids my love and tell them to call me soon. Especially Zac, he's getting very slack. Chloe's quite regular. Anyhow... I'll let you go. I love you.'

'Love you too.' She races to her bedroom, picks up her phone and curses as she sees lots of missed calls and messages. *Oh, fuck a duck!* She turns the volume button back on and instantly a call comes in from Aisha who sounds frantic. 'Where have you been? Everyone has been trying to call you all day! It's your birthday, if you haven't forgotten, and I'm picking you up in about a minute!'

'Okay! Okay! Thank you. Sorry, the day just got away from me. See you soon.' Melissa balances her phone on her shoulder as she tries to pull her jeans on, then listens to Billy's voicemail message: 'Happy birthday, honey. I'm so sorry I'm not there with you but I couldn't let this opportunity pass. Make sure you spoil yourself and I'll make it up to you when I get back on the twenty-ninth. I love you. Bye now.' *Well, that is just fine with me, Billy!* She checks the phone and sees several missed calls from her mother. *I better call the kids too.* She calls both their numbers, but neither of them answer. She stops in the hallway and texts them: "Just a little reminder that your old mother is one year older and I'm going out for dinner with Aish and Elle. Last minute thing. Anyhow, I'll see you both soon. I love you both. Mumma."

Aisha comes running into the house. 'Happy birthday, beautiful friend. I'm sorry I was stressing; we were all just getting worried about you.' She kisses Melissa on the cheek, grabs her friend's coat and bag and forces Melissa into her car. 'We've got to run.'

~~~

When they walk into Gaston's, Lucien greets Melissa with a huge cocktail heavily decorated with fruit and sparklers. He tries to encourage everyone to join him as he sings loudly, 'Joyeux anniversaire à toi, joyeux anni...' He laughs, kisses her on both cheeks and then on the lips.

Zac and Chloe run out from where they've been hiding behind the others, and hug her. 'Did you really think we'd forget our old mum?' Chloe laughs.

'Well, I nearly did,' Zac admits. 'Luckily, you have a daughter who remembers these things. I'm not good with dates; I barely remember my own birthday. November eighteen, isn't it?'

Melissa taps him gently on the side of his head. 'No, November seventeen, as I recall.'

Elle comes running in from the garden. 'Ah, sorry, bloody new smoking laws. Ridiculous, aren't they? Happy birthday, lovely woman!'
~~~

After weeks of listening to Billy's complaints and worrying that her children were really concerned about her, Melissa finally relents and reluctantly agrees to see James again. She'd been feeling so great for a while and begun to think she was better, but the nightmares and her confusion had recently become unbearable again.

Zac is keen for her to visit Lilly and do the PLR in India, and she would have loved to do that with her kids. Although she isn't sure she would be up to travelling and the hustle and bustle of India, and Lilly has also spoken of possibly moving to Bali.

The Castillo Clinic seems to be the much better option. It is only a few hours away, and she has read hundreds of positive testimonials. Melissa is hoping that with this visit to James, she may convince him to talk Billy around about past life therapy her husband is so vehemently opposed to. She's worried that if anything goes wrong, she will never hear the end of it. Although the hallucinogens and release pods are freaking her out, she's desperately hoping that this Clinic may be able to fix her.

*Here we go.* She rolls her eyes before entering James's office, and he jumps up and comes around from behind his desk, greeting her in his usual manner. He puts his hands right around her waist and kisses her directly on the lips. Turning her head slightly, she endures the kiss and sits down quickly.

They chat for a while until she almost breaks down. 'I've tried so many things, James, but nothing is working. Despite all the medications you've given me, nothing has changed, I was good for a while, except now I look like and feel a bit like a junkie again.'

James wears his sympathy well. 'We need to get you back in here, Melissa. We need much more information about what's happening in your brain.'

'I can't do that again, James. I think I'd rather dic.'

'Melissa, there's something seriously wrong with you. We could possibly give you a stronger sedative to take before you go to bed, but if I were you, I'd come back in for more tests, that way we can make sure we have the right medication.'

Melissa shakes her head and bites at her bottom lip. 'Well, I can't.'

James sighs. 'Then the only thing I can recommend is the psychiatrist and the medication we've already prescribed, and please take them as directed.'

'That first lot of meds was terrible, James; you saw what they did to me. There was no way I was going to continue with them. I was a total wreck. And the second lot... well, I honestly thought I was going to become addicted. They certainly made me feel good, but—'

'Melissa, you really need to pay attention to this. Your condition is severe. I've seen it myself. It's not something your family needs to be subjected to, either.'

'My god, James—'

'I'm sorry, Melissa, it's just that Billy told me you've been getting violent with him. The medication you are on is perfectly safe and you have to admit, your nightmares occur much less frequently when you take them properly.'

'Well, I really don't know about that, James. I couldn't actually—'

'Well, I really think you also need to see the psychiatrist we recommended, Dr Pymble.'

'I can't even remember you mentioning his name. I can't remember anything anymore! I manage to go to bed and wake up in the morning, but it feels as if my memory is being erased over and over again.'

James looks away from her, apparently finding his stapler extremely interesting.

Melissa sighs loudly and tries to appeal to him again. 'I'm tired of not being able to remember anything and feeling like a junkie, James. Isn't there anything else that can help that won't make me feel as if I am going mad?'

'The only thing I can recommend is to get you back here for some more tests. And to also have regular sessions with Pymble. He's a man I trust. He's helped many of my patients.'

Disinterested in James's suggestions, she asks hopefully, 'Have you heard of the Castillo Clinic? Apparently, they have cured a huge range of psychological disorders and—'

'Ha! That crackpot? He uses hallucinogens and god knows what!'

Melissa ignores him and continues. 'He's even cured people of schizophrenia and psychosis.'

James sneers. 'The man is a maniac!'

'Maniac or not, he seems to get results. There are so many positive testimonials on the internet by all sorts of people and I'd like to explore it as an option.'

'You do know he's been struck off the medical register, don't you?'

'No, I didn't know. But... um... isn't the proof in the pudding? There are literally hundreds if not thousands of testimonials and people are giving their full names and contact details.'

'Well, in my professional opinion,' James replies in a deeply patronising tone, 'I believe Castillo is a very dangerous man. Even after being struck off, he continues to practise—'

'But, James—'

'He's in and out of court every other week. What he's doing isn't certified and I don't believe it's safe. I wouldn't let my wife go to see him, and I imagine Billy wouldn't be happy about you going either. Don't believe everything you read on the internet, Melissa. Honestly, there are a lot of crackpots out there who can make themselves sound quite credible. Now, our Dr Pymble has had some great results. I'm sorry but the only thing I can suggest is that you give him a try and stay on your medication. You are not going to end up an addict. It's not heroin.'

*Oh, yes, that's the party line, isn't it? Shut up, woman, and take your meds! Yes doctor, no doctor, three bags full, doctor!* She raises her eyebrows and sighs, trying to keep her disgust at his patriarchal bedside manner, hidden. 'Well, can you give me Castillo's—oh, sorry, I mean *Pymble's*—details, then? I have to do *something*.'

James pushes a referral in a sealed envelope across his desk. She hesitates before picking it up.

CHAPTER 22

Life seems to pass in a blur for Melissa. She's been seeing Dr Pymble every Wednesday for months now, but it's painfully clear he isn't helping. The only tangible thing she can remember lately is being at the ocean and feeling an overwhelming urge to be swept away by it. She stares at herself in the bathroom mirror. 'What little nightmares have I created for myself today?' She washes her face and slowly musters the energy to go and check the house for any damage she may have caused.

She sighs as she nears the sitting room. 'Okay, what havoc have I caused in here?'

Melissa's happy to see that Billy's drinks trolley and all of the alcohol is still intact. She checks the bar fridge is stacked, straightens some cushions and as she goes to walk back out of the room, she feels dizzy and grabs the side of the couch before falling onto it.

She closes her eyes and cringes as she remembers coming out of the ocean, naked, at Third Point again. As much as she loves being at the shack, she shouldn't have gone there alone again. *What is it that I'm looking for? What is beyond the breaking waves that I desperately need to get to?*

She slides from the couch to the floor to steady herself and try to remember what it was that she was searching for beyond the swell. As a feeling of lightness envelops her, she inhales deeply and allows her body to relax as she is carried away by this intense sensation of soaring through the water as she drifts off...

...Melissa is happy here in his arms as he holds her just above the water. She breathes in slowly enjoying the gentle caress of his fingers circling her navel. 'Our beautiful baby... notre beau bébé.' She knows this intense love. She knows this experience well and she allows herself to be taken away with it as she falls into a deep sleep.

Hours go by and a nagging feeling disturbs her sleep. *Am I supposed to be somewhere or doing something? I just want to stay here!* She tries to stay in her dream, but that nagging won't go away. Focusing hard at the clock on the shelf, she sees it's already four o'clock and she drifts back into a sensual sleep until something stirs within her again. *Oh god, I am supposed to be somewhere.* When she opens her eyes once more, it's now 4.30. 'Putain! I'm supposed to be at Pymble's at 5.30!'

~ ~ ~

Matthew watches from the window of Dr Pymble's room as Melissa's bright aqua car pulls into the carpark – like clockwork, 5.30pm every Wednesday. The rain striking the windows makes it difficult for him to get a good look at her, but it's unmistakable that again she is distressed. Tears stream down her face as she stares through the windshield and straight through the window to where he is sitting. For a quick moment, it feels like she is looking at him but he soon realises she is not, or at least she gives no hint of it. He suddenly realises that Dr Pymble has asked him a question. He quickly answers and continues trying to make the man understand that the prescribed drugs are driving him crazy. Matthew's made his mind up that he must take control of his life, and this so-called expert in the field is making him even more depressed.

He glances out the window again, realising that tonight will be the last time he'll see that little aqua car pull up. He's tried so often to speak to her, but the time was never right.

~ ~ ~

Melissa is mesmerised by the tracks the rain is making on the windshield. She forces herself to breathe deeply, trying hard to calm her nerves. The last thing she wants to do is go through with another one of these stupid appointments. If Chloe and Zac hadn't encouraged her to continue to see Pymble, she probably wouldn't be here right now, but she knows she's running out of options.

The sound of a car door slamming nearby rouses her from her daze. She leans over to look at her reflection in the rear-view mirror. 'Oh no. I look as bad as I feel.' She grabs a tissue from her bag and wipes the mascara stains from under her eyes. 'Oh, fuck it's five-thirty. Do I have to go in there?' She pulls the keys slowly out of the ignition. In her mind she can still hear the last thing Billy said to her before he went away.

'You're as mad as your sister, Melissa. How do you think this makes me look? Honestly, I'm beginning to think you're schizophrenic.'

*Am I schizophrenic? Maybe I am. I guess I wouldn't know if I was.*

The memory of Billy's voice won't go away, 'Make sure you don't miss another one of Pymble's appointments. He's not going to be so forgiving next time. Just bloody go!'

*You just bloody go, Billy! Bloody go and don't come back. I know I'm confused, I know you all think I'm mad. I don't know what's wrong with me, but you don't help, that's for fucking sure!*

The huge embarrassment she'd felt only days ago when she'd walked naked from the ocean sends a rush of heat to her face. 'Fuck a duck! Great. Now I'm bright red.' She quickly runs her hands over the windows and places them over her face, trying to cool herself.

*It's official. You are stark raving mad. Tu es complètement fou furieux. You have to do something.* Melissa looks once again at Pymble's office. *Okay I'm going! This is only for you, Zac and Chloe!*

~ ~ ~

The nondescript building that houses Dr Pymble's clinic is no preparation for what confronts Melissa each time she goes in. There are altars, religious icons and paraphernalia dotted around his rooms, and there seem to be more of them each week. To Melissa, it's obvious who runs the clinic – his wife, who insists on being called Mrs Pymble.

'Melissa!' Mrs Pymble's tone is easy to read and not just because Melissa has been coming regularly for appointments. With Mrs Pymble, you always know where you stand. 'Please do try to get all the water off you before you come in from the foyer, dear. The last patient left an awful mess when he came in.'

Melissa shakes herself off and does her best to find Mrs Pymble's soft spot. Moving over to the reception desk, she takes a deep breath, biting at her lip, and asks as gently as she can manage, 'Mrs Pymble, how long do you think I will be coming here? It's just that I've been coming every week for months now and nothing has changed. I'm just curious, do people just come back week after week for a long time? I'm sorry, I don't mean to be rude. I'm just exhausted and frightened and I don't know how long I can keep doing this.'

The old woman stiffens, raising an eyebrow and fingering the string of pearls around her neck. 'How long is a piece of string, my dear? It depends on so many factors...'

*I knew you would say something like that. Don't you feel bad taking all of this money week after week and giving people false hope? Not to mention the amount of our time you're wasting...*

'Oh really, could it take that long?'

Mrs Pymble looks outraged. 'Yes, that long!'

Accepting this admonishment, Melissa backs across the reception area and sits on one of the straight-backed chairs. The seasoned receptionist only tightens her lips further and goes back to her paperwork. Sighing deeply, Melissa closes her eyes and waits her turn.

She doesn't have to wait long. Loud, muffled sounds of an argument coming from Dr Pymble's office reverberate through the reception area, and the voices get louder and more raised. Mrs Pymble jumps up and bustles around behind the reception desk, opening and shutting filing cabinets in an obvious attempt to cover the altercation. This amuses Melissa, as does the woman's apparent discomfort.

Melissa does her best to make out what the two men are arguing about but can only hear the odd word here and there. 'Tired of... Why not... I feel like they are making me mad...' And then she hears a man with a deep voice clearly saying that he is going to go to the Castillo Clinic.

*The Castillo Clinic? What? Did he really say that?* Just as she is trying to get her head around what she heard, this man rushes out of Pymble's consulting room and pulls the door behind him. He looks straight into Melissa's eyes and hesitates for a moment. Melissa blushes and quickly looks away. The man hesitates again, just for a moment, and then departs. *What... what just happened? Who was that man? Who was he? Who?* An unfathomable urge for answers overtakes her. *I have to know who he is. Well, he definitely said Castillo Clinic. I'm done here too. I'm done with the ridiculous Pymbles too.*

Mrs Pymble's mouth had turned into a thin frown, 'Trouble with a capital T, that man. Has been since we first laid eyes on him. I told my husband as much, but he wants to help everyone. *You* can go in now, Melissa,' she says, stressing the initial word.

'No. No, I don't think I will,' Melissa states bluntly and rushes out the door after the other patient. She's determined to catch him. *God, am I gonna get an earful about this. Well, fuck you, Billy and James and your dad and my mum and anyone else I've forgotten to acknowledge, fuck you too. Va te faire foutre aussi.*

The rain pelts Melissa as she runs to catch up to the man, determined to ignore Billy's words that spear into her head as she does so. 'You are not going to Castillo's, Melissa. He's been struck off; he's a known nutcase! He plays with dangerous hallucinogens and weird technology. You'll end up more psycho than you already are.'

*Well, Professor Castillo couldn't be any worse than Pymble and Press!*

Each one of Billy's words hits her like the hard slap of rain on her face, searing into her mind. Her hatred for Billy grows with each drop, urging her on as she runs down the road.

*Fuck Billy! Fuck James!* She's going to check out Castillo whether they like it or not. It's her life and nothing else is working for her. The mind-numbing drugs are driving her crazy. Fuck the lot of them. She's going!

Finally catching sight of the man, Melissa calls out, 'Excuse me!'

He instantly halts and turns. It catches her off guard, and she skids along the wet pavement, flailing her arms wildly to regain her balance. 'Ooohhh... fuuuuuucccckkkk! Putain de merde!'

The man grabs her arm to steady her, and he laughs loudly. 'Putain de merde. Ha! I know what that means.'

She laughs with him, recovers herself quickly but feels embarrassed by her clumsiness and her swearing. Her face flushes but his smile relaxes her and they both stand there while she catches her breath.

'Well... that was a little embarrassing. Sorry. I've been chasing you since Pymble's. I thought I'd never catch you.'

'Oh really? I'm not in the habit of being chased by beautiful women.'

Her face heats up again. *Stop blushing, Melissa, he's just teasing! His eyes are so intense. And why does he look kind of familiar?* Their eyes fix onto each other's for an uncomfortable amount of time and Melissa blushes again. *Why am I so damned nervous? Because it feels like he's looking directly into my soul.*

A group of people, escaping the rain gather around them and he smiles awkwardly. 'I was just going in here for a drink. I need a stiff one after this afternoon.' He points at the bar they've stopped in front of. 'Would you like to join me and get out of this rain?'

She smiles and nods, following him in through the door to an old, renovated warehouse called Le Monde. *Le Monde... the world... Tout le monde. What on Earth does tout le monde mean? Ah it doesn't matter. I'm just so nervous.*

~ ~ ~

The bar is busy, and the rain continues to pour down, echoing off the high tin roof. People are pushing and shoving and shouting to be heard. The man looks over his shoulder to make sure she's still following him, and, in the crush, he grabs her hand tightly and guides her towards the bar. A tingling sensation rushes through her body. *He's so self-assured.* Nervously, she attempts to begin a conversation, 'I just heard you mention Castillo...'

'Sorry, what did you say?' he asks, leaning closer so that he can hear her.

'Back at Pymble's office, I heard you mention the name Castillo.'

He looks at her and smiles, 'Yes. That's right. The Castillo Clinic.'

'I've been interested in going to see him for a while. I've read hundreds of testimonials about how brilliant he is. And he's here... unbelievably here, in Australia.'

'I know, I know. He does sound amazing, doesn't he? A little bit freaky maybe, but I think I'm going to give him a shot.'

'Do you know much about him?'

'Just that he might be able to help me out and Pymble has been wasting my time for ages now. He's been trying very hard to put the fear of god into me about Castillo, which just makes me more likely to go.' He smiles wryly.

'Yes, Mother Theresa Pymble has tried to put the fear of god into me as well.' Her voice quavers slightly and her face heats up as she notices he's watching her lips as she speaks.

'And how hilarious is Pymble's hypnosis technique? I always end up in fits of laughter and he gets so upset; I feel a bit like a naughty schoolchild.'

Melissa chuckles with him. 'Yes, it's so weird. I certainly never go under either. It's all been so—'

A loud crack of thunder reverberates through the warehouse, and she jumps in fright. They look at each other and then burst into laughter.

'Perhaps they're trying to strike us down for storming out!' His intoxicating smile lights up his face. 'They're a strange couple, aren't they? I should have trusted my instincts and left the day I arrived.'

The rain eases a bit, and Melissa sighs, echoing his sentiments. He is about to ask her another question when he's momentarily distracted by a woman's voice with a strong accent calling him. 'Matthew! Matthew!'

*So that's your name, Matthew. Matthew. What a beautiful name.*

It looks like he's trying to ignore the woman, and asks Melissa a question but the voice persists.

'Matthew! Maaaaaaathew!'

He finally looks up and acknowledges the striking Latino woman calling out to him. 'I'll join you shortly, Matthew.'

He quickly responds. 'Okay.'

Melissa is mesmerised, drinking in his profile as he turns. He looks so unlike the man who rushed out of Pymble's office; his clear, sparkling eyes paint an image of a man full to the brim with energy and life force.

'I'm Matthew, by the way, in case you missed that,' he says, looking into her eyes expectantly.

His eyes are so intense, she doesn't know where to look. Melissa stutters slightly as she responds, 'Sorry, Melissa… My name's Melissa.'

'It's a bit hard to hear in here!' He smiles, and then he says something about Castillo that she doesn't catch. Noticing her confused look, he places his hand on her cheek and leans in close to her ear. 'Don't worry it's a bit loud. Can I get you a drink? What would you like?'

'That might take a while.' She motions to the packed bar. 'I'd love a white wine, thanks, and I might just find the bathroom.'

Melissa makes her way through the crowd to the bathroom and heads straight for the mirror, and almost recoils in horror. *I look a mess! Bugger, bugger, bugger.* Her hair is dripping and flattened to her head and what's left of her mascara is completely smudged under her eyes. She looks around for some paper towels to wipe her face with. Once done, and no longer looking like a drowned rat, she heads to one of the cubicles, trying to ignore her growing excitement. She locks the door, and just as she is about to sit, her phone vibrates. She rummages around in her handbag, and seeing Aisha's face on the screen, she takes the call, whispering, 'Yes, yes. That's all organised. I did it this morning. But hey, I… just met the most beautiful man.'

'How did you manage that? I thought you had your psycho appointment this afternoon?'

'Long story. I literally just chased him down the street. Oh god, but I'm a wreck! Aish, the way he grabbed my hand… I don't know how to describe it... He gripped my hand so firmly... my entire body... I don't know... it was so exhilarating... so intoxicating. My entire body was all jittery with excitement... he was just so strong and protective and self-assured and—'

'What? Liss, where are you? Why are you whispering?'

'I'm in a bar down the road from Pymble's office. He's buying our drinks and I'm in the bathroom. There was this stunning Latino woman calling him... so she's probably his wife or his girlfriend. I really need a drink. Oh, Aisha, he's just gorgeous. I'm so nervous.'

'I'm absolutely intrigued. Now Liss, listen to me. Take a deep breath and get back out there. I've never heard you like this. Go find out more, and I want to hear all about it in the morning, remember?'

'I just ran away from Pymble's—literally.'

'This is the best thing I've heard all year, Liss. Pymble is a weirdo. I think you need to see that other guy you told me about. Anyhow, go, I want all the details in the morn—'

A loud banging on the cubicle door interrupts them.

'Okay; gotta go. See you in the morning. Bye.'

The noise from the bar has lessened by the time Melissa returns from the bathroom. The rain is now just a pleasing white noise. She spots Matthew making his way from the bar, and when he notices her, motions to a table that has just become empty in the corner of the room. He puts their drinks on the table and pulls two stools close together. 'Is this okay—'

Loud music starts up, and Melissa leans in closer to him, 'Sorry, what did you say?'

'I said...' He begins to talk and then nods towards the rear of the building as the music gets progressively louder. She turns around and looks over a high ledge to see lots of people dancing.

He says loudly, 'Maybe the Pymbles are really working against us, it's very hard to hear in here.' He smiles at her cheekily, 'Perhaps we should go and dance to spite them!'

Melissa blushes. *Stop blushing! He's joking!* She smiles and tries to humour him, 'Okay, I love dancing! Let's spite them!'

He grabs her hand and she laughs as she pulls back. 'I was kidding! I do love to dance but I haven't danced for a long time.' She hears the lyrics to the song playing.

*"Oh my love, I wait for you in this light*
*I know you'll be here soon*
*My sweet meat pie."*

She smiles as she watches people dancing. 'Oh, I love this song!' He grabs her hand again and holds it firmly as he teases. 'Come on then, this must be a sign.'

She smiles shyly. 'I don't think—'

'Are you sure?' he says, smirking at her cheekily before very slowly releasing her hand. 'So, you're thinking of going to Castillo too?'

'I've wanted to since I first heard about him, but my husband—' Melissa stops abruptly. She hears her own voice, like that of a child, scolding herself for wanting something she isn't allowed to have. She's completely smitten with this man, beyond anything she can comprehend, and the last thing she wants to do is to mention her husband. Cringing slightly, she goes on. 'My husband works in the medical industry. He and his colleagues think Castillo is dangerous. But I don't think what he's offering could be any more dangerous than the pharmaceutical concoctions I've been on.'

Matthew nods sympathetically. 'I agree.'

'I guess I'm scared about doing it, to be honest. My husband makes it sound like it's the work of the devil.' She flinches as an image rises of Billy screaming at her about how terrible it will be for him if she has her mind messed up even more than it is by Castillo and his hallucinogens.

'It does sound very unusual and a little scary.'

Melissa nods enthusiastically. 'Totally scary, but when I heard you mention Castillo's name tonight, it was like something inside me woke up... a lightbulb moment? I don't know, but I've read countless testimonials and I've been so keen to do it but I've been wanting some kind of reassurance or something.'

'That's great. Really great.' Matthew looks deeply into her eyes. 'I got to the point today where I've had enough too. Pymble just doesn't listen. I'm sure some of these doctors don't actually want us to get better. They just want us coming back week after week for years.' He looks at her a little sheepishly. 'Oh, sorry... your husband and all.'

When she smiles again, he continues, 'I told Pymble today that the drug he's prescribed for me makes me feel like I'm going mad. And all he said is that I have no choice, that I should stay on them regardless of how I'm feeling. And then he ridiculed me for suggesting Castillo again. That's when I lost it.'

'I feel exactly the same. The drugs are making me like a zombie. My husband would have everyone on prescription meds if he had his way. It's like they close their minds the minute they get their medical degrees.' *I'm so tired of it all. The meds and the marriage.*

'From what I understand about Castillo...'

Melissa can hear him talking about Castillo and she takes in snippets here and there, but she has lost concentration again. She catches a few words and tries to engage again, 'I heard he lived in a remote village in Peru and studied all their traditional herbs and medicines for something like twenty years.'

If the conversation hadn't been so relevant to her current situation, Melissa would have had a hard time following it. She finds herself having to look away every so often just so that she can concentrate on what he is saying, so mesmerised is she by his lips and the way they curl at the corners, smiling as he speaks, and by the way his eyes sparkle with almost every word he utters.

She finally hears what he is saying, 'Apparently, these plants are supposed to activate your memories, and then they somehow tap into your brain and make your memories... I don't know... tangible? Accessible, somehow.' He raises his eyebrows. 'You don't have any dark secrets or any skeletons in your closet, do you, Melissa?'

The way he says her name with such familiarity and confidence sends a shiver through her. Internally, she tries to replicate how he said it, playing with different intonations and tones. *Melissa. Melissa. Melissa.* She repeats it silently several times and enjoys the sound of her own name as she has never done before. She repeats it again. *Melissa. Melissa.* Her thoughts are going wild, and she finally shakes her head in response to the question he's just asked her.

He smiles at her cheekily and continues, 'From what I hear, if you do, then this is *not* the treatment for you!'

She laughs along with him. 'No dark secrets or skeletons that I know about, anyway. But I do want to delve into some issues I've been having.'

'I have some issues I'd like resolved too.'

'Well, we may both have an interesting journey ahead, Matthew.' It feels great to use his name and she repeats it silently and, with a French accent, she loves the sound. *Mathieu, Mathieu... what a beautiful name!*

'You look far too lovely to be the local mass murderer!' he jokes.

Melissa can't stop herself from blushing and grins awkwardly. *I'm so nervous, he must be getting tired of me! Where is that striking Latino woman?* Melissa returns to the safety of the clinic conversation. 'Yes, so it seems Castillo is quite the genius. I hope all the positive testimonials are true.'

'Yes, me too. The testimonials are amazing, aren't they? Unbelievable... I read that people with no knowledge of history can afterwards describe all these historical facts with complete accuracy. And some people can sing in pitch-perfect baritone, even though usually they're tone deaf. I think there's got to be something to that, if it's true.' Excitement lights his eyes.

Melissa smiles. *Okay, he said something about singing and history.* She responds finally, 'Yes... yes it all sounds quite amazing, doesn't it? I also read that people have spoken fluently in a foreign language they claim they don't know. As you heard earlier, I don't know where it comes from but I keep coming out with bits and pieces of French, unfortunately mostly swear words. I've tried to learn French for a long time, but it just doesn't seem to click with me somehow. I'm definitely not the brightest cab off the rank when it comes to languages!'

He looks at her curiously, and smiles sweetly at her. 'No, I'm not the brightest with languages either.'

She has totally lost her concentration again. She cannot stop this internal dialogue.

Matthew notices she is distracted. 'Have I lost you, Melissa?'

'No. Sorry, I just remembered something.' She feels her face blush and quickly tries to return to the conversation, but she cannot concentrate as she is finding everything about him so attractive to her, and she feels he's somehow familiar. She asks him another question about Castillo, trying to take the heat away from herself but when he answers, she hardly takes in any of what he says, mesmerised again by him as he speaks.

As the crowd begins to thin, more people recognise Matthew and stop by their table for quick catch-ups. Between interruptions, Melissa learns that Matthew has a business in the area. She isn't quite sure what type of business, however, as she is too busy being enchanted by him. *Concentrate, Melissa! Now where is that stunning woman with the sexy accent?*

Matthew is clearly excited by the prospect of going to Castillo's and tries hard to engage her in the conversation. 'Yeah, it is amazing. Maybe, Melissa, you and I could go together?' he suggests with a laugh, but he looks at her intently.

She blushes again. *Fuck! Stop blushing!* At this moment, she wants nothing more than to do anything with him. Anything at all.

When she doesn't respond, it's clear he thinks she's uncomfortable with the suggestion, and continues quickly. 'I've found all the testimonials fascinating. I'd love to get there, but I've been apprehensive. I had several bad acid trips...'

Melissa tries desperately to stay in the conversation. 'Oh, sorry, what did you say?'

He begins again and she can hear bits and pieces but her stomach drops as she hears somebody announce that it's just after 8.30. *What!! Billy is due home tonight.*

Matthew is saying something about years ago having lots of bad acid trips, mixed with all sorts of illegal party drugs, which were disastrous, but she cannot focus at all. She bites down on her bottom lip trying to pretend she is listening, but she is consumed with fear about the impending argument she knows awaits her at home. *What am I going to say I was doing? Fuckkkk, Billy's going to freak out, I was expected hours ago! God, I'm so late.* Her heart pounds heavily. *Shit. Merde. Merde. Sue and Nigel are coming for dinner, and Billy is counting on them investing in his wonder drug.*

A vision comes to her prominently now of Billy, Sue and Nigel sitting angrily at her empty dining table. She can still hear Matthew talking but cannot even pretend to hear what he's saying now. Melissa is pleased the tall Latino woman has joined them and is almost completely blocking her from Matthew's view. He tries to introduce the two of them, but the other woman is too busy talking to stop and greet Melissa. Matthew tries to cut her off, but she's a force to be reckoned with. 'Darling, the Mertons have arrived, I think we should...'

*Well, that definitely sounds like they are a couple.* Matthew tries again to cut this woman off, but Melissa feels slightly relieved that she can quickly sneak away as she's now consumed by memories of Billy undermining her with her kids. Billy will make her life a misery if he hears where she's been. She still doesn't know if the kids believe his last lie about her trying to seduce one of his male friends.

Melissa isn't sure whether Matthew saw her trying to say goodbye, but she runs out of the bar without looking back, fear gnawing heavily at her gut. When she reaches the pavement, she remembers her car is still outside Pymble's. 'Great. Just great.' She takes off her shoes and runs through the rain. 'Putain de merde! Fuck, I'm gonna get it!'

With each step, more and more images of Billy freaking out flash through her mind, and as she nears her car, another image hits her hard – of Billy storming towards the front door with Chloe on his hip and Zac grasped tightly around one wrist, the two of them pleading for their mother. Billy calling her a terrible mother as he loaded the kids into the car. She remembers chasing after the car, the sting of bitumen beneath her knees as she collapsed to the ground, grief-stricken. Even though they've left home, the thought of losing her kids to him still terrifies her.

Mustering all the strength she can find; she does her best to calm herself on the drive home. Each corner she takes reveals a new excuse she can use to explain her absence, but by the time she drives into her garage, she can't remember which idea makes more sense.

As she steps out of her car, she's surprised to find there are no lights on in the house. When she unlocks the door, she's sure nobody's home. But there's a nagging sense, a fear that Billy is going to jump out at her in a rage.

Melissa tiptoes nervously inside, and panics when something touches her thigh. Her heart is pounding as she reaches down and realises it's her phone vibrating through her bag. With no small amount of trepidation, Melissa pulls it out, her hand trembling when she sees Billy's name. Deep dread runs through her at the impending tirade, and she holds the phone right away from her ear as she answers it.

'I'm going to be very late tonight, honey. I have so much to do here before I leave for Copenhagen in the morning.'

Partly relieved but incredibly angry with herself for racing out of the bar, she asks, 'What about Sue and Nigel?'

Instantly, Billy pounces on her. 'I left a message for you hours ago. They couldn't make it. Nigel has to leave for— What the hell? Where have you been since your appointment with Pymble?'

She manages to placate him with a convincing mixture of lies, and exhales when she finally gets him off the phone. The adrenaline of the last hour courses through her veins, making her dizzy. She slides down the fridge door onto the floor. 'Putain de merde... Holy fuck; what did I just do?' Why is she so frightened of Billy? 'I am an idiot. Je suis une imbécile! I'm so very... very... Je suis très... très... très fatiguée.'

Resting her elbows on her knees, she presses the heels of her hands into her eyes and weeps. The excitement, the intrigue, the fear, the pain and the disappointments of the past year come flooding out. She curses herself over and over. 'Why did I race out of there? This could have been the best thing for me. He was even interested in going to Castillo's! Fuck, this could have been great. And he was so beautiful! Maybe... just maybe that woman is only a good friend, doubtful but maybe.'

She doesn't know how long she sits there but manages to eventually pick herself up from the floor and fill a water bottle when Billy bursts through the front door fuming.

'My father said he saw you with a man, and it looked to him like you were more than just friends!'

Melissa's heart pounds and her face flushes, but she stares at Billy defiantly, almost relieved that it's finally come to this. *This is good. I've had enough. We have to break up. We have to!*

Billy watches her, waiting for her response, and as she breathes in, about to tell him everything, he talks over her. 'Well, Melissa? Who would that be? And really, at *Gaston's?* Where so many people know us?'

She stops herself and realises. *Ahhh... Gaston's! Lucien! Should I just tell him anyway about where I've really been?* She takes a deep breath and finally responds, 'Well, perhaps your father needs to get some more details before he worries you like this. It was Lucien. We're working on his new restaurant at the Point, and you know what he's like... he kisses everyone on the lips. Even you, if I remember correctly, and you were not too happy about it. It's just his nature to be affectionate—'

The anger dies quickly in Billy, and he gives her a small apologetic smile, picks her up and spins her around. 'Sorry, honey. I love you so much, I can't stop myself, I just think every man in the world wants you—'

'Ha, yeah, I'm sure you do! Not! I remember now Lucien was over the moon because he liked the new concept for his menus...' *Yes Billy I'm sure every man in the world wants me!* She becomes distracted as she reflects on Billy's words. *In the world... Le monde... Le monde... Dans le monde... Tout le monde... I wish I was back at Le monde.*

She trails off deep in thought as Billy races to get a whisky and yells back to her, 'I'm leaving for Copenhagen at four in the morning. Did you get my suits dry-cleaned and the shirts ironed? And did you get the new razor I asked for?'

Anger surges through her, and she responds through gritted teeth. 'Yes, no, and yes.'

He races back down the hall and stares at her. 'What?'

'*Yes,* I got your suits dry-cleaned. *No,* I didn't iron your shirts; they'll be creased by the time you get there, anyway. And *yes,* I got the razor.'

He looks at her incredulously and shakes his head. 'I don't know why we can't get more help around here if you're not going to do everything I need you to do.'

~ ~ ~

Gliding through the water as he navigates his way through a complicated maze of underwater caves, he surges quickly through the rock passages towards the light. Melissa holds on tightly around his neck, to this man she shares a deep love with. The sense of familiarity when she opens her eyes to see the bright sparkles on the turquoise and golden corals in the cavern all around her, send tingles through her. She wants to stay here with him, but this voice is nagging at her... pulling her away from this place where she feels this total euphoria.

'Why? Why? Why?' This voice keeps persisting until she recognises, with some confusion, that the voice is her own. It curses her and curses her until finally she wakes and the reality of everything that's happened the previous evening hits her like a hammer blow. 'Why the *fuck* did I race out of there? Why the fuck? Je ne le reverrai jamais. Jamais! I'll never see him again. Ever!'

She tosses and turns for a while, tormenting herself as she tries to go back to sleep until frustration drives her out of bed and to the bathroom. She sits on the toilet and screams at her reflection, 'Why the fuck did I worry! Billy is off on a bloody trip to Denmark with Janet, I bet. Oh, and I'm sure those condoms in your suitcase really were Gerry's. I'm sure Gerry just didn't have that *tiny bit of space* in his suitcase for them!'

Melissa takes calming breaths that really don't help at all. Why does she care what Billy thinks? 'He's going through so much of the Trust money that he should be on his knees thanking me. How many times has he said, "This is going to be the big one, babe!? Ça va être le grand, bébé! What bullshit! Quelle merde!"'

She screams at her reflection. 'He's as bad as his father!'

If only she and Lilly could get their heads around all the finances. They could take control. And then it would be a matter of keeping their mother out of it. At least Dad was wise enough to put it in the hands of trustees, who are keeping it under control. Melissa is sure Billy and her mother would have sent them broke by now. 'Thank you, Billy Blatt and mother dearest!'

She stomps up to the mirrored wall, and fumes at her reflection. 'Melissa, tu es une imbécile!! Mathieu! Mathieu! Why didn't I get your number?' *Why couldn't I focus on what he was saying?* She has no idea what sort of designer he is. Website? Interior? Graphic? *That would be nice, we could have a graphic design company called Together Forever! Ensemble pour toujours!*

'Mon dieu! You are such a child!' She yells at her reflection.

Aisha is going to give her so much grief. She has to calm down. Melissa is just going to have to tell her friend that Matthew is married or something. Maybe he *is* married to that beautiful woman. *Oh, fuck, I'm supposed to be meeting with Lucien again this morning to show him the new ideas for his new seafood restaurant.* She's still shocked that he's going with her suggestion, Stunned Mullet. If only he knew where she came up with it from.

She washes her hands and catches a glimpse of her face, still smeared with the remnants of her mascara. Stepping under the shower, her mind returns to Billy and her fear of him. Her fear that he'll turn her children against her. He uses Zac and Chloe as weapons against her, and that only makes her blood boil. Yet the fear remains.

Once dressed, she races down to her study only to curse herself for not having Lucien's designs prepared. There's still a few months before the opening, and she hopes he'll forgive her. She sends him a quick text saying she will have them to him in a couple of days. 'Best client in the world,' she says as she locks up the house behind her.

~ ~ ~

Melissa is heading for Le Monde, irrationally hoping that Matthew might be there. Many people seemed to know him, so maybe it's his regular haunt. She knows that Aisha will be happy. The best thing she could do, according to Aisha, would be to leave Bully altogether. She'd started recommending this soon after she met him. *Why didn't I listen to her? Why didn't she stand over me like my mother did?* 'Because she's a better person than my mother, that's why,' she chastises herself.

She slows as Le Monde comes into view and does her best to see if she can spot him through the large front windows, but a line of cars builds up behind her and before she knows it, they are beeping their horns. 'Oh! Pour l'amour de dieu! Oh, for god's sake! Pourquoi les gens ne sont-ils pas plus patients? Why aren't people more fucking patient? Can't you go around?'

Driving on a little way, she looks in her rear-view mirror, hoping to glimpse the bar again. 'Great. Now I'm a stalker. You're a married woman with two beautiful kids you adore. What on Earth are you thinking?' She catches a glimpse of herself. 'And you look like shit!'

The cars behind her are still beeping their horns. Some stalker she is, in her bright aqua car. Frustrated and embarrassed, she gives up and heads in the direction of the beach. She parks near Whale's Inlet and walks down to the sand and sits in a daze, staring at the ocean for hours. She'd been enlivened by her conversation with Matthew. It had certainly stirred something deep inside her, and now, more than ever, she wants to have that amazing feeling again in her life.

Maybe she is losing it. *Stop it, Melissa, just stop!* She's married and has two beautiful kids who would never forgive her for leaving – Billy would make sure of that, and if he didn't, Brian or Jean would.

She takes a few deep breaths and tries to bring herself back to the present, but all that resides in the present are thoughts of Matthew. The way he took her hand and led her protectively through the bar... and then when he whispered in her ear... it sent tingles through her body. And he smelt so good! *Fuck, Billy, why don't you just leave me?* Billy was barely ever home, anyway. Between sport, work, international conferences, and a girlfriend—not that she minds him having a girlfriend, at least he doesn't hassle her for sex as much—he rarely spent any time at home. Maybe if she goes to Castillo's, he'll be pissed off enough to leave? No, he'll likely just have a psychiatric restraining order put out on her. With James's help, of course.

Thoughts of Matthew ignite her again, she can no longer resist the temptation to return to Le Monde. Her heart pounds heavily at the thought. She desperately wants to see him again. *I can't think of anything I would like more than to go to Castillo's with you, Matthieu.*

She drives past Le Monde several times before eventually finding a parking space. She quickly checks her reflection. *I look terrible!* She rubs her lips together, pinches her cheeks, ties her hair up and wipes mascara from under her eyes. The likelihood of him being here is so remote, and she doesn't know why she's so nervous. *Pour l'amour de dieu! For god's sake... I like the sound of that. Oh well, fuck here goes.*

Taking a deep breath, she makes for the entrance but her phone rings. It's Aisha, and Melissa is grateful for the distraction. She whispers as best she can to her friend, 'I can't talk now. I'm back at Le Monde. I don't know what I'm doing.' She gets the vague sense that people around her have stopped their conversations and lowers her voice a bit more. 'Oh, you are so sweet but no, I don't expect you to stop what you're doing and join me.' Grateful for her friend's reassurance, she ends the call and self-consciously makes her way to the rear of the building.

She can't see Matthew anywhere. *Well, I guess I didn't really need to pinch my cheeks after all. A bit of embarrassment will always do the trick. Oh, why didn't I just get his number?* She could have avoided all this desperation.

Melissa takes a moment to look around and sees a dark-haired man towards the back of the bar. It's not Matthew, so she orders a drink. One drink, then she's leaving. The charade has gone on long enough.

# CHAPTER 23

*I just can't get you out of my head! I have to see you just once more. Are you married? Es-tu mariée? No, you're not married... are you? Why did I run out of there!* Melissa dives deep into her pool wondering how on Earth she can see Matthew again. Her mind latches onto how she's in need of drawing materials since she had destroyed a lot of them recently. It just so happens that the biggest art supply store in the area is just around the corner from Le Monde.

Feeling like a teenager whose hormones are out of control, Melissa drives straight to Le Monde. It feels like the world is watching her. She really needs to do something more constructive with herself rather than thinking about Matthew all day long!

Anger wells up inside her, and memories of the months after Billy's accident, surge to the surface. Her mother's grip as Melissa was dragged through those cold hospital corridors to Billy's bedside and ordered to pay penance.

'Billy's accident is all your fault.'

'Mum, it wasn't my fault. We'd broken up.'

But her mother would only pile on more guilt. 'What if he dies? God! What if he never walks again?'

After all this time, just remembering this interaction leaves her cold. How could Melissa have allowed her mother to have so much power over her? Even back then, Melissa had known she could never be happy with Billy; she'd broken up with him because there were so many things she couldn't stand about him—his arrogance, his competitiveness, his jealousy to name a few—but seeing him in a coma, looking so peaceful and gentle, her heart had softened. Deep down she knew his accident wasn't her fault, but she'd worried terribly that he would die. And there'd been guilt, believing in some convoluted way, she had been the cause.

She had tormented herself for so many years about letting her mother have so much control over her life. The ballet lessons were one thing, but to marry someone she wasn't in love with? Melissa always consoled herself with the fact that without Billy, she wouldn't have her two beautiful children, but was secretly pleased neither Zac nor Chloe resembled him physically or emotionally.

*Stop thinking about your mother, for fuck's sake. C'est le passé, passe à autre chose! It's the past, move on!* With a deep breath, Melissa makes her way inside. She finally finds a table near the bar and pulls out her laptop. Embarrassment has her face redden as she pretends to work while subtly scanning the room. How she wishes they had table service as the thought of now having to make her way to the counter is daunting. She finally musters the courage and as soon as she stands, she sees him coming quickly towards her.

*He's here. Oh, Pour l'amour de dieu... Oh, fuck. Fuck. Fuck. Fuck.*

He smiles and imitates the skid she did the night they first met out the front of this building. 'We really should stop meeting like this!' He grins mischievously.

They awkwardly greet each other with an intense embrace, and his gaze remains fixed on her for what might ordinarily be an uncomfortably long time. She blushes and he adds, 'I'm sorry if I offended you about my illegal-drug-taking days.'

Melissa is confused. 'Sorry?' Then vaguely recalls he did say something along those lines. 'Oh, god, no it wasn't that. I'd realised I had visitors that night. I did try to say goodbye, but you were busy,' she says, and can feel the heat rise to her cheeks.

'You look really lovely when you blush, and you do it a bit, I've noticed.'

Feeling even more embarrassed, she pushes him away, but can't help smiling as she blushes even more. In an effort to turn attention away from the colour of her face, she tries to resume their conversation, 'So have you been to Castill—'

'Hey, Matt!'

A tall, thin man approaches, and Matthew introduces his friend. 'Melissa, this is Charlie. Charlie, Melissa.'

'Hi, Melissa.' Charlie politely offers her his hand then turns straight back to Matthew. 'You're getting harder and harder to catch. Is everything okay? I saw Jane the other day; she's really worried about you, man.'

Melissa notes the concern in Charlie's eyes and looks to Matthew to see if she can gauge what's going on.

'I know, mate. That's just Jane creating drama. I'm fine.' He faces Melissa. 'Jane is my sister, by the way.' Melissa blushes slightly at the added attention and he focuses back on Charlie. 'Anyhow, how are you doing? Is the partnership working out?'

Charlie winces. 'It's a bloody nightmare, to tell you the truth. Why did I ever think I could work with my brother? I should have followed your path, man.' He looks to Melissa. 'Matt and I studied architecture together. This smart man here dropped out and I slaved away for another couple of years and his business is booming—'

'Actually,' Matthew interrupts, seeming somewhat uncomfortable with the adulation, 'I got really lucky that my aunt let me design her a new home. That helped so much—'

'Yeah, well, I couldn't have pulled it off. I don't know how you knew so much—'

'Just lucky I guess. Drink, anyone?'

'Rubbish! Talent, you mean!' Charlie insists he gets the round of drinks, and heads to the bar.

'So,' Melissa starts, 'it's Matt, is it? Is that what you prefer?'

'Not really. It's a bit close to "mat", you know, as in doormat! Or so my mother said, and she always insisted on Matthew when I was very young. It's funny, it's one of the few things I remember about her. And you? Is it Mel?'

'No, I hate Mel, truth be told. I only get it occasionally and it is okay, but I prefer Liss or Melissa.'

'So, which would you like me to call you?'

*This sounds like we're going to meet again. Am I going to see you again? Oh, la la I hope so. I hope you're not married, Matthieu! No ring so that's a good sign.* She looks into his eyes and realises he is waiting for an answer. 'Oh sorry, whichever feels right for you is great.'

'Mel it is, then,' he says with a grin. 'Actually, that doesn't suit you at all. I like Melissa.'

Charlie returns with their drinks and immediately fires questions at Matthew.

Melissa excuses herself and heads off to the bathroom to call Aisha. 'Aish!' Melissa does her best to whisper, but her excitement is difficult to control.

'Liss? Where are you? What's happened?'

'I'm in the toilet at Le Monde again. He's here and we're having a drink. I'm a nervous wreck but I'm melting inside!'

'Oh, I'm so happy for you!'

'Aish, he's so beautiful; way more beautiful than I first thought. I want him so badly. I can hardly breathe.'

'Slow down, babe.'

'Oh, what am I doing?'

'You're living your life, that's what you're doing!'

'Aish, I'm scared and I... I feel guilty!'

'You're a grown woman and you've met this beautiful man. Enjoy yourself. And don't feel guilty, *Janet*... oops, Melissa! This man may encourage you to have a treatment that may save your life, this clinic sounds amazing.'

~ ~ ~

When Melissa returns from the bathroom, Charlie is still firing questions at Matthew, who tries several times to change the subject. It's only when Charlie finally goes to the bathroom, that Matthew can apologise.

'Sorry about that. He's got a few business problems. So, tell me, are you going to try Castillo's? I'm really keen. I'm wanting to go down next week to do the basic medical they require and get all the forms. Are you in?'

Excitement and nervousness have Melissa's stomach flipping. 'Yes, I'm keen... but I'm not sure I have the guts.'

He nudges her. 'Ah, come on. Let's look into it, anyway. We'll have to do this together, don't you think?'

Melissa takes a breath, fortifying herself. 'Okay. I'm keen. I have to go to Brisbane next Wednesday, so I could go then. God, I'm nervous just talking about it.'

Charlie returns with more drinks. 'What are you nervous talking about?'

Matthew smiles at Melissa, and answers for her. 'She's not! You're going to do it, aren't you, Melissa!' He nudges her again and flashes a cheeky smile. 'Aren't you?'

Melissa nods but she is annoyed and distracted by the constant vibration of her phone. Finally she responds. 'Well, yes but the hallucinogens are—'

Charlie scoffs. 'What hallucinogens? Are you serious? Did Matt tell you about when I met up with him in Bolivia when we were younger?'

Matthew raises his eyebrows and tries to change the subject, but Charlie continues loudly. 'It was in these beautiful mountains about fifteen years ago. We were with a small group of travellers and we went to these amazing cliffs with incredible views down to the ocean. We'd all heard about this local hallucinogenic ritual and we decided we'd experience it later that night. Well, it didn't quite agree with Matt. We almost lost him.'

Melissa turns to Matthew. 'Really?'

Matthew nods. 'Yes, I guess so.'

Charlie slaps Matt on the shoulder. 'Definitely, mate. You were so close to the edge.'

'Don't you worry, Charlie, I know. I was absolutely petrified.'

Charlie shakes his head. 'You'd run off, and I was worried but after I drank the hallucinogenic tea, I couldn't stop vomiting. Can't remember what happened until the next morning.'

Matthew sighs. 'All I remember is having this incredible urge to jump off the cliffs into the ocean. I was terrified when I came to the next morning. How I hadn't fallen off the cliff is still beyond me.'

Charlie slings an arm around Matthew's shoulders. 'No more cliffs, yeah?'

'Promise,' Matthew tells him then turns to Melissa. 'We'll be okay won't *we*, Melissa?'

'Y-yes, we'll be fine,' she says, when he nods for her to agree.

Annoyed by her phone, which has been continually vibrating since Charlie returned with more drinks, she reluctantly looks at it and sees a message from Billy: "Where are you? I'm back early. I've left messages for you."

*No... Non.. Not now! You were supposed to be away for a week.* Her phone vibrates again, but now he's calling her. *No, go away!* She wants to ignore Billy but he continues to call, and panic sets in. Frightened that Billy is going to come bursting through Le

Monde's front door any minute, she turns to Matthew with an apologetic smile. 'I'm sorry, but I have to go. I'll let you know about Castillo's.' She wants to ask for his number but she feels awkward, and her panic is rising. 'Okay, I'd better go.'

Matthew calls after her. 'Would it be okay to get your number, Melissa? Are you serious about Castillo's? Are you going to pick up the forms?'

Her eyes light up. 'Yes. Yes, I will. I'll go next Wednesday.'

'That's great! That's really great; really, really great. How about we meet up after to compare notes?'

'Okay, let me check my calendar.' She opens her phone and tries to remember various dates, knowing that her calendar is not up to date. *Okay calm. You have to do this. Billy is off again next Wednesday and definitely won't be back till after the weekend because of his big cycling competition. And Zac and Chloe aren't coming up until the weekend after that as they are going to a big festival on the 30th.*

Matthew waits for her response and finally she smiles. 'Yes, if all goes well at Castillo's, that would be great. I could probably meet up on Friday.'

'Great. Let's meet here at one or two in the afternoon?'

'Two sounds good.'

'Is it really okay to get your number?'

'Of course.'

Her heart races as he inputs her number into his phone and immediately calls her. *I can't believe I have his number now! I'll have to save it under another name, or I'll have to memorise it!* She says her goodbyes and leaves, heading quickly to her car. She drives past the art supply shop but is too panicked to stop. Why the fuck did Billy have to come home early? She exhales loudly, turns the stereo up and sings along:

*'I want to hold you in my arms, I want to never let you go,*
*I want to hold you in my arms, and I want everyone to know*
*This love, this love, this love like ours is...'*

# CHAPTER 24

Melissa's nerves had got the better of her again. She'd spent way too much time and gone through so many different outfits until finally deciding on a simple pair of jeans and a t-shirt. The paperwork from Castillo's she'd kept hidden in a cupboard sits on the passenger seat of her car as she makes her way to Le Monde. *Oh, I'm panicking. Ah, je panique.*

As they spot each other outside in the carpark, they each hold aloft a sheaf of papers and he gives her the thumbs up. Entering the bar together, Matthew mimics her skid, flailing his arms and clutching at her arm to steady himself. She laughs. *Never let go.* 'So, did you meet the man himself?' she asks.

'The notorious Castillo? No, I didn't get past his annoying assistant. I think he only works where they actually do the procedure, which is miles away.'

'I didn't meet him either. His assistant *is* difficult, isn't she? I'm dying to know what he looks like. I imagine this little nutty professor with thick-rimmed glasses, a balding head and olive skin.'

Matthew disagrees. 'With a name like Castillo, I see him as a tall, strong, fair-haired, fair-skinned man, ha not really! Actually, I don't know what to expect.'

'How did your medical go?'

'It went well. And you?'

She nods. 'Yes, I got through, but it was quite intense.'

After ordering their coffees, they sit together at a table at the rear of the bar and try to make sense of the forms in front of them.

'Wow.' Melissa flicks through the pages. 'This is going to take a bit of time. There are so many questions.'

They both get to work on filling in their personal details, and then Melissa reads out the first question, 'Okay, "List all your loves/hates/fears." All right then.'

Melissa makes a list of all of the people she loves, and she pauses, chewing on the end of her pen and pondering for a moment as to whether she will put Billy, Brian and her mother on to the hate list. With a shake of her head, she continues filling out the form.

'My mind is a bit blank,' Matthew says, looking over to her. He reads out his list of loves. 'Monty, surfing, designing, kitesurfing, building, reading. And I have my aunt and my sister and a couple of friends... That's all I have so far.'

'Monty?'

'My German shepherd. I depend on him for my sanity. He's twelve now and he hasn't been doing very well lately.'

'Oh, sorry.'

'Ah, he's strong; he'll be okay. Do you want another coffee or anything to eat? I'm starving.'

'Something small to eat, and another coffee would be great.'

He returns carrying a tray with two coffees and two cakes. He asks which of them she would prefer.

'Too hard to choose. They both look great.'

'Okay, I'll sort that out.' He cuts the two cakes in half so that they can share each of them.

Eager to get the paperwork out of the way, Melissa skims

through the list and reads out a couple more of the questions. 'Okay, traumas in your life... significant people... guilt that may have a hold over you... um, unfulfilled expectations... whoa this list goes on and on.' They both roll their eyes at each other.

Matthew puts his hands behind his head and stretches. 'There's a lot to get through here.' He frowns as he tries to hear a song playing in the background. 'Do you know this song? I like this song...'

'Yes, I love this band!'

They begin talking over one another and laughing about why a particular song is better than another. Melissa picks up her forms again and flicks through all the pages. 'Unfortunately, we still have a lot to fill out.'

Matthew groans dramatically. 'Okay, let's begin again.'

'I'm still stuck on some of the first questions. I don't know what my greatest fears or phobias are... I've got so many. Nightmares... paralysis... claustrophobia—'

They both make jokes about the Castillo Clinic being high on their list and then she reads on. '"List the events in your life that have been the most significant to you".' She sighs heavily and moves on. 'And the one after that wants us to list any losses we've endured.' They quietly write down their thoughts and feelings and the atmosphere around them deepens as the questions become more and more personal.

After a while, Matthew drops his pen on the table and pushes his forms away. 'How about we talk about something else for a while?'

'We were supposed to have these back *yesterday*, remember?' Melissa says with mock sternness.

He knows immediately who she is imitating. 'There's something definitely wrong with Nurse Edwards. She lacks any kind of... of...'

'Empathy? Maybe Castillo feels sorry for her, or perhaps

she's his wife? Or nightmare mother or sister?'

Matthew rolls his eyes. 'I have one of those. I love my sister but she's a lot of work.'

Melissa smiles and finishes her paperwork. 'Okay, I think I deserve a wine. Can I get you a drink?'

'Ah yes, just a lager would be great. I'm just finishing off.'

As Melissa heads to the bar, she hears him read the next question aloud. 'Any recent traumas?' He sighs loudly.

When she returns, it's clear he's upset. She puts the drinks down, takes her seat, and hesitates before asking if he's okay.

'Sorry,' he says in a quiet voice. 'I've been really messed up. A woman I was with for a short time killed herself in my home.'

Melissa takes his hand and squeezes it gently. 'I'm so sorry.'

He closes his eyes and she watches him take control of his breathing before continuing slowly. 'I really don't know how we got together. My sister, Jane, almost...' He sighs. 'I was doing quite a lot of recreational drugs at the time and somehow, Katryn and I got together. The next minute, she was pregnant. I mean almost the next minute. I think I saw her three times at the most.'

He takes a long sip of his beer, and sighs heavily. 'Katryn was an acquaintance of Jane's, and my sister really laid it on me that I was solely responsible, and somehow, I bought into it. Katryn moved into my place and we had a tumultuous relationship. I asked to see the pregnancy test, and she flew into a rage. Then... then she *allegedly* miscarries, and I'm living in this extremely volatile relationship.'

'I'm sorry,' Melissa tells him again.

'She was jealous all the time and would often become quite violent The relationship clearly wasn't working, but Jane insisted I had to stay.'

Matthew stares at the table as he continues. 'I love my sister, I do, but she's high maintenance. Our parents died when we were both young, so I've been watching out for her as best I can. I really did try to do the right thing by Katryn, but she knew I didn't want to be with her.'

Melissa understands his need to purge his self-imposed guilt, and encourages him to keep talking.

Hours go by as Matthew tells her of his early depression, his South American sojourns, and how it all culminated with Katryn and the calamity that followed. As tough as the subject matter is, there's an easy trust between them, confident that there'll be no judgement.

They move closer, divulging the stories of their lives to one another. A waiter starts doing his rounds, putting small lanterns on the tables, and the soft candlelight illuminates their faces with a warm glow and their conversation grows even more intimate.

Matthew sighs loudly and looks insecurely at Melissa. She has no idea what he's about to say, but she puts her arm around his shoulder and encourages him to keep talking. She can feel his body shaking slightly and his voice quivering, 'I hope you don't think I'm bad! I don't know… but I hope you will understand… if you knew the situation….' He rolls his eyes and takes a deep breath before continuing. 'Anyway, as I said, it was an extremely tumultuous relationship. She would call me constantly and make all these threats, and I mean *all the time*… sometimes ten or twenty times a day. Anyway, they were constant. And initially, I reacted as she wanted me to react – by running home to save her. But after weeks of this, I'd had enough. She called me seven times this night. I'd been in a meeting and missed the calls, and when I came out of the meeting, I was tired and….' His voice falters, and Melissa rubs his arm warmly, encouraging him to continue.

He takes a sip of his lager and looks Melissa directly in the eye before continuing, 'I was so tired of the calls and all the threats, so when the phone rang again, I saw it was her... I threw it... I threw my phone so hard against a wall wanting it to break and for the calls to end. I'd had it. I threw it so hard, and it smashed, but the ringtone continued on and on, so I picked it up and held the button in until it went off. I felt so relieved. I guess I was hoping it would all go away... I'm sorry.'

Melissa smiles at him and encourages him once again to keep talking.

He clears his throat before continuing. 'But it didn't. I got back to my place, and just the sound of my dog crying helplessly through the front door... I knew... what I'd done... I knew she had done what she'd threatened to do so many times...'

He bangs his fist up against his mouth firmly. He does this several times before he continues. 'It was so... so surreal and sad. And I will probably never be able to forgive myself...'

Melissa stands up and puts her arms around his shoulders, and whispers. 'It wasn't your fault.'

He looks up at her, stands, and they embrace.

Melissa melts into his strong embrace, her entire body tingling. Her yearning for him is so fierce, she can hardly contain herself. She breathes him in, and this familiar euphoria rushes through her. Even if she wanted to, she couldn't pull away. It's so right here in his arms, but somewhere in the pit of her stomach, fear stirs and slowly rises.

She tries so hard to stop the voices in her head but her fear of Billy keeps nagging at her: 'The kids know you have serious mental problems, Melissa. They'll never forgive you. Never forgive you.'

Melissa imagines Billy driving away with her kids as she chases after them. That's all it takes for her to pull away from Matthew.

'I'm so sorry, Matthew. I'm so sorry, I'm not ready for this. My kids... I can't.'

'No, it's me who should be sorry. I know you're married—'

She places a finger against his lips. 'No, no… please don't apologise.' She closes her eyes, puts her head down, covers her mouth as she begins to cry. 'I am so angry with myself. I'm… I am so angry with myself because you're all I think about, but I just can't betray my kids. He would turn them against me. I'm sorry. I'm so sorry.'

Melissa dares not look at him again and quickly grabs her handbag and runs from the bar. As she runs out, she bumps the elbow of someone at a table near the door, and when the man looks up, it's Charlie.

'Hey…'

She shakes her head and rushes out the door.

~ ~ ~

Dragging his eyes from the door, Matthew follows the sound of the familiar voice and sees Charlie waving at him. He tries to shake the image of Melissa's back disappearing through the doorway but Charlie is soon walking across the room, his friend's expression morphing into a frown as he nears.

'Whoa, are you okay, man? What happened?' He turns to the front door, then slowly moves his attention back to Matthew. 'You're a bit taken with her, huh? What was her name again?'

'Meli…' He clears his throat. 'Melissa. Her name is Melissa.' Still staring at the exit, he quietly continues, '…and yes… I've been taken with her for a very long time.'

~ ~ ~

Outside the bar, Melissa finds no comfort waiting for her. Once again, she's sitting in her car not wanting to leave but knowing she must. Tears stream down her face. Her urge to stay is so strong, she finds it hard to put the key into the ignition. She wants to go back inside but forces herself to drive away.

Melissa is thankful that Billy is away at his bike race and arrives home to an empty house. She races straight to the sitting room, grabs a glass and a bottle of wine and heads back out to the pool. With her feet dangling in the water, she opens the bottle and pours a large glass, drinking it down quickly. *Oh mon dieu qu'est-ce que j'ai fait? What have I done?*

Staring out at the forest, tears well in her eyes again. She pours another glass, drinks it down just as quickly. 'I've got to get him out of my head. I have to.' But she can't. Every time she pushes his image away, it returns. Stronger and sharper.

'What am I going to do?... I don't know what I'm going to do. I know... I know... What do you know?' she asks herself, then provides the answer. 'I know that my life will... Your life will what, Melissa?... My life will be so messed up.'

A laugh escapes her, and it sounds a little hysterical. 'Stop fucking talking to yourself and stop thinking of him. *Right now. Tout de suite!*'

Melissa runs back into the house and grabs another bottle of wine out of the fridge, and just as she is about to take it out to the pool, she stops, pours a small glass of wine and puts the bottle back in the fridge. She'll just have this little bit and then go to bed. 'I'll get up bright and early in the morning and visit the kids.'

She lies down next to the pool and cries, waking hours later shivering as she hears Billy calling for her. She sees two empty bottles of wine, *Oh fuck! I don't remember getting that second bottle out of the fridge.* Melissa hears Billy getting nearer and curses herself for not getting rid of the bottles. *Here we go.* But she's surprised by Billy's tone, he sounds genuinely compassionate.

'Oh my god, honey, I was really worried about you. I've been trying to call you. We have to get you better. I love you so much.' He crouches and holds her against him for a moment and then tenderly picks her up and carries her to their bed. He lies down behind her and pulls her in close. She tries to move away from him subtly. *This just feels so wrong. So, so wrong. Oh, Billy, please don't touch me! Please don't breathe on me. Your voice, your smell, your touch, everything about you is so, so wrong. You disgust me. Tu me dégoutes.*

Billy groans and pulls her into his body once again. Melissa reluctantly relents. She is not up to another argument; she knows well enough that she'll still get an earful about dumping the psychiatrist and failing to take her medication correctly.

CHAPTER 25

For weeks after Melissa had run away from Matthew at Le Monde, she is overwhelmed by a deep sadness. How could she have run out after he'd poured his heart out to her? She shouldn't have left him like that. Melissa stares at herself in the mirror. 'You know why you ran out of there. You're terrified of what Billy would do to him, or to you or the kids. Why does he have this fucking hold? Other people just break up. Why can't I?'

She doesn't speak about Matthew to anyone, but he invades her every thought. Though she spends a lot of time with her kids and her friends, her mind drifts back to him, always trying to imagine where he is and what he may be thinking, and secretly hoping he is thinking about her. *Ne sois pas ridicule... Don't be ridiculous, Melissa. I'm sure he's moved on.*

And then as clear as the day they were uttered only a few months ago, Elle's words float through her mind. 'Sorry, my darling, but men really *do* only want one thing. They're not interested in just "loving us up" unless they think they'll get something more. They want sex and nothing else. And I don't think you're ready for that.'

*You're stuck with your lot, lassie! Suck it up!*

She constantly replays the day she last saw Matthew, always

hoping she would run into him somewhere, but it hadn't happened. Melissa didn't want to call him; she wouldn't know what to say… but she's desperate to see him again. She slams her laptop shut. 'Fuck it. Just one more time. I'm not getting any work done anyway.'

She's going back to Le Monde and that's that.

Melissa races into her bathroom, and stares at herself in the mirror. It's her grandmother's voice she hears, asking if this is really what she wants.

'I so want to see him again, Gran. His face, his eyes… just everything. But I shouldn't. I just… I can't get him out of my head. I'm not. I'm not going to Le Monde again. I can't! Not ever!'

# CHAPTER 26

Melissa jerks suddenly, and her heart pounds. Billy has once again woken her by slamming the toilet seat back. *Who invented ensuite bathrooms? First the toilet seat then the loud peeing, then the guttural sounds, and then the heavy snorting and coughing and spluttering! Mon dieu! You would have to be the most inconsiderate man on Earth!* After her initial annoyance subsides, she rolls over and wills herself back to sleep... back into this other reality where she feels loved.

Little bits of her dream come back to her. Of this elusive man tenderly kissing her stomach, her breasts, her neck, and finally her lips—

She frowns heavily as she hears a strange noise and then someone's voice getting louder and more aggressive. 'Melissa! Melissa! MELISSA!'

She clutches at her neck and jolts away from Billy, standing over her in his bike gear.

'For Cahrist's sake. Have I ever tried to strangle you? Have I?' He imitates her melodramatically, clutching at his neck, and before she has time to answer, he continues. 'By the way, Sleeping Beauty, you've got some more tidying up to amuse yourself with this morning. You've destroyed the sitting room again, and this time I cut my foot quite badly on a piece of ceramic because you smashed that new sculpture or whatever you call it that Lilly made you for your birthday. You managed to find my good whisky again and smashed that, too. Funny how it's often the whisky and not your white spirits! I'm sure all this will help me in the race this morning, thank you very much.'

*Really? Just the whisky? Am I so discerning?* She wouldn't have a clue. And she's the one who has to buy the whisky, so she doesn't understand how he thinks it benefits her.

She closes her eyes tight and tries to remember what she had done through the night but nothing comes back to her. Burying herself under the quilt, she can feel some painful cuts on her knees, and she sighs as she is forced to contemplate her nightmarish existence once again.

As soon as Billy's gone, she makes her way to the sitting room to find the smashed bottle of Royal Salute; the vodka and gin bottles stand unharmed on the glass drinks trolley. But the ceramic sculpture Lilly made for Melissa's birthday is broken beyond repair.

'I've had enough! I can't do this anymore!'

CHAPTER 27

*Les stalactites sont magnifiques... Je suis enceinte...* These words linger as Melissa begins to wake. *Magnifiques... What is enceinte? Why can't I remember...* Melissa tries to remember the rest of her dream, but the more she tries, the faster it disappears.

She slowly stirs. 'Ah well, I have to get ready.' Words from her dreams linger. *Enceinte... enceinte... je suis enceinte... I am with child... Ah, that is it. I am with child. That was such a beautiful dream.*

After days of feeling utterly bleak, Melissa feels embarrassed that her kids think they must look after her while Billy is away yet again. Zac's turn this week. At least the surf is up, which will make him happy, and he did say that he was looking forward to some home-cooked meals.

Melissa gets some vegetables from the fridge and stares into the garden. *Je suis enceinte... I am with child?* She continues to stare as Zac arrives. 'Zac, do you ever wake up from a dream that feels so real you think you're really a part of it?'

'Wow, Mum, you were somewhere else.'

She blinks rapidly, her eyes adjusting to the sudden awakening, and then instinctively wraps her arms around him. 'Sorry, I was trying to hang onto this... this scene, this image or this memory perhaps...' Melissa sighs. 'Sometimes my dreams feel so real, like I'd really been there and when I wake up, it just… evaporates. Does that happen to you?'

'Yes, maybe, but I think I just let it go. Come on, let's swim. I've been doing a bit of free-diving training, and I think I'm gonna beat you now.'

Melissa watches him dive in and remembers when she was a child, and that massive wave at Third Point spun her over and over. She was sure she was going to die that day. When her kids were young, she often played games and encouraged them to hold their breath for as long as they could so that if the situation ever arose, they could survive the dangerous waves.

She dives in towards Zac at the other end of the pool. 'Okay; show me how good you are.' They breathe deeply, dive to the bottom together, and hold onto each other's arms. She holds on for as long as she can, then propels herself swiftly from the bottom of the pool and bursts out of the water.

Zac comes up just behind her and triumphantly pounds the water with his arms, elated that he's beaten her. 'I've been trying for so long, and finally, I've beaten you!'

Melissa is delighted. 'I'm so happy you won. That's brilliant! You can beat me at everything now!'

He laughs and climbs out of the pool. 'I think you can still draw better than me. I need a drink; I'll bring some water.' He runs inside as Melissa's phone rings, and before she can ask who it is, Zac shouts back that it's Aisha.

'Coming!'

Zac puts the phone on loudspeaker. 'Hey, Aisha.'

'Hey, Zaccy; nice to hear your voice. Sorry to hear that you and Olivia broke up. Your mum said you were pretty upset.'

'Oh, you know Mum; if she wasn't worrying about one of us or fussing over us, she wouldn't feel like her life's… um, her life's work is complete… Oh, you know what I mean.'

'Yes, I do know what you mean. She adores you kids. Well, I

hope you're okay.'

Melissa comes running in and grabs the phone. 'Yes, I'll be there... I'm looking forward to it.'

Before hanging up, Aisha adds suspiciously, 'I didn't know Jean and Brian were so chummy.'

'*What?* Brian and Jean? No, they're not. They hardly know each other.'

'Oh well, perhaps it was someone else. It's just that I saw Jean getting cosy with some man in Blythe's the other day, and he had a Friar Tuck hairstyle, like Brian's. And I'd just seen Billy driving away from nearby, so I thought maybe it was him. Oh, I gotta go!'

Zac smiles at his mother as she hangs up the phone. 'Mum, I promise you, I am over Olivia. Please don't worry about me. You need to look out for yourself, not worry about us.'

'I'm sorry. I was worried about you and thought you were putting on a brave face. Heartbreaks are a terrible thing and—'

'And what would you know about heartbreaks, huh, Mum? You've been with Dad forever. I promise I'll let you know if I have a problem. Anyhow, what was that Aisha was saying about Brian and Jean?'

'Oh, I don't think it was anything.'

'Are you sure?'

'Yes, I'm sure!'

'Hey, Mum. I wonder whether one of these big overseas holidays that Dad has been proposing for a while now may be good for you. He said you're not up for any of them because of your work, but I think it may do you some good, and we can all be there.'

'Sorry, what are you talking about?'

'Dad said he keeps asking you if we can all go on a big European holiday, but you keep saying no.'

'Zac, your dad suggested a few trips a while ago but nothing recently. I would give up any of my work to go on holiday with you kids.'

CHAPTER 28

Melissa links her arms with her friends and draws them into her as they emerge from the cinema. 'Thanks, girls. I really needed a night out. That was a great film. I love that actress. What's her name again?'

Aisha answers, 'You mean Lily Bell Tindley?'

'Yes, that's it. God, she's wonderful. So natural; I got the feeling she was playing herself.'

'She totally made that film,' Elle chimes in. 'She's amazing. And talking about amazing, I'm amazing! No alcohol or cigarettes for "Sprightly September" and I am feeling remarkably well.'

Aisha pulls Melissa in the other direction and yells back to Elle, 'What a shame, we're off to have a drink. You'll have to miss out!'

Elle chases after them. 'Oh, come on, it's not set in stone. Wait for me!'

Aisha hurries along, pulling Melissa with her. 'We don't want to wreck it for you. You're doing so well! It must be about the second or third already!'

Elle catches up to them. 'Well, it feels like the twenty-third to me. Who's silly idea was that, anyway? Of course, I'm in!'

The trio walk arm in arm, taking up the entire pavement as

they re-live the film's most magical moments. Melissa frowns as something farther down the road distracts her.

Aisha looks in the same direction. 'Did we lose you there for a minute, Liss? What is it? Are you okay?'

'Huh? Sorry, what did you say? I thought it was Billy… no… it's okay.'

'Elle was asking you if you're hungry. Apparently, she's starving.'

Elle nods. 'I am. I haven't eaten since breakfast.'

Aisha scoffs. 'If you don't count the choc top and popcorn at the cinema.'

'No, they don't count,' Elle says firmly. 'They didn't touch the sides. What about you, Liss?'

'No, I'm not hungry at all. Jean forced me to eat at her place before the film and, surprisingly, it was quite good. She's on some new diet, but it wasn't too bad. I'd love a glass of wine, though.'

'We could go for Thai?' Elle suggests.

Aisha nods. 'Bombetta's is just up here. Why don't we go there for a drink and then head to the Thai place?'

'Excellent,' Melissa says. 'I did a bit of work for them a while ago..'

Elle grins. 'Done. Bombetta's it is. I'd love to see some more of your designs. I absolutely love the installations at Gaston's.'

'Well, go easy on me,' Melissa replies. 'The owners seemed happy but I'm not so sure. It is a bit unusual.'

Aisha scowls at her. 'You're too hard on yourself. I bet they're great.'

'Oh, well, we'll see.' Melissa guides the pair into the busy bar while they continue their conversation. 'Hey, Aish, did Elle tell you what she said to Jean the other day?'

Aisha turns to Elle. 'No. What, pray tell?'

'Well… I didn't mean it. She seemed to be waiting for me to

give her a compliment, so I just said, "You're doing very well for your age!" and she instantly snarled at me. I thought it was a compliment but it seems not.'

They all laugh, and Aisha turns to Melissa. 'It's so good to see you laughing, Liss! You seem a lot better again.'

'Yes, I've had Zac with me for the past week, which has been divine. He just left this morning. And I've had quite a lot of work on, which has been good. And—'

'Wow!' Elle interrupts, pointing to the Bombetta's logo of a man in a bowler hat with a dove covering his face. 'I love it!'

Aisha agrees and they both stand in front of the large canvas. 'Yes, Liss, it's great! Where on Earth did you get the idea?'

'Thank you, lovely friends. Well, Bombetta means "hard hat", and I embellished the design from a famous twentieth-century painting.'

Elle keeps drawing attention to the design, saying loudly, 'Wow, it's really great!'

Melissa tries to usher them away, but Aisha stops her and agrees loudly, 'Yes, it is really great; you should be more proud of your work!'

Melissa finally steers them away towards the bar. 'Thank you, I will in future. Now, what can I get you both to drink?'

Aisha pinches Melissa's cheek. 'I am so happy to see you looking so well. You'll have to get Zac or Chloe back home permanently.'

'I wish! And yes, I have been pretty good. Billy's been away quite a lot and that is always a welcome reprieve, as I'm sure you both know.' Her friends nod enthusiastically. 'I've been able to focus on—' Melissa stops short.

'On what...?' Elle prompts. 'Have we lost you again?'

Melissa blushes. 'Yes! No! Oh, mon dieu! Don't turn around!'

They both immediately turn around.

A group of men in suits enter the bar, followed by a dark-haired man in casual clothes and a strikingly attractive tall woman.

'It's him. It's Matthew. With the stunning Latino woman.'

Aisha and Elle instantly stare while Melissa tries desperately to stop them. 'Don't stare! Oh my god, stop it!'

Aisha and Elle try to oblige, but the compulsion to look is beyond them, and the fact they are so blatantly obvious, it makes Melissa even more uncomfortable. 'You two are so obvious. Well, at least you've kept your tongues in your mouths.'

Elle chuckles. 'I can hardly keep mine in. Whoa, she is gorgeous!'

'I know,' Melissa says. 'Look at every man ogling—'

'I'm kidding!' Elle says. 'He is gorgeous. This isn't fair.'

Melissa tries not to look at Matthew and turns her head away. 'I can't stop thinking about him,' she whispers. 'He's in every thought I have now. I try so hard to get him out of my head but the more I try, the more I think about him.'

Aisha places a reassuring hand on her arm. 'Oh, Liss, you haven't said anything about him for so long. I thought you were over him. I wouldn't be trying to get him out of your thoughts. Dieu il est très, très très... magnifique. Ah, I'll never get French but he is very, very, very damn gorgeous.'

Elle nudges her. 'Oui, très, très, très beau. Very beautiful! I'd be doing a lot more than just thinking. I'd be going for it, Liss. I think we all know by now that Billy's getting his rocks off with Janet. Vomit, vomit!'

She watches as Matthew's group heads towards a large table, and as he manoeuvres himself to a seat, he catches a glimpse of Melissa across the room. Instantly, his face lights up and he smiles at her. She can't help but smile shyly back, but quickly looks away again. She tries as discretely as possible to sneak quick glances at him, but it seems that every time she looks at him, he catches her. 'I'm so nervous, do I look all right?'

'You look fine, honey, except for the drool on your chin,' Elle replies, taking a cursory look at Melissa and then she turns back to Matthew and continues, 'You didn't let on that he was this... this... well, I see what your fascination with him has been about now. He's really gorgeous, isn't he?'

Aisha agrees. 'Yes. Very, very cute. How did you manage to meet him again?'

Elle's shoulder's slump. 'Why don't I ever meet guys like him?' She suddenly sits straighter and pulls her top down a little to reveal a bit more of her generous cleavage. 'Okay, girls, we can't let this one get away!'

They laugh, and Aisha pulls Elle's top back up.

Melissa cannot look away any longer, she wants to see his face again. She is somehow hoping that she can negate anything her friends faces might be giving away. When she looks over at him and smiles, he immediately gets up and heads over.

He subtly mimics the skid and pretends to stumble over the empty chair beside her, looking into her eyes expectantly. 'Hello again, stranger,' he says. Melissa continues to smile at him but doesn't say anything so he adds cheekily, 'We met a while ago... Melissa, isn't it?

'Oh sorry, yes, we did. Matthew, isn't it?' She glances at her friends. 'Um... Matthew, these are my friends, um... this is um... Aisha and Elle.'

Matthew makes a joke and Aisha and Elle laugh a little too enthusiastically and it takes everything Melissa has not to roll her eyes at them.

Elle fires questions at him that he answers politely. He seems to be looking to Melissa for reassurance. 'Can I get anyone a drink? I know I need one. I'd love to escape these clients.'

Aisha clears her throat, stopping Melissa's answer. 'Ah, no thanks. We're just off to have some Thai food, hey, Elle? Melissa's already eaten, so maybe you could look after her and you can escape your clients just until we get back?'

The set-up couldn't have been more obvious and although Melissa feels like she might die of embarrassment, she's also happy Aisha took an opportunity to give her some time with him.

Elle leans in to give Melissa a hug and whispers, 'He is totally into you! If that stupid guilt takes control of you again, can you pass on my number?'

The noise in the room masks Elle's comment and Melissa quickly whispers back, 'Oh god, Elle… do I look all right? I look like a desperado, don't I?'

Elle jokes, 'Oh, yes, you look disgusting, as always! Now, we won't be too far away if you need us, and I will happily take him off your hands if you need me to. Has he got a twin brother, by any chance?'

Aisha is keen to move the situation along, grabs Elle's wrist and pulls her. 'Okay, then. We shouldn't be too long.'

~ ~ ~

Deep in the crowded bar at Bombetta's, Melissa and Matthew are having trouble hearing each other. He gently guides her mouth closer to his ear, a smile forming on his face as he listens intently to her words. Before she can speak again, they are interrupted by his name being called loudly and the crowd part as the larger-than-life Latino woman presses through towards Matthew.

'See you next week; I've got to go. They are all happy with everything. This is going to be another big one.' She leans over and kisses the air by his cheek.

Reciprocating, he smiles and thanks her. After she leaves, he turns his attention back to Melissa and apologises. 'Sorry, I would have introduced you, but I didn't want her to hang around. I've had enough of work for one day. She's a bit of a pain in the arse but she's great at what she does.'

Melissa smiles. *She's so stunning. A pain in the arse? Well, that's good!* He looks at her, expecting some sort of response, and finally she says, 'Ah, no problem. What does she do?'

'She handles the clients, the marketing, the books and whatever else needs doing.'

'You have a design and building company, is that right?'

'Yes, and it is a bit out of control at the moment as we've just taken on a huge eco-friendly retirement village and quite a bit of other commercial work.'

'Wow, an eco-friendly retirement village sounds interesting.'

'Thanks. Yes, it's coming along well...'

Melissa is distracted. *I need to apologise for walking out just after he had poured his heart out to me. How do I do it? He may not want to be reminded. I've got to say something.* 'Um... um... I... I'm really sorry for running out—'

He shakes his head. 'Please don't be sorry. I completely understand. Completely. I'm sorry I shouldn't—'

Melissa puts her hand up, gesturing for him to stop apologising. 'It's noisy in here, isn't it?'

They continue talking for a while, struggling with the noise level and laughing at their misinterpretations of what each other is saying. Matthew says something several times that she just cannot understand, so he grabs her hand and leads her through the busy bar to the outdoor courtyard where an energetic crowd is dancing. They are almost forced apart by the crowd, but he tightens his grip and ushers her protectively near to the dance floor.

'It's way too hard to talk anywhere here anyway and you said you loved dancing,' he smiles cheekily. 'Come on!'

He takes hold of her hands, encouraging her to dance. Self-consciously, she begins to move a little, following his lead. He laughs and encourages her to close her eyes and she does so, smiling. The music becomes louder and the crowd becomes more enthusiastic. They begin to move faster and more freely together until they are totally a part of the crowd, swept away by the music. She can feel his strong hands around her waist, and he lifts her up high as the tempo of the music picks up. They dance until they are exhausted.

Out of breath, they take their leave from the music and exertion of the dance floor and make their way to a quieter corner of the courtyard, near the carpark. They stand close together and he stares intently into her eyes; she feels as though he is looking for something or expecting something from her and she looks at him curiously. The intensity with which he stares at her seems to caress her entire body, to the point where she feels she has no self-control. He completely envelopes her in his arms and she melts into him. She breathes him in and feels an incredible lightness that she has never felt before. Slowly, he cups her face in his hands and moves closer so that his lips are almost touching hers. His breath caresses her lips, and she's filled with an intense yearning for him as he whispers, 'I am so mad about you.'

~~~

Melissa's bedroom is alive with reflections from the pool, creating shimmering patterns all over her naked body. She breathes in, and a feeling of ecstasy flows throughout her body. She smiles down at Matthew, lying beneath her. His eyes are closed as he reaches up to kiss her breasts. A tingling sensation goes through her body as she remembers when Matthew first kissed her beside the pool, the two of them oblivious to the rain pelting down on them. She's deliriously happy he's with her, in her bed, and he tells her again, 'I am so mad about you.'

They hold tight to each other, savouring the intensity of the moment. Her desire is insatiable now as he moves slowly
~~~

around her body, kissing every part of her, enjoying the tension building within her. They move in harmony, connected in ways she's never experienced.

His lips almost touch hers as they stop breathing, about to climax when they suddenly hear a noise. They stop moving, remaining perfectly still. Hearts pounding, their desire overtakes their fear, and they begin to move again, slowly as one.

She closes her eyes softly, prolonging this moment for as long as she can... until a euphoria sweeps through her and consumes her. A deep fulfilment wraps around her, more than she could ever have imagined. She lies back blissfully until loud, angry footsteps near, and the bedroom door bursts open.

~ ~ ~

Melissa clutches at her neck and jerks back forcefully as she looks up to see Billy's face. Terrified, she curls her body up, closes her eyes and puts her arms up to protect herself. She waits expectantly, her heart pounding, but nothing happens so she opens her eyes again slowly, jumps up, rushes past Billy and searches frantically for Matthew. She cannot find him.

'What have you done?' she screams. She throws herself on the bed and wraps herself quickly in a sheet.

Billy watches her, confused. 'For Cahrist's sake, it's like you're schizophrenic! One minute you're going nuts and the next you're an innocent little... god knows what! I was just watching you sleep. You looked so angelic. And seductive, I might add...'

He leans in to kiss her and she flinches back from his unexpected advance. Still feeling the intensity of what has just happened, she is confused and out of breath. Her face white with fear as she asks him. 'Mon dieu... What's happened? Why are you here?'

'Calm down, psycho queen! The conference was cancelled at

the last minute. I've just got back from Melbourne and found you asleep looking so beautiful lying there wet and naked. I was hoping you might be pleased to see me.'

Seeking the safety of the bed, she pulls the sheet tight around herself as he quickly undresses, lies down behind her, caresses her breasts and kisses her neck gently. She cringes. *No! Go away! Don't touch me! Ne me touche pas! Tu me repousses. You repulse me.* She lies still, squeezes her eyes closed and imagines she is away from him... that she is with Matthew... that it is Matthew in bed with her now.

She tries to return to her dream state but cannot. She is fully aware that it is Billy in bed with her. She pushes his hands away from her breasts aggressively. 'Please, Billy, leave me... laisse-moi.'

'That fucking French.' He rolls onto his back, and she waits for more complaints. When none are forthcoming, she realises Billy is masturbating and breathing his damned whisky-breath throughout their bedroom.

*You make me feel so, so sick.* Disgusted, she jumps up, grabs a towel, runs out onto the pool deck and dives into the pool. She swims deep under the water until, at last, she is exhausted.

Floating peacefully, she closes her eyes and relives her evening at Bombetta's. A huge smile lights up her face, and she feels a yearning when Matthew's lips got so close to hers that she could hardly contain the urge to kiss him. *'I am so mad about you.'* The words send tingles through her body again, and she stays in the pool, floating happily, not wanting anything to destroy this memory. *I am so mad about you! Je suis tellement fou de toi! Fou de toi!*

She swims for long enough to ensure Billy will be sound asleep before she goes back to bed. She checks that his snoring is constant and makes her way to the bathroom, she quickly brushes her teeth, messes her hair up, and pulls an insane face at herself in the mirror. *Melissa, you're ridiculous. It just can't happen with Matthew. It could be dangerous. Very, very dangerous. Très, très dangereux.* She sneaks into bed quietly beside her husband.

As soon as she lies down, a tingling feeling washes over her again. She tries to hold onto this vison of him when they were standing at Bombetta's near the carpark but suddenly she felt like she was being watched.

She shakes her head. *No! That must have been my imagination! There are lots of dark, little sports cars... there was no stripe... I'm sure of it...* Her heart sinks, and she tries to think about it logically. *If it had been Billy, he wouldn't be like this now. He would be out of control. I must have imagined it... maybe I had too many wines? Fuck, I can't remember!* She closes her eyes and tries to go to sleep but in a nightmarish vision, she's chasing after Billy's car as he drives towards the headland. She can hear him telling her children, *'Kids, your mother has serious psychiatric problems!'* as he drives over the cliff with them.

She breathes in deeply and sighs, forcing herself to change her thoughts. Billy is still snoring peacefully, and she has seen enough of his jealous rages in the past to know that he mustn't know anything. *He would have murdered me by now or he would have stormed out of the house. He certainly wouldn't be sleeping so calmly.*

Billy's snoring is regular and rhythmic. *He's fine. God, why do I scare myself with all these horrible thoughts? Pensées horribles!*

~ ~ ~

Just as the first signs of light appear across the sky and the birds begin to stir, Melissa finds herself naked, wet and shivering, lying on the deck outside her bedroom. She is desperate to move but she's paralysed, and she feels as though she has just escaped from an intense struggle. *I'm sure someone was trying to drown me in the pool... but I can't remember how I escaped. How was I able to pull myself out? Why am I paralysed now? Am I really imagining this?* She tries to move her limbs but they refuse to obey. *How did I get out here?* Melissa stares at a little globule of blood erupting on her fingertip. She can vaguely remember smashing her head again.

As the paralysis slowly subsides, she raises her hand to the lump on the right-hand side of her forehead. *Why would I smash my head into the mirror?*

She makes her way back to her bedroom and sees Billy sleeping. *Oh bugger... bugger... I wish he wasn't here. I hope to god he hasn't seen me.* She crawls quietly into bed, trying desperately hard not to disturb Billy. She huddles into herself. *Merde... merde... why does this keep happening to me?* She feels so helpless.

~ ~ ~

Billy's screams wake her with a fright and she panics. *Oh, fuck, oh, fuck; what have I done?* She looks out from under the bedcovers to a beautiful, bright, sunny morning. She knows this incessant yelling won't stop until she deals with it, so she grudgingly drags her cut and bruised body out of bed in order to placate him. This has been their routine for as long as she can remember now.

Given the pain she's in, she manages to get out of bed surprisingly quickly and as she gets nearer to her bathroom, the smashed mirror triggers the memory of the night before where she was sure someone was trying to drown her.

Billy scowls at her. 'What the *fuck*, Melissa?'

She tries to tell Billy of the near-drowning but he looks at her in despair, shaking his head as he pulls a shard of glass out of his foot. 'I tried to help you but you were even more aggressive than usual.'

All she can remember clearly is brushing her teeth and cleansing her face, after that it's all a blur. She tries to apologise, but his constant yelling drowns her out.

'Look at the trail you've left all the way out to the pool. Okay,

Miss Natural, what are we going for this week? I suppose we're off our medications again? What are we trying now? Fucking drops of seawater mixed with rose petals and scorpion nails, or some other bizarre homeopathic concoction that fucking Aisha has recommended? Unbelievable!'

'I'm *trying*, Billy. I'm trying so many things I can't keep up, but nothing is working... and the pharmaceuticals—'

'This is a regular event! You've certainly got some cleaning up to do. Maybe we should get the decorators in on a full-time basis to keep fixing the house? And you might want to replace all the photos you keep destroying, not to mention our other possessions, many of which have sentimental value, at least to me! And while you're at it, maybe you should find a priest to exorcise the demons out of you!'

'Do you think I'm enjoying this?'

'Well, do something about it. I'll be away again next week. I've asked the kids to get here as much as they can. You could go to your mother's—'

'No. No way. Don't even go there. I don't know what to do—'

'Well, I don't know what we're going to do. I give up trying to help you. I should have called the cops or an ambulance at least. I can't take any more time off and we can't expect the kids to take any more time out from their studies. We can't keep going on like this...'

He puts a band-aid on his foot and then reaches over to kiss her on the lips. When she recoils, he says. 'I don't know why I bother trying to kiss you anymore. Would you rather I didn't?' He doesn't wait for her to respond, just puts his shoes on, and leaves.

Relieved that he's gone, Melissa sits on her bed staring out into the garden. *Yes, I* would *rather you didn't kiss me anymore. In fact, I'd love it if you didn't come anywhere near me. Why can't I leave... or better still why can't you leave me!* She can hear her phone vibrating on the bedside table but ignores it. *Putain! Putain! Putain. Fuck, I am sick of this shit!*

She lies in her bed for hours, trying to focus on what happened last night after she finished brushing her teeth, but nothing comes to her. She rolls over and buries her head in her pillow and cries. Her phone vibrates again, and she sees she has eight missed calls from Billy. She listens to the most recent one. 'Please, honey, call me. I've been trying to call you all day. I'm sorry I blew up again this morning, I just get frustrated when I have so much on my plate and I have these disturbing... anyway, please let me know you're all right. We're going to get through this. I love you so much and I do really care about you. Please call me back so I know you're okay.'

She texts him back, *I'm fine, Billy, see you tonight.*

Melissa pushes the sides of her mouth up trying to smile. She grabs her laptop and sets herself up for a day of watching films in bed, but feeling as battered and bruised as she does, she decides to have a bath first.

As she undresses in front of the mirror, there are bruises all over her body, particularly on the back of her neck. *How did I bruise myself there?* Melissa puts her fingers to it, and the pain jogs her memory. Flashbacks of a struggle in the pool in the middle of the night. Of crawling out on the deck trying to get away... Someone chasing her... trembling legs. Trying to dive into the pool but yanked back by her hair... intense pain in her ribs.

She remembers struggling with someone under the water, who she was sure was trying to drown her but then she was heaved out of the pool and then... and then...

And then she remembers waking, absolutely positive someone was watching from the forest. *What was that! There was someone there I know it!*

She bathes for a long time, and as she dries herself, she feels again the pain from the bruising. *Why is this happening to me?*

*What happened last night? I have to do something!* Feeling totally frustrated, she grabs a pair of jeans and a jumper, races to the garage and puts on her gumboots before heading outside. She walks around the pool, looking for any kind of clue, but there isn't anything apart from a lot of fallen leaves. She continues on to the forest at the back of their property and walks through it slowly. There are some empty beer bottles, but they look old and dirty. Melissa continues her search and sees something deep in the forest. *What in god's name is that?* Going closer, she finds a huge mound with a variety of colourful mushrooms. 'Wow, it's so beautiful in here.' She meanders past a small clearing where Zac used to have little bonfires and drink with his friends when he was a teenager, but she can't find anything else of interest.

She creeps quietly along the little creek that separates the properties until she is close to the two neighbours. *Maybe it was someone from one of these houses, they weren't happy when we built here.* She sits for a while until the constant barking from a large, old German shepherd trying to get at her through the fence becomes too much. She tries to shoo it away but it won't stop. It barks loudly and constantly until finally she has to leave.

As she nears the house, she sees a truck manoeuvring in reverse onto the grass. She'd ordered a replacement mirror for her bathroom weeks ago. *Oh, this couldn't come at a worse time... not now... Okay, Melissa pull yourself together.* She directs the glaziers to her bathroom, humouring them as they make jokes about having only replaced this same piece not so long ago.

~ ~ ~

Melissa watches Zac wax his surfboard, 'Honestly, Mum, I want to get up here more when Dad goes away. I only have classes three days a week, which I loathe, and I can't exactly surf in Brisbane. So, I'm happy to be here whenever I can, and Coke can cover the other days when I can't be here.'

Chloe stops talking on her phone, smiles and nods in agreement.

Leaning heavily on the kitchen bench, Melissa smiles at Zac's offer. 'It's really not necessary. Just come when you want to, not because Dad tells you to. I know you're both busy. I promise I'll call you, but I really am fine.' She wants to show them that she really is okay, but her body feels so heavy she can't even begin to pretend that she is. She'd tried to take her gumboots off earlier but that was too much effort and now looking at the peeler and potato in her hand she's afraid that's too much too. *And look at the dishes all over the bench. I'm not sure that I can pretend.*

Zac takes the peeler and potato from her and he and Chloe help her to the sitting room and onto the couch. He yanks her gumboots off and Chloe wraps a throw around her.

Her son gives her a quick hug. 'How about Coke and I fix some dinner for us all?'

He looks to Chloe for agreement and she smiles back at him, tears in her eyes. 'Yes, Mum, you just have a rest. We'll cook up something easy and—' She stops short when she sees the lump on her mum's head. 'How on *Earth* did you get that big lump on your head?'

Melissa is about to reply when Billy arrives home and calls out loudly to his kids. Zac and Chloe roll their eyes. Billy keeps up his yelling as he approaches and when he enters the sitting room, they rush to quieten him.

Happy to see his kids, he gives them both a quick hug, heads to the drinks trolley, and pours himself a large glass of whisky. He grabs some ice from the bar fridge, glances at Melissa, and then whispers to Zac and Chloe, 'If she would take all the bloody meds she's supposed to take, she'd be better by now. She keeps halving them, not bothering to take them at all, or taking some hippy magic Aisha gives her. It's her own fault.' He sits on the edge of the couch and cuddles her. 'Isn't it, Missy? But you're about to be a big girl and take them as prescribed. Aren't you? I know they can fix her. I know it.'

Melissa feels the blood drain from her face.. *Your voice makes me sick, Billy. I wish you would just shut up and go far, far away. Putain de merde... merde... merde.*

Chloe turns the overhead fan on and gives her mother some water. Zac ushers his father into the kitchen and Chloe follows, pleading. 'Dad, she looks dreadful. She looks so drugged out. There must be something we can do. What's wrong with trying something more natural? She looks terrible. And what about—?'

'What about that healing place,' Zac says. 'The one that does the... the... Oh I don't know but I think it was Costello's... Castello's or something like that. She showed me some information about it and it sounded awesome...'

Billy rolls his eyes. 'Maybe she just needs to stick to the prescribed medication, and she will be fine? We could all get some bloody sleep around here. I'm really suffering too, you know.'

Zac and Chloe glance discretely at each other, clearly irritated by his self-pity. Billy is oblivious.

'We're really worried about her, Dad. There must be some alternative treatment she can try. She's been on and off these medications for so long now.'

Billy raises his voice slightly to his daughter. 'As I just *said*, if she had stuck to the prescribed medication and taken it as directed, she'd be better by now. It's embarrassing for me when Dr Press tells me that she's quartered the dose or whatever the hell she does. James is a specialist in the field, but your mother would rather listen to Aisha, who knows nothing about this kind of thing. She thinks her hippy magic...'

Zac and Chloe look away and Billy changes what he was about to say. 'Listen, Dr Press has told your mum to see this great psychiatrist – Dr Pymble. But I don't think she gets to her appointments. I don't have the time to take her.'

Sensing that his audience is not impressed with his ideas, he changes his tune completely. 'So, Coco, Mum said you did really well in your portfolio assessment. I'm sorry I missed the opening. When can I come along and see it?'

Matthew's attention is dragged from the fine detail of a design he is working on at his drafting table, when he sees his sister pull up in her car. *God, why can't she leave me alone?* He jumps up immediately and switches off the lights. The house is set back behind a small forest, so he hopes she won't have seen him yet. As soon as she gets out of the car, she calls his phone and he runs quickly through the house, trying to find it to turn it off, but the ring tone begins to blare, and now Monty is crying for her through the door.

Realising she knows where the spare key is anyway and that any moment, she'll be using it, he answers the door, gives her a quick hug, explains how busy he is, and walks back to his drafting table.

Almost as though he hasn't even spoken, she launches in. 'Come on, you need to get out and meet people.'

'No, I don't. And I'm so busy—'

'Well, I think seeing this woman again after so many years is really going to mess with your head! You need to get over her. *She* messed you up when you were young, and it took you so long to get over it. Please don't do this to yourself again.'

Disinterested in what she is saying, Matthew studies the

designs on his drafting table. Jane grabs his face and speaks right into it. 'Will you get over *her*, for fucks sake! It was so long ago! She's probably a haggard, old Mumma now with a million kids and—'

'Actually,' Matthew interrupts and looks at her seriously. 'She's really beautiful, has two kids, and is going through a really hard time.' He holds up a large sheet with a design on it and indicates for Jane to hold one end as he examines an intricate part of the design.

'You've been through a really hard time too. I just don't want you to get hurt again, that's all. I love you and I care about you. Listen, just come to this party, it will do you good.'

Matthew is now consumed by what happened all those years ago. He is still trying to piece it all together, but with his sister annoying him in the background he can barely concentrate. He asks her if she would mind taking the dog for a walk while he finishes up his work for the day. Reluctantly, she agrees, and he watches her go.

He still can't determine why Melissa's mother had always been so threatening. He still remembers clearly the phone conversation he had had with her. 'Ah, Matthew. Well, you've got a nerve calling here, haven't you? After everything you've done. This nightmare is all your fault, you know. My daughter and Billy were having a small break. Melissa doesn't want to talk to you; she wants you to go away and not bother her. She is traumatised enough after her boyfriend's near-fatal accident! If you continue to bother her, I will call the police.'

He frowns, trying to remember the course of events. *Why, after Billy had got out of the hospital, did he heavy me... it was weird, especially since I hadn't had anything to do with Melissa again after the night of the accident.*

When Jane returned with Monty, she immediately started in on him again. 'Do you really want to go there? I mean, it was such a long time ago.'

'I don't know, it all just felt so wrong. It was just so messed up.' He closes his eyes, trying to remember but Jane is only interested in getting him to the party.

'Okay, big bro. Pick me up on your way, around nine! Okay?'

Understanding she won't go away until he says yes, he nods. Still absorbed in his thoughts, he reflects painfully on how he has now messed it up with Melissa again. *Why did I try to kiss her? Why did I have to fucking mess it up? I'm a fucking... I'll probably never see her again. Why did I have to blow it?*

Jane stands at the door demanding his attention. He waves goodbye, assuring her again, 'I'll be there at nine. Go!' Monty jumps at him and he responds, 'Okay she didn't give you much of a walk, did she? Let's go out the back into the forest, I've got to get Melissa out of my head.'

Despite his attempts to stop thinking about her, Matthew finds that more and more memories of Melissa keep resurfacing, many of which are baffling. He vividly recalls spending days at the beach after the accident, desperately longing for a chance encounter with her. Even after her mother threatened to involve the police, Matthew lingered for months hoping to meet her again, but she seemed to have vanished. He'd hoped to run into her again for many years, but it didn't happen.

It wasn't until about ten years later that he unexpectedly spotted Melissa at Third Point. As he emerged from the surf, he was shocked to find her playing with her children near his towel. Matthew stared at her, longing for her to acknowledge his presence, but she was engrossed in her kids and utterly oblivious to him. She looked so beautiful as she played with her young children on the shore; they were all so happy... her world was full. Matthew didn't exist for her. When she eventually glanced in his direction, he initially believed she still held him responsible for Billy's accident. However, it became evident that she didn't recognise him at all. Over the past decade, Matthew had changed significantly; he had grown about a foot taller, and his hair had transformed from sun-bleached white to dark brown.

For days after Matthew had seen her, he couldn't get Melissa out of his head again and went to the beach regularly for weeks. When he finally encountered her again, she was utterly absorbed in her young children once more. Although she briefly glanced in his direction, she had clearly forgotten about him. Disheartened, Matthew walked back along the trail from the beach, still desperately hoping that Melissa had moved on from Billy. However, his hopes were shattered when he passed by the shack and saw Billy standing on the veranda, dressed impeccably in a tailored suit, one arm leaning on the post as he glared at Matthew with pure hatred.

Matthew was stunned; Billy recognised him while Melissa hadn't. Billy's glare held the same intensity as the time Matthew had beaten him in the surf comp. How on Earth could Billy still feel such intense emotions so many years later? Especially since he was still with Melissa and they had two kids.

It was shortly after that, Matthew had taken off overseas for many years, and while he did cross paths with Billy over the years, the man was always weird.

# CHAPTER 30

With two large wine glasses and a bottle of red in her hand, Elle steers Melissa into her living room, where they immediately plonk down on the floor in front of the couch.

'Cheers, my dear; I haven't had a drink all week. Well, nearly all week, not counting the weekend, but you can't count the weekend, can you? Or hang on Monday… or…' She laughs, before taking a big gulp. 'Ah, who cares? I needed this! And I deserve it.'

'I'm sure you do,' Melissa says with a laugh. 'It's Wednesday, so that *is* a long time.'

They clink glasses and continue the conversation they were having in the kitchen. Elle asks again, 'Are you really sure the medication is helping? I'm not seeing it.'

Melissa grimaces. 'I don't know, one minute I think they *are* helping and the next… I'm so messed up with them.'

'Well, be careful because sometimes you're a total zombie on them. In fact, I've been thinking… well, actually, I've decided. You're going to Castillo's with that really rather cute man you had a thing for and who definitely had a thing for me, ha ha! No, but seriously, Liss, what did happen there?' Jovially she pushes Melissa, who loses her balance and almost spills her red wine on the white shag pile rug. 'Oh, woops!'

Melissa steadies herself. 'I don't know. I was determined to go to Castillo's with him but... I was... scared. I was really worried about what Billy might do. Oh, I don't know, I really don't, but I had to literally force myself to stay away from him. Then the nightmares returned thick and fast, and I lost any sense of time. He was going to Castillo's, I remember that much, but that was about six months ago, I think.'

'Sorry, darling, but I insist you get in touch with him. At least he'll be able to tell you if Castillo's treatment works – if he's done it.'

Melissa smiles and wriggles in excitement at the thought. 'No matter how hard I've tried, I haven't been able to block him from my thoughts but at least I stopped driving past Le Monde, which I was doing regularly. So eventually I gave up any hope of going to Castillo's clinic with him.'

Elle reaches past her and grabs Melissa's phone. 'Okay, where is his number? Ah, what is your code... no wait a minute, I know 1709. Yep! Zac and Chloe's birthday combinations.' She scrolls through Melissa's contacts and asks, 'What was his name again?'

Melissa refills their glasses. The thought of seeing Matthew again is incredibly exciting. 'To be really honest, I'd love nothing more than to call him, Elle, he's still so vivid in all of my thoughts, and my daydreams. It's really sad, I know. I just can't help it. I try so hard to get him out of my head, but he's there all the time.'

Elle gives her a sympathetic cuddle. 'You worry too much, Liss. I think we should let fate take its course. Come on.' She continues scrolling through Melissa's contacts, smiles and asks, 'So where is his number? What's it under again? Margaret, was it? No, here it is – Martha. That's his code name, right?'

Melissa nods. 'Yes, that's him. My lovely old friend Martha. I wonder what happened to her?'

Melissa wants to make the call. Mustering all the courage she can, she takes her phone from Elle, breathes in deeply, and breaks into her gran's Irish accent. 'I am tragic to be sure, to be sure!'

They both laugh hysterically as they come up with lots of ideas about what she should say to him. Melissa practises seriously. 'Hi Matthew, my name is Melissa. I don't know if you remember me but—'

Elle chimes in. 'But if you have forgotten me, I am sure you would remember my friend, the lovely brunette with the generous cleavage. You really seemed taken with her, ha ha. No, I know. Hello, sexy Matthew, I was just wondering if you'd be up for a ménage à trois? Or what about... Hi Matthew, I was just wondering if the nutty professor is really as nutty as Big Billy and his little lapdog, Little Jamesy, say he is?' Elle gestures with her little finger to indicate the size of James's penis.

Melissa laughs. 'Eww! I can't believe you ever went there!'

Defensively, Elle retorts, 'It was a long time ago! I was drunk! I was desperate! Oh, all right, I have no excuse. I'm guilty as charged and he wasn't so bad either. It was very small, but he knew what to do with it!'

Melissa blocks her ears. 'Ew, I don't want to hear about it, I promise you!'

Elle empties the bottle of wine into their glasses, leaves the room and returns with another. Melissa puts a cigarette in the side of her mouth, grabs the bottle in one hand and her phone in the other, and begins to wobble around the room, slurring drunkenly, pretending to make the call.

They laugh, and Elle tries to be serious. 'Come on, it's getting late. I mean it, you have to call him. You know you want to.'

'There is no way I am ringing him now!'

They both lie on the floor in hysterics, creating lots of drunken imitations of the call. Finally, Elle hiccups and slurs tragically, 'I think I have to agree. Tomorrow will definitely be better for the call.'

'Let's watch this film, it is wonderful. I've already seen it three times.' They Huddle together on the couch, and laugh and cry and sing loudly along to some of the lyrics by Rodriguez:

*'Sugar man, won't you hurry...*
*...All those colours to my dreams...'*

~ ~ ~

Melissa wakes with a thumping headache in Elle's spare bedroom. Fearful that she may have wreaked havoc during the night, she scours the apartment, happy to find only the usual mess – a few empty wine bottles and an ashtray overflowing with cigarette butts. The sun pouring in through the windows onto the kitchen bench almost blinds her, she searches her bag for her sunglasses, puts them on and makes herself a cup of coffee.

Moments later, Elle bounces energetically out of her bedroom in her gym wear. Melissa peers at her over her sunglasses, 'You don't look like you've ever had a drink in your life. Do you want a coffee?'

Elle grins. 'I'm a seasoned drinker, honey. Now, I'll go and sweat it out of me so that I'm ready for tonight. Okay, where's your phone?' She grabs Melissa's phone off the bench, scrolls through her contacts quickly and calls Martha's number.

Melissa laughs, thinking Elle is joking, and panics when she sees that her phone is already calling his number. 'Oh god!' She fumbles, trying to turn it off, holds the phone away from her body, and shakes it. Her body trembles and she grins to Elle as she hears his deep voice, loud and clear saying, 'Hello?'

Realizing that she has to say something, she nervously replies, 'Um... hello, this is... um... Sorry, is this—?'

Matthew's deep voice talks over her. 'Melissa?' He waits for a moment. 'Hello again.' As she doesn't reply, he keeps talking, obviously not wanting her to hang up. 'So... ah... are you ready for Castillo's?'

'Um... I'm thinking... um... haven't you been already?'

'No, I didn't really want to go on my own, but I'm really ready now and I definitely think we should go together...'

She cannot concentrate on what he is saying. Melissa cannot believe after all this time that he still wants to go there with her. *Okay, Melissa concentrate. Say something intelligent.*

Nervously, she paces around the apartment while they talk.

After watching her for a moment, Elle kisses her on the cheek. Looking really chuffed with herself, she waves and exits for the gym.

~ ~ ~

Elle returns a while later covered in sweat, and smiles proudly when she sees her friend still happily talking and laughing on the phone. She showers and dresses and when she hears Melissa wrapping up the call, she excitedly pounces on her. 'Wow, you two sure did have a lot of catching up to do. You must have been talking for two hours! So, tell me, tell me, tell me do – what's the plan?'

Melissa looks at her curiously and checks her phone. 'Wow, eighty-nine minutes. My heart is still thumping.'

'Well, he certainly ticks all your boxes, doesn't he? And he had you in hysterics.' Elle starts singing to her friend, 'It must be love, love, love...'

'God, how I'd love him to take me in his arms right this second. I feel so right with him.'

'Is there *anything* wrong with him? Well, darling, you haven't experienced very much of anything in your life... apart from Billy Boy. Enjoy, for once in your life.'

'I must admit, Elle, I'm terrified about what Billy could do.

You know he can get nasty when he's jealous.'

Elle rolls her eyes. 'Of course you're not going to tell your narcissistic husband that you are going with anyone. But you *are* going to go, aren't you?'

Melissa breathes in, closes her eyes, hugs herself and quivers. 'Yes, I am, and as soon as possible. Matthew's seeing if he can get us both in quickly before one of us changes our minds.'

'That's great, Liss. Before Billy gets back from Copenhagen. That's where he is, isn't he?'

Melissa nods. 'Yes, Copenhagen. Until the end of the month. I just hope we can get into Castillo's quickly!'

'Yes, fingers crossed! Well, you'll be as good as new. Finally able to stand up to Billy. Your kids will be proud of you.'

CHAPTER 31

Naked, floating face down on the perfectly still surface of the pool, Melissa finally releases the last few bubbles of breath, and slowly sinks to the bottom. Sinking deeper and deeper, her heart pounds and she can no longer hold on. Kicking off the bottom, she bursts out of the water, gasping for air. *Oh, that feels good!*

Catching her breath, she holds onto the side of the pool. *I wish he'd hurry up and call. I'm so nervous.* The loud music from the house drowns out the sound of her phone and as she checks it again, the screen lights up. Her heart races when she sees Martha's name on the screen. 'Calm down, calm down you've been waiting for this.' She tests her voice before answering: 'Hello. Hello. Hi...' Clearing her throat, she breathes in and answers, 'Hello. How—'

'We're in Saturday week; the fourteenth and we have to—'

Matthew's giving her the details but she's distracted as the music reaches its crescendo, *This love, this love, this love like ours is—*

Suddenly the screeching of tyres reverberates through the house. She almost collapses and drops her phone. *No! Non! Non! Putain!* Shaking all over, she quickly picks up her phone and whispers to Matthew, 'I have to go! I have to go!' and disconnects.

'What the hell! Que diable!' Her body's shaking uncontrollably as she creeps wet and naked through the house. Her heart is pounding wildly as she approaches the door to the garage. She reaches down for a throw to cover herself when suddenly Billy bursts through the door. She jumps back and screams, 'Merde!'

Billy notices her face drop when she sees him. 'Lovely to see you too, Melissa.' He looks her up and down, raises his eyebrows at her naked body and as he approaches her, she wraps the throw around herself. She tries hard to smile but her mind has gone into panic mode, desperately worried now that she is going to be forced to cancel Castillo's. She leans against the couch, feeling crushed and powerless when an inner voice rises up inside of her. *Fuck you, Billy, I'm going to Castillo's.*

Happy that she's found this inner strength, she finally finds the words to greet him. 'Sorry, Billy, I'm just shocked that you're home. I wasn't expecting you till the twenty-ninth.'

He quickly kisses her on the lips. 'Yes, well, our meeting was sabotaged by some overly conservative board members and...'

Billy looks downtrodden and she feels genuinely sorry for him. 'Oh, I'm sorry. I'm really sorry. Well, I guess there are a lot more fish... in the sea...'

He feigns a smile. 'Yeah, honey; that doesn't make me feel much better but thanks for trying. Anyway, I have to do some work and I've got calls to make so can you keep that bloody music down. And can you cut the French bullshit.'

She whispers. 'Vraiment charmant! Really charming!' As Billy heads up the hall, she dutifully turns the stereo off and imitates Billy childishly, 'Keep that bloody music down and cut the French bullshit. It's so lovely to have you home again, Billy. It's a real delight. C'est un vrai délice. You want more French bullshit... I think I'll study it, and soon I won't speak any English at all.'

She dives back into the pool. *Why did he have to come back now? Putain! Putain! Putain!* Feeling sorry for herself, she swims lap after lap deep beneath the water, trying to work out how she's going to get away now that he's back. She can't think straight and the thought of telling him that she's going to Castillo's frightens her. She swims vigorously until she is physically exhausted, then rests with her head on the side of the pool while her mind goes into overdrive. 'How am I going to do this now?'

She's determined to go, just doesn't quite know how it's all going to happen now... but it *will* happen.

Melissa tries to think of something else but Aisha's words come back to her: I didn't know Brian and Jean were so chummy; those words had been playing on her mind a lot recently. *Did Mum have an affair with Brian? Oh, shut up, little voice, I don't want to go there. It's ridiculous! Oh, please don't go there now.*

She tries to focus on something else but can't get the thought out of her head. It's weird how Mum was always kind of nervous around Brian, as though she was in awe of him. He was very successful back in the day and always in the social pages, which of course Jean read religiously. But would she really go there? Melissa's mind races. Was she having an affair with Brian before Dad died? She closes her eyes to try and block the thoughts but she cannot stop thinking about it and finally she shouts out. 'Whoa... Jean's relentless requests... Why don't you and your sister put Billy in control of your Trust money? What do you girls know about money?'

Jean was right about that, but that's where the trustees came in. Melissa doesn't know how she allowed it but somehow Billy weaselled his way into controlling her share. Why did Jean put so much pressure on us all the time to force the trustees to release more and more money for Billy's so-called wonder drug? If only Jean knew how much he had blown over the years, she'd probably die. She yells out into the garden angrily. 'God, I hate my mother! Dieu, je déteste ma mère!'

She sinks deep into the pool. *Stop thinking all these negative thoughts... oh here we go another one, the night I caught Billy and Janet in the city, getting out of his little sports car. Even with so much guilt plastered all over his face and hers, he bailed me up.*

Billy's pompous voice rings clearly in her ears. 'I despair of you, Melissa. You must be insane. Dear god, I work with the woman! She's a highly regarded physician and I respect her. What have I done wrong? I work so bloody hard! Why do you look at me like that and try to make me feel guilty? Your own mother thinks you and your sister are both crazy and I am starting to think she's right!'

She screws up her face and shakes her head. *Stop thinking about him! Oh no, what now? Why can't I stop having all these negative thoughts?* But her thoughts return to the day, months ago, when a crowd of people gathered on the beach, watching her as she stood naked, being smashed back to shore by the incoming waves. She's embarrassed just thinking about it. *What was I doing? How did I get there?*

She looks towards the house and feels a deep pain in her stomach, worried about what this day is going to bring. Billy was already settled into the couch with a whisky, casting videos of his latest bike race, from his laptop to the TV screen.

Melissa glides through the water, trying to block out the constant stream of negative thoughts, trying to drown them out by singing the song to herself that was playing earlier.

*I want to hold you in my arms, I want to never let you go,*
*I want to hold you in my arms, and I want everyone to know*
*This love, this love, this love like ours is...*

She remembers the first night she'd met Matthew outside Le Monde and the tingles that rushed through her when he grabbed her hand. She swims lap after lap deep under the water, wanting to stay with any memories of him.

When he held her face in his hands, and his lips were almost touching hers and he whispered, 'I am so mad about you.' Every part of her wanted him. She's never felt like that before. Ever. She's determined to go to Castillo's but Billy's arrival has completely thrown her.

The thought of going back inside to be around Billy churns her stomach. She grimaces when she sees him coming down the hall with yet another Grand Salute in one hand and his phone in the other. Why can't she leave him? She's so sick of this life with him.

Melissa tries to think of something positive, but apart from the kids, Billy is just anger and jealousy and derogatory comments. She cannot stop the horrible memories as she watches him through the glass doors, heading up the hall to his little drinks trolley and then back to watching himself racing. That must be his fourth whisky. Why did he have to come back so soon? *Go to Janet's! Go anywhere! Go away! S'en aller!*

She's so tired of these terrible memories. She leans on the edge of the pool and stares out at the forest, trying to find something to distract her but nothing works.

Melissa drags herself from the pool and heads to her bathroom, standing close to her reflection in the mirror. 'Fucking stop it! You're a misery-guts!' She tries to snap out of it, but Billy keeps dominating her thoughts and she is taken to another horrible memory.

The kids were very young, Billy had been at a conference overseas, so she had taken them to the shack. She had just put Chloe and Zac down for a nap and was wandering around the house in her bikini when Billy arrived unexpectedly. Melissa had been so frightened when Billy had burst into the house. He was furious, accusing her again of trying to seduce other men. Her fear had turned to anger at being accused *again,* and she told him to 'go fuck himself.'

He'd grabbed her, pulled free all the ties of her bikini so

she stood naked in front of him and spat his accusation of her having an affair. The abuse had never been physical before, but that day he'd pushed her against the wall, her hair fisted in his hand as he screamed into her face.

She'd tried to leave him that day. So why hadn't she? *You know damn well why!* Billy would turn the kids against her forever... or maybe even kill himself and them too.

Melissa shudders as she tries to stop her imagination from creating image after image of Billy's sports car spattered with blood, of Zac and Chloe dead with him. She squeezes her eyes tight trying to make the images go away. 'Stop it! Why do you let your thoughts go there?' Melissa angrily tries to pull off a ring Billy had given her. *How many guilt gifts over the years? This hideous guilt ring! The guilt car! The guilt holidays! Why didn't I leave him? Why? Pourquoi? Pourquoi? I have to leave him!*

~ ~ ~

Sitting on the edge of the bath mesmerised by the screen on her phone, Melissa hangs up when she hears Elle's answering machine message for the third time. *I don't want to leave a message. I just need to talk to you. Oh god, I don't know what to do. I'm going to do this Castillo thing, I'm going to, but I'm scared. Please pick up Elle, please pick up. I need your amazing advice.*

She begins to dial Elle's number again and then remembers her friend was away for a 'dirty weekend' in the country with her new man. She had tried Aisha's number several times but hadn't been able to get on to her. Now that Billy is back, she doesn't know how she's going to make it to Castillo's. *I need your help Aish and Elle. Okay, I need to eat and then I'm going to the beach. I need to be away from here.* She was feeling so strong earlier and now she feels weak again.

As Melissa heads towards the kitchen, Billy calls out to her. 'Have a look at this honey... hang on... it's on this other one.' He grabs his laptop and plays a different video onto the TV screen. 'Ah, this is the one. Look how I take off up the hill. I'm on fire, even if I do say so myself!'

'On fire, Billy!' She agrees sarcastically and then she looks again. 'Wow, you really are getting away from them up that hill.' She shakes her head curiously as she walks past him to the fridge.

Billy gets up off the couch, kisses Melissa on the cheek and asks, 'I don't suppose you feel like making one of your delicious home-made chicken pies, do you?' He pulls a cutesy face and heads up the hallway to replenish his whisky.

She imitates the face he just pulled and mutters to herself as he walks away. 'It's actually the last thing I feel like doing for you, Billy. But to keep the peace and because I'm hungry, I guess I will.'

There is chicken in the fridge, but for the life of her, she can't remember what else is in it. 'What was it called... Mumma's mornay pies or something like that.'

She grabs Billy's laptop off the couch to quickly look up the recipe and groans as she is instantly stopped. 'Bugger, bugger. His computer needs a code... Of course, it needs a fucking code!' Deep down she knows she probably shouldn't be on his computer; he's normally guarded with it, but since she's making his favourite pie, she's sure he won't mind. She just can't be bothered going to find her own.

Melissa can faintly hear Billy up in the sitting room, pouring himself another drink and talking quietly to someone on the phone. *Who are you whispering to, Billy? Would it be Janet by any chance?*

She quickly tries a few codes on his laptop; Billy's birth date, 2411, and a combination of their kid's birth dates, and it opens. While she waits for the recipe to open, she flicks to another screen.

Her world screeches to a halt.

*What the fuck?*

*No! NO! NON!*

Melissa staggers, unable to draw her gaze from the horrifying images, and she falls onto the arm of the couch.

She is shaking as she hears the sound of ice blocks clinking in Billy's whisky, getting louder and closer, as he comes back down the hallway. She quickly clicks onto one of the videos. She panics. *Fuck! Fuck! Why won't the fucking thing open?* Her heart pounds as the loading symbol spins and spins for what feels like forever.

The clink of ice in the glass nears, and she almost drops the laptop as Billy glares at her from the other side of the room. She scowls back and glances down as the video finally opens on the screen.

Billy drops his glass, steps towards her and even with guilt plastered all over his face, he yells, 'I've told you before not to… I hope you haven't lost any of my really important work—'

'Don't. You. Come. Near. Me!'

She stands, grasps the laptop to her.

He stops as she edges closer to the garage door. Melissa can't stop shaking, and then the video finally opens, and she sees Billy standing over her naked in the mirrored wall, pulling her up by her hair, taunting her.

Billy yells and charges towards her, tripping drunkenly over the arm of the couch as she fumbles over the keyboard. In a blind panic, Melissa manages to send the video to her sister overseas. She slams the laptop shut and stares at Billy venomously, 'I just sent whatever *that* was to Lilly and if you come near me, I will call the cops. Get out of this house! Get out of my life!'

She grabs her bag, coat and shoes and races out with his computer under her arm. She slams the door as hard as she can and hears him pleading through it. 'I'm sorry, honey, I just got so jealous. I didn't ever want to hurt you! I just wanted you to love me!'

Shaking all over, she quickly gets into her car and locks

all the doors. She has to get away from him and this fucking nightmare right now.

She puts the car into reverse. Her legs are shaking so much that her foot slips off the clutch. Immediately the car slams straight into the cement wall, smashing one of the panels. 'Fuck! Fuck! Putain de merde!'

She restarts the engine, jams the gear into reverse again, and revs the engine hard.

Terrified that Billy is going to pounce on her at any moment, she screeches loudly out of the garage, and races down the road. The sound of the broken panel scraping on the road becomes louder and louder, and she turns the music up and screams with frustration.

The noise and the damage attracts the attention of onlookers, making it impossible to keep going. She pulls over and yanks up the handbrake. 'Putain! Putain! Putain de merde!'

From somewhere deep inside her, an inner strength emerges, and with it, laughter that borders on hysterical. 'This is great! I'm finally going to get rid of this fucking horrendous guilt-gift!'

Ignoring the stares, Melissa drives straight to the nearest car yard, grabs her belongings, and tells the salesman she wants to do a deal right now. 'A small, automatic, dark-coloured car. And I want you to keep this one and do with it what you like, but I need to drive out of here right now.'

She negotiates a deal quickly, and within a short time is speeding away in her new car.

It doesn't take long for the reality of the situation to sink in. The image of Billy, naked, pulling her up by her hair, taunting her, keeps coming back to her.

*Oh god that makes me feel ill! I am such an idiot! But why now? Why after twenty-plus years? Oh why didn't I fucking realise!* 'FUCK! Seriously! Did this really happen? Is this for real!' She grits her teeth. 'Merde!'

What is she going to do? Where is she going to go? Elle is away, and Aisha must be somewhere in Africa by now. Melissa pulls to the side of the road and takes a few deep breaths to calm herself. *Oh, merde, Lilly.* She calls her sister several times, but it goes straight to message bank, so Melissa sends a text.

URGENT. PLEASE DON'T LOOK AT EMAIL UNTIL I HAVE SPOKEN TO YOU.

PLEASE CALL ME ASAP.

Melissa stares out towards the headland. What the hell is she going to do? She's not even sure if she should tell anybody about this. The last thing she wants is for anyone to see this, or for the kids to see it. She picks up her phone to dial Lilly's number again and finds endless calls and texts from Billy. 'Fuck you, Billy. Leave me alone. Laisse-moi tranquille.'

Her phone vibrates with an incoming call. 'Oh no, it's Zac.' She can't talk to him now. She just can't. She quickly texts him.

Sorry Zac, I'm out of range staying with Julie my old school friend on her farm. I'll call you soon. I love you, Mum xxx

She glances at several texts from Billy and reads a few sentences from each.

It's not how it looks honey I promise. For months I kept finding you in the bathroom or the kitchen cowering in a trance! You kept doing it week after week…

Honey I never meant to hurt you. You just went to some weird place and you wouldn't go back to Chevallum and so I had to…

You were always hurting yourself. All those times you trashed…

I adore you I never wanted to hurt you. I just want you to love me…

Please come back and we can talk…

I can't live without you Melissa… you know I can't live…

Repulsed by all of his texts, she throws the phone onto the passenger seat. 'Not another fucking suicide threat! I never want to see you again! Ever! Fuck! Never! I don't give a fuck what you have to say. You disgust me! Tu me dégoutes!'

She looks down at the laptop, 'I feel like throwing this fucking disgusting filth off the headland into the sea.'

~ ~ ~

As Melissa pulls into the shack, a calmness settles over her. She loves it here. She just needs some breathing space and then she'll book a hotel or something. She closes her eyes and breathes in the sea air. *Fuck it. I'll be okay. I need to work this out.* As she gets out of the car, she throws the laptop into her bag, still shocked that Billy actually let her take it. *Now I'm gonna find out what the hell has been going on.* Fear spikes through her. When Billy sobers up, he'll realise how incriminating it is. She has to hide it.

Melissa panics, runs inside the house and slams the door behind her. She runs from room to room, searching the house for somewhere to hide the laptop. She throws open the oven door and puts it on one of the racks and then she pulls it out again – she's just as likely to forget it's there and put the oven on. She opens the clothes dryer door and carefully puts the computer inside. 'That will do. I don't think I've ever used this dryer.' Melissa slams the door shut and leans back against it. 'God, I feel sick.'

Her heart is pounding as she races around the house locking all of the windows and doors. 'Fuck, fuck, fuck.' As she slowly approaches the front door she gasps. 'Oh fuck!' It won't lock. She pushes hard against the door but it makes no difference. She looks around the room panicking and finally she pulls a chair up against the handle of the door. She pulls it again and again to make sure that it works. 'Okay, okay. Everything is locked. Dieu merci! Thank god!'

She sits at the kitchen table, and a moment later, her phone lights up with a call. 'Not again, Billy! Leave me alone! As she declines the call, she catches sight of a text and reads it.

I'm moving out of here now… I just wanted you to love me and you never could, could you Melissa? Honey I never meant to hurt you. I just wanted you to love me and you just kept going to some weird place. James can confirm…

*Weird place? What weird place? Well, I guess that was a weird place in my own bathroom. Thank fuck you're moving out, you fuckhead! That's the least you could do.* She scans quickly through to the end of his text.

Please can I have the computer back it has some very important work and hopefully I can explain some things to you…

'Fuck you! Fuck you! Fuck you!'

She quickly scans through lots of texts, all of them begging her not to show Zac and Chloe. Did he really think she would scar their beautiful kids? To show them their father involved in such an act? Or for them to see her in such a condition?

Oh how I would love to see Matthew right now! But… No… Putain! Non, I need to sort this shit out. I should send him a text as he must be wondering.

Sorry about hanging up on you earlier. I have to sort a lot of things out, but I am really keen to go with you to Castillo's on the 19th. Let me know if you chicken out again as I probably will too. But I think at the moment it would be a great thing for me to do and for you too hopefully.

I'll call you in a couple of days to confirm.

Warmest regards,

Melissa

She sighs. 'I'm exhausted.' Melissa grabs a bottle of water, heads to her bedroom, and buries herself beneath the covers. She closes her eyes, breathes deeply, and the sound of the ocean calms her as she drifts off...

...A beautiful calmness surrounds her as she glides through the water in the underwater caves just past Third Point. She hears whispering and as she turns her head slightly to listen, she sees it is dark outside. She can't see anything, but she can still hear the whispering of somebody trying not to wake her at the end of the bed. Her eyes feel heavy. She tries to move but it's as though she is stuck to the bed

The muffled sounds and whispering continue. Melissa cannot understand what they're saying but she knows it's *them*. She *knows* Billy and James are standing at the end of her bed.

A faint tapping sound.

*They're preparing the syringe.* Terrified, she forces her eyes open and sees their shadows lurking, ready to inject her. She can't move at all. Can't hear what they're saying but she knows they're still there. She's too frightened to scream.

Tears streak down her cheeks; she won't be able to fight them off. *Fuck you, Billy and your little lapdog, James!* Anger at herself churns through her, but she has no energy and finally resigns herself to the situation. Waiting for the sting of the syringe, cold air brushes her legs as the covers are lifted. Melissa waits and waits for the jab until finally, she finds her voice. 'Help! Help! Please, somebody help!'

She jolts upright in bed, screaming, and can't see anything. *Fuck!* Her heart beats hard as she gets up slowly and edges towards the light switch. With trembling fingers she turns on the light.

The room is empty.

*A nightmare. Just a nightmare. It was so real! Merde, zut, damn what if that email didn't send to Lilly?* Melissa has to remember what Billy has done. Why didn't she write a note to herself? She has to remember! *The dryer. The dryer.* She hammers this into her memory, then grabs her phone and writes a note, hiding it amongst others on her phone.

Melissa! Remember BB has been drugging you. All of the evidence is in the laptop in the dryer.

Adrenaline still surges through her body. She has to make sure the video has definitely been sent to Lilly. She runs to the clothes dryer, throws the door open and reaches down into it for the computer. *Where the fuck is it?*

Tears well up in her eyes, and she waits for Billy and James to pounce on her. *No! They were in my room and now they are locked in with me. They've got the laptop and I don't know if Lilly has received the file! And now I won't remember anything again.*

She muffles her cries as she crouches in front of the dryer, terrified as she waits for them to attack. She cries profusely as she waits and waits in terror.

When the tears finally clear, she sees something shiny on the base of the dryer. She frowns and wipes her eyes and immediately sees the Apple logo of the laptop; the computer has wedged itself perfectly into the base. She should really get out of here just in case he comes. But surely he's gonna be too frightened that she's already called the cops.

~ ~ ~

Melissa grabs a bottle of water, sits down with the laptop and slams her fingers harshly on the keys, entering the code. She scowls at the thumbnail image of herself again. She clicks on it and is immediately confronted with a frightening image of herself cowering under the bathroom vanity. Melissa slams the laptop closed. 'You animal! Tu animal! Okay, okay I'm busting.'

Melissa races to the toilet, and as she is sitting there, she panics. 'I must check that the email has been sent to Lilly and warn her not to open it.' *Oh, Lilly'll be horrified… she's always hated Billy. Oh, why wasn't she around then…*

As she sits down again at the laptop, she grits her teeth. 'Oh, thank god, the email has been sent.' She quickly sends another, asking Lilly not to open it and to call her urgently.

'Okay… Okay… D'accord. What do I do now?' She types her name into the search bar and scrolls through the results. Melissa closes her eyes, breathes in and out heavily, and then reads a few lines from emails sent to James Press.

Hey mate.

For Cahrist's sake. Don't get so serious. You won't get struck off. I thought I could trust you. Don't forget mate, I'm still sworn to secrecy and I've been true to my word all these years. I haven't told a soul! And by the way, you don't want me or the company getting any bad publicity, your dad's already invested a LOT of money…

…I know you detected benzo, ketamine and a huge range of concoctions in her bloods. Obviously, I know that is what is triggering these reactions but I need to take the heat off me. And I want to know what the fuck she is doing….

…So I'm gonna send her in and you're gonna assess her, just as you do with all your patients but you just give her the doses I give you. It's not gonna kill her, I've been giving it to her for over a year on and off. Well, since I first caught wind that she was gonna leave me…

…I want it all on film so that there is no more finger pointing at me. Her friends never stop looking at me as if they know, and she's started looking at me suspiciously lately. So I need you!

…If you only knew what I have to put up with, mate. My lovely wife despises me. Basically, if I didn't force her we'd probably have sex like once a… once a farkking never.

…Initially I was just having a bit of fun with her and then these weird reactions started happening to her…

…I tried putting it in her wine but it wouldn't dissolve so I ended up putting it into the toothpaste – she always cleans her teeth at night so I just had to put the tube out before she'd go to bed. But faarrrk that wasn't easy especially when I couldn't find the farrrking tube and then I was freaking out that the kids would get it. I finally worked out she'd taken it to the shack and that's why she ended up naked at Third Point. I never leave her alone on it…

…Honestly, it wasn't meant to hurt her and now I just want you to tell me what the fuck is going on with her and all this babbling. She's certainly not in this reality, she is in some other dimension. It's gotta be interesting to you in your field of work.

…Don't worry, mate I'm always with her. I know she thought I was overseas but she didn't look closely enough at the date of birth on my passport. Not exactly my birth date. I'd never leave her alone. It was an accident with the toothpaste. You know how much I bloody love her.

Check this video out. Bill

Melissa groans as she opens the video attachment. She shudders as she sees Billy in his suit standing at the back of their bathroom, videoing her as she methodically strips off all of her clothes, folds them neatly and hides them under a basket. He zooms into her eyes and asks, 'What can you see? Where are you? What are you doing?' She stares straight through him and babbles incoherently.

Melissa scowls at the video. 'What in god's name am I doing? What am I saying?'

She clicks on another video to see Billy standing in his suit in the background while she stands naked before him. Billy's voice comes through clearly. 'I accidentally smashed a bottle of my whisky the other night and you totally believed it was you. You just never question it. You're so nice to me when you think you've fucked with my stuff, I feel like doing it all the time. You just do my head in. I just fucking hate the way you look at me. You fucking despise me, don't you, honey!'

Melissa screams at the screen. 'God! You are right there, Billy. I do despise you and you totally disgust me! How could you...' She puts her hand to her mouth, and turns the video off before returning to the emails—

Yeah, I tried lowering the ketamine and mescaline mix so that she doesn't get so out of it but she still didn't shed any light on where she goes.

...Yes, I'll try that. I always have a little mix for myself to enhance my experience too...

No problem, mate. I don't mean to hurt her. I just fucking love the bitch. I won't do it again. She only married me out of guilt.
Bill

'You're right, Blatt.' She screams at herself. 'How could I have been so stupid!' She clicks on another video attachment and fast-forwards to where she can see Billy in the mirror, getting dressed, complaining. 'They've blocked the funding again. Fucking Trustees! Fuck you, my beautiful wife. Why can't you get rid of them?'

Billy looks closely at her. 'Are you sure you have no memory of anything, Missy? Sometimes you look at me and I'm sure you know something. I guess not. I've got to stop panicking. The benzo works a treat, I know you have no memory of anything cos I can make shit up, and you don't doubt it for a minute, and then you're so nice to me. Which, Missy, is how you should always be.'

Billy reaches down and picks up her arm, which flops down heavily when he releases it. 'If only you wouldn't struggle so much, I wouldn't have this paralysis problem.' The video cuts out and she reads the email attachment.

I'm gonna give her a break for a while, she's been like a zombie again and the kids are freaking out. Thank god I found that blasted toothpaste. I'd bloody die if anything happened to her.

Melissa wipes her tears and sees an email from Billy's father. 'What on Earth do *you* have to do with your deviant son, Brian?'

For Cahrist's sake, William, why haven't you gotten rid of those meddling trustees. We need this money urgently or we're going bust again. Can't you tell Melissa to get rid of them? Why isn't bloody Jean in control… isn't it time Melissa put something into trust for Zac and Chloe… you need to do something quick. If we lose any more of our investors we're history.

As she skims through more of the emails, she curses herself. 'How could I have been such a fucking idiot? Well, no wonder they were all rushing us down the aisle. Your entire family are a disgrace. Thank god, my father set up the Trust.'

Melissa clicks on another link. 'What the fuck?' She shudders at the sight of herself standing against the mirror, staring and muttering incomprehensible words. Billy is standing before her, naked and crying. 'I adore you, Melissa! Why could you never love me? Why? You just couldn't give a damn about me. And by the way you will never—'

Melissa slams her hands on the table and shouts over him. 'Oh yes, Billy, you just adore me! How could you do this? How could you do this to the mother of your kids. How dare you!'

She grimaces as she watches more of the video. Billy kisses her all over her face and neck then he moves her in front of him in the mirror and whispers into her ear, 'Go on, tell me you love me! Tell me you love me! I could have had anyone. Our family were important! You are non-compos mentis, Melissa! You're insane! Non compos mentis!'

He moves around to stand before her again. 'You'll never have anyone else and every time you go near someone, I guarantee you, I will go crazy! I fucking love you and you are not going to do this to me! Our kids are never going to forgive you! Never! Do you know how it makes me feel when I see you—'

Melissa stops the video. 'Your self-pity makes me sick!'

She takes a large sip of water and skims through more emails to James.

...Well, if my little wife wasn't so feisty, she wouldn't end up so bruised all the time. I honestly don't mean to hurt her but I couldn't let her get away.

...I know. I know. I was a bit out of control. Sorry, mate. I lost it. But I've got it under control... I've got myself on, funnily enough, these sleep calm tablets and they're helping me to control myself. I didn't mean for her to slam on the deck, I just had to catch her. If she gets away, I'm fucked!

...Yeah, I know. I won't smash her head into the mirror again. I just get so messed up when I feel she hates me. If she just didn't look at me that way but I promise it won't happen again...

...Yeah, I know, I know she's really out of it but I just feel she's looking at me like she hates me. I really won't let it happen again. I have been busting a gut trying to get more investors—

'Your self-pity makes me want to vomit.' Just as she's about to shut the laptop, she sees Castillo's name on one of their earliest communications. *What the fuck? Castillo?* She opens the email.

She's still talking about Castillo's again and she'll probably go just to spite me. I've talked her into making an appointment with you so tell her anything, will you, but stop her from going there. She'll be all over me if she sees him.

...Not sure how Castillo's still practicing as one of the big players spent millions trying to shut him down. I don't know how he's getting so much good publicity, someone's got his back. You gotta keep pushing Pymble. It might not be easy but you gotta do it.

'She will be all over me...' Melissa whispers. 'What on Earth does he have to do with Castillo? She'll be all over me if she sees him. Well, that's cemented it. I'm going to Castillo's on the nineteenth.'

Melissa twists her hair, ties it into a knot on her head, and gulps down lots of water. She pushes her chair out from the table, and just as she is about to close the screen, another email subject header catches her eye: —She Wanted Me.

The low battery warning flashes on the top of the screen. *Oh blast, I don't have a charger.* She slams the computer shut, picks it up and just as she is about to put it back in the dryer, she stops and curses herself. *Melissa! Enough! Enough! Assez! Assez! She wanted me? What the fuck? I feel absolutely repulsed and completely sickened by all of it, but I can't stop myself... I have to see what this means.*

Her index finger trembles for a moment before she presses the touchpad to open the video attachment. She can hardly recognise herself. She looks possessed. Muttering incomprehensibly and cowering under the basin in her bathroom, the camera zooms in tight to her eyes, which appear to have an opaque, gold-coloured glaze over them. As the camera pans out again, she is methodically stripping off her nightdress and underwear, folding them neatly and burying them under a basket.

Billy laughs. 'Look, at you. You're stripping off again! Maybe you do just want me?' The room becomes steamy quickly as Billy quickly strips off and adjusts the shower so the warm water sprays up all over them.

He grabs a bottle of coconut oil and pours it all over Melissa's body. He stands behind her and holds her by her breasts. He gently kisses her neck and caresses her breasts as he rubs his wet, naked body against her. He breathes in deeply and mutters, 'I'm really buzzing from my little mix. God, you're beautiful.'

Melissa stands in a trance-like state as Billy resumes kissing and fondling her. Slowly, he moves up, kissing her stomach and sucking on her breasts. He kisses her neck and slowly moves up to her face and as he gets near to her lips, she jumps back and spits back into his face. She stares straight through him screaming, 'Luca? Où es-tu, Luca? Qui est cette créature méprisable? Where are you, Luca? Who is this despicable creature?'

Billy wrenches her by the hair. 'What the fuck are you saying?' He tries to kiss her lips again, but she pulls away from him and he bellows, 'Even in this state you despise me!' He drags her to the mirrored wall by her hair and smashes her head against it until the edge of the mirror cracks, and shards fall to the floor.

Billy then whispers in Melissa's ear, 'Hey, honey, I just want to pick you up and take you to bed and cuddle you.'

Melissa slams her hand onto the table. 'Your psychological manipulation makes me want to scream.' She closes her eyes but can hear Billy making childish jokes, and when she opens her eyes again he's rubbing himself against her. She struggles again and slips from his grasp to back herself into a space between two cupboards. He laughs, crouches slowly in front of her, and looks closely into her eyes. 'Oh, fuck. I need to up your dose. Uh-oh,' he says with a childlike voice, 'looks like you're back with us. If you remember this, I could be struck off. But that's rubbish. I saw you undress for me. You wanted me! You wanted me!'

Melissa slams the computer shut, runs to the sink, throws water over her face and screams aggressively. 'You are so *sick!*' She grabs the computer, places it back in the dryer, and slams the door closed.

She frowns and holds her hand tightly across her mouth, trying to contain her emotions as she runs down the hall to the shower. Her whole body shakes as she crouches beneath the steady stream of warm water. 'Oh god…' Melissa stifles a sob.

She feels so... so violated... so dirty and disgusting.

Melissa scrubs herself until the water runs cold, then continues to scrub herself, trying to get clean, trying to rid herself of... of *him*.

Shivering uncontrollably, she quickly dries herself off and falls onto the bed. She curls up and wraps herself in the thick quilt for protection. She has to get the images of Billy molesting her out of her head.

*Luca!* This word reverberates through her head. *Luca, Luca, Luca!* A feeling of calm washes over her, and finally she falls into a peaceful sleep.

~~~

Early the next morning, Melissa wakes to the sound of the ocean and the fond familiarity of the creaking roof beams in the shack. The birds are loud as the sun breaches the horizon... and suddenly she remembers why she's here. She curls up in pain. 'Fuck you, Billy! I *will not* let you destroy me!'

Using the breathing method Lilly taught her, Melissa returns to an *almost* sense of calm. 'Okay, okay. I'm going to get through this.'

The first thing she has to do is block Billy's access to any funds. Then she'll make sure Billy is stopped. And *then... then...* 'Fuck!' She needs help with this. Fuck! How did this ever happen! 'Lilly call me. I really don't want you to see the video!'

Melissa takes some more calming breaths, and decides to head down to the beach, hoping the ocean air and water will help clear her head. Within minutes, she is walking to Third Point, enjoying the same sandy bush track she had taken since she was a child. She has a quick swim and then sits on the rocks thinking of all the things she needs to do. 'A list. I need to make a list.'

She checks her phone to see if Lilly has called and sees a
~~~

message from Billy saying that he has moved out. She doesn't respond and a short while later, another text arrives. She reads the first few sentences and feels disgusted, but she can't help herself and reads more of it out aloud in a childish voice. 'No matter how much I achieved, you were never impressed. Nothing I could ever do would make you proud. You could never love me, and you have never loved me, have you, Melissa? I have tried so hard to make you love—'

She slams her phone shut and screams at the screen. 'No, what you and I had was *not* love! It was evil! Extrêmement mauvais! Extremely evil!'

*Oh god, what am I going to tell the kids?* She stares out over the glistening ocean. *This is where I want to live. This is where I want to be, and I'm going to do it.*

# CHAPTER 32

Sunshine filters through the trees and shimmers onto Melissa's wet hair as she drives along an almost deserted country road. She hasn't passed another car for about an hour. *I hope I'm going the right way! Why wouldn't the satnav work out here? Why didn't I bring the mud map they gave me? Bugger! It'll be okay. Calm down.*

Determined to shake off her sadness, she changes the music and sings along. Her mood lifts as she cycles through more and more upbeat songs.

'I'm really doing this! I'm really going to the Castillo Clinic.'

Melissa reflects on her morning with Zac and Chloe, of her daughter's words. 'Stop worrying about us, Mum. We've known about Janet for a long time; we just didn't want you to be hurt. I don't know how many times Zac called Dad and he would say that he was in the apartment in Melbourne and Zac could clearly see on his phone that dad was actually on the coast or in Auckland where Janet has her holiday apartment.'

Chloe grinned cheekily. 'By the way, I have to fess up about the tattoo... I only came up with that excuse just before I got to Gaston's cos I knew Dad would freak out. I actually just liked the design. It was going to be that or a little lotus, and I can assure you I will not be getting a family tree either. Can you imagine me having to go through pain to have Jean's name on my hip or Brian's name? Ha ha. NO way!

Her children had hugged her as she got into her car. 'The new car's hell grunt, Mum, grunt good that is,' Zac had said. 'We knew you hated the old one. You're looking great already, Mum, and you haven't even got there. We read up about Castillo's and while it sounds pretty freaky, the testimonials sound amazing! You'll be rippa in no time.'

Melissa wanted to reassure them that she was already better but couldn't tell them what had happened or what their father had done to her.

Watching them in the rear-view mirror as she drove away, she hoped they'd never find out, that they'd never have to suffer for the sins of their father. Thank god they knew about Janet, and that she is the reason Billy gave them for moving out.

Finally, after driving for miles, a majestic, old building surrounded by a manicured garden comes into view. 'This must be it!' There are no signs out the front, but this has to be Castillo's. There hasn't been any other buildings for more than an hour.

Melissa navigates the tree-lined driveway until she emerges into a large carpark at the front of an imposing, whitewashed, Georgian mansion surrounded by miles of rolling green hills.

She turns off her car and looks up at the building, getting the strange feeling she is being watched. 'I'm going to pull the pin any minute if you don't turn up soon, Matthew. I am *not* going in there on my own.'

In her rear-view mirror, a large four-wheel drive enters and pulls into the park next to her. She looks up to see Matthew smiling at her and she smiles back and mouths: *Thank god*!

He quickly gets out of his car, and opens her door. 'Come on, out we get! No chickening out now!'

They embrace and he asks, 'How are you... Are you okay?'

Melissa blows her hair out of her eyes. 'I'm... I'm pretty good now. Very, very nervous though.'

'Yes, me too. Do you have the feeling we're being watched?'

They scan their surroundings suspiciously and look up as the monumentally tall front doors open and tiny Nurse Edwards races towards them with hurried little strides. Her bright red hair blazes in the sunlight and she is muttering something as she approaches, 'Excuse me, are you coming inside or are you staying out here all day? We are waiting for you both!'

They *were* being watched, and they apologise in unison as Nurse Edwards turns on her heel and scurries back to the mansion.

Melissa chuckles softly. 'Well, we're off to a good start. How late are we?'

Matthew checks his watch. 'Only about half an hour. We were meant to be here at four, but after a long drive to the middle of nowhere without the aid of a satnav or a proper map, what did she expect?'

They grab their suitcases, hurry inside and are again accosted by Nurse Edwards. 'Did you bring everything, then?'

Melissa and Matthew hand over the extra paperwork, their payment details, their suitcases—which she says she will have taken up to their rooms—and finally their sentimental possessions. Matthew tries to explain that he hasn't brought anything sentimental. Nurse Edwards raises an eyebrow and snatches everything Melissa has with her. Without another word, she leads them down an ornate corridor to a large door and indicates that they should go in and wait.

Nurse Edwards scurries off again and Melissa whispers, 'Do you think she heard us?'

'No, I think that's just her way, but I couldn't think of anything to bring that has sentimental value. I thought that was optional?'

'Yes, it was optional. I just threw a few things in at the last minute. The rug and the large teddy bear just makes it look like a lot. You should have brought your dog.'

'Yes, I'm sure Nurse Edwards would love Monty.'

~ ~ ~

A huge formal portrait of a judge in full robes hangs prominently behind Castillo's grand oak desk in his massive office. The large room looks like it would have originally been the library. Several rolling ladders are dotted around the walls against the ceiling-height bookshelves, enabling access to the overflowing books on the top rows. Large windows allow the afternoon sun into the room, highlighting the cobwebs and dust on almost every surface. Large glass terrariums are scattered about adding some colour to the otherwise oak-coloured palette.

Melissa and Matthew glance at each other, grinning, as they finally catch sight of Castillo talking to Nurse Edwards in the corridor. Melissa whispers, 'Exactly as I imagined him.'

'You were almost spot on – the thick-rimmed glasses, the olive skin, and he is quite short. But you didn't pick the goatee and ponytail.'

'No, I missed that—'

She stops as Castillo enters, studying some papers and muttering to himself. They both greet him and Matthew comments, 'Wow, what a great place this is out here in the middle of nowhere.'

Castillo, not registering what has been said, sits behind his desk. He continues examining the records in front of him. 'All your physical and psychological tests, etcetera, are good.' He finishes looking through their additional paperwork and then looks up, and smiles with a sparkle in his eye. 'You are both definitely healthy enough to handle the procedure.' He finally acknowledges Matthew's comment. 'And yes, this place is a classic. It was actually gifted to us by a very happy client, a judge, Edward Brampton, who had suffered from varying degrees of psychosis for most of his life.'

Castillo motions to the painting and smiles at them. 'That was his great-great-grandfather. There's a long line of judges in this family. Even with Edward's bouts of psychosis, he was still able to work quite adequately, but he suffered quietly. My mother was a trained nurse and became his live-in housekeeper. He'd tried every type of cure and one day my mother told him about my work.

'I was overseas at the time and as soon as I got back, he let me work with him and we had great success. Unfortunately, by this stage, he was too old to have a family so when he died, he passed this property and his Brisbane property on to us, so that we could carry on with our work. Nurse Edwards came to work for him after my mother died, and she and her husband, Nico, stayed on after the judge passed. They were part of the deal, so to speak,' he says with a grin.

Melissa and Matthew nod as they take a seat, and Castillo continues, 'The judge was also instrumental in keeping us out of court for quite a long time, which was wonderful. That helped us to get on with our work.'

Matthew crosses his leg and adds. 'That's great. There are certainly a lot of people wondering how you continue practising since you keep getting dragged back into court all the time.'

'Yes, it's been very annoying, very annoying. The powers that be—or rather, *shouldn't* be—have been trying to shut us down for years. I'm sure these large corporations, corrupt authorities and very powerful, greedy pharmaceutical companies will one day implode.'

He studies the roots of a small plant lying on a sheet of old newspaper as he continues. 'Anyway, I worked hard for the medical title and I intend to keep it until the day I die.' He adds jokingly, 'Not that I use it, mind you, all my colleagues simply call me Castillo, except Nurse Edwards of course! Anyhow, where was I? Ah yes, many of these major players are just money-hungry thieves. Luckily, everything we use here comes from nature, which cannot be chemically replicated by the pharmaceutical companies. If they could charge you for the air you breathe, I am sure they would. They just haven't worked out how to yet.' He raises a hand, gives them a short grin. 'Please excuse the outburst, but they do get up my nose. Fortunately for us, though, we've had a lot of success with a great many influential and kind-hearted people, so we still have a lot of legal support.'

Melissa and Matthew encourage him to continue. 'Now the procedure we are going to take you through, may or may not be a particularly pleasant experience, but I can almost certainly guarantee the results will be very good indeed. We do want your stay to be pleasurable and we hope you enjoy all the facilities and the gardens and the meals and everything else.. Oh, and we also inherited an enormous wine cellar, enough to last us into the next century, although I would advise not to have too many. You don't want to feel unwell for the procedure. Oh, and there is also a gym and pool.'

'That all sounds great,' Matthew says. 'Perhaps could we put the procedure off for a few days?'

Castillo grins back cheekily. 'That could possibly be arranged as we are running very behind schedule, which is usual here. The Releasing—which is what we call it—is a very individual thing. It can be relatively quick for one, and for another, quite drawn-out. We can never know.'

Getting up from his desk, he goes over to a side-table, picks up a tiny plant cutting with a pair of tweezers, moves to another terrarium, and carefully grafts the cutting onto another plant. He glances at Melissa and Matthew. 'And as you have probably heard—stop me if you have—'

They both nod at him to continue.

'I lived with a very remote tribe of Peruvians in the Amazon rainforest and studied with them for over twenty-five years.'

Melissa asks, 'Is that where your family are from?'

'No, my parents are Chilean. My father died when I was a child, and my mother and I came out here to live with an aunt of hers. After completing my medical degree, I was drawn back to South America where I travelled extensively until I came across this Peruvian tribe who entrusted me with a knowledge that has been passed down through many generations to only a very few. I have been fortunate and feel very privileged to have this knowledge. The herbs and plants we use are simply "weeds" that grow wild all around the world. All around us.' He raises his eyebrows and with a grin he adds, 'Although they can be extremely dangerous if they're not taken in the right quantity and under the right conditions. We've had incredible success with all sorts of psychological disorders—dementia, schizophrenia, depression, obsessive-compulsive disorders— the list grows every day as new patients come to us. Obesity is one of the latest. We hope, in time, this work can spread all around the world.'

He continues to explain his work and life as he wanders around the room, flicking through old diaries for information and, with a small pair of tweezers, grafts another cutting onto another plant. Melissa and Matthew smirk at each other, impressed by his incredible multi-tasking. As they listen and watch him closely, a very small, hunched-over man with a bald head and dark features comes into the room.

'Ah, this is Nico. Nico will escort you to your rooms. As I mentioned, we are running a bit behind but at this stage we should be able to get you both started in the morning. So, live it up a little as very soon we will be doing some serious work. Please enjoy an evening meal, which will be at seven in the dining room. And, of course, make use of any of the facilities.'

Without a word, Nico leads Melissa and Matthew out and up a massive, intricately carved stairway. They pass a huge, ornate lead-light window at the landing, giving colourful glimpses of the extensive gardens around the property. On the first floor, Nico opens a door and mumbles, 'Laing,' indicating they have arrived at Melissa's room. It is brightly lit with beautiful, high ceilings, and a door that leads to a modern-looking ensuite bathroom. Several pieces of antique furniture are scattered around, but it is otherwise sparsely decorated. Matthew follows Melissa in, sits on the bed and bounces up and down on it. 'More like a five-star hotel than a clinic. Very nice! I could get used to this. I'll be very happy if we don't get a start for weeks.'

Melissa grins and looks towards Nico who, it seems, is not a very humorous man. Matthew jumps up, 'I have to just check over a few things that I didn't get done before I left and we can meet in the dining room at seven.'

Melissa nods and he quickly follows Nico's lead out the door.

~ ~ ~

As soon as Matthew arrives to his room, he quickly turns on his laptop, checks over some work he had done earlier and responds to some emails. He closes it again. 'Okay, hopefully that is all done, and now I am out of action.' He turns off his laptop and his phone. 'Now please don't bother me, Manuela!'

He falls on to the bed and tries to relax but this commercial building that is under construction is nagging at him and he reopens his laptop, checks over a couple of things and lies down again. 'Okay, wow that was much easier than I thought. I'm done! Relax!' He tries to enjoy the calm and quiet of his surroundings but a memory he wants to avoid keeps nagging at him. He tries to focus on the birds he can hear in the distance but the image of Katryn's dead body and the sound of Monty's whimpering is still with him. He sighs loudly. 'Go away, go away.'

He tries to distract himself. 'Hallucinogen! What a weird word… Ha-lu-ci-no-gen! Hal-you-see-I-no-gen! Lucigen!' He plays with the word for a while until the memory of his near-fatal hallucinogenic experience in Bolivia comes back to him. 'Oh fuck! Here we go. One bad thought after the other.'

He lies still, trying to calm his mind, listening to the sounds of the birds outside. 'This is nice. It is so quiet out here, just the birds… no cars.' He smiles and focuses his mind, reminiscing about the first time he ever saw Melissa.

It was a hot, sunny day, and Melissa and her sister were jumping off the rocks into the water at Third Point. She was so cute and always laughing loudly. So vivacious! He remembers so clearly feeling that he was in love from that first day he saw her. He had never been in love.

Matthew had loved that time when thay had come to stay at his aunt's house for the holidays, just down the road from Melissa's beach house. To see Melissa and her sister jumping off the rocks together and swimming out to their father. Matthew was so shy and there was no way he had the courage to talk to them.

Those years had always been his fondest memories – the long, lazy summer days when his parents were still alive. After they'd died, he and Jane had come to live with his aunt, and he would often see Melissa at the beach from afar, and his feelings for her grew stronger over the years.

He stares out at the trees and tries to hold on to the memories of her. Of the first time he saw her up close. She was about sixteen and had come to one of the local surf competitions. Matthew was with a group, waiting and watching the other competitors when he saw her standing on the shoreline. He couldn't take his eyes off her. Then her boyfriend, Billy, came up to her and she tried to console him about his poor performance in the competition.

Neither Matthew nor Melissa had seen each other up close before but as she walked past, their eyes met, and she stopped and smiled at him. He was so nervous, but the connection was severed instantly as Billy frowned at her, then at Matthew, and pulled her away.

Weeks later, Matthew finally plucked up the courage to talk to her, and they'd chatted all the way over the sand-dune and down the track until they reached her house. As she walked slowly up the path towards her door, Matthew desperately wanted to ask her out, but didn't have the guts.

He'd turned, cursing himself and finally she called out. 'I broke up with Billy, by the way. And just for the record, he doesn't take too kindly to losing a competition, as you could probably tell.' And then she laughed loudly.

And then he'd laughed maybe a bit too heartily. 'I could certainly tell. Everyone on the beach could tell!'

Matthew was nervous, but he'd found it so easy talking to her and they talked for hours. He'd even awkwardly admitted to playing in a band but then her hideous mother drove into the property and immediately yelled for Melissa to get inside.

Melissa apologised for her mother's incessant yelling, and before she reluctantly made her way inside, he had plucked up the courage to invite her to a party on the beach the next night. 'It's the second cove just past Whale's Inlet.'

Matthew remembers that night so clearly. Of being nervous playing guitar in front of her but she beamed at him and danced excitedly with her friends to all of their songs. And at the end of their set, he and Melissa danced until they were exhausted.

They had sat away from the others and shared such intimate stories of their lives in the very short time they were together. He'd felt such an instant closeness with her, which he'd never felt with anyone else.

Then out of the darkness, Billy appeared in a rage, hands

clenching and unclenching, jaw jutting as he glared with pure loathing. Billy grabbed Melissa by the arm and dragged her away. They'd all wanted to help her but she kept telling everyone not to get involved.

Everything had happened so quickly. Billy yelling and shoving Melissa into some bushes, then running off. Melissa returned looking fairly shattered and all her friends gathered around her and told her to come back and enjoy the party. Only moments later they'd all heard the screeching tyres and a huge bang shattering the night. The night Matthew had lost Melissa forever.

He tries to get rid of this memory, to replace it with the earlier part of the evening, before the crash – this last time when they were both young and free, and for a short moment he'd been with this girl he'd been mad about since he was young.

Matthew had wanted to comfort Melissa the night of the accident, but the way she just stared straight through him... he had felt that she thought he was to blame as he knew that Billy's jealousy had caused the accident. And then later, her mother insisted that it was Matthew's fault.

Despite her mother threatening to call the police for harassment, he'd still tried desperately to contact Melissa but it was as though she had vanished off the face of the Earth.

None of it made any sense. Matthew was sure Melissa had broken up with Billy before the accident but her mother insisted they were just on a break. It was all too weird. And after that, he hadn't seen her at the beach or anywhere else until that day at Third Point with her children, about ten years after the accident.

He'd never forgotten her.

Realising he has been lying on the bed for hours, and that it must be getting close to seven, he jumps in the shower and tries to imagine how the evening will unfold. *Should I tell her everything? Surely, she didn't blame me for Billy flying into a rage and nearly killing himself. Surely not!*

~ ~ ~

Frantically searching through her bag for something to wear, Melissa holds a sexy black dress up against herself. She looks in the mirror and screws up her face. *No. That's tragic.* 'Okay, this…' She holds a long-sleeved top and some jeans up to herself. 'Now you look like you're going to milk a cow!' She rummages around in her bag again. *Not too casual. Not too overdone… but better too casual than overdone.*

She grabs a lace top and jeans and stands in front of the mirror in the bathroom. Images of Billy begin to flash before her eyes. 'No, not now! I don't want to think about that despicable creature… créature méprisable.' She closes her eyes tightly but despite her best efforts, she cannot shut Billy out.

Melissa shudders and can almost feel his hands all over her. 'Merde. Stop thinking about him!'

Wanting to escape her inner voice and feeling the need for someone to help her calm her nerves, she grabs her phone and calls Elle, who immediately answers, 'Are you hallucinated yet?'

'I… I'm so nervous!'

'I'm sure it will all be fine. You've certainly done your homework.'

'I'm not actually nervous about that. I'm just about to meet Matthew for dinner. Oh god, he's so gorgeous! I'm shaking.'

'Calm down. Scull your first drink and then another, lean over the table, kiss him and then drag him back to your room and have your way with him. That's what I'd do!'

Melissa laughs heartily. 'You're so funny. And I know that is what you'd do. And as much as I'd love to, I'll have to resist, I'm afraid.'

'Oh, go for it, woman. Go and grab him! Call us as soon as

you're back and by the way, I am taking full credit for getting you there. Um well, that is, if it works out well. If it doesn't then I had nothing to do with it... nah... it's going to be brilliant!'

Melissa sighs, unsure of how the future is going to play out but relieved that everyone except her mother has been so understanding and happy about her breaking up with Billy.

As if conjuring him, a text comes in from Billy with a heading "Important re Zac and Chloe." She opens it hesitantly.

I know the kids are upset with me about Janet but could you really blame me? I hope one day you will tell them that you never loved me and that no matter how much I achieved you were never proud of me. I could have had anyone. I tried so hard to make you love me—

*There is something wrong with your brain, seriously wrong... gravement tort.*

She scrolls through her phone and reads texts from Zac and Chloe wishing her well.

As she closes her phone, she sees another text with photos of Aisha standing with a group of elephants somewhere in Africa.

Go for it, Liss... You deserve the best life. I love you. Oh and you won't believe what I just found out about Matthew he just happ—

Her phone suddenly dies. *What about Matthew... What were you going to say about Matthew! Bugger! Bugger! Oh, blast, I forgot my charger!*

# CHAPTER 33

Melissa heads down to the grand dining room, every step echoing. She turns to footsteps coming up behind her and smiles as Matthew approaches. They share a look, surprised that it is so deathly quiet and there is no-one else to be seen. Matthew's voice seems to reverberate. 'Where is everyone? Why are there so many cars out front and so few people around? Maybe the rumours are true, and they are all out the back, cutting up people's brains for science.'

Before Melissa can comment, a jovial young waiter comes running up the stairs towards them. Melissa smiles and asks, 'Are we the only ones here?'

Out of breath, he responds, 'You may be the only ones for dinner tonight; it depends. Sometimes people come here to eat, and other times they recuperate in their rooms.'

He leads them into the dining room, sits them down and cheerily runs through the menu. Music begins to play in the background, which adds some warmth to the otherwise austere surroundings.

They eat and drink and laugh and a while later, the waiter clears away their dinner plates and returns with another bottle of wine. 'Would you like to order anything else? The chef is about to finish for the night.'

'No,' Matthew says with a shake of his head. 'That was great. Thanks.'

'Yes, I think we've had enough food to sink an army. Thank you, it was beautiful.'

The waiter chuckles, and heads back to the kitchen.

Matthew raises his eyebrows. 'Yes, a lot of armies would have been sunk by so much food, wouldn't they, Melissa?'

She pushes him away. 'I'm afraid these sayings just blurt out of me. I have to blame my grandmother.'

'Yes, I've noticed. You said one the last time I saw you... "You need to be tough skinned"... I think it was. And there was another... Oh, I've got it. "Brightest cab off the rank".'

She laughs and asks, 'Oh, really? Well, what should it be?'

'I think it is the first cab off the rank, but I like brightest cab better.'

She laughs. 'I think I have a serious problem! I speak before I think!'

He joins her laughter. 'I know another one... I think you said, 'Let the elephant out of the closet! I like them, they're funny.'

'Well, that is a change... some... ah it doesn't matter. I've noticed that you have a bit of a nervous twitch.'

'Really? And what is that?'

'You play with that plaited leather on your wrist a lot.'

'Really? I've never noticed. It's one of the few things I have from my father.' He smiles at her and cautiously places his hand on her shoulder. 'I was so sure you weren't going to make it, and I was so—'

'After what has just gone down at my home, nothing would have stopped me. I don't want to go there, though.'

He senses her upset and softly squeezes her shoulder.

She shudders thinking about Billy and apologizes. 'Oh, I'm sorry. What were we talking about before my stupid sinking armies comment? Oh that's right, I was showing off about my wonderful kids.'

He smiles and agrees. 'Yes, you were telling me about your son smashing your arse under the water.'

She laughs. 'I'm not sure I said smashing my arse, but yes, he probably could have smashed my arse, but he was too excited to come out of the water to brag!'

The young waiter waves as he departs, and they are left alone in the huge dining room. Matthew inhales deeply, smiles, and pulls his chair closer to hers. 'I can't believe I'm really here with you.' He holds her hands in his and confides, 'You know, I actually saw you many times before the day you... you, um... the day you fell all over me.'

Blushing slightly, she replies, 'Really? Oh, rubbish. You're just trying to make me blush.'

'No, I'm serious. A long time ago.'

'Really? Where?'

He thinks for a moment, and then suddenly, he's unsure how she'll react if he mentions the night of Billy's accident. He is just about to tell her and then hesitates. 'I... I um... I actually saw you the first day you arrived at Pymble's. It was my second session, and it was about to be my last and then I saw you in your car in the car park. You looked so distraught and I would have liked to... I don't know... to save you.' He smiles and squeezes her hand gently.

'It was as if you were moving in slow motion, getting out of your car and wiping the tears from your face. Then I saw you at the counter filling out their forms as you kept wiping your tears. You looked so sad. And in that moment, I decided Pymble wasn't so bad after all!'

'Really? You're just teasing, aren't you?'

'No! I really did. But no matter what I did week after week, I could never get your attention.'

'God, I can imagine. I was a total mess. It took a lot to get myself there, but I knew I needed help when my kids thought it was a good idea to see him. I was in a really bad place at that time and I was not very happy about having to see a psychiatrist.' She rolls her eyes and smiles. 'But really?'

He smirks. 'You came every Wednesday at five-thirty, so I always tried to get my appointments for around that time too so I could run into you—'

Melissa blushes. 'I don't—'

Matthew puts a finger gently against her lips. 'Didn't you notice how many times and how loudly I said Castillo that night you chased me down? Mind you, I didn't expect you would follow me, but I did want you to know about Castillo.'

'Oh, rubbish; you're just trying to make me blush! I don't believe you—'

'You look very beautiful when you blush. Your eyes get a little watery and they sparkle. I am going to have to try harder to make you blush more.'

She pushes him harshly, almost shoving him off his chair.

He laughs. 'I'm sorry for embarrassing you. I won't do it again for at least a few minutes, I promise.'

'Good! Don't!'

Feeling relaxed after all the wine they've consumed, Matthew decides he wants to tell her everything. He stares into her eyes, trying to gauge her reaction as he tells her he'd been with her at the beach the night of Billy's accident.

~~~

Tears instantly well in Melissa's eyes. *Oh god... oh god... what? What? It's him... the boy that broke my heart.* She stares at him incredulously as he explains that he and his friends used to call each other by their surnames or nicknames. 'There was Johnno, Stevo, Jacko... ha ha. I hated Matt as a nickname, so I was known
~~~

as Christo, or Christos, back then. Short for Christensen, my surname. I tried over and over to contact you, but your mother was so vehement that you didn't ever wish to see me, that the accident was all my fault, and then she threatened to call the police if I didn't stop harassing you. And I—' He stops short as she pulls away.

'I'm sorry.' Melissa suddenly feels dizzy and races to the bathroom. She looks at herself in the mirror, takes a deep breath and throws water over her face. She closes her eyes to try to stop the dizziness and makes her way to sit on one of the toilet seats. *Dammit, Mum. You lied to me about him! How could you? I had so many sleepless nights running to my window, hoping he would have tried to contact me. God knows how impressed you were with Billy's family, but would you really go this far? Fuck you, Jean! I told you I had broken up with Billy weeks ago! We were finished. And I told you about this new boy...*

She feels dizzy and confused as she tries to remember how her mother had been. Her mother's words return clearly. 'Well, if that boy really cared for you, Melissa, don't you think he would have tried to contact you by now?'

Those words had cut her so deeply at the time; that he didn't feel the same way she did. Melissa had really fallen for him and was devastated he didn't ever try to see her again.

Reflecting again on what Matthew has just told her, how could he think she would have ever thought he was responsible for Billy's stupid accident? How on Earth...? She does remember thinking he and everyone else there thought it was her fault.

Wiping her eyes, she races straight up to the mirror, blows her hair out of her face and smiles at her reflection. 'Fuck you, Mum. I'm going to enjoy this night to spite you.'

Melissa apologises when she returns to the table. 'I'm sorry about that. It's just such a shock to discover my mother betrayed me. I'm so sorry for what she did. She is... is... well, she's really messed up, but I'm shocked she would have gone that far. I can't believe that she told you it was your fault. How on Earth could it have been your fault? How—' She shakes her head.

'Well, I'm so glad to hear the truth. It baffled me for years. Your mother was so insistent, and then you disappeared. It took me ages to accept that you blamed me, but I just thought you didn't want me in the way, and if I hadn't invited you to the party, he wouldn't have nearly killed himself.'

'She is sooo devious. She also told me it was all *my* fault. Anyway, I am glad we've sorted that out.' She squeezes his hand and smiles. 'So, we have about twenty or so years to catch up on, Christensen. Tell me, what happened to the white-haired surfer?'

'Phew! Yes, the hair changed soon after I went travelling and I wasn't doing so much surfing.'

'It's weird, now I'm wondering how I couldn't have seen it… your eyes and your mouth. I don't know… I suppose I would have expected you to tell me—'

'I just wasn't sure. The way you looked at me… and your mother was pretty convincing that you didn't want to ever see me again.'

'God, she's a horror! I was in a really bad way after the accident. I don't know what happened to me. That time is such a blur… before I had the kids. After I had Zac and Chloe, my life lit up again.'

They continue to talk about their childhood years on the beaches and what they had done since. Matthew pours some more wine into their glasses and goes to the bathroom. She takes a sip, blows the hair out of her face again and thinks quickly to herself. *Okay, okay. Should I tell him? Will it turn him off me? But… I need to talk… I haven't been able to talk to anyone about what happened. I need to talk to someone. J'ai besoin de parler à quelqu'un.*

'What is it?' Matthew asks when he returns to the table.

'What's that face for? Come on, tell me.'

Melissa chews her bottom lip then sighs. 'I feel really awkward telling you this... but I just...' He smiles, moves closer and encourages her. 'Well... you know...' She exhales and starts again. 'Well... well, recently, I was using Billy's laptop for a quick internet search, and I saw this small image of myself... of myself naked. I clicked on the icon and this video opened up and... and I... I was standing naked in some sort of trance-like state as he filmed me in my bathroom. I could see him through the mirror injecting himself, and then he began to molest me whilst I was totally out of it. It was frightening... I looked like I was almost possessed. It was horrible. I....' She puts her hands up to her cheeks to cool her face down and sighs loudly as tears well in her eyes.

Matthew looks horrified. 'I'm so sorry. That's so fucked up! I'm just so sorry... Are you sure you want to keep going?'

Melissa nods, inhales deeply and continues. 'Yes, I do. I need to get it out of me because I just don't know what to do. I haven't spoken to anyone yet. I was in total shock when I saw the video, but I knew instantly I had to get proof. I sent it to my sister overseas and then he knew he was busted. I wanted to call the police, but I kept worrying about Zac and Chloe and their reaction, and would they hate me if I was responsible for getting him sent to jail. I just... I don't know if I want to press charges against the father of my children and have the world know what he's done to me. The thought of them having to go and visit him in jail...'

'It must be hard. Jails are ugly places and they do often treat the visitors as though they're criminals too.'

'I know. The thought makes me sick.' She bites down on her lip. 'There were so many times. His jealousy... I don't know how I didn't realise he could have been involved. He was always out of the country, and I'd even check his passport, so I thought it couldn't possibly be him. I don't know. How could I be so stupid? How did I keep going back?'

'You are definitely not stupid, Melissa. You're probably way too soft but not stupid. You were with him for a long time, of course you couldn't imagine something so horrible happening after such a long time.'

She takes a large sip of her wine. 'I should have realised as it only started to happen as soon as the kids had left home. The timing was perfect, but I didn't think about it. I guess... I mean... he would have known I was seriously thinking about leaving him when the kids were no longer at home. But I know now that he was trying all sorts of drugs on me, and I would end up with really strange reactions. That's why I ended up over at Third Point, naked. I really thought I had totally lost the plot then.'

Matthew squeezes her hand reassuringly.

Melissa breathes in deeply, trying to settle herself before continuing. 'I don't know what happened, but for many years he was fine... well, as fine as he could be. We've always kind of lived separate lives. But then a couple of years ago, this insane jealousy started up again—'

'You know what's strange? You didn't recognise me at all at the beach but he instantly recognised me even after I'd been away for years. I probably wouldn't have recognised him but he was so hostile, I realised who he was. And... I've crossed paths with him in so many random places—'

'Really where?'

'At the cemetery when we were burying my aunt. Um... near my office, which is a bit out of the way. And I've seen him recently at Le Monde—'

'Really? A funeral? I'm sorry—'

Matthew shakes his head. 'It's not a problem. Please, I interrupted. You go on.'

'I think he's psychotic. He made this video when I was completely drugged out and he was professing his love for me and then cursing me at the same time for not loving him.'

Matthew embraces her as tears roll down her cheeks and she sighs. 'It feels so good to get it all out. I've been feeling this shame. Logically, I know I shouldn't, but I've been... humiliated and I feel such a fool for not realising what was going on.'

'You are not a fool. I don't think anyone would expect their partner to be suddenly drugging and filming them. And as you said, especially since you were still having episodes when he was away overseas, of course, you wouldn't have thought it was him.'

She looks up at him and smiles. 'Thank you. I feel so much better now... I really needed to get it off my chest. Thank you.'

Melissa refills their glasses with the last of the wine, and suddenly all the lights are dimmed. He nods towards the tiny red camera lights in the corners of the room, grabs her hand and leads her out to the balcony.

She shivers from both the cold and her nervousness, 'You probably think—'

'I love you.' He stares intensely into her eyes. 'I think of you from the moment I wake up till the moment I go to sleep. I think of you constantly and I have done for so long now.'

Melissa buries her head into his chest, and just as she is about to respond, he lifts her face and kisses her. *Oh god, I love you too!* She melts from the tenderness and the passion of his kiss. *I could die in your arms. This feels so right. Oh, mon dieu, mon amour.*

Rain begins to fall, first lightly then more heavily. Matthew manoeuvres her under the protection of the awning before kissing her again. They embrace, their kisses deepening until the wind picks up and makes it almost impossible for them to stay outside.

He cups her face in his hands and looks into her eyes. 'I am so happy.'

She smiles at him. 'So am I.'

They creep in quietly, completely saturated. Melissa tries to cover herself when she notices her lace top is now completely transparent, revealing her almost transparent lace bra. Only a few floor lights are on in the corridor and they stumble and squeak with every step. They try to muffle their laughter but the more they try to stifle it, the louder it becomes. He guides her towards their rooms, and they joke about feeling like naughty school children, afraid Nurse Edwards will pounce on them at any moment and reprimand them.

They get to Melissa's door, and she glances up at the tiny red camera light. Matthew pulls her into his arms, and they hold tight to each other. He breathes in deeply. 'I love your scent... and... and... and so many things.'

Faint morning light suddenly filters through the window on the landing just beyond Melissa's room. 'Oh dear. I guess we have to get some sleep.'

They kiss again and finally agree to part.

As Melissa shuts the door to her bedroom, she leans back against it for a moment. *How could I have ever resisted him? That took a lot of strength.* Smiling, she inhales deeply and closes her eyes. A shiver surges through her body as she quietly whispers his words. 'I love you... I think of you... I think of you from the moment I wake up till the moment I go to sleep...' She sighs happily and adds, 'And I think of you constantly too.'

# CHAPTER 34

It is a cold and grey, rainy day and Melissa and Matthew shiver as they're led out through the garden. Their white cotton trousers and shirts provided by the clinic doing nothing to fight against the frigid conditions. As they follow Nurse Edwards and Nico, Matthew leans over and whispers, 'Where the hell are we going?'

All Melissa can see is miles and miles of green fields with a few trees dotted here and there. 'No idea, but I'm freezing. I think we were probably supposed to wear the dressing gowns they left in our rooms as well. Thankfully, I remembered my big woollen scarf. Do you want some of it?' He nods and she drapes one end around Matthew's shoulder and they laugh as they stumble over each other, trying awkwardly to share it.

As Nurse Edwards turns around and looks at them disapprovingly for about the third time, Matthew whispers, 'What the hell is her problem? And where the hell are they taking us? There are no buildings out here. I don't dare ask her, do you? She's already reprimanded me this morning, did she reprimand you too?'

Melissa nods.

Matthew squeezes her around the waist. 'I would love nothing more than to kiss you right now.'

She beams at him. 'And I would love nothing more than to kiss *you* right now.'

Matthew smiles mischievously. 'Come on, let's go.' They both look back at the mansion, which is now almost a pinprick in the distance. 'Oh blast, it's a long way back. Maybe these two are taking us to a dungeon and *they* are going to have their way with us; ooo-aaahh!'

Melissa laughs and pushes him. 'I must admit, I'm starting to freak out a little. Where are these Release Pods?'

'I'm sure it's okay.'

'I would have been terrified here on my own.'

Matthew nods and confides, 'Don't worry, I don't think I'd ever have come if you hadn't. I'm not terribly brave, I'm afraid. Can't we just run away together right now? Did I mention I would just love to kiss you? I'm finding it very hard to keep my hands off you.'

She smirks as she looks at him intently. 'I still can't believe that you were the surfer boy who broke my heart so many years ago.'

'And you were the girl from the rocks jumping into your dad's arms that broke mine! Do you remember that song that I played on my guitar for you that night?'

'Oh my god, yes! How could I forget it! "Oh Melissa".'

'Well, I am going to have to confess. Believe it or not, I didn't make that truly unique song that night. I actually made it up when my aunt first gave me the guitar when I was just thirteen!'

'You're lying! You're just trying to make me blush.'

He laughs. 'I was sure that night that you could tell. I cursed myself for a long time thinking that you must have thought I was such a dick—'

She squeezes her arm around his waist. 'Definitely not a dick... actually the sweetest boy I'd ever met.'

Melissa nods back towards the mansion when suddenly, Nurse Edwards holds out her arm and warns, 'Mind!' She points down to a moss-covered stairway leading to a solid metal, vault-style door. Nico turns and begins heading back without a word, and Nurse Edwards indicates for them both to descend.

They look at her warily and she snaps, 'You simply pull the handle and make your way through that door.'

They look at her curiously then climb down slowly into the darkness. Matthew opens the thick door as Melissa whispers to him, 'Can you please check that the door will open again from the inside?'

Once he does, they both enter, raising their hands to protect their eyes as they're confronted by an intense brightness.

'Whoa,' Matthew says. 'It's like entering another world.'

~ ~ ~

Melissa and Matthew shake their heads as their eyes adjust to the overwhelming brightness and the heightened activity in this bunker-style lab. They are surrounded by all sorts of scientific paraphernalia and large terrariums with plants growing under bright lights. In the centre of this vast, underground building is a glass-walled central observation area filled with monitors and people in white coats. On the far side of the observation area sit a number of vault-like doors, each with a name and a green or red light above. Matthew whispers, 'This looks like a scientist's fantasy world!'

Melissa nods. 'It's amazing all of this out here in the middle of nowhere. Look at all the large glass vessels filled with colourful liquids. It looks like an art piece.'

'Yes, I wish I could take photos for this new building—' He stops short as Castillo comes out of the central observation area to greet them.

'Welcome to the Castillo Clinic! I hope Nurse Edwards found

some suitable transport to get you down here. We have several golf carts but somehow, all of them are out-of-action at the moment.' He smiles at them cheekily before continuing, 'We usually get an early start, but you two were night owls last night, I hear. So, we thought you might appreciate a bit of extra sleep.'

'Sprung,' Matthew says under his breath.

Castillo smiles and nudges Matthew. 'It makes me happy to see young people enjoying themselves.' Gesturing towards the central area, he adds, 'This is the Hub, where we film and monitor your procedure, although we prefer to call it "The Release Experience". In the large terrariums are numerous plants where we are constantly developing specific hallucinogens that will further enhance the Experience. Behind us is the recovery room, and the rooms on the far side of the Hub are what we refer to as the Release Pods, where your Experience will take place.'

Two of his colleagues, carrying small vials of the colourful liquids, confer for a moment. 'I think we will need to throw these out as they are losing their potency; we can tell by this yellowing. What we would be aiming for in these ones is a pure turquoise colour. You can match it perfectly on the chart under the particular plants you are working with.'

Castillo leads Melissa and Matthew across the room to the entrance of the Hub. He motions towards his colleagues inside, most of them engrossed in excited discussions and several others staring intently at the monitors. 'We have the entire spectrum of health physicians, psychoanalysts, neuropsychologists, herbalists etcetera, and most of us are multi-lingual, which can be very important with this work.' He pauses. 'I'm sorry but it looks like I am being called away. I'll just quickly introduce you to Paco, who is my right-hand man.'

Paco smiles. 'Hello and welcome. I'd like you to meet Hélène and Eric who will be the main people looking after you during your Experience. And this is Gus and Arjun; we will all be working closely behind the scenes.'

Matthew quietly reads a quote he sees above the door of the Hub, '"There are wonders beyond belief, there are truths to be revealed, if one can remove truth's protective layers".'

Eric looks up at the sign. 'Ah, yes, that is a quote from Neil Armstrong somebody put up a few years ago. During the Experience, everyone has one of these... "divine" moments, where they literally cannot describe what they are experiencing. They try, of course, but always end up saying they can't describe it. So, many years ago a colleague brought that in and now we call it the "Armstrong Moment".'

Hélène smiles at them. 'Or the Magical Moment.'

Castillo returns from the Hub and explains the procedure to Melissa and Matthew. He has obviously said it many times before and continues rapidly. 'We will be attaching something called Senstimulators or SEMS to all the major and minor chakras of the body. These are an amazing new technology that penetrate deep into the psyche and alert us to any connection problems. They reveal to us when people intentionally block. Often, memories can be torturous *but* these are the most important to experience in order for the Release to happen. Our job is to prompt you to stay with it. This amazing piece of technology when used with the Camoiiteh is an incredible combination. The Camoiiteh is the hallucinogen we have specifically developed from a variety of roots that grow wild in most parts of the world. The Camoiiteh will open your mind and produce real-life visions from earlier time periods in this life—and, from all of our own personal experiences and our research has shown us, from past lives too— that may be creating problems for you.'

He waits for them to nod their understanding before continuing. 'The SEMS stimulate specific parts of the brain to help conjure past experiences. Your mind becomes the projector in your own private theatre. We monitor you constantly, and from the information you give us, we try to decipher as much as we can to help you stay in the moment. When some people get to a place they find disturbing, they often close up, so we assist you to remain because we believe that ninety-nine-point-nine percent of the time this is the most important experience to confront.'

Castillo becomes distracted by another colleague who is holding up a vial of bright indigo liquid. He nods, mouths his approval and returns his attention to the group. 'Now, where was I? Ah, yes. So, this is not a conscious process on your part. The SEMS are directed by your brain. Just as your brain tells your body to breathe without you being conscious of it, this is also an unconscious process. The SEMS are tiny and very fiddly to deal with, but once they are attached you won't know they are there. They work something like electrodes, except about a thousand times more sophisticated, working on the totality of the human mind and body – the conscious and the unconscious. The Camoiiteh is a brilliant aid in opening your mind to anything that presents itself.

'So it may be a combination of past experiences that are adversely affecting you. The Camoiiteh will open up all your memories and help you to see things clearly without any filters—'

Matthew asks, 'What do you mean without any filters?'

Castillo smiles at the question. 'It is hard to explain. You will encounter moments from your past in the first-person in the present time and, rather than how you would have experienced them in the past, you will get to see these times without any filters almost as though you are an observer of your own life... so you can break from learned behaviours. The clarity this brings to people is very beneficial, so they can continue their lives and escape these learned behaviours. Sometimes, we have been very close to people through our lives, and we don't see how destructive they are to us.

'During the Experience, we will try to unravel what you project. This could be from some time in this life or it could be from a past life. This unravelling will enable you to reconcile whatever is causing you problems and holding you back in this life. You get to see your relationships clearly without any filters. You will undergo the problem just as you did in the past, but by bringing unconscious memories to consciousness in the present moment, you will free yourself and move on.'

Melissa nervously chews on her thumbnail. 'How do you know that people are seeing into past lives?'

Castillo smiles excitedly. 'You certainly know! Especially if it is another century... things are just different. I have personally been through the process many, many times and all our staff and literally thousands of people over the years have come through the Experience and we know that we were in another century.'

'Does everybody go back to other centuries?' Matthew asks.

'No. Some people only connect with this life, but as many of our staff have found, the more times they went through the Experience the further back they went. About the earliest we think anyone has gone would be to about the late-1700s. And this is only based on what we understand from history books. And how reliable they are is another... never mind.'

Castillo smiles at Melissa and Matthew. 'We work diligently to keep you immersed in your Experience. You will be aided by us activating the SEMS and by us verbally encouraging you to feel deeply all the events you are confronted with. You will benefit by describing your Experience in as much detail as you can, using all your senses, which will be heightened from the Camoiiteh. Wherever your mind takes you, whatever memory comes up for you, you will become immersed as though you are living it in real time. You are not able to change what happened in the past but the SEMS will allow you to release the hold it has on you. And if you can convey to us exactly what you are experiencing, that will help us to provide you with the SEMS stimulation in order to keep you there in that precise moment. We want you to really become a part of wherever each projection takes you. Go to that Experience. Feel the fear or whatever it is that is there for you, while we continue to unlock different states of your consciousness.'

Castillo stops for a moment as several staff rush towards a door that has just changed from red to green. 'It is very busy down here. Now, please try to stay with the projections, however unpleasant. We may gently intervene, especially by prompting you when we know that you are trying to block something, because this very place, this Experience, will be where you get the most benefit from the Releasing process. We will be tapping deep into your brain to get it functioning as it should and freeing the cellular memory held in the body so that you can leave the past in the past and strengthen your path for the future. It will be a total Releasing.' He smiles at Matthew. 'We will be monitoring your body constantly and we take your safety seriously. We do have a backup procedure, but I am happy to say we haven't needed to use it for many, many years now.'

Matthew asks, 'And the backup procedure is to be sedated? Right?'

'Yes.' Castillo smiles and puts his arm up around Matthew's shoulder. 'We would only do that if your Experience got out of hand and your mental and physical health was at risk, but I am happy to say we haven't needed to sedate anyone for at least ten years now. You have full control with the buzzer to open the door and put a stop to it at any time. On very few occasions we have had people do this, but they have nearly always ended up returning and going through it again. Matthew, I can assure you that you are in very safe hands, it will be nothing like the bad experience you had in Bolivia.' He puts his arms up around both of their shoulders and smiles. 'I wish you both abundant health and vitality. I will get Eric and Hélène and they can get you set up.'

They smile at him and as he walks away Melissa tries to comfort Matthew. They talk quietly to each other amongst the many conversations and clinical sounds surrounding them. Matthew jokes, 'Should we just make a run for it now? I am feeling a lot better all of a sudden. Come on, Melissa, let's go.'

She smiles nervously. 'I wish.'

'Okay, then; let's make a run for it.'

Melissa calls his bluff. 'Okay, come on!'

'Really?'

'No, *not* really!' she laughs.

He pouts. 'Oh, bummer! What if someone comes screaming out of one of these doors? I assume the red light means someone is in there.'

'Yes, I suppose so. The doors with the red lights are closed and the doors with the green lights are open slightly. I'm sure they know what they're doing and—'

'But, god, I'm still scared. Not very manly, am I?' He looks to her for reassurance and she squeezes his hand as Eric and Hélène approach. Gripping Melissa's hand tightly, Matthew continues, 'Are you sure about this? We could still—'

'Looks like it's too late.' Melissa nods as Eric comes towards them. 'I think he's waiting for you. Good luck; it's going to be great. Remember all the testimonials we read. Twenty years of counselling unravelled in a session.'

Eric quickly leads Matthew around to the other side of the Hub. Matthew tries to mouth something to Melissa as he is being whisked off. She shakes her head and shrugs, and he tries again but Hélène is now ushering her off in the other direction.

'Hello, I'm Hélène. I will be assisting you with your

Experience,' she says with a very strong French accent. 'We have you set up in this pod here.'

As they walk towards the door Melissa asks, 'Why do they call them pods?'

Hélène raises her eyebrows and grins as she opens the door.

Melissa can't help but laugh. 'Ah, because it is shaped like a pod... an ellipse. Wow, this is so spacey.' She jumps in and out through the door like a child, noting the loud hum of clinical sounds outside, and the heavy and deafening silence inside. 'The energy is so different; it feels so heavy in here; I feel the weight of the world. These walls are so thick.'

Hélène looks on, amused, and replies, 'Yes, these are sensory deprivation modules, designed specifically so there is absolutely nothing to distract you from the intensity of the Experience.'

Melissa anxiously fidgets with her hands. 'I'm so nervous. Are you sure I can get out if I want to? I get terrible claustrophobia sometimes. I felt a bit freaked when I came down the steps and saw that huge door. I had to check that I could get out again before I felt safe to enter.'

Hélène pats Melissa's shoulder. 'I get a bit of claustrophobia too, so I can assure you, you will be fine. You are able to open the door from the inside whenever you want. Just press this buzzer and it will open immediately.' Melissa presses the buzzer several times and the door springs open. She sits on the edge of the bed and tries to distract herself. *What on Earth have I got here in my sentimental memorabilia? I'm not quite sure about any of it! Why did I bring this Moroccan rug and the large teddy bear?* She fidgets nervously at the fringe of the rug. 'I feel like I'm in a padded cell but at least it's a cool, elliptical padded cell.'

'Yes, it is... for your protection of course. Over there is a small basin built into the wall with a water hose that you can drink or shower yourself with. And there are several towels and blankets scattered around the room.'

Melissa points to a small medicine cup with bright turquoise liquid sitting on a soft white pouf. 'I assume that is the famous Camoiiteh that has been designed specifically for me?'

Hélène nods and smiles as she begins unwrapping the SEMS. Melissa steps up close to one of the walls. 'And what are all of these miniscule circular disks all over the entire room? Your state-of-the-art monitoring cameras?'

Sensing Melissa's nervousness, Hélène nods. 'It's very unusual for us to have a couple attending the clinic.'

Melissa blushes. 'Ah... we're not a couple, just good friends who happen to have some problems at the same time. And to be honest, we were both too frightened to come alone.'

'Yes, the procedure does sound fairly confronting, but I can assure you, it is the best thing you can ever do for yourself. We can't actually work here unless we have gone through the Experience ourselves, as Castillo believes we need to truly understand what is happening when others go through it. So, don't worry, I know from personal experience it is the most amazing thing and you will be totally safe.'

Hélène proceeds to get Melissa ready. 'Okay I need to attach the SEMS over the chakras of your body. So, firstly, if I could get you to lie down and lift your top up, then I'll sit you up again as there are a lot that need to be attached to your head as well.'

Melissa does as she's asked. 'Cordless. I am very happy about that. They nearly strangled me to death at Chevallum. Well, I nearly strangled myself. Anyhow, I really shouldn't go into that now.'

Hélène winces. 'I have heard some weird stories about Chevallum.'

'Yes, I can imagine. Everything here is state-of-the-art, isn't it?'

'Yes, I don't think there is anywhere else in the world with such incredible facilities and technology. We do get amazing results here. We have thousands of testimonials attesting to the brilliant work we do, and there would probably be a lot more if mental health wasn't still a bit taboo.'

Melissa nods. 'Yes, I've read hundreds of testimonials; thank goodness some people are brave enough to admit they had a problem.'

Hélène continues attaching the SEMS and replies proudly, 'I love the work here; there are a lot of people on the waiting list wanting to work with Castillo. He is hoping that in the not-too-distant future the work we do here will spread around the world.'

Melissa begins to feel more relaxed as the conversation takes her mind away from her fears. 'It's amazing how he still gets such bad press.'

'Yes, well, I think that is about to change, thanks to some very satisfied and very wealthy media moguls that have been with us recently.'

'Wow, that's great. You know, over this past year or so, I have been coming out with bits and pieces of French. Je ne comprende... I don't understand most of it, and I must admit that it's mostly cursing or swear words. I hope I don't offend you if—'

Hélène smirks. 'That is very interesting, and no, you would never offend any of us. We hear a lot of swearing and cursing, so relax.'

Hélène smiles and gives her a gentle hug. 'I hope you have a great Release Experience.' She points to the Camoiiteh beside the bed. 'Drink it when you are sure you are ready. Oh, and by the way, you are welcome to recuperate back at the mansion for as long as it takes when you are finished. Just ignore old bitch Edwards if she tries to move you on. Castillo encourages people to stay as there are many rooms and facilities, and we can only have ten people down here at one time.'

Squirming at the sight of the turquoise drink, Melissa hugs the large teddy bear tightly. *Do I have to drink that?* She breathes in and smiles as she remembers the previous night with Matthew. *That was divine!*

Rotating her head around at all of the cameras, she scowls. *I feel like a monkey in a circus... a performing monkey... or whatever it is they say... this is so weird.* She closes her eyes tight, and sighs happily thinking about her kids. *I'm so happy Zac and Chloe are so cool. That's such a relief. I hope they never find out what really happened.* She tries to focus her mind to more memories of them, but the thought of what she had just learned the previous night about her mother keeps hounding her. *'Well, if that boy had cared for you, Melissa, don't you think he would have tried to contact you by now?'* She frowns. *Stop! I don't want to think about her!*

She shakes her head and as she hugs the large teddy bear tighter, another negative memory comes back to her. *Oh god, here we go. It was the first time I'd felt the full power of Mum's animosity when Dad came home with this bear and lots of other gifts for Lilly and I. Mum was so angry with him. The tension in the house around that time and the arguments because he was refusing to accept his inheritance from his parents had been so awful. I can't work out how she had so much power over us all. Not so much power over Dad though when it came to his inheritance. But why were we all so frightened of her?*

Melissa buries her head into the bear. 'I feel so ashamed.' *Why did I let her stand over me all my life? Why couldn't I stand up to my own mother? To do ballet for so many years when I hated it is one thing but letting her convince me to stay with Billy, well that is ridiculous! I don't know why I was so afraid of her. I don't know... somehow... I think I just needed to feel she loved me. I had no other adult in my life.*

Melissa curls up on the bed, closes her eyes and frowns as another memory returns. One of her most shameful. Why was she so weak? Zac would have only been about two, and for some absolutely ridiculous reason, Mum smacked him. He'd never been smacked and was so upset. Melissa was furious. *Why didn't I have the strength to challenge you, Mother?* Instead of demanding her mother leave and never lay a hand on Zac again, Melissa sheepishly told Jean about the documentaries that said speaking to a child about their behaviour had far better outcomes than smacking a child. 'So, I will be doing that with our kids, if and when it is necessary.'

Finally, Jean had scowled. 'You have to discipline your children, Melissa. How will they know right from wrong if you don't?' With that, she had handed Zac back. Then added gleefully as she left, 'I imagine Billy will be happy about this new idea of yours!'

After Jean left, Melissa had held Zac tightly, furious with herself for not grabbing him away from her mother instantly and comforting him. She'd berated herself incessantly for a long time after that incident. Why was she so fucking weak around her own mother? What was she so afraid of?

When had Mum become so vile towards us all? When did she change so completely? Or was she always like that? Melissa vaguely remembers her dad returning home one day when she was about six or seven. Melissa had never seen him so angry. There'd been another huge argument with his mother and father, and he'd sworn he would never touch their fortune, no matter what. *Did Mum really resent us all our lives because of the Trust?* But there'd been plenty of money coming in from Dad's investments. Was she so obsessed with money?

Swallowing drily and looking once again at the turquoise liquid in the container beside her bed, she grimaces. *I have to get that down. Oh, god, I didn't make any plans for after this is finished. What if I finish before Matthew? Relax. I'm not going to knock on his door now!* She sits up, takes a steadying breath and drinks the turquoise liquid quickly.

'Oh, ohhh.' She raises her eyebrows and smirks. 'Actually, that wasn't so bad.'

~~~

The lights dim as Melissa waits nervously for the Experience to begin. She lies down, closes her eyes and within minutes is feeling lightheaded. *Oh, god, what am I doing? What's that noise? Birds? Seagulls and children playing somewhere off in the distance?* She frowns as the room becomes brighter and brighter, and as she opens her eyes, she sees hundreds of childhood memories projected vividly all around her. *Oh, these are the best memories. Wow!* She rises, smiling, and spins excitedly as more and more projections come to life.

*Where do I start?* She focuses in on a projection of children playing on a beach. *Oh, that's Lilly and me jumping off the rocks... and there's Dad treading water waiting so patiently so he can help us onto the waves to ride them back to the shore. God, I was so happy. My life was so blessed. Oh... oh no, what's happening? I want to stay here.*

The memory disappears but as she turns her head, she sees Zac and Chloe playing on the beach when they were very young. 'I can see my babies! Hear their cute little voices as they
~~~

play in the waves. I know they can feel me here with them. Chloe is hugging my leg and Zac keeps splashing us. They're so cute. This is so wonderful.' She relaxes as she is immersed, playing in the shallows with her children.

As this day with her children begins to fade, she stands once more and begins to spin as more and more memories come to life all around her.

Hélène prompts Melissa gently as she sees her spinning.

Melissa looks worried and becomes transfixed on one of the projections. After several minutes, she responds. 'We're walking back to the shack from the beach... Zac is very young... he's telling us a story about a jellyfish, and... I'm distracted. I know my kids are trying to get my attention, waiting for me to respond but I'm staring into space, and I can't snap out of it. I know what's about to happen, and I want to get us all away.'

Melissa shouts, 'I want to intervene! Argh! This is so frustrating! Okay, okay I realise I can't change anything. I finally snap out of my daydream and I give my kids my full attention, I answer them and Zac continues his story. And then... and then my mind goes blank and I can't remember at all what I had been thinking. I know my kids can feel me. I am really there with them. They are so, so cute.'

As another projection dominates the pod, Melissa is instantly transported to a different time. 'I wanted to stay with my... ahh, this is okay. I can see my father at Third Point. I'm so happy to be back with him. I feel deeply that he's with me. I can smell his familiar scent, and the sound of his voice is so comforting. I know he can sense me too. I'm teasing him, calling him Jeffy and he retaliates calling me Missy Lissy. We laugh together and he picks me up and throws me onto a wave. He's so happy. I want to stay here. Dad, I love you...' She lies down on the bed and enjoys this past.

Loud, squealing noises and the brightness from a new

group of projections force her to open her eyes again. 'There are seagulls everywhere fighting over some leftover food on the beach. My mother is playing with Lilly in the water and my father is just about to push me onto a wave. We are all so happy... it's so much fun...' She drifts off and rolls over on the bed with a smile on her face.

As this day on the beach with her parents fades, she sits up on the side of the bed, drinks some water and smiles as she sees her young kids again. 'Oh, I loved these times. I'm telling Zac and Chloe a story about—' She lies back and closes her eyes; *I'm so happy—*

Hélène prompts her again gently and she resumes her commentary. 'I'm so happy, and I can feel my children's joy. We're lying on Chloe's little bed and they're snuggling into me. As I breathe in, the sweet smell of their skin and their hair... it's so familiar... so beautiful. I just want to savour this moment but they're waiting for me to continue the story they know so well, and they wriggle free and stand up on the bed, flapping their arms. A huge surge of joy envelops us all as I continue the story.'

Melissa begins to giggle. 'Wow, I'm in complete ecstasy. Wow... this is amazing! This is... This is... This is better than any drug. Better than anything I have ever felt! This is how we should feel... should feel alwaaaaays. Thisssss issss beauuuuutiful. So warmmmm and fuzzzzzzzy and soffffffffft. Everythinggg is slowwww... sofffft... tinnnggglyyy...'

Sitting up, Melissa sways from side to side and shivers as she raises her hands and gently lifts her hair away from her scalp. She begins to speak slowly. 'I feel so euphoric... Ooohhh, I have tingles everywhere.' She keeps gently lifting her hair from her scalp and smiling. 'I'm floating. Out of my body. Floating. Everything is light. Everything is beautiful. Pure.

'All my darkest memories are becoming light. This is beautiful. The colours are... and the people are... *Everything* is beautiful. *Beautiful!* I want to be like this forever. Floating. Just... bliss. Perfect. So perfect.'

~ ~ ~

Sitting closely at Melissa's monitor in the Hub, Hélène gently encourages Melissa to describe her experience in more detail. She records what she understands into a small microphone. 'The colours are indescribable; colours I've never seen before. I'm seeing images I can't describe but they're beautiful. I'm feeling... I don't know how to describe how I'm feeling. Euphoria? Ecstasy? It's incredible! Like all my darkest memories are changing to light...'

Hélène turns to Eric. 'Okay, looks like she is enjoying it now, and she's gone quiet. I think she will be like this for a while. Her vitals have all slowed and are steady, I'll wait a bit longer, and then I'll get a bite to eat.'

Eric looks over to her monitor. 'Bring on "the Revelation", Melissa. Describe it!'

'Maybe you'll have to get back in there and do that for us, Eric.'

Eric laughs. 'Actually, I was thinking just that the other day, that if you went through the process enough times and completely emptied yourself of all your baggage from your whole existence, then perhaps that would be all you'd be left with – the "Almighty Revelation".'

Gus takes a look at the screen. 'Yes, Melissa certainly looks happy. Maybe we need to invent some new words to describe the *Experience* fully. I mean, if we can see it and feel it... I just think that maybe it is our languages that are lacking. Castillo has been through it so many times and he still hasn't been able to describe the Magic Moment. If only we could record the images and scenes people experience when they are in that euphoric moment.'

Hélène nods. 'Hopefully, the technology won't be too far off.'

'What do you think he means by the "protective layer"?'

Hélène sips her coffee, contemplating. 'Yes, what is the protective layer, Neil Armstrong? Is it language? It's the trillion-dollar question.'

Castillo returns to the Hub, does his rounds of all the monitors. 'And how are Melissa and Matthew doing? Are all their vitals under control?'

Paco quickly checks his computer. 'Well, Melissa is really enjoying it. She has been lying there smiling and hasn't moved for about two hours. I think she may be in there for quite a while. She didn't start for about an hour initially; we thought we might have to offer her the Camoiiteh intravenously, and then she threw it back and seemed to enjoy it. Matthew got into it fast and is still in the euphoric stage.'

Castillo moves down the line of monitors. 'And how is Aleksey doing? He's just about to break the endurance record, isn't he?'

Gus looks up and smiles. 'He's done that. We just clocked him at twenty hours. We've been monitoring him closely and he's doing nicely.'

~~~

Melissa's eyelids flicker as new, larger-than-life projections appear. Opening her eyes fully, she smiles.

A kaleidoscope of colours fills the entire pod and a flickering sound starts up, like the end of an old-fashioned spool of film running out of steam. 'Euph... euphoria. Wow...'

She stands and sways in slow motion, her hands moving slowly through her hair. 'My head is tingling... I can hear soft music.' She moves to the music as another memory rises around her. 'Billy is away and Aish and I have taken some ecstasy tablets, we're having so much fun dancing freely with
~~~

flashing strobe lights in this smoky nightclub… I'm lost in the crowd, dancing on my own.' *Oh, I was enjoying myself there.*

Her eyes are forced open by the brightness of a huge projection of a large baby's head. 'I can hear echoes of loud, slow-motion groans… Aisha and I are in a birthing pool on the deck of my house. I'm groaning and crying tears of joy. Zac has just been born. My baby boy lies on my breast. I feel so joyous; he is so tiny and perfect. I want to stay here and hold him and enjoy this moment, but I can feel Billy lurking behind me. He doesn't approve of home births, and his animosity is almost a physical thing. But as I show him our beautiful baby boy, he softens and tears well in his eyes.' Melissa lies down and reflects on this time with her new baby.

~ ~ ~

Seagulls screech and squawk loudly, filling the pod with their cries. An image appears of young children leaping off the rocks into the ocean. Melissa frowns as an overwhelming number of memories begin to play out in every direction. Hélène's voice resonates in her mind, urging her to concentrate. She focuses on Chloe and Zac, back when they were toddlers. The joy of holding her young children in her arms is euphoric.

'I pick Zac up and squeeze him tightly before I put him back down. He wants to give his sister a horsey-ride. I pick up Chloe and prolong the moment, enjoying the smell of my young child and I hug her tight before helping her onto Zac's back. I am so happy to be back at this time, listening to my children's laughter, the purity of their joy.'

She sighs as this memory fades. 'I just want to stay here and enjoy my children at our beloved shack… but I'm… being drawn to another time.' She closes her eyes and relaxes as distinctive smells and sounds come to her and she recognises her bedroom at the shack. 'I'm here with Lilly. The music in the background is so familiar and so is the sweet scent of Lilly's freshly washed hair. She's just applied make up to my face, and I'm nervous as I apply the last touches to hers. Lilly opens her eyes, grabs a mirror. "What have you done to me?" She laughs and tackles me on to the bed.

'I can feel deeply my beautiful sister's joy as we jump up and down on the bed and sing a bunch of old sixties classics at the top of our voices. I want to stay here with Lilly; it's so wonderful to see her so happy, but it's fading... Lilly is disappearing into the darkness. I run through the house searching for her, but she keeps disappearing! I want to be with my sister when she was happy, before our mother became so divisive and I hardly got to see Lilly at all. My sister stayed in her room most of the time and I had to go along dutifully as my mother forced me to do ballet and whatever other activities she felt she'd been deprived of in her childhood.'

Melissa tries to savour this happy memory of her sister, but a huge image of Jean's scowling face remains.

She can hear Hélène prompting her to continue and finally she responds. 'I keep searching and searching for Lilly and I've found her in her bedroom in the shack. We're happy until Jean arrives and stands in the doorway. Lilly is frightened of her, but defiant, so Jean ignores her and berates me.'

Melissa tries to shut her mother out but the more she tries, the more Jean's voice increases in volume.

'When Mum finally leaves, we imitate her voice, and then we pout and run around the room flailing our arms, singing, "I must, I must, increase my bust!" We laugh and laugh at our mother's new breast implants and her over-inflated lips.'

Lilly fades quickly and Jean's scowling face and voice are inescapable. "'If that boy had been interested in you, Melissa, don't you think he would have contacted you?'"

The anger wells inside of Melissa, and she surges from the

bed to confront her mother's image. 'How could you do that? You forced me to go back to Billy! WHY WAS I SO AFRAID TO STAND UP TO YOU?' She falls back onto the bed, still cursing her mother, and weeps.

~ ~ ~

Lying exhausted in the dark, Melissa rests and waits. Slowly, the subtle sounds of a crying toddler become more and more audible. She sits up. 'Chloe is only about three years old and I cradle her in my arms and wipe away her tears. Zac looks worried about her and offers her a lolly to cheer her up. The next minute she gets straight up out of my arms and says cheekily right into my face, "I love you Mummy! Boom, boom!" And then she says right into Zac's face, "I love you, Zaccy! Boom boom!" How I wish I could stay here with them.

'I can hear a song playing,

> *Take off your dress, oh, oh.*
> *It is nothing more than just a game.*
> *You led me to believe you were someone you're not, oh, oh...*

'I know this song well. It's getting louder and louder and the projection of my kids is transforming into a new one. Aisha and I are laughing hysterically at each other, falling all over each other, drunk, as we are singing along very badly to the song:

> *Take off your dress, oh, oh.*
> *It is nothing more than just a game.*
> *You led me to believe you were someone you're not...'*

Melissa jumps off the bed and with a huge smile on her face, sways slowly from side to side. She turns her head slightly back towards the bed and sees hundreds of images playing out on the top of her Moroccan rug, creating kaleidoscope-like patterns as her memories fade in and out and in and out.

She focuses in on a disturbing image of Jean snarling just after Lilly had given her the rug. Melissa squeezes her eyes shut, trying to erase this memory as she encounters a new, slightly blurred, scene. 'I remember Dad saying this so clearly. "I will not accept their stinking money! I swore to them my entire life that I will not accept my inheritance and I stand by my words. We don't need it, but I will accept it on behalf of our girls in Trust for the future. If you do not sign, Jean, I will relinquish my rights to it."

'I remember Mum scowling at Lilly and me as she walked past us and went back to the kitchen table at the shack to sign the document. The irate echo of my mother's voice rises. "I hope you girls are happy!"' Melissa cowers. *I want to get my mother out of my head! Go away!*

Hélène sees that Melissa is blocking and prompts her gently.

Melissa exhales loudly, and then continues with a high-pitched voice imitating her mother. '"This is all your fault, Melissa! All! Your! Fault!"' Melissa pauses and then resumes in her normal voice. 'I can feel my mother's hatred. I feel so guilty, I feel so ashamed and I am begging her, "Mum, Billy and I had broken up—"' She stops as she is transported back to the scene of Billy's accident. Piercing sounds and horrifying visual snapshots of the accident slam into her, forcing her there, to experiencing this frightening time. 'I can see Billy's body in his smashed-up, bright-yellow car with blood all over it. My heart pounds heavily. "Billy! No! NO!"

'The boy I'd only just left at the bonfire stares at me. I want him to comfort me, but the intense shame that this accident is all my fault, forces me to stay silent. Still. This is all my fault! Oh, god, what have I done? I'm sure everybody thinks it's my fault... but now... right now, I can clearly see that this boy... that this boy and Aisha and all of my friends are all trying to comfort me and reassure me, but I cannot hear them, I can't believe them. The boy is trying to get to me but stops. I want to go to him, but I can't, I'm too ashamed. The accident is my fault.

'Out of the darkness my mother's face appears and her words confirm my belief. "This is all your fault, Melissa. What if he dies? What if he dies? If you hadn't raced off with that other boy so quickly, this wouldn't have happened."'

The sound of her mother's voice rings in her head and she covers her ears, pleading. 'No, no; I didn't. It's not my fault. It is NOT MY FAULT!'

Crying, she collapses to the floor and as she opens her eyes, she sees Jean hours after the accident, offering her a hot chocolate saying. 'Here dear, you've been through this huge ordeal take this.'

*God, I remember wondering what the hell was going on... One minute Mum was telling me it was all my fault and the next she was concerned about me. It felt very strange.... Like I was living in this alternate reality but I thought it was just from the trauma.*

She watches her mother grinding tablets, and as the projection begins to fade, sees her putting them into a cup and handing it to her. 'Why, Mother? Was it so important for me to be with Billy? Why?'

~ ~ ~

*Where am I?* Melissa wakes with a fright. Her legs are cramping and she crawls back onto the bed and closes her eyes. *I'm so tired. Très fatiguée. Oh, what now?* She tries to keep her eyes closed but a bright light forces them open again and she finds herself completely immersed in a luminescent underwater world.

'Oh... oh... this is divine. I'm holding on to a man's shoulders and we're gliding smoothly through schools of fish that dart out of our way as we weave our way through a maze of underwater caves.'

*I know this man. I know this intense love. The shimmering colours are so beautiful.*

'I can hear a hollow, underwater sound, and the colours are beginning to fade and now I'm alone, deep in the ocean amongst a myriad of caves. I can sense him, deep in the darkness of the caves and I try to follow but he keeps moving farther and farther into the darkness. The image phases out and I can no longer feel myself in the water.'

As this projection fades, Melissa is overwhelmed and exhausted. She wants to escape the staggering volume of memories that surround her. *Focus on the now.* 'Okay, where am I?'

A very vague image of Castillo comes to her, as does a quick image of Nurse Edwards scurrying back into the mansion.

She sighs heavily and closes her eyes; there are still memories lurking that she is wanting to avoid. Melissa is relieved when a sudden brightness lights up the pod and she stands up and smiles. *Wow, I'm back with the kids at the beach.* 'My kids are so cute, playing on the beach. A tall man is coming out of the surf and I see him, but I look straight through him. I can see him looking at me but I'm totally oblivious to him. He drops his board and picks up a towel right near us. He's watching us, trying to get my attention, but he knows I don't recognise him. Oh, if only I had have seen it was Matthew... I would have loved to have seen him. But I am totally caught up in the joy of my children, and as we leave the beach, he is talking to someone near the sand dunes and we walk straight past him on the path to the shack.

'Oh, this feels so amazing... oh I can feel the joy of being with my beautiful children. Wow, Zac talks a *lot*.' She laughs quietly to herself.

But the laughter soon fades, and Melissa shudders now as she cannot avoid being dragged back to what happened after she left her children sleeping. 'I can smell Billy's sweat and anger as he bails me up against a wall, fist in my hair and yelling into my face, "Look at you in your little skimpy bikini, trying to seduce every man that comes near you!"'

Melissa backs up against the wall of the pod, trying to escape him. 'He is *seething*... I am so frightened of him—' She drags herself away from this Experience. 'Why didn't I leave him? Why?' Her thoughts become muddled as she tries to remember how she could have stayed with him after so many of his jealous rages. Did he see Matthew at the beach? 'How could I have been so stupid? How? The ridiculous apologies every other week, and the guilt gifts all the time. How could I have been that stupid?' She curls up on the bed and finally drifts off to sleep.

~ ~ ~

When Melissa wakes, she looks around confused and slowly realises she is back in Bombetta's with Matthew. She sits up, instantly rejuvenated. 'I'm so happy as I follow Matthew's lead through the busy bar, and I cling to his hand so that I won't lose him. God! I love his scent! It is so, so subtle but familiar... so fresh, like he has just stepped out of the ocean. I feel so awkward at first, dancing in front of him, but I can feel his love as he encourages me. Oh, I love dancing with him. I don't want this night to end. His strong hands encircle my waist, lifting me up so high as the tempo of the music picks up, and we dance as one with the crowd until we are exhausted and he leads me out into the courtyard garden.

'We are alone amongst some potted trees. He pulls me close and I melt against him. His lips almost touch mine. I want nothing more than for him to kiss me, but we stay still, breathing and holding onto this moment. I want him so badly, but I'm scared, and feel someone is watching me. But... I want him and I don't care anymore. Billy has Janet, why should I care? But as a car drives past, its headlights light up a dark sports car. It can't be Billy, he's in Denmark, but I can't stop worrying. I'm terrified, and I race away from Matthew.

'At home, I quickly change into an oversized t-shirt and

bury myself in my bed, waiting nervously for Billy. I try so hard to stay awake, but eventually fall to sleep, fall right into an incredibly visual, sensual dream about Matthew.

'I'm dragged from this dream by a strong odour. Something is wrong. Billy stands in the doorway, in a fit of rage. The dream was so real to me and I panic that Matthew is with me. I pretend to be asleep but Billy pulls me out of the bed by my hair, rips off my shirt and screams into my face. "You bitch! You fucking still want him! But you'll never have him—never! You will NEVER HAVE HIM!" He holds my face so tight and forcefully kisses me. I pull away from him and he throws me aggressively onto the bed—' She stops and buries her head.

Hélène prompts her gently and Melissa responds. 'I had no recollection of this. Oh god, I was so frightened—' She stops suddenly trying to escape the nightmare.

Hélène says gently. 'Take your time. You are doing so well. Try to stay with it.'

Horrified, Melissa sits up on the edge of the bed as she becomes immersed again in what really happened that night. 'I'm terrified! My entire body is shaking as I desperately try to crawl out of my bedroom onto the pool deck towards the forest... I've hidden out here so many times before. He's coming! I try to run, to make it to the pool, but he grabs my hair and yanks me back. Billy is holding a syringe. "This is what you get, Melissa! You can blame Christensen for this! Do you know how fucked up I've been over him? My whole fucking life! I saw the way he looked at you that day of the surf competition and I saw the way you looked at him! Do you know how humiliating that was? You bitch! You never got over Christensen, did you, Melissa! Or should I call him *Martha*? Ha! You think you're so clever!"

'I can hear Billy ranting as the force of the paralysis takes hold, and my memory is slowly erased.'

Tears stream down Melissa's face as this projection slowly

fades. She can still feel herself collapsed on the deck in a trance-like state while Billy continues to rant in an angry, jealous rage. She watches him now without pity.

'Billy, you disgust me! You are sick! YOU ARE SO FUCKING SICK!'

This terrifying night fades and she sighs with relief. She closes her eyes and curls up on the bed.

~ ~ ~

Another intense brightness shines onto Melissa's eyelids. *No! I'm so tired! Go away! Va t'en!* She tries hard to keep her eyes closed and resume her sleep. She has no idea where she is being led and she doesn't care anymore. *I just need to sleep. Leave me alone. Go away Hélène, I've had enough!* The bright light continues to intensify, forcing her eyes open, and she is confronted by a huge image of her mother in a bikini at the beach. *Not my mother again!*

Memories lurk in her peripheral vision, memories she knows she wants to avoid. She focuses on some familiar film footage that had been shot on her father's old-style movie camera. She can see her mother, her father and Lilly flickering on and off, faster and faster, and she remembers that she saw these films when she was young, when her father was alive. She smiles as fast-motion footage shows her father holding Lilly's hand, proudly pointing at her mother's pregnant stomach. Melissa smiles as she watches some footage of her mother building sandcastles with Lilly. More projections from the movie camera begin to inundate her until she becomes dizzy and flops happily onto the bed again.

The light from a huge projection of a naked baby is so intense, she is forced to open her eyes again. She puts her hands up defensively as life-size images of famous people from history appear all around her. They are all hunched over and tap-dancing in this tiny roof cavity.

'What? What is this?' The sound of their shoes tapping is deafening, and she screams as she tries to respond to Hélène. 'I... I don't know what's happening; there are famous people... I don't know but it looks weird in here! It's as though the pod is wobbling and changing shape, getting smaller and larger and smaller again!'

The images come to life one after the other in a clockwise direction around the pod. She can't make sense of any of them. *I know I don't want to go here. Get me away! I'm not going here!* Her body begins to tremble and her face slowly contorts as the muscles collapse like jelly. Sweat drips off her. 'My god, this is painful!' She stumbles to the bucket and leans over it. 'I'm going to be sick.' She waits, sweating and trembling, but nothing happens, so she sprays herself with water, and the sound of the tap-dancing finally dissipates...

# CHAPTER 36

Hélène yawns, leans back on her chair and asks Eric how Matthew is doing.

'Okay. He was very freaked out at first; I thought he was going to do a runner. Definitely blocking for a long time but I think he will get there. Do you know the relationship between the two of them? I assumed they were a—'

'Me too,' Hélène smirks. 'They are just good friends *apparently*, but they are a lot more than that by the looks of things.'

'Yes, I think so too,' Eric says, raising his eyebrows and grinning.

Hélène grins back. 'Yes, well, Melissa has been up and down. She is doing very well at really feeling everything. On a scale of one to ten, I would give her a ten.'

Eric turns back to his screen. 'Oh, have a look! What do you make of this?'

Hélène looks over at his screen and sees Matthew grabbing at something up at the ceiling.

Paco calls to Eric. 'Keep your eye on Matthew, his heart rate and blood pressure are right up.'

Eric nods as he watches the monitor. 'Yes, he looks distressed. He keeps jumping up at the ceiling. I've tried to get him to speak but haven't had any luck yet.' He tries again to prompt Matthew. 'Stay with it…'

Matthew is sweating and jumping at the ceiling. He finally screams. 'Monty is howling… I'm trying to unlock my front door but I can't get the fucking key to work. Something is desperately wrong, I've never heard him like this. When the door finally opens, I scream. "No! No! No!" I try to lift her down, but this fucking chair is broken, I keep falling over the broken pieces as I try to hold her body up. I keep trying to balance on the broken chair but it keeps collapsing… this fucking chair… I don't know what to do—'

Matthew stops suddenly.

Eric waits a couple of minutes and then prompts him gently.

Out of breath, Matthew finally resumes, crying as he speaks, 'I know it's too late but I try to hold her body up while I try to pull another chair over closer with my foot—'

Eric prompts him again.

'I can't look at her! I… can't! I can't! Her hands are stuck under the rope and she keeps spinning… spinning… Monty is whimpering. I try desperately to stop myself from looking at her face while I am trying to lift her down, but she keeps spinning around, facing me. Oh god, Katryn, why did you do this? Why? I struggle to lift her lifeless body down. You look so sad. So, so sad. As though you know you made a mistake. Why didn't I answer your calls? I'm so sorry, Katryn. I'm so, so sorry. I can't untie the damn rope; it's so tight. I can't get it off. Ah, finally it is loosening, I'll just gently lower you down and we can lie on the rug next to Monty.'

He closes his eyes and sighs loudly. 'Ah, this feels incredible… I feel… God, this feels so good at last! I don't even think she meant to do it… I think the chair broke.' He breathes out loudly and forcefully. As he begins to drift off to sleep, he mutters, 'Okay, this is good. This is all I need. I'm not going through anymore.'

~ ~ ~

Matthew gasps for air as he wakes to bright projections slowly evolving all around him. *Fuck, I don't want to go here. This keeps lurking somewhere in my subconscious, but I know I don't want to go here.*

He can hear Eric prompting. *I know you are just doing your job, Eric, but I'm sorry, I've had enough.* Matthew showers himself in water from the hose, wipes himself off and yells, 'I can't take any more! I can't do this!'

Eric responds gently. 'I know it's very hard, but this is important.'

The brightness within the pod forces him to look, and he is relieved. 'Oh, thank god... I'm so happy. Melissa has finally arrived at the party. We dance and have so much fun and then we talk so deeply... it's amazing... amazing that I have confided in her what I've never told anyone in my entire life. I've finally revealed the guilt that's haunted me all my life.

'Out of nowhere, Billy's arrived. He glares at me with such hatred and pulls Melissa away. When he starts to push her around... I want to help her but she won't let me. He won't stop pushing her. I am so angry! I want to help her but she doesn't want anyone to help.' He frowns and stares curiously as more and more memories with Melissa progress.

Matthew smiles and concentrates. 'Ah... this is the song Melissa loves, "My sweet meat pie", she looks so pretty and we're about to kiss but then she disappears. I try to follow her and at last, I find her... This is so confusing, I don't know where we are now, I grab her hand, hold it tight and run with her towards the light but she disappears. I run and run and as I turn, I see her following me I want to tell her that I know her, but I'm afraid. I don't want to remind her again of that horrendous night. I don't want to lose her again. I want her to stay here with me, but she keeps running away. I hold her hand again as tightly as I can… I don't want to ever lose her again… I don't know what's happening… I feel like I am being transported all over the place… Melissa keeps disappearing.'

~ ~ ~

A loud smashing reverberates throughout the pod and Matthew shudders. 'This is too hard… I can't do this… Not my parents! Not my parents! I cannot go back to this time, it's too painful.' He buries his head under the pillow but the sound of a car skidding and finally smashing are so disturbing. 'NO!'

He grips his head. 'No! No! No!'

Eric gently prompts him again. 'You can do this, Matthew. Just take it slowly.'

Matthew sighs, and after a long pause, responds. 'I'm terrified. I'm in the back of our family car and my mother is screaming. "Don't hit the brakes! Don't hit the brakes or we'll keep skidding." But my father keeps braking and the car keeps skidding out of control. We're so close to the edge of the cliff… it won't stop… and I can see we're just about to go over the edge. I close my eyes and then suddenly I am jerked forward and there is this loud smashing sound… and then everything's dark and silent.' Matthew breathes heavily and sprays himself with some water. He pauses while he gets his breath. 'All I see is black… and I can't move… I can hear something getting louder and louder and when I finally see again, there are huge metal blades coming close to my head as this heavy machinery is cutting our car apart.'

Matthew keels over and holds his stomach in pain.

Eric prompts him gently again and he continues. 'I want my mother to turn around to us, but she's perfectly still. I wait and wait but she doesn't move. The blades are getting so close to her head and I'm frightened they're going to cut her. I can't see her face. I need her to look after my sister and me, but she still doesn't move. I can't see my father; the roof is caved in and my sister is crying. I try to comfort her, but I can't move. I'm trapped.' Matthew sniffs. 'When the car is finally pulled apart, my mother's seat falls back...

'Oh god! Oh god! Her bloodied face is on top of my knee... her eyes are just fixed... staring. I want her to say something but she just stares.'

Matthew falls to his knees, leans over the bed and covers his eyes. 'No. I don't want to see her again. I can't...'

Eric encourages Matthew once more.

After a long silence Matthew resumes. 'She's right there in front of me. Blood dripping from her forehead. She doesn't say anything. She just keeps staring.' He shakes his head. 'No! I don't want to be here. It's too painful!'

'It's okay, you're safe,' Eric says kindly. 'Just take your time.'

Matthew takes a shuddering breath. 'I'm screaming. People are taking us away from our mother and father. They don't listen, they cover our eyes and take us away. There's lots of blood on my leg, but I can't feel it. My sister is lying on a stretcher and I want to go to her... but I can't get to her.'

He curls up on the bed 'This is excruciating. I've relived the guilt and the shame of this nightmare so many times.' He closes his eyes and sighs loudly as he is transported back to just before this tragedy. He gets up from the bed and smiles when he sees his mother. 'Oh, I loved my mother. She's smiling at Jane and me with such tenderness. She's just peeled a mandarin and as she turns, she passes my sister and I a segment each and says. "It's a beautiful sweet one and I've pulled the pips out for you both. We'll be at the beach soon, kids. Aunty Helen is so excited to see you both." We drive on for a while and then my sister starts to whinge and kicks her legs onto mine. I push her legs back away from me and she whinges louder. My father keeps yelling at me to leave my sister alone, but she keeps kicking and kicking and won't stop. I finally push her and growl at her to stop. My father yells at me, turns around and looks me directly in the eyes as he swerves into the side of the cliff—'

Matthew stops abruptly and buries his head into the bed, sobbing. 'Oh god! What have I done?'

Eric's voice is soft and smooth. 'You're doing really well. Stay there.'

Matthew lifts his head from the bed and resumes. 'These adults just drag us away from the accident scene. I needed... I just want to see my parents... just one more time. Just one more time! I want them to know I'm so sorry I caused the accident. It was my fault. I want them to know how sorry I am.' Matthew closes his eyes and weeps into the pillow.

~~~

The sun reflecting brightly onto the ocean wakes Matthew.

Eric sees him stir and asks, 'Are you ready to keep going?'

Matthew pushes his hair out of his eyes, focuses. 'Yes. I'm feeling so much better. Wow. Yes, I think this is... Yes, this is just after the accident and I'm walking down to Third Point on my own. Replaying the accident over and over, trying to block the nightmare. I'm so grateful my aunt offered to look after my sister and me. I know she's devastated after losing her sister. I love her so much and feel so guilty and I want to tell her that it was my fault but I'm too frightened. I wished I could tell someone.' He pauses and sighs heavily.

Matthew squints as he focuses in on the projection. 'I'm walking from my aunt's and I can see them. They're here nearly every day, this man and his two daughters. As usual, he's treading water in the surf as his two young daughters jump off the rocks to him and he helps them onto the waves, so they can surf back to the shore. They don't notice me at all, and I'm too
~~~

shy to go near them. There's this strange… affection I have for the younger girl. It's something I've never before felt. I don't understand this feeling. It's totally foreign but is so real. It builds as I watch her smiling and playing so happily here every day. I wish I had the guts to—' Matthew lies down on the bed and becomes immersed in this time when he had first seen Melissa.

~ ~ ~

Hélène yells to Paco and Arjun who quickly switch their screen views to Melissa's pod. 'She's obviously trying to block. Looks like she's really trying to avoid something huge.'

Paco checks another computer. 'Her heart rate and blood pressure are high, but they're okay at this point, given the amount of spinning she's doing…'

Melissa's voice comes softly through the speaker. 'I don't want to go here… I want to get out of here. I feel so heavy…'

Paco gets up and says to Arjun. 'She'll be okay but keep an eye on her vitals.'

Desperately searching for the buzzer, Melissa tries to call out, but no sound emerges. She can see Billy through thick steam and realises she is now in her bathroom. 'I can smell Billy's stale whisky as he tries to kiss me. I'm sickened by the smell of his sweat and the alcohol. I spit at him and manage to get away only to back myself into the mirrored wall as he comes right up to my face until his lips are almost touching mine. He screams, "Oh, fuck—I've got a problem!" Billy grabs a syringe from on top of the vanity and says, "Don't worry; you won't remember a thing."

'I struggle and struggle until finally Billy injects something into my spine and says, "Hey, honey, I just want to pick you up and take you to bed and cuddle you. Now back to sleep and forget everything that's happened." I'm so confused… I can't see where Billy is… the steam has turned into a thick fog and now there are dirty soldiers pulling my head up by my hair... by my extremely long hair. My head is hurting as they pull me higher, screaming and spluttering into my face in a foreign language. My limbs are about to fail... and I drop heavily onto the bathroom tiles.'

Melissa sighs in pain. 'I want to get away from here, but I can't escape. The cold from the tiles penetrates my naked body. As he leaves the bathroom, Billy says snidely, "You'll never have anyone else, Melissa. Never." He turns off the bathroom light, shuts the door behind him and I am paralysed, stuck with this lingering stench. When some movement comes back to me, I cry out, determined to remember what's just happened. But it keeps fading from my memory no matter how hard I try to hold onto it.'

Sitting up on the edge of the bed in the pod, Melissa forces herself out of this nightmare. She is out of breath and takes a large drink of water and curls up on the bed. Covering her head with her hands, she forces the memory away. Every time she sees Billy, she strains to push him away. 'GET AWAY FROM ME!'

She stifles a sob. 'When are these nightmares of Billy going to stop!' She sits up on the end of the bed and stares with a cold intensity until finally the projection fades and she sighs with relief before falling back onto the bed.

~ ~ ~

Castillo congratulates his colleagues in the hub. 'Well done. You're all doing an exceptional job. It can be very tedious waiting while the client's psyche is searching.' He does his rounds of the monitors and when he gets to Hélène's, he stops. 'Looks like you have some activity in there again now. It's obvious she is blocking, judging by all that spinning.'

'Yes, she Released something maybe an hour ago, which was

huge. Her body showed large signs of stress and she shouted Billy's name a lot, which is her husband. I think she did a lot of releasing through that experience. She's been great at staying completely in the moment, wherever it is taking her. A lot of these recent events have not been pleasant, unfortunately, but she's staying with them and allowing the pain of her emotions to Release. She has picked up the buzzer several times but stops just before pressing it.'

Paco calls to Castillo. 'Melissa's vital signs are worrying.'

Castillo sits at Melissa's monitor and asks Paco to turn the lights up in the pod. 'Okay, we'll give her a couple of minutes and if she still wants to get out, we may have to intervene. Whatever it is she's trying to avoid will be vital to her success of this process, but she is very distressed. We will need to turn down the SEMS for the moment and keep monitoring her closely.'

They watch Melissa staring straight into one of the cameras as though she can see something through it. And they record the unusual sounds coming through the speakers. She's mumbling and appears to be terrified. Finally, she pleads into the camera in English and French.

Paco looks worried as he studies another computer screen. 'Her heart rate is really high again. We're going to have to keep a really close eye on it.'

Arjun nods at Hélène. 'Okay, now we're getting almost full sentences in French, which is great, as we have the right person in place. Paco, are her vitals okay yet?'

Paco nods unconvincingly and moments later, he gives a more convincing nod.

Hélène and Arjun put headphones on and turn up the volume from Melissa's pod. Hélène gently encourages her to describe what she is experiencing in both French and English.

Melissa huddles herself. She's totally confused and repulsed by what she's experiencing. 'Va t'en! C'est tellement horrible... It is so horrible.' She screws up her face and frowns heavily, taking a moment to respond to Hélène's questions. 'Um... there are people... people just lying on these... these low benches. It looks like they're... Oh... Oh god! They're being decapitated! It is horrible!'

She cries profusely, closes her eyes, and tries to block this Experience, but the more she tries, the more she feels herself being drawn back to this time. Her eyes fill with tears and she jumps between French and English. 'The air is so dirty and smoky. I can't breathe. Je ne peux pas respirer... Dead people... personnes mortes... are piled on top of each other. Oh god; oh mon dieu! Young children... jeunes enfants... are piled on top of each other. They are being burned, and the stench is horrendous... La puanteure est horrible! There is so much sadness everywhere. Only sadness... seulement la tristesse...'

Arjun raises his eyebrows to Hélène. 'She's definitely regressed into a past life where English and French are the dominant languages.'

Paco announces loudly, 'Okay, her adrenaline is skyrocketing. She's avoiding a Release at the moment.'

'What is this?' Melissa suddenly jolts as she feels herself being forced back to this time. Nausea swirls as she recognizes the fat, bald man above her, forcing himself on her. She knows him well, and tries to fight him off, but feels suffocated, unable to yell out.

Watching Melissa closely on her monitor, Hélène asks her gently, 'What is worrying you? What can you see? Que peux-tu voir? What are the smells? Quelles sont les odeurs? What do you hear?'

Melissa closes her eyes tightly, trying to make herself invisible. She can hear Hélène prompting her but is terrified to stay back in this time. Melissa tries to force the memories away.

*I'm not going here. No. I can't go here. I can't!*

Hélène waits a while before prompting her again. Melissa presses her face into the mattress and covers her ears with her hands. 'I do not want to be back in this time. I have to get out of here! *Now!*' She shudders as the memories overwhelm her and cries out in a mixture of English and French. 'The noise... et le bruit! The noise est horrible! It is screeching... il crie! It sounds metallic...ça sonne métallique! It is the cries of people... people being tortured. Desperate mothers, and les cris des enfants... So many desperate, destitute children...'

Melissa weeps. *I'm not going here... No way! No way! Non! No way! This is too much! I've got to stop this!*

Hélène can see Melissa is blocking, and softly reassures her. 'There is nothing that can harm you now, Melissa, and the more you can endure, the more they will be Released.'

Melissa looks slowly all around her, and grimaces at what she sees. Her voice shakes. 'No... I can't do this... Non! I do not want to be back here! Mon dieu, je ne veux pas être ici! Even the air doesn't feel right. It is thick, and a rusty orange colour... and it smells so heavy... l'air est lourd. It is putrid and it's hard to breathe. There are people everywhere and... and... ils sont... they are... so dirty. And la puanteur... the stench is unbearable...' She pauses. 'My clothes sont noir... my clothes are black and they're heavy and uncomfortable. Ils sont serrés... they're tight... et je ne peux pas respire. I can't breathe. The stench is thick, and I'm suffocating under these clothes.' She sits up, gasping for breath. 'Il ne reste plus d'air! There is no air left!'

Her voice falters, as though she's being strangled, and she strains to breathe. 'It is... I don't know... it's like you can taste the air. It's so thick with... with... mort et décadence... death and decay... with rotting corpses.'

Melissa falls to her knees. 'I feel physically ill... No more! No more! I don't want to be here!'

Hélène can see Melissa's distress and waits until she calms down. When she sees Melissa pick herself up from the floor, she encourages her again to Release. Hélène can see from her actions and the SEMS feedback that Melissa is still blocking.

Melissa paces manically back and forth in the pod. *I can't be here! Get me away from here!* She suddenly groans loudly and heavily as though she is exorcising something out of her. And then, something wells inside of her, and she feels an overwhelming compulsion to describe everything she is experiencing. 'I know this place! I know this time! I've been here before! I can feel the coarse fabric on my skin, it's so tight around my neck! I can feel the pain of the bruises my husband, Guillaume, has inflicted. He is brutal... a brutal savage...'

Melissa instinctively pushes down on the hollow of her neck. She's done this regularly for as long as she can remember, ensuring that her pendant is safe. There's a long pause and then Melissa stands. 'It's hard to get enough air to breathe! Il fait chaud... the air feels hot... as it enters votre bouche... as it enters your mouth. It feels contaminated and it doesn't move, even as we move through it. You can't feel it on your skin, it's so thick and stagnant. I'm sitting in an open carriage surrounded by dirty people... peasants... just pleading with me... paysans... implorant avec moi!'

She closes her eyes, screws up her face and feels around her body, reluctantly describing what she is experiencing in a slow, strained voice. 'The seat feels like... like it's made of coarse hay... under... under something like velvet. It makes such a noise as we move, and we're moving quite jerkily. A carriage. I'm in a carriage... horse-driven, and there are soldiers on horseback riding alongside. I'm eating something... I don't know what... Oh, it's... it is *disgusting!* It tastes very much like the stench of the air. There's an old, fat woman asleep in the seat opposite me, wearing an ornate, jewelled gown. She's slouching and has dribble running down her chin. This woman is known to me... And now somebody rides up beside the carriage and he's calling to me. I think he's calling me Marianne... Yes, Marianne... He seems to be waiting for me to give him some kind of order and meanwhile, all these people are crowding around the carriage, pleading with me for something...'

Melissa pauses, confused, and suddenly her voice completely changes from sounding hesitant and confused to loud and commanding. She raises her head, elongates her neck, and proclaims in a loud, pompous English accent, 'I DESPAIRRRR of these peasants! I DEMAAANDD that you get them away from me!

'All these people... they're begging me! Pleading with me! I am the powerful one and I care not about anyone! My horrid mother is lying opposite me, drunk as usual, and I'm happy she's sleeping because she lets me alone. I'm hungry and I want to eat, but this meat tastes disgusting. I'm gorging myself on fruit and morsels of meat, but everything is rancid, so I spit it out. The noise of the carriage, and the horses, and... and all of these people crowding around is overwhelming.'

This Experience is all so vivid that Melissa becomes even more distressed. She knows now that she is truly a part of the reality where she feels she is trapped. Melissa has now become Marianne; she can feel it to her core. She reaches manically for the small pendant around her neck, presses it firmly into the hollow between her collarbones. She slides her hands around her neck ensuring that the chain is still intact; it had been ripped from her neck by her husband many times but was never broken. When she looks at her fingertips, there's a tiny trace of blood.

She takes shallow breaths as she continues to describe where she has found herself, and once again she hesitates to breathe for fear of being contaminated by the stench; by this smell she knows so well. Melissa is completely immersed in her surroundings and she knows her presence is definitely felt by the people around her – they are awaiting her command on this country road in the south of France in 1743.

Melissa looks confused. 'I can feel these people waiting for me, but... I'm caught up in some kind of dream or another reality and finally I nod, and the horses move much faster. I can truly feel the uncomfortable pull of the horses struggling to drag my carriage across the rugged terrain as we pass horrific scenes of dead bodies just strewn about like garbage. And there are people... people just lying lifeless... and rotting animal carcasses.'

A heavy, rusty fog lingers low in the air and Melissa feels herself drawn deeper into this arrogant, imperious woman. It feels completely natural to her that she *is* Marianne; but she also wants to escape this selfish, horrid person whom she despises. Melissa cannot assimilate at all, but somehow feels unable to escape this duality.

In a confused, strained voice she begins again to describe where she is. 'Marianne is pulling... I mean, *I* am pulling pained and arrogant expressions in the carriage. She grabs... I mean... *I* grab my cloak to cover my mouth from the stench. I am... I am like... a spoilt child. I totally despise this life and I despise everyone in it.'

As the Marianne persona takes hold, Melissa's voice becomes more and more arrogant. 'My cape is heavily laden with gold and precious stones and it is scratching the skin of my neck. It is so tight... it is suffocating. I am thirsty and I am hungry, and I have no care for what is happening around me, or for these peasants. I care only for my own hunger and thirst. The carriage is moving quickly through the drab, grey countryside. "Hurry!" I order the coachman, and the horses start to falter in the muddy terrain. I just want to get away from this misery. I am shouting, I am impatient. I need to be away from this contamination!

'I drink some wine but it is also sour, so I spit it out of the carriage window. I have not a care in the world. I spit upon one of the peasants and throw the bottle without caring it may hit someone. I look back as we drive on and see people pushing at each other to get to the wine bottle and I laugh heartily. I am so happy my mother is totally out to it, lying uncomfortably on the seat opposite me.'

Melissa pauses, exhausted and sickened by Marianne's obnoxious demeanour. She struggles to rid herself of the feelings of this inner tyrant. Tears roll down her cheeks as the memories become clearer and she finds she still can't escape this arrogant, heartless character that is now taking over her. 'I feel some pleasure at last about the game I have devised. They are like savages... like wild animals, and I laugh when I throw meat and it falls in the mud and they fight over it! I find more things in the carriage to throw at them. Je suis vivante! I am alive!'

Melissa draws her legs up to her chest and wraps her arms around them. *Who is this vile person and why am I a part of her? I need to get out of here!* She is pained by this Experience and is determined to escape this creature festering inside of her. She searches for the buzzer again but is unable to find it. She rocks back and forth until this overwhelming urge to Release overpowers her.

Hélène notices Melissa's heartbeat increasing rapidly and she watches closely as her demeanour seems to change dramatically as she returns to Marianne, struggling as she tries to separate herself and speak as an observer.

Melissa's voice falters. 'I... I can feel... her... Marianne, inside of me. It's sickening but I can't seem to escape her.'

Hélène gently coaxes her. 'It can be extremely difficult but please try to stay with it. I am sure this is where you are needing to go.'

There is a short silence and Hélène waits.

Melissa straightens her back and sits herself up on the side of the bed. She smiles arrogantly, composes her face, flares her nostrils and continues to describe the game Marianne has just devised. 'We are going up a steep hill now and the horses are stumbling and faltering. The peasants are making way for me, bowing their heads. I love this power; it is glorious. I care not for their misery. I long to be home. I want to eat *fresh* meat... and drink my mulled wine... and most of all, I want my pure, specially refined opium!'

The Marianne persona takes over Melissa completely. 'I hate this world! I despise this world! Je déteste ce monde! Je méprise ce monde! I abhor this world and everyone and everything in it! How I long to be at home again in my clean, white nightgown away from all of this.'

Melissa is suddenly overpowered by Marianne's memories of her ornate bedroom. Hélène prompts her and she responds softly, 'Marianne is standing in her white nightgown, brushing her waist-length hair aggressively in her ornate bedroom. She's staring at herself in the mirror, with each brush stroke she is thinking angrily, 'I wish this horrendous nightmare of what happened three years ago would go away but it won't! That horrific night! The night I regretted for so, so long. I had inhaled as much opium as I possibly could. I did this often to ease the pain of my existence. My face was covered in the white powder and as I was brushing my hair, I felt so much anger with my husband and his obsession with me, so I shaved off all my hair. As I looked at my reflection, I smiled and despised myself intensely until all my hair was gone. I had hoped this would stop Guillaume's delusional obsession...'

Melissa closes her eyes as she remembers the pain of this time. 'I regretted this for three excruciating years. My opium supply was cut off until my hair grew. Oh, how I suffered during that time. Extreme withdrawals. After that day, I knew I would never do anything that could sabotage my opium supply ever again. The thought still haunts me. I discard my brush on the dresser, and quickly fill my nostrils with as much opium as I can inhale.

'I had just picked up my brush again when I spied Guillaume standing in the doorway with a large bottle of whisky. I shuddered. The light was dim, but I could still see his short, slovenly, half-naked body, with his childish smirk. *You are so repulsive. So disgustingly hideous. I feel nauseous at the sight and smell of you. The stench of your whisky makes me want to vomit. La puanteur de ton whisky me donne envie de vomir.*

'He looked me up and down and snarled, "Your distaste for me, mon amour, only drives my sadistic nature even wilder…" He stood in the doorway with his gold-embroidered dressing gown open, exposing his grotesque, hairy stomach. He raised his eyebrows as he looked my body up and down. "I am intoxicated by your beauty, mon amour." I screwed up my face with distaste and he raised his eyebrows, acknowledging my reaction. Then he smiled as he slowly curled the hairs on his stomach around and around his navel as he masochistically enjoyed seeing my repulsion. Drunk and staggering, he held my hair in his hand and sniffed it, "Why do you tend to your hair yourself, Marianne?"

'I glared at him defiantly, "I cannot stand to have *your* people fussing over me." He then forced me over to my four-poster bed. As he pushed me down, he tripped and almost fell into the large fireplace. He looked up at me and put out his hand for me to help but before I could move, he scowled and rolled over onto his hands and knees and struggled to pull himself up off the floor. He yanked back the curtain that surrounded my bed, pushed me down and then climbed on top of me. I did not struggle. I am completely powerless as I endured my fate.'

Melissa begins to cry, closing her eyes tightly and trying to make this horrendous Experience go away. She shudders violently before she continues. 'I can feel him and now I can see him on top of me! I can see Guillaume's hairy back covered with sweat and varicose veins in the mirror built into the ceiling of my bed. I can see his bald head with a bit of auburn-coloured tufts of hair at the sides. I can't breathe... I feel claustrophobic. I feel like I am suffocating under the weight of this horrendous creature.

'He screams at me over and over. "Vous détendre! Vous détendre!" Tears stream down my face and I clench my pendant as he tries to kiss me. I try to endure his kiss, but his breath is so detestable, I can't help but spit. He laughs, grabs my neck, and almost chokes me.'

Melissa feels this pain as her own, and with deep empathy continues to describe what Marianne is forced regularly to endure. 'She's powerless to do anything to stop him. He controls her. He's drunk and he is... raping her. Her hair is trapped under his elbow, pinning her to the bed, and she says repeatedly, *"I detest this slothful, sadistic creature."* She can do nothing but lie there and accept her fate. She's tried so many times to escape but each time she's suffered horrendous punishment afterwards.'

Melissa remembers clearly resigning herself to this torturous life, which was only made barely tolerable due to her endless supply of opium. It took almost two years for her hair to grow back past her shoulders, and after several suicide attempts, Guillaume unblocked her access to her supplier.

Melissa shudders as she sees the image again of herself in the carriage. She desperately does not want to go back to this time. She forces her head into the pillow, trying to escape. Hélène's constant prompting is annoying and frustrating as Melissa is determined not to return to this day.

CHAPTER 37

Hélène stands up and stretches. 'Hey, Eric, I really think she needs a break and so do I. This is very intense. Can you keep an eye on my monitor? I need a bit of fresh air, but I have my beeper on.'

Hélène is concerned when she returns soon after and sees Melissa rocking back and forth manically. 'It's okay. It's okay. Nothing can hurt you... just try and stay with it.'

Melissa takes her time, staring violently as the image of her ornate bedroom is still fading. She shudders, repulsed by the horrendous memories of her husband in this room, and desperately wants to avoid going back to this day in the carriage. Taking her time, she allows the memory to settle.

She sighs loudly as she allows herself to re-live this horrendous time again when she's back in the carriage as it jolts over a rut in the road, and Melissa becomes one with Marianne. 'I shake my head and shut my eyes tight, desperately trying to get this memory of my husband out of my head. My drunken mother slouches opposite me, just about to fall to the floor. I would love nothing more than to throw her from the carriage but I fear her wrath, so I make sure she is supported. Ma mère est une imbécile. My mother stirs and wipes the dribble from her chin and falls back into a drunken slumber.

'I would like to get drunk, but the wines are sour, so I spit out another mouthful of wine and throw another bottle out of the carriage, laughing uproariously as it hits someone on the head. The man is angry as blood starts dripping down his forehead. He picks up the bottle and shakes it threateningly in my direction. I am outraged. All around him people are urging him to put the bottle down. He ignores their pleas, staring into my eyes – the eyes of this creature that has not a care in the world for who she trespasses against. He dares to look so defiantly at me? Incensed by this provocation, I order the carriage drivers to stop and the horses clatter to a halt.'

Melissa stops, she's feeling Marianne's emotions as her own. She presses her palms firmly against the hollow of her neck and tries to centre herself. This Experience has become completely invasive, and Melissa knows that she has no choice, she has to be back here, at this time.

She closes her eyes and breathes deeply at the intensity of Marianne's feelings penetrating her body, and the memory of what happened next becomes clearer and clearer to her. 'Marianne demands that this insolent man be brought before her. People rush away from him in fear as he stands defiant, alone and powerful.'

Melissa jumps off the bed quickly. She knows exactly what happens next and she wants to stop Marianne. 'NO, NO! LET HIM GO!' But no matter how much she wants to stop Marianne, Melissa knows she cannot change what happens next.

Deeply melancholic, Melissa continues observing what she wishes she could stop. 'Marianne is even more outraged now. Again, she orders her horsemen to bring this man to her. The man stands his ground, but the horsemen finally overpower him and he is brought before her, blood dripping from his brow. He has no fear. Marianne cannot see him clearly through the foggy haze. From her carriage, he looks like any peasant but as he nears, it becomes clear that he is strikingly handsome; his long, dark hair pulled back from his face, wearing a clean, white linen shirt.

Marianne's persona and Melissa meld together as one right at this moment when she sees him clearly. Tears instantly stream down her face, and Melissa describes Marianne's thoughts, which are so profoundly her own.

'Oh god… I know this man! He is the man I would never forget. The man I have longed for my entire life. I love him as I've never loved another. Mon dieu; how did this happen? How can this be… to find you here now? Non! Non! Non! NON! Il est mort! Il est mort! He is dead! He is dead!' These words had haunted her since that tragic day. 'This can't be! I *know* he is dead!' She cries, her hands gripping the carriage window frame. 'Luca… is it you? Luca?'

Melissa reaches again for the hollow of her neck, deeply grief-stricken. The pod becomes completely dark. She sits still, agonizing over the guilt and deep remorse.

~ ~ ~

An intense brightness forces Melissa's eyes to open. She squints as she tries to adjust to her new surroundings when a strange sense of familiarity seems to waken something deep within her and she embraces this time with Luca when they were young. *I remember this time so clearly. We were so in love and so happy.*

Melissa sits up happily, eager to be revisiting this earlier time. She allows herself to be swept away, responding quickly to Hélène's prompting. 'We are naked in the glistening ocean, laughing and happy. Luca lifts me just above the water, kisses my stomach excitedly, puts his mouth to my stomach and whispers. "Notre beau bébé, mon amour… Our beautiful baby, my love." He slowly moves his lips around my body, up to my breasts and my neck, to my face and lips. We are so happy as we wait and watch the tide recede from the cliffs of the headland. We wait for hours, until finally he smiles. "It is time." Slowly, he manoeuvres me onto his back. We have practiced many times to make our way to the caverns beyond the headland. Today we must go farther, we must get to our cove. Our sanctuary!

'We both breathe in deeply as we dive deep beneath the waves and together, we are carried briskly with the outgoing tide. Once we are beyond the headland, we swim toward the strong ocean current ahead. The force draws us in until we are at onc within it. Wc love this exhilarating experience as we are swept along. But suddenly, I lose my grip on him, struggling to hold my breath. He holds me tightly with one arm, fighting the force of the water with his other arm, and changes our course. He turns me on my side, and I gasp for breath. I almost lose consciousness as he lifts me out of the water into this golden cavern of rocks hidden within the headland.

'"Ah, mon amour! Mon amour!" He kisses me tenderly. He lies behind me, cradling me into him. Shivers pass through my body as he kisses my neck, and soon the movement of our entwined bodies becomes synchronised with the ebb and flow of the lapping waves...

'We lie for hours, waiting for the tide to change again. We know the ocean is the only way to reach our cove, where we know we will be safe. It's impossible for the soldiers and horses to pass. "We can't ever go back, Rianne."'

Lying down on the bed, Melissa closes her eyes and smiles as she allows herself to cherish this time. She snuggles back into Luca's naked body, enjoying the moment, until the shattering memory of what Marianne said next comes back, and she relays it to Hélène. 'Marianne says, "I have to see my mother once more so she knows I will be safe, mon amour. Then we will return." Luca looks into my eyes, shocked. "Oh, non mon amour! C'est trop dangereux! Your mother has forbidden us to marry. She will make you marry her cousin."

'"No Luca. My mother would never do that, and when Guillaume finds out I am with child, *your* child, he will not wish to marry me. No man would wish to marry a woman carrying a child of another man."

'"Non, Rianne! He is obsessed with you! Il est obsédé par toi!"' Luca looks at me sadly and shakes his head. "Oh non, mon amour. Your mother is devious. Ta mère est sournoise. Sournoise!"'

'Tears well in his eyes, and he looks at me pleading. '"Non mon amour. Tu vois la vie en rose. La vie en rose, Rianne."'

Melissa groans loudly. 'Through rose-coloured glasses, that is for sure. Going back was a devastating mistake. How could I have been so blind to my devious mother? Oh, how could my own mother betray me?' She sits on the bed and wraps her arms tightly around herself. 'Why did I return... why... for my selfish mother's sake!'

Feeling once again the deep pain and regret at the massive mistake she had made by going back, Melissa does not want to remember. She wants to block, but the brightness of the sunny day forces her eyes open again, and she can see Marianne and Luca the day they had returned, walking hand in hand through the busy marketplace as they had done so many times before.

'We were so young and naive and in love. It was a beautiful, bright, sunny day and I had just been back to see my mother, to tell her that I was with child, Luca's child and that we would be safe in our cove on the other side of the headland. We were so happy but I knew Luca was still worried about my mother. People were busy buying and selling their wares; the marketplace was alive with all sorts of entertainers and musicians; children were playing; and animals were wandering freely. We enjoyed the lively music and entertainment, and we were excited as we were heading back to our cove, to our sanctuary. Then, in the distance, the sound of horse's hooves hammering on the clay road. In a flash, the ambience of the market changed as these soldiers appeared, thundering into the marketplace, knocking people out of their way.'

Melissa feels the full intensity of this moment now. 'Luca grabbed my hand. "Oh non, mon amour… Your mother must have told her cousin. We should never have returned, Rianne!"

'I was so frightened and angry with my mother and I cursed myself over and over. "This is all my fault… all my fault! Tout est ma faute… c'est ma faute! Ma mère… my mother has betrayed me for her own greedy gain! My own flesh and blood. So that I will marry her despicable cousin. She knows I am pregnant with *your* child. Oh, ma mère! Ma mère! I am so, so sorry, mon amour!" The disturbing squeals of the horses reverberate through the marketplace as the soldiers descend upon us. People scurry away in droves.'

Melissa takes a shuddering breath as she continues. 'We run together, our hands clinging tightly to each other until the horses physically force us apart. The horses rear up in front of Luca, but he manages to throw something to me. I hold it tightly to my chest and hide under a table with other people who have been unable to escape. Huge soldiers' boots surround the table where I am hiding, and I wait nervously for what feels like an eternity. When they finally leave, I carefully open my hand and see the intricate, complex, spiral-inspired pendant and chain Luca had spent months designing and forging for me. I quickly hide it in my chemise—

'Whoa, this is incredibly intense.' Melissa stares and places her two hands over the hollow of her neck. She breathes out loudly and continues. 'I search the streets frantically and eventually I find Luca in the hollow of a dead tree, bloodied and bruised. "Non! Non! Mon amour." I am sure he is dead. I cry on his chest and listen and I hear a faint heartbeat. I fetch water and dab it onto his lips. I clean the blood from his face and he looks into my eyes, 'I thought they took you, Rianne… I thought they got you.' His kiss is gentle, filled with relief. "Mon amour, we must go now, or we will never get another chance."

'The skies are turning grey and the ocean is whipping up ferociously as we reach the beach. We are frightened of the soldiers returning as we wait on the shoreline for the tide to recede. Shivering, we huddle together, fretting as the waterline on the cliffs lowers so slowly. The sky darkens, the waves have become almost wrathful, but we know this is our last chance to escape. We take off our clothes; they will hold us back.

'I pull out the intricate spiral pendant that I had hidden earlier. "Mon amour, this is the most perfect pendant I have ever seen. It's like… um a treble clef or… or… or maybe it's an ampersand and chameleon's tail." He smiles, clasps it and pats it into the hollow of my neck. We look out at the wild, grey ocean. And hope.'

~ ~ ~

Blinking slowly, Melissa is overcome with emotion. She can feel the fear of entering the huge, grey ocean and she can deeply feel her intense love for Luca. She knows this Experience. She's lived it. Melissa shivers at Luca's breath near her ear. "'Once we are past the headland, Rianne, we are free. Suis les marées… follow the tides and the currents will carry us to the caverns."

'The frigid water laps at my feet. My heart races and my body trembles as the ground vibrates beneath us. I'm too frightened to turn around as I know the horses are very close. We run naked into the wild, grey ocean holding tight to each other, desperately pushing against the waves.

'The soldiers are almost upon us when suddenly their horses rear high into the air. We dive deep, knowing the force of the waves will abate if we can only get under them but the next wave spins us into violent somersaults. This wave is never going to let me up again but finally it releases me amongst the thick sea foam.

'I can hear Luca calling my name as I fight to stay above the water. I'm going to drown, but he launches himself towards me and holds me above the water while I catch my breath. I can feel Luca's fear but he assures me we will make it. Again, we fight against the waves, but we are pushed back closer to the shore. We dive deep again, but the next wave separates us. When I surface, he is calling desperately for me but I am forced back to the shore by the waves.'

Falling to her knees in the pod, Melissa groans painfully, yearning for Luca and this love she knows so deeply. 'I try desperately to get to him. I crawl to the water, but the soldiers come after me and grab me by my hair. They lift me out of the water and scream angrily into my face, "Il est mort! Il est mort! He is dead! He is dead!"

'I can hear the sombre cries from the horses, the soldiers swearing and cursing. Finally, they ride away and leave me lying naked on the shore. Shivering and terrified, I wait until I am sure they have gone. I lift myself on to my elbows and scan my surroundings but the beach is deserted. I force myself to my feet and I search for Luca. I walk deeper and deeper into the ocean screaming and begging for it to take me to him, when suddenly a huge wave envelopes me entirely, and I am spun out of control...'

~ ~ ~

Loud screeching birds and bright sunlight in the pod forces Melissa's eyes open, and she looks up to see hundreds of birds hovering over the seaweed-covered carcasses. She cringes as she feels the enormity of it all. Completely disoriented, she tries to steady herself and finally responds to Hélène's constant prompts. 'The last thing I remember is being spun out of control by an enormous wave and now I'm alone, naked, curled up in a ball on the shoreline. There is carnage all around me. I remember everything that happened, and I can't get the soldiers' words out of my head. "Il est mort! Il est mort! He is dead! He is dead!"

'I look at the horror around me. "How? Why? Why was I born into this tyrannical family? Ma mère... mother... WHAT HAVE YOU DONE?" I try to stand but stumble; my body is badly battered and bruised. With fierce determination, I push to my feet. I will find Luca's body.

'After hours of relentless searching, I'm exhausted, dehydrated, and finally fall to my knees. I know that it is hopeless and I howl and scream. "I no longer wish to live! I have no purpose in this life! This is no place for a child!"

'Looking out across the ocean, I feel a strong urge to be taken out into it. I cradle my stomach, our unborn child. I know our child no longer lives, and I plead with the ocean to take us both to where Luca is, to be with him in death. I can feel it dragging me out quickly, and I totally surrender to it. "I am going to die now," I tell myself... but a huge wave envelopes me and I am spun over and over and forced back to the shore once again.

'I am shattered and disoriented. An angry voice is yelling at me. "Marianne! Marianne! You must forget this... this inferior peasant! He is dead! You must marry my cousin, Guillaume! You must!" I finally open my eyes and see my mother standing over me, surrounded by soldiers, holding my cape. There is no escape.'

Melissa falls to the bed and scowls at the image of her mother holding her cape.

~ ~ ~

'No, I don't want to go here! No! Non! Non!' Melissa shakes her head vigorously as she is dragged back once again to that fateful day straight after she had thrown that bottle. 'Oh god, I can see him... I can see Luca with blood dripping from his brow, looking up to me in my carriage.'

Melissa is desperate to escape this time. She tries to pull the SEMS from her chest but they won't come off. She keeps digging at them, but they're stuck down tightly. She tries to escape the hallucinogenic effects by talking to herself. 'Okay, I'm here at the Castillo Clinic... okay... okay... my... my name is Melissa Laing and my children are Zoe and Cl...' She frowns and says it slowly and carefully. 'My children are Chloe and Zac! Ah... no... I can't stop this.'

She looks down from her carriage and sees Luca standing defiant and strong. *There is no escape! No escape from going back to this time when I foolishly threw that bottle from the carriage! This day I would tragically regret forevermore... the nightmare of this day that has been indelibly stamped in my memory for eternity!*

Melissa can hear Hélène in the background, but she takes her time as she recognizes Luca and feels herself drawn back to that horrifying day. She inhales and continues. 'Luca is angry and defiant as he looks up to my carriage.' Melissa frowns and puts her fist up to her mouth as she chokes back the tears. 'I am mortified with myself as I see him, and I realise what I have done. My cape falls to the ground, and I pull my hair free of its binds. Luca instantly recognizes me and he sighs painfully in shock.

'He closes his eyes at the horror of what is happening. His face pales as I cry out to him: "Il est mort! Il est mort! Il est mort!"

'He shakes his head, pushes away from the soldiers. "Non,

mon amour! Je ne suis pas mort! I did not die! I blacked out and got caught in the current and it dragged me past the headland. I came back for you... and then you were gone. I tried to find you... I tried for so many years... and I waited on the beach, Rianne, I could not give up! Not ever mon amour—"

'Angry cries from the horses interrupt him and the soldiers drag him away.'

Melissa buries her head in the bed as she is overwhelmed with a sense of remorse and anger. Hélène prompts her again.

'I am furious and run to put myself between Luca and the soldiers. My thin nightdress and slippers are spattered with mud. The soldiers look to my mother now for their orders. With the sleeve of my nightdress, I wipe the blood from his brow and he flinches when he sees the pendant around my badly bruised neck. "Oh non, mon amour!"'

Outraged at what she is experiencing, Melissa speaks out angrily. 'I look back up to the carriage to find my mother is now taking command of the soldiers and I curse her. I lash out at the soldiers and scream, "Spare him. Spare him! Find your humanity... votre coeur... your hearts!" The soldiers ignore my pleas. Luca tries to fight them off and the soldiers strike him down and quickly tie his hands in front of him.'

Melissa sobs. 'I want to be with him... I want to run away with him. Please, god, what have I done? How can I save him? Mon dieu... I died long ago when... when I believed Luca was dead... and... and on that same day, our child died inside of me after the brutality of my husband's soldiers.' She pauses for a moment and yells, 'I have no care for my fate. Please take *me*! Spare him. He does not deserve this. Oh, why is this happening? Pourquoi? WHY?'

Marianne desperately pleads with the soldiers. 'I beg you! Spare him! My family destroyed his life as a young man, please spare him now, he should not suffer anymore. How did

I become such a despicable creature? I have caused this... this destiny de la mort... this destiny of death. Spare him. How did this happen? All I ever wanted was to be with this man.'

She wipes the tears from her face and continues. 'I try to physically stop the soldiers and I plead with my mother. "Please, Mother! I implore you! Find your humanity! You know he does not deserve this. He has done nothing more than challenge the cruelty of the detestable monster I have become! Mother, this is my fault and mine alone. Please, I beg you, leave him!"'

Melissa rocks back and forth, holding her stomach. 'My mother ignores me and she cowers as Luca stares into her eyes and yells to her, "How could you do this to your own child? *You* are the despicable creature – you alone! And, be warned, you tyrant. Every guilty person is his own hangman!"'

Melissa wants to run to him. She wants to save him but she knows she has no power to change anything. She trembles as she continues. 'I stare softly at Luca and our eyes lock. Right at this moment a terrifying glimpse of both our fates flashes before my eyes. I am overcome with fear and rage. I stand between Luca and the soldiers. "I *demand* you leave him be. I... I fall at your feet and beseech you to spare this man!"

'They push past me and try to drag Luca away but again he strikes back. He turns towards me and pleads, "Pourquoi, mon amour? Why didn't you come back? Why did you never come back?"

'"I could not escape. I could never escape, not ever! My mother escorts me everywhere! I was forced to marry him. Pas le choix! No choice!"

'He looks up to my mother and shakes his head. "You are despicable!" My mother looks down ashamed, and then nods for the soldiers to take him.'

Melissa is overwhelmed with emotions. She falls to the floor and cries out loudly. "Oh, mon amour, I was beaten and raped and forced to marry him. I could never get away from him... oh, there are so many things I want you to know. So many things..."'

Melissa weeps and weeps and continues softly. "'I want you to know you are all I ever lived for. We lost our beloved child on the same day I believed *you* died. I tried to end my life, to be with you, my love. I tried to meet my death in the ocean where I believed you had died, but my Mother was waiting. It was *she* who betrayed us. I am so sorry I did not listen, I did not believe my own flesh and blood would betray me! I have regretted that day for my entire life. Oh, mon amour... I never knew love until I knew you... and I will never know love again...'

Melissa yells. 'I can't endure this anymore! Please! PLEASE STOP!' She tries to move up on to the bed, but she feels trapped. 'LET ME GO! LET ME GO!'

As she tries again and again to move, she passes out.

~ ~ ~

'Let me go! Let me go!' Melissa tries to get onto the bed, but her head, it feels stuck. *What the hell is happening? I can't move my head at all! Oh god, no... I'm trapped...* She screams out, 'I don't know where I am... I cannot move my head.' She strains and strains to try and move but she cannot.

She sobs loudly. 'They've taken Luca away. They beat him up so badly he is hardly recognizable. Oh, my mother, my detestable mother! How she hid her head in shame. And now what's happening? Where am I? I'm scared. I don't know what's happening. I don't know where Luca is. I can't move my head. What have I done? Why did I throw that bottle? Why? Je suis un imbécile! This is all my fault! C'est ma faute!

'I am lying naked in the centre of a candlelit, sandstone cell with just my black, jewel-laden cape draped over my legs. Tears well until I can no longer hold them in, and they spill down my face. My long hair is laid out on the ground, trapped beneath a large rock so I cannot move. I desperately want to tell Luca of these torturous nineteen years since we were barbarically separated from each other.

'I am devastated as I reflect on his last words before the soldiers dragged him away from me. "Rianne, I tried for so many years... and I waited on the beach. I could not give up! Not ever, mon amour." The distant echo of Luca's words torment me. I cry for hours until I finally fall into an exhausted sleep. I dream. I feel so much a part of this dream, and I am happy, as it takes me far away from this horrifying reality. I am totally swept away... Luca is with me, we are happy as he holds me in his arms above the lapping waves in the glistening ocean around us.

'I want to stay in this dream, and I do so for many hours until a strange, distinctive odour stirs something in me. It is so ghastly and disturbing. I force my eyes open and gasp at the horror of Guillaume's huge face staring closely at me. I wrench at my hair, but it is still pinned beneath the huge rock, and I scowl at Guillaume. He snarls then he smiles, enjoying both my disgust at the sight of him and the terror that fills my eyes when I see the axe in his hand. An all-consuming fear fills me as Guillaume stands over me and hefts the axe. He enjoys watching my fear; it flickers in his eyes. And I close mine and scream as I wait and wait for the axe to fall.

'I wait and I wait.

'Finally, I open my eyes to his laughter. Like a child, he holds the axe higher, taunting me, and the more fear I show, the more he taunts. At last, the rage that boils deep within me, erupts. "I HATE YOU! JE TE DÉTESTE! I HATE YOU!" I close my eyes and wait, until at last, I hear a loud thud as the axe falls and I almost feel relieved that this is the end. I feel the last breath leave my body; my head falls forward.

'The urge to breathe again is dizzying, and I suddenly realise my hair has been cut. I am alive. I scamper quickly away from Guillaume, and he laughs maniacally. He gathers the rest of my hair carefully from under the rock and closes his eyes as he puts the remnants to his nose, breathing deep before tucking it inside his shirt. I curse and scream at him as I cover myself in my cape. He stalks towards me, grabs me by the arm, rips my cape away and laughs as I huddle naked in front of him. He pulls my body close to his face and breathes in deeply. He holds my face and kisses my cheek before whispering into my ear, "You will finally be reunited with your lover, Marianne!"

He shoves me away, and calls to his soldiers waiting outside the cell. They throw my cape over me before dragging me away down a dark corridor. I am scared to death as they open a large door and I am confronted by the intense brightness of the sun. As we pass through a large gathering of people, I see Luca. He has been beaten so badly his face is almost unrecognizable, but I know his tall, strong body instantly. Despite the blood and bruises covering his face, his eyes still sparkle. I cry out, "Oh non, mon amour! NON!"

'The soldiers throw me at Luca, and we embrace for an intense moment until suddenly we are violently separated again, forced to our knees before two large, heavy blocks of wood. The fear, the sorrow, the regret, and the guilt make it hard to breathe. Luca turns to me, smiles softly and says, "It is not your fault, Rianne." I smile back at him as the axe falls upon his neck and I begin to weep uncontrollably. I close my eyes for the last time, and I, too, am swallowed by the blackness...

'Noir... Noir...'

The light of day is harsh in Melissa's fragile state as Hélène helps her up the moss-covered steps. She covers her eyes, almost blinded by the brightness of the day. 'Wow, how long have I been in there?'

Hélène smiles. 'I'm not exactly sure, about fifteen hours I think, and then you slept in one of the recovery rooms for quite a lot more.'

'Really? When did you get to sleep?'

'We get food and sleep breaks when we know you are not blocking... when we don't need to keep prompting you. We do try to follow people through the entire procedure if possible.'

'It's amazing this work you do here. Oh, I am so glad to see that golf cart, I've been lying in the recovery room wondering if I would make it back if I had to walk.'

'No, we would never do that to you. It is about a kilometre back to the mansion.'

Melissa raises her eyebrows and grins.

As they get near to the mansion, she sees Matthew sitting alone on the rear deck reading. As the cart pulls up, he spots her and runs down to help her. They embrace for a moment, and she whispers in his ear, 'That was so amazing... so, so amazing but so intense!'

He squeezes her hand. 'Yes. It was amazing. And I'm so happy to see you.'

She nods slowly at him and smiles. 'Me too, but I think right now, I might collapse. I don't think I've ever been so exhausted. I really need a hot bath.' Both Matthew and Hélène help Melissa up to her room. Hélène runs a bath for her as Matthew helps her onto the bed. 'Let me know if I can do anything.' As he leaves the room, she smiles and nods, her eyes closed.

Hélène helps her to the bath. Melissa thanks her, then lies calmly in the hot bath and sighs loudly. She breathes in deeply and then forcibly exhales. 'What an Experience… oh, god what an Experience!"

She drifts off to sleep only to wake hours later, shivering, because the bathwater has turned cold. Melissa pulls herself out, wraps herself in the bathrobe, dives under the quilt and drifts back to sleep.

She begins to nestle back into the warmth of the body lying behind her, but as she opens her eyes, she realises she has been dreaming. 'Oh, putain, how long have I been sleeping?' Melissa stretches then gets out of bed and makes her way to the window, relieved to see Matthew's car is still there. She has a quick shower, dresses and wraps her hair in a towel. She wants to go and find him, but she feels dizzy, so she lies down again. Exhaustion hits her once more, and she can do nothing except snuggle back under the covers. *I can barely move. I think I have to get some more sleep.*

~ ~ ~

Matthew knocks gently on Melissa's door and listens for a response. He is about to knock again when Nurse Edwards walks up to him and scowls. 'Let her rest! We have been monitoring her and she is sleeping peacefully. I can pass a message on to her when she wakes.'

Matthew sighs, 'She's been in there since yesterday afternoon, is this normal?'

'Yes. Some people sleep for days after the procedure. There is a pad and pen at reception if you would like to write her a message and I will pass it on to her once she is up again.'

'It's okay, I'll send her a message.'

'However, you like Matthew. I really need to get your room made up now. Have you got all of your belongings out yet?'

He nods reluctantly, and Nurse Edwards ushers him towards the stairs. He tries several times to text Melissa, but the messages will not send. When he gets to the reception, he writes a message and grudgingly passes it to Nurse Edwards.

As he gets to his car, he looks back up to check Melissa's window one last time, but there is still no sign of her.

He drives away slowly.

~~~

Melissa opens one eye and sees that she is still in the mansion. She curses. 'I bet he's gone by now! I just could not stay awake.' She rushes straight to the window, and there's no sign at all of Matthew's car. 'Oh blast, he's gone.' She stares out at the empty car space and reminisces about her first night here with him.

She breathes in and smiles as she relives the overwhelming sensation she'd felt when he'd held her face in his hands, kissed her and told her he loved her. As she gets ready, she whispers the song he had made up for her when he was only thirteen. 'Oh, Melissa, you make me happy... Oh, Melissa, you may be close to home... Oh, Melissa, you... Okay stop. Come on, get going.'

She smiles at her reflection while she fixes her hair. 'What did he say again? I love you! I think of you from the moment I wake up till the moment I go to sleep. I think of you constantly...' She shivers wildly and smiles happily at her reflection.
~~~

~~~

Hélène helps Melissa to her car and asks how she's feeling.

'Really good,' Melissa grins. 'Actually, I couldn't feel any better.'

'C'est merveilleux! J'espère que vous êtes bien reposée et prête pour votre nouveau voyage!'

Melissa looks at her curiously and Hélène chuckles. 'I am kidding! I said, that is wonderful, I hope you are well rested and ready for your new journey. During your Experience, you spoke a lot of French.'

Melissa laughs. 'I do... I do remember that. Well, I hope I retain it. Let me see... oui... merci... bonjour... that's about all I've got for now! Oh, wait...' She opens her mouth as though she is about to say something in French, but nothing comes out.

They laugh, and Hélène adds, 'I think you will enjoy reading your report.'

Melissa nods. 'La vie en rose. Peut-être? Whoa, I don't know where that came from or what it means.'

'Perfect pronunciation by the way. La vie en rose. Peut-être? Means life seen through rose-coloured glasses. Perhaps you may find that the language comes back to you.'

'Ah, that would be brilliant. Yes, I look forward to reading the report. I actually know that I did block. I was so exhausted but now I feel this... I don't know. I'm not sure how to describe it. All I can say is thank you so much for everything. It was truly amazing and you are truly amazing.'

'And you are too. You have incredible stamina. As you will see in your report, Castillo picked up that you blocked a couple of times, but he thinks that was because you were more determined on getting back to this intense time. That was such a big Experience for you. You had such a big Releasing from it!'

'Yes, I think that must have been where I needed to go. It was
~~~

so incredibly intense. But now… now I feel so much lighter.'

'Je suis si contente pour toi… I am so happy for you. Je pense que vous avez peut-être un lien beaucoup plus fort avec Matthew que vous ne le pensez'

Melissa grins with a quizzical look.

Hélène smiles. 'I think you may have a much stronger connection with Matthew than you realise.'

'Yes… yes… je pense… I think so too now. I really hope so. J'espère vraiment. It's coming back, huh?' Melissa reaches over and hugs her tightly. 'Je suis très heureuse!'

As Melissa drives down the long gravel driveway, she looks back at the mansion with a smile. She turns the stereo up loud as the lyrics of the song resonate with her and she sings louder and louder along with it. She scrolls through her playlist and chooses another song and sings along excitedly. Tears begin to run down her face as she feels the lyrics penetrate right to her soul, and she yells the words.

> *I am strong, I am strong,*
> *And I know now where I belong,*
> *Oh I am strong, I am strong.*

*Go on, cry it all out! This is good! Cry!* She rewinds the song several more times and sings out loudly and vigorously feeling stronger with each line,

> *I am strong, I am strong,*
> *And I know now where I belong,*

As she drives along the deserted country road, this inner strength wells up inside her. Suddenly, she slams on the brakes, comes skidding to a screeching halt and pulls off the road. 'Far out, it's him!' She jumps out of her car and races out into the field to where Matthew is standing. He picks her up, holds her high above his head, slowly lowers her, and kisses her strongly and passionately.

He looks her closely in the eyes. 'I am so happy... so, so happy. I have loved you for so long Melissa Laing.'

Tears well in her eyes and she smiles. 'And I have loved you for so long Matthew Christiansen.'

Matthew takes her hand, kisses it gently, then leads her through a forest to a small clearing beyond. She looks up to him and he gently shifts her hair away from her face. He looks deeply into her eyes as he lowers his hands and cradles her breasts. Every part of Melissa wants him and she encourages him. She sighs happily as she undoes her bra. Their desire for each other is intense and they make love with a tenderness neither of them had ever experienced before and in their moment of ecstasy, they both shed tears. Tears of joy.

CHAPTER 39

The late afternoon light glistens on the water, broken only by the silhouette of two lovers talking and laughing just beyond the waves. Sweeping her into his arms, he nestles his face against her neck and inhales deeply. 'I love your scent... I've probably told you that many times before... it's just so grunt... good grunt ha ha.' Matthew supports Melissa as she floats on the water, her arms outstretched. With one hand under the small of her back, he gently swirls the water over her breasts. A grin spreads across his face, and he sings, 'Oh, Melissa, you make me happy!' He kisses her passionately and then he raises her body above the water and kisses her pregnant stomach.

Melissa smiles as she stares through a window to the sea beyond, watching the love of her life getting ready to head off to the beach with her beloved kids. 'Life is so grand! So... so grand.' Her life is almost perfect except for something niggling at her. Jean's persistent phone messages, texts and letters. *I don't know why I have to even bother but somehow, now, I am feeling sorry for her.*

She looks back at her computer, sighs, and rolls her eyes. Grudgingly, she walks back to it, clicks 'Reply' and begins typing.

Dear Jean,

You are an intolerable, selfish piece of—

She deletes these words and starts again.

Dear Mum,

I am happy to hear you are settled in Florida and I'm sorry you've had to have so many skin cancers cut out, but you probably deserve them and it is very suspicious that you left the country so suddenly—

Melissa deletes these last lines and continues.

Lilly and I both forgive you, and we would like to leave it at that. I am not sure either of us believes you. And I am particularly confused about why you were giving me sedatives without telling me.

Again, she deletes the last two sentences.

We don't hate you, hate only hurts oneself. Lilly and I want to leave the past in the past. We are both so happy in our lives and we do not intend to wallow in what has happened. I think you should try writing to her if you are still worried. That 'Weird Therapy' as you described it, that I underwent healed my pain.

Anyhow, Lilly is doing really well with her art, selling to prominent galleries all around the world. She has her own little place in Ubud, Bali. She visits us a lot now, but she says Bali is her home. Above her door sits a carved wooden sign that reads: Happily Ever After.

You keep asking about what happened with Billy. I never ever want to even think about him. He wouldn't stop harassing me until I finally threatened to press charges. Thankfully, that is well in the past now. But I can tell you, the Trust lawyers took your pin-up boy to court and they managed to get most of the money back that Billy had been syphoning into his own personal account. Apparently, his 'wonder drug' was banned very early on but he hid that extremely well; it had so many serious side effects it would make your skin crawl. But somehow, the Trust lawyers sold Redlicht's for a good profit.

I am not sure what he is doing now but he can't practise anymore. As far as I know, he has settled in Auckland with Janet. Chloe and Zac don't have much contact with him or their stepbrother, Tim, who is the same age as Zac — that was a bit of a shock that they haven't really got used to yet. All that Zac and Chloe know is that Billy left me for Janet. I think perhaps Billy has found it hard to face them, considering all he's done. The distance makes it easier.

Lilly and I made a swap on some property and she is happy we've renovated the shack to live in. We raised the back and get a beautiful view from Whale's Inlet to Third Point.

As she types, Melissa hears Matthew and her kids getting ready to go to the beach. She sighs again and types faster.

Zac dropped out of his studies and started working with Matthew, and is loving that. He's been getting involved with a bit of the building design work and loves to get on the tools as well. Zac is madly in love with a beautiful girl, Sienna, she is an absolute delight. They are so happy together.

Chloe finally broke up with Oscar and is going out with a lovely young man from the coast. It is early days, but we are hoping that he will lure her up here again too. We do a bit of graphic design work together from time to time, which is great. Lucien has really taken her under his wing and manages to get her a lot of work with all of his contacts.

Matthew and I have a divine little girl, Tosho, and an equally divine little boy, Jakey. Jakey is so cute, he is a big boy – "six and a half and three-quarters", according to him. He reminds me so much of Zac when he was young. And our beautiful Tosho is almost four. She reminds me so much of Lilly but with really white-blonde hair.

And as for me, Mum, Matthew and I are blissfully happy. I didn't know I could ever be this happy. I didn't know it was even possible. I do bits and pieces of my design work and Matthew involves me in his work too, and I love that. I am not used to having a partner who appreciates my ideas.

I am not sure that we will get to the US in the near future, but you are always welcome to visit us. I will send some photos soon. Melissa

She backspaces and writes,

Love Melissa xxx

P.S. My beautiful friend Elle is having her first baby in July. She finally settled down with Sam and is blissfully happy. Aaron and Aisha are, as always, madly in love and very happy too.

'That's enough. Or should I take out "you are always welcome"? Ah, leave it. She won't come anyway. I think for the first time in her life she does feel ashamed about the lie that kept Matthew and I apart for a huge part of our lives.' She drums her fingers on the table for a moment and exhales loudly. 'Leave it in the past, Melissa, and get ready.'

She puts on her bathers, grabs her towel, then races back to the computer and presses 'Send'. Running down the stairs, she finds the house empty. Melissa grabs her sunglasses, hat and water bottle, before running out of the house to the beach.

~ ~ ~

Seagulls drift lazily on the warm sea breeze, rising and falling in unison with the tide. The glistening water makes it hard to see, but the silhouettes of Matthew and Zac treading water just beyond the swell, are unmistakable. Jakey and Tosho jump off the rocks, and Matthew and Zac help them onto the waves to surf back to the shore.

Melissa drops her things next to where Chloe and Sienna are lying on their towels and asks Chloe, 'What's that on your lower back?'

'Another four-leaf clover, I got it at the same time as the one on my wrist, it's meant to be good luck. But as you can see the M is for Melissa and the inverted M is for Matthew. Ha!'

Melissa squeezes her daughter's arm affectionately.

Chloe shades her eyes from the sun. 'Are Elle and Aisha coming tonight?'

Melissa grins. 'Je ne sais pas.'

Chloe responds. 'Ha. Are you sure you don't know? I've been practicing up on my French ma chère douce maman. Ha ha my dear sweet mum.'

'Ha. Well I'll have to practise up on mine too, ma belle fille. Au revoir.'

Zac has just put Jakey onto a wave, sees his mother walking out to the edge of the rocks, splashes her until she is soaked.

Matthew swims closer and calls for her to come to him. She dives into the water, climbs onto his back and whispers in his ear. 'I'm so happy... Je ne pourrais pas être plus heureuse.'

'I couldn't be happier either.' He holds her tight as he treads the water. 'Okay, here's the perfect wave.' He swims hard until they are at one with the wave and glide to the shore. In the shallow water, they smile at each other. Melissa looks around at her family... *Je ne regrette rien. I have no regrets.*

THE END!

## ACKNOWLEDGMENTS

Thank you to everyone who helped me to produce this book. It has been such a long time coming, so I am bound to forget so many people, but please know that I appreciate so many of you. Also, thanks to Assisi Chant, Lyvea Rose, Joanne Lance, and Deb Carlyon, who contributed along the way. A big thanks, particularly to Melissa Bland, who helped and encouraged me to have this published.

Thank you to all my dear friends who have inspired me to keep going over the years. Egi Selja, Stephanie Leo, Mia Taffin, Mary Heenan, Gabriella Erb, Mark Fry, Jodie Stewart, Sandy Kelly, Kerrie Jackson, Anja Morgan, Colleen Packham and Nicola Turschwell.

And a huge thank you to Mia Daskula, whose kindness and encouragement were my driving force.

Thank you to Luc Turschwell and Fabia Novak for all your help with the French.

And also a big thanks to Amanda Spedding and Julie Postance. I would not have got here without you both.

Big thanks to the best husband, sons, daughters-in-law and nieces anyone could wish for.

# AUTHOR BIO

Mandy, a self-proclaimed black sheep of her family of eleven, didn't think her life was particularly interesting until a film producer insisted she write her life story for him to produce—an extremely challenging task that is a work in progress but may take her a lifetime.

Mandy has a BA from Deakin University. Her dedication and intense passion for writing came about when she had two sons in the early '90s. Every night rather than reading from books, they insisted Mandy create 'magination' stories, as they called them. Since then, she has written hundreds of adult stories, all at varying stages of completion and all with an element of romance.

Most of Mandy's characters are based on real-life people. In *A Guilt Within*, Elle and Aisha bear an uncanny resemblance to her best friends, both in appearance and demeanour. And Liam, the romantic lead in one of her upcoming stories, is based on when she first met her husband on an overnight train. In the morning, after they had parted, he came running back to the train station searching for his wallet, quickly finding it again, and then offering to shout her and her sister out for beers (it was 6 a.m.). He confessed a week later to lying about losing his wallet, and, to Mandy's horror, he'd overheard she was a few years older than him, so he'd also inflated his age by ten years.

She now lives with her slightly 'younger' husband and a somewhat neurotic dog. They have two amazing grown-up sons who regularly visit their extremely lively home on acreage in the Noosa Hinterland, where they happily share produce from the fruit and veggie gardens with the regular visiting wildlife, including ten king parrots, hundreds of rainbow lorikeets, and dozens of free-roaming kangaroos.

www.ingramcontent.com/pod-product-compliance
Lightning Source LLC
Chambersburg PA
CBHW020259120726
47904CB00001B/267